MASTER OF SECRETS, HERALD OF DOOM

He was a renegade spy, a seeker of truth—dreamer of a nightmare that could destroy mankind. He had lost touch with himself, his past, his identity. There was only his work and his country.

And then one day his best friend was suddenly killed in an automobile accident. His apartment and all personal effects were eliminated in a mysterious fire. The newspapers and government were silent. His memory was obliterated in one day.

But Katzhak knew his friend's death was no accident. It was the beginning of a very secret and very diabolical conspiracy. And Colonel Katzhak was the only man in the world who could prevent it.

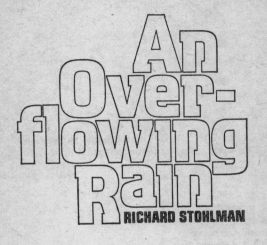

An Over-
flowing Rain

RICHARD STOHLMAN

AVON
PUBLISHERS OF BARD, CAMELOT AND DISCUS BOOKS

AN OVERFLOWING RAIN is an original publication of Avon
Books. This work has never before appeared in book form.

AVON BOOKS
A division of
The Hearst Corporation
959 Eighth Avenue
New York, New York 10019

First Avon Printing, December, 1979

AVON TRADEMARK REG. U.S. PAT. OFF. AND IN
OTHER COUNTRIES, MARCA REGISTRADA,
HECHO EN U.S.A.

Printed in the U.S.A.

1

Colonel Vladislev Tovarish Katzhak took his second heavy pull from a small glass of warm, straight vodka as he sat on the desk in the tiny, drab gray cubicle that was his office. In his hand was a manila folder encasing an inch-thick sheaf of papers that comprised yesterday's intelligence gatherings gleaned by his small, hard-pressed, and very efficient staff. Katzhak, as he was called, owed much of his success, and perhaps even his life, to the thorough and meticulous habits that had become a way of life to him and which he demanded from his subordinates, as well as to the boundless energy which had placed him in his office shortly after four A.M. this late-October morning.

Katzhak was tall, lean, and well-built. His face showed each of his forty-seven years, but his posture and demeanor did not—his age was hard to determine by visual inspection alone. Blue eyes bright and alert, sandy hair not yet grayed were augmented by a square jaw, high cheekbones, and a Roman nose, which, acting in concert, lent his face a classic, ethnically nondescript aspect. His past was equally enigmatic, and it was his past which troubled him now.

The words leaped out at him from the yellow page before him. Dead: Major Arno Tuskov . . . Auto accident . . . Moskva . . . KGB . . . 28 years in the party . . .

Stunned, Katzhak leaned forward, deep in thought. Disbelieving, he continued reading: No state funeral . . . Interment Tuesday, October 29. . . .

He glanced at his American-made watch. Today! The brief continued: Replaced, Major Vicktor Brasslov. . . .

1

Agitated, he finished his vodka at a gulp and quickly perused *Pravda* and *Izvestia,* both party organs, for the mention he knew he would not find.

What he did find bristled the hair on the back of his neck. At the bottom of a page was a terse account of a quickly contained fire in a small block of apartments, coupled with a denunciation of smoking in bed. Intuition told him what a phone call would later prove. Tuskov's flat was among the few destroyed.

2

He had obviously been murdered. No. Assassinated. But why? How? By whom? What was so important that a war hero and party member in good standing, relatively high up in the strata of senior KGB officers, was killed for it, his personal effects destroyed, and his memory obliterated in a day? It was incredible. Fantastic.

The fact that it was big, whatever it was, was readily apparent. Someone had gone to a hell of a lot of trouble. An auto wreck. A fire. Gagging the papers. And, of course, the murder itself. The order had to come from someone higher up than Tuskov. Higher even than Katzhak, as he had had no inkling, and would not have had for some time, were it not for his vigilant diligence and that of his hand-picked staff. God, security was incredibly tight! It had to be someone with a good deal of pull, able to pull strings in several areas at once. It smelled like KGB, but why hadn't he known? The killing and the subsequent erasure of Tuskov's life had to have been authorized by someone immensely powerful. But who was more powerful than the secret police? He dismissed that thought as ridiculous.

Further speculation on that point was useless. It was overwhelming, beyond sense.

His mind turned to the reason for the slaying. No power struggle had preceded it. It was too big to be personal, the act of a single individual. If it were an ideological deviance, it would have been much more effective to depose him and humiliate his memory than to destroy him. They had even dispensed with the superfluous formality of a kangaroo trial. Perhaps Katzhak was not informed because the decision to eliminate Tuskov was made too quickly. No, the plans were too well laid, even down to the selection of the heir-apparent. Yet it must have been a fairly recent development, as Tuskov himself had had no idea, at least not as of their last communication. Last communication? Of course! Katzhak turned off the light, locked his office, and hurried down the basement corridor.

He consciously slowed his pace. If he had any chance of getting the answers to the multitude of questions now churning in his uncharacteristically anxious mind, he must unhurriedly pursue, in utter nonchalance, his race against time. The irony of so much deceit in order to learn the truth had been lost on him for nearly three decades.

His face, an impassive, inscrutable mask when he so wished it, reflected a carefully calculated hint of boredom, in direct opposition to his inner upheaval, as he signed for one of the identical black, domestic, compact sedans which stood in neat rows in their underground hive, the literal vehicles of Soviet bureaucracy.

Katzhak waved aside the offer of a driver, and motored out of the concrete catacombs, squinting against the increased light of the outside world. An ice-water rain plummeted down and chilled him deeply, though in cap and overcoat he should have been quite warm. He shivered as he slowly guided the car through familiar Moscow streets, heading for his home village of Sovetsk.

3

3

Sovetsk, like Katzhak, had not always been Soviet. It had changed loyalties, face, identity. Known as Tilsit before the war, it had belonged to Germany. Founded around a Teutonic castle in the thirteenth century, it had been occupied by Russia once before. The invaders were repulsed after only seventeen days in 1914, and it had remained free of Soviet control until January 20, 1944, when it was recaptured by Soviet troops. Katzhak had been part of that second, successful invasion, and it had wholesalely altered the course of his life.

Katzhak had been born Dieter Heinrich Kirchenstein on April 14, 1928, in what was then the village of Tilsit, a German Jew of Russian and German peasant ancestry. He had grown up a part of the brassy grain fields, musty lumber mills, and plentiful horse stables that were the mainstays of the city. It was a town of leather workers, tobacco shops, delicatessens, and breweries. It grew out of the earth, and its sights, smells, and sounds were in Katzhak's blood, were part of his flesh, bone, and spirit. The rhythms of his heart. It had always been his home and would forever remain so. It was this sanctuary that restored Katzhak and which was therefore worth the infrequent but fatiguing thousand-kilometer commute to his home there. On this particular journey, the distance was a welcome opportunity for reflection and study of both his past life and the events of the last few hours.

As he drove, the Red cityscape was not the Russia of the 1970s, it was the Russia of the war years, vintage 1943. Katzhak was staring into a kaleidoscope of images of people and places existing now chiefly in his memory.

4

He was now in his home with his family, clustered around the radio, listening with rising alarm to the demented ravings of Adolf Hitler. The vision dissolved, and another rose and took its place. He and another young Jew were fleeing for their lives, fleeing the Nazis, fleeing the concentration camps, fleeing the ovens, fleeing their pasts and families, fleeing what neither would ever escape, the shameful scourge of being a Jew. Katzhak was lost in reminiscences of that headlong flight. He and the future Arno Tuskov had been just boys, Katzhak fifteen and Tuskov seventeen. Both hated fascism, as did the Communists across the border, and it took no great rhetoric or bullying to inspire their revolutionary zeal. In the chaos of war they had joined the Soviet Army and mutually decided to conceal their origins. They had created fictional new identities for themselves, sticking roughly to the truth, which had served them long, and, Katzhak admitted with pride, quite well. Both he and Tuskov were aware that they were most probably at the zenith of their respective careers, as there were limits to the advancement of the man who could not document his every breath. Still, he mused, they had come a long way, a hell of a long way. A distance, Katzhak thought, again with pride, quite respectable.

The images flickered before him now in more rapid succession, dim and somewhat overfast, like a newsreel. There had been several months of hard fighting for his home village in the bitterly cold winter of '43. He saw the trenches, felt the crush of dead bodies upon him, heard faintly the distant concussions and the staccato sounds of small-arms fire. He recalled how he had wept at the massive damage done to the beautiful village he had left just months before. He remembered with renewed waves of tenderness and sorrow the months of attempting to locate his parents, finding finally that they had been deported to Poland and had died in the horror and stench that was Krakow.

His remembrance accelerated still further: bits and pieces of his rise to his present position, then more notable and relevant highlights darting in and out of his mind, bringing him slowly up and out of the past, advancing him to the present.

Katzhak drove for a short while, thinking of nothing, before resuming his reflections, which now turned toward his wife, Tash.

Born Anne Natashye Solevske, she had spent most of her life in the hot, brazen grain fields of Soviet Kazakhstan. Her home village of Chelkar was located in the heart of this great wheat belt that girded the agricultural underbelly of the Soviet Union. Unlike many Soviet cities, Chelkar had a railroad that went directly through town. From this relatively small and otherwise unremarkable point was shipped one of the mainstays of the high-carbohydrate Soviet diet.

This rich, golden cargo traveled as far west as Poland, Czechoslovakia, and Romania; as far as Murmansk to the north, near the northeastern tip of Norway; it reached as far as Afghanistan, Iran, and the Caspian Sea to the south; and extended eastward all the way to the seas of Okhotsk and Japan.

In the past two decades there had begun the cultivation of thousands of acres of virgin land, yielding hundreds of thousands of tons more wheat, to be funneled along the iron pipeline and channeled to feed the hungry millions of Russians in the vast, sprawling giant just feeling the first tentative stirrings of its massive, quaking strength.

There was a certain distinct feeling of pride in surveying the endless expanses of sun-soaked stalks, their heads large and laden with grain, first green, then golden, now white. Pride in causing life to spring from the earth. Pride in feeding an empire, in making possible the end of the centuries-old hibernation of the great Russian bear. Pride in submitting an invaluable contribution to the state. Pride in being productive, fertile, alive.

It was in her native grain fields that Katzhak had first laid eyes on her. His mind seeped slowly under the barrier of the last twenty-five years, and once again he found himself in the past.

He had been a young officer of twenty-two, she a girl of seventeen. He had been touring some of the local collective farms and he had not been in the fields for more than an hour when he had caught sight of her.

She was five and one-half feet tall, and deeply tanned, but golden, not dark. She was lithe, strong, and slender, but

6

not muscular or unduly slight. She was tawny, sleek, healthy, and exciting. The golden grain, brassy sun, and honey sky were the perfect setting for this beautiful creature of the earth, and the hot golden radiance of sky, earth, and woman blended and flowed, became united, made inseparable, connected, one shimmering, blazing, harmonious whole. Highlighted all, by richocheting rays which glanced and danced and sparkled. Everything gleamed and shone, hummed with a common life and consciousness. Nothing was dull or inanimate. It was dazzling in its fire and brilliance, stunning in its effect.

Transfixed, his eyes took in more detail. She wore a scarf to hold back her light brown hair, lightened still further by the sun. Her face was a small oval with hazel eyes, straight, diminutive nose, and full pink lips. Her cheekbones were high but not pronounced, and her beauty sprang more from her plainness and humility, an innate, natural, simplistic grace and a spirit that was somehow visible in an aura of peace which surrounded her, than from any combination of external features. Her loveliness, defined, was nonetheless deep and definite.

She was sweating, and Katzhak watched the beads from her face, throat, and chest suddenly merge and trickle down, eventually disappearing in the valley between her breasts. He took these in, as he did her arms and neck, lean sides, and gently curving hips. He absorbed her legs as well, and his eyes traveled along them, willingly following them with both interest and enthusiasm to their conclusion. Her clothes were covered with a fine dust and dotted with chaff and an occasional locust, which she shook off without flinching or particular notice. She was working hard, with bare arms and cotton work gloves. Katzhak watched, hypnotized and aware of neither the fact that he was staring nor how long he had been standing there. He might have stood there much longer if she had not, once alerted by the intensity of his gaze, stopped her work and spoken to him, bringing an abrupt and embarrassing end to his trance.

"Comrade, what do you think you are doing?"

Her words jolted him out of his thoughts.

"What?"

"Are you having difficulty with your eyes?"

7

"No, I . . ." he stammered, groping. Had he been that obvious?

"This is the dry season, comrade. Smoking is permitted only in designated areas or indoors. Didn't you read the signs?"

He was practically leaning on one. He realized angrily that his face was flushed. Struggling, he tried to change the subject. "No, no, I didn't. I'm sorry. I was so engrossed in watching your work."

He managed a smile, but knew he was unconvincing. He cursed himself for unconsciously lighting a cigarette, and wondered when he had done it, as he elaborately stabbed it out on his boot.

"Are you that interested in our work, comrade?"

Her tone was one of slight amusement, and only mock severity. He smiled again, this time more confidently.

"I find . . . your work . . . most interesting."

The pronoun had been subtle, not emphasized, but it was not wasted. She flushed and smiled, looking down. Slowly, from an angle, she lifted her head and surveyed his face. She looked into his eyes, studying. They were gentle eyes, honest eyes; they seemed to smile with a life of their own. His whole being seemed to smile at her. She was disarmed and was not afraid of this man.

She smiled more freely. "I am glad."

Suddenly self-conscious, he took off his cap. "I did not get to meet you properly. My name is Katzhak."

She was silent.

"What is your name? I may want to mention it in my report."

Her eyes narrowed. "I am Anne."

"Anne . . . ?"

She looked at him again. That smile, his kind eyes. She could not be suspicious. "Solevske," she said.

"Good, then. Return to your work, Anne. My observation will not disturb you?"

She colored again, deeply. His eyes twinkled; he was playing with her. She held his gaze for a long moment.

"I hope you enjoy our farm," she said. And walked away.

Katzhak thought, accurately, that all those years had failed to dim her beauty and graceful charm. He recalled

8

his wedding, his joy at being married to this girl to whom he had been so irresistibly drawn, of the way her peace had gentled, calmed, and quieted his soul, given it rest. Inwardly, he hoped that it would work its magic on him again, slow his life down, elucidate his thoughts, and sort his jumbled feelings.

In the last few years Katzhak and Anne had drifted some distance apart. His world was constantly changing, accelerating, becoming outrageously complex and increasingly difficult to cope with. Her world was simpler, slower, more peaceful somehow, and less sophisticated. The pressures on him had become too great; the trickle of sharing talk about his work, which had gone on before, had of necessity dried away to nothing.

Katzhak had lost his roots. Had lost touch with himself, with his past, his identity. His world was so demandingly complicated that the manifold elements of personal identity—past, relationships, masculinity, race, origin, and perhaps even humanity—could not be considered in addition to his job. Indeed, the strains of survival and of functioning at an adequate if not successful level in his job (which absorbed all his time and energy) were difficult to cope with. A broad, overall view was impossible. It had to be scaled down, narrowed somewhere, somehow. One's energies had to be focused, or else they would be quickly and hopelessly drained and dissipated. Katzhak was an efficient entity in his capacity as agent and sometime bureaucrat. While he did not like the alienation and exorbitant personal cost of such an arrangement, it was vital to his survival in his job.

The foundations of his world had been shaken. He had to return home. He was losing focus, perspective. He was trying to assimilate and process far too much input at once.

Katzhak yearned deeply to merge again, to unite with the simple, quiet, and peaceful creature he remembered his wife to be. He must find peace and rest, restore order and rationale. He was going home, and the prospect filled him with quiet elation. He had not seen his wife in months, and had not slept with her for much longer, but he knew that this time he would. He had to. He wanted to.

His mood brightened considerably as he boarded the

9

train that would rush him still closer to home. Suddenly
he was very tired. He settled down in his seat, watching
his reflection in the window for a long moment before
shutting his eyes and almost at once dropping into a fitful
sleep.

4

Katzhak stood near the left-hand side of the cobblestone
street, just off the curb. The sky above him was gray and
solid with clouds, some almost black. The sky was a bit
too low, like a heavy, oppressive blanket; it hung dismal
and foreboding. It rumbled, distant thunder coming closer,
closer. The air was warm and moist, almost stifling, and
thick with electricity. It looked like rain. A terrible, total,
overflowing rain. Funny, to be frightened by the rain. His
anxiety mounted. It was dark, dark, dark—and getting
darker by the moment. Suddenly he realized with alarm
that there were no people in the street, no cars, bicycles,
carts. Nothing. Not even a dog would brave the evil sky.
He looked upward toward the faces of buildings. They
were yellow. A dirty yellow, like the sun through smoke.
An eerie, diffused light glowed from them, and their outlines were blackened, as if scorched. He turned his head
and looked down the street. He heard the noise of some
distant tumult approaching him slowly. He peered out,
staring at the spot where whatever it was would soon
become visible. Curious, he watched as a small band of
people bearing something on their shoulders wound their
way up the street. As they came a fraction closer, Katzhak
saw that most of the people seemed to be carrying an
object on a platform or bier; the others were shouting and
beating sticks together, making a loud rhythmic music to

10

accompany their chants. The object seemed to be the center of attention, and he saw that it had the appearance of a small bear down on all fours.

From time to time, those leading the procession would offer food to the bear, fresh meat which they would lay at his feet. He took the meat greedily, hungrily, and devoured it. Each time he would eat, he grew and became larger and heavier. His weight became more difficult to support. At first others joined the ranks, joined in the praise of the great bear. Soon the people needed more help to shoulder their burden. The number of volunteers dwindled, and the people groaned with the weight of the thing. All the while, the bear grew bigger and stronger, louder and hungrier, more threatening and insistent. Some of those in the crowd, partially from loyalty and partially from fear, began to call to the people in neighboring houses to come and join them in supporting the bear. Some few did come. It was not enough. Many strong men in the crowd broke away and ran into the houses of others, dragging out the struggling inhabitants, forcing them to support and serve the bear. Those who did not, as well as those who wavered or were caught shirking what the leaders saw as their duty, were knocked down and trampled by those who carried the bear, and by those who praised him, and some were fed to the bear. He roared and growled. He stamped on his enemies and on those who refused to support him. He shredded them with the claws of his feet, and ground them between his terrible iron teeth. He dropped their bones into a deep pit which yawned before him. And for the first time Katzhak heard the groans which came up from out of the pit. He watched in horror and fascination. He could see better, now that they were closer.

The bear was made all of stone, with iron teeth and claws. He was immobile, a stationary statue when he was not hungry or devouring the offerings sacrificed to him. He stood now on his hind legs, rearing. When he roared, growled, and fed, his eyes were yellow. They gleamed, as if sulfurous fires burned behind the fixed forward set of the staring, glassy eyes.

The music was getting louder and louder. The crowd of people cheered, praised, shouted, and extolled the bear

11

for his great strength and size. They worshiped his fero-
ciousness, his power, his invincibility. Katzhak heard the
shouts of triumph, the clacking of the sticks, the groans
from out of the pit.

All the while, the bear grew larger; he was monumental,
awesome, terrifying. He growled, threw back his shaggy
stone head, and roared his hunger, greed, and lust. He
needed to be fed almost constantly now, and even as he
ate one offering, he eyed others. He seemed to have a life
of his own, to be the master, not the mascot. He was tyrannical in his demands, out of control. It was clear the
people served the bear. Everything worthwhile was sacrificed on his altar. There was no limit to his appetite. They
were slaves to a monstrous magnification of themselves.
And all the while they praised the bear and worshiped
him.

The leaders singled out the next offering. He was smaller
than all the others, tiny. He was scarcely a mouthful.
Katzhak was choking on his anxiety now. He did not know
why, but he knew that there was some incredible, some
fantastic hidden danger in this small sacrifice. Why didn't
anyone see? It was so plain. He heard himself shouting,
screaming. Above the noise of the music and the praises he
could not be heard. He was running. He talked to dozens,
tried to explain. They laughed and offered him sticks. He
shoved them away. He tried to reach the leaders. They
ignored him. A group of strong men walked toward him.
He ran. As soon as the bear reached out to take his
minuscule prey, there were thunders, lightnings, voices,
and an earthquake. There were strange sounds—screams,
horses neighing, derisive laughter, angry shouting, the
noise of war—all carried on the winds. It turned suddenly
colder and darker. The shadow of a cloud passed over the
bear. No one felt the shaking, heard the sound. The bear
raised the meat to his jaws and bit down. The noise of the
crowd was almost deafening. They were jubilant. Almost
frenetic with triumph. A deep growl of exultation swelled
throughout the crowd and upward toward the bear.

Suddenly it was quiet. The stunned crowd drew in its
collective breath at a gasp. They watched in horrified
disbelief as the teeth of the great bear broke, crumbled,
and fell out. His claws snapped like brittle twigs, and he

released its prey, letting it fall from his paws. His great yellow eyes turned back to stone. The stone eyes rolled slowly backward, up, and to the right. His jaws and posture froze upright. The crowd was hushed. The groans from the pit ceased.

Simultaneously, it began to rain. Water poured uniformly from all over the sky. The people stood still and mute, watching the bear. Again the crowd drew in its breath. Someone screamed, and then Katzhak saw it. It began as a trickle from inside the mouth of the image of the beast, fell on his stone chest, and trickled over his full, inert belly. Suddenly it poured out like a burst wineskin, cascaded down, covering the beast and his leaders, splattering the worshipers. From the mouth of the beast was pouring . . . blood.

It was then that Katzhak noticed the cracks in the statue of the bear. Across the paws that supported the hind legs, on which he was standing. He started to shout warning, but it was too late. It was all too late. The cracks widened, deepened, and connected. The image tilted, tottered, and fell into the crowd. Great hailstones fell from the sky, and some were pounding Katzhak as he watched the image and the people under him crash into the street.

He awoke feverish and sweating. His head ached, not with hailstones, but because it tapped against the window of the train car. The others in the car were staring anxiously at him. Shaken and embarrassed, he mumbled an apology and turned away, looking out the window.

The dream Katzhak had just seen had been frightening, even to him. It was puzzling, in a way, as he had seen more terrible things, he thought, in reality. Yet there was something distinctly different about this dream, which made it unique among the relatively few he had recalled in his lifetime. It was reality, somehow. Or it might become so.

It had been so vivid, but again, with a quality of alarming realism which distinguished it from others, therefore meriting it special attention. Why had it frightened him so? He had felt so alone, a spectator to fantastic destruction, struggling futilely to warn the unsuspecting of some

13

danger—of a magnitude which none realized, and from a source which none expected. Why had he felt kinship with those people, almost as if he were one of them? If he were one of them, what had set him apart, how had he escaped the destruction that had come upon them all? Katzhak noticed that his stomach was still knotted with fear, his hair still bristled. He could not shake the awful gut feeling that he too had been warned. That somehow he must stop this entire horrible, bloody nightmare from becoming reality. He knew instinctively that if he did not, if he failed, the things he saw would come to pass. He was agitated, and he felt the full weight of an awesome responsibility. One he dare not shirk, even if he were to lose his life. He knew, somehow, that this challenge would require all his strength and inner resource. It would test all of his convictions, drive him to the limits of his endurance. It would take everything he had to beat this thing. He knew that somehow he must. He was engaged in a mortal combat for incredibly high and frightening stakes. It was winner take all. Either the nightmare would die or he would, trying to stop it. The faces of the people reappeared in his mind. They seemed, in their helpless ignorance and blindness to the overwhelming danger, to implore him, to solicit his help, even though it was clear that he might not succeed.

Automatically his well-trained and disciplined mind began to slow down. He had to put things into perspective, regain his mental composure, his calm, his rationale. He realized with a measure of self-disgust that he had almost characterized this dream as a vision. He was overreacting. This thing with Tuskov. Yet, after twenty-five years in the business, he had developed a "sense" that rarely, if ever, failed him. He trusted that intuition, and he felt justified in being upset. Still, he was not a man who gave much credence to dreams. His very survival had rested on the fact that he was not a dreamer, not ruled by the Joan of Arc voices of conscience. Katzhak was a hard worker, a realist, pragmatic. He succeeded, not because of providence or idealism, but because he did his homework. He did his job with his might, which was considerable. He lived his job, leaving nothing to chance. He wanted to be good, and he worked hard at it. Drove himself relent-

14

lessly. It was a formula that paid off. He was alive. Many of his enemies, co-workers, and former superiors were not. He was a formidable foe. He was clever, tough, resourceful. Self-confident and self-reliant. He was a professional. And one of the best.

Dismissing the dream for the present, Katzhak returned to dealing with the concrete, a world he felt more sure in, a world he could handle more easily. His mind turned now to the primary reason for his journey—the last words of Arno Tuskov. It was for this reason he had left Moscow. He wished to ascertain whether or not Tuskov had sent him a last message before his death. What if he had not? It was the best lead—indeed, the only lead—Katzhak had. What if Tuskov had? Katzhak pondered what the brief note might contain. Did Tuskov know he was going to be killed? Did he know why, or by whom? Was there danger in it for Katzhak? Could he get hold of the message before Tuskov's assassins did? Would they be at his home, waiting for him? Had they altered the message to destroy Katzhak and implicate others? He could only wait and see. He began to relax, and, as usual, filled his spare moments with routine paperwork.

In order to communicate sensitive information while minimizing the risk of that information being monitored, Katzhak and Tuskov, from their homes in the country, just miles apart, had communicated through the use of carrier pigeons. These silent couriers were hard to trace, could not defect, would never reveal the identities of their superiors under interrogation. To the untrained eye, most pigeons looked alike, and pigeons were abundant in Sovetsk. Just birds. There was some risk involved in any procedure, and this system had its flaws too. In Katzhak's work, one had to guard not only against the discovery of a connection between contacts but also against the mere suspicion that such a connection exists. From the moment someone begins to suspect, security is compromised. The trick is not to prevent discovery, but to prevent suspicion. Katzhak knew that the chance of discovery of anything at Tuskov's home by his slayers was, optimistically put, dismal. The odds on the correct interpretation of the minuscule clue that they might find, and then managing to trace that tiny shred to Katzhak, were even more remote. While the possibility for error was always present, according to his careful calculations the margin of safety was broad enough to preclude excessive worry on his part.

As he worked, the thought struck Katzhak that after a thorough search, Tuskov's house had unquestionably been utterly destroyed too. He shook his head imperceptibly, in farewell to a man who no longer existed except in the fleeting memories of a few like himself.

5

It was late afternoon when Katzhak opened the small wooden gate and walked down the pathway of broad, smooth, flat stones toward his house. Natashye stood about a hundred yards distant to his left. She was shoveling earth from the roots of a small tree stump into a wheelbarrow. Katzhak watched her with a tenderness he had not known for a long time. She was still beautiful, still a hardworking woman, and he found, without surprise, he still loved her. His eyes flickered to the row of tall trees which ran beside and behind her, which they had planted together as a windbreak. He quickly surveyed the cottage-style house they had bought so long ago. He saw the shutters he had built and the window boxes he had made for her flowers. The swing he constructed for their porch. He observed, unprofessionally, that he loved this house, their small acreage, their life together. Why was he so sentimental, so deeply satisfied to be home? He shook off the questions. He was happy; he had earned that. And that was very logical.

He stood looking at her, and finally she looked up and saw him standing there. She stood frozen, wondering. Slowly her arms dropped to her sides. She waited for him to speak. He did not. As he approached her, she could

16

sense that something was different, something had changed. He was smiling at her, the way he first had so many years ago. His eyes traveled over her, drinking in the sweetness of this long-anticipated moment. His gaze returned to her face. He was searching it for some clue to her feelings, some small flag of hope that she still loved him. She was obviously puzzled by his sudden appearance, confused by the look on his face. He smiled. He smiled deeply, joyfully. He was unabashedly glad to see her. His eyes looked at her, greeted and caressed her with such apparent love and unaccustomed tenderness she scarcely could take it in. She was baffled, and she had not the faintest idea of what to do or say. Before she could react, he solved that problem for them both. He did something totally unexpected, something which shocked and pleased her. Something she was totally unprepared for. He kissed her. As they held the kiss, Natashye let the shovel fall from her right hand, and responding to the embrace, put both arms around him, each drawing the other closer and basking in the warmth of love. Drawing apart, they held each other's gaze, quiet. The wind blew through the trees above their heads and rustled leaves beneath their feet. Her lips trembled, as did the fingertips of the hands with which she now held his face.

"Katya?"

"Tash, I . . ." He fumbled, groping for the words. Her eyes darted all over his face.

"I had to come. I had to come home."

"Oh, Katya, it's so good to see you! You've been away so long."

"I have missed you, Tash."

"Katya, what's wrong? Why do you look at me like this?"

"I had to come home. To see you again. Arno Tuskov is dead."

"Arno Tuskov! His house burned down this morn . . ." Her voice trailed off. "So that is why you came." Her eyes and head lowered with the weight of crushed hope, and her hands began to slip from his face. He caught and held them.

"No. No, you mustn't think that. That is part of it, yes. Of course. But I wanted to come home. A man must come

17

home to be with his wife. . . . I have been so far away . . ." He let the words fall. She saw he was near tears. She believed him.

"Oh, Katya! It is so good to have you back." She hugged him. "How selfish of me," she said. "You must be so tired. Don't stand out here like a stranger. Come in. Come . . ." She took him by the hand and led him up the steps to the porch.

"A man should not be a stranger in his own house." Her words were meant to both chide and comfort him. On the porch he stopped her.

"I do not want to come halfway home, Natashye. It would be better for me to return to Moscow." She understood.

"I want you to come all the way inside, Katya. It is where you belong. Accept my invitation. Please."

Their eyes once again met and held.

"Thank you, Tash." He sighed deeply. "It is good to be home." With that, he kissed her, and putting his left arm around her, walked smiling into the house.

She cooked for him. A small stew which contained meat, and vegetables grown in their garden. There was tea with their dinner, and hot vodka with lemon afterward. Katzhak spoke almost as little as his wife ate. She watched her husband much of his meal, and they rocked gently together on rocking chairs, his right arm curved around her shoulder; his left, glass in hand, rested on his thigh.

Sighing softly, she put her head on Katzhak's chest. She was silent as she gathered the courage to ask him the terrible questions she feared to have him answer. Finally she began hesitantly, "Arno—was . . . was he . . . ? They murdered him, didn't they?"

"Yes." Katzhak shut his eyes.

"Did you know? I mean, did they tell you? Did you hear rumors?"

"No. Nothing."

"You were completely surprised?"

He nodded, and said nothing.

"Then they will kill you, too," she said. Her head sank in conjunction with her spirits.

"No, Tash. I am a careful man. They will not get me. Erase me, as they do everyone else. I promise you that."

"I cannot accept your promise, Vladislev. You cannot guarantee that tomorrow they will not snuff out your life like a candle. I am not a child that you can pat on the head. Do you really think that you can protect me from the world with a few transparent lies? I am not a fool, Katya. Even I can see that you may be in grave danger, and yet you rock me in your arms, sing me soothing lullabies, and promise your little girl everything will be all right? What do you take me for? Katya, you are an intelligent man. You do not flatter me with this kind of treatment. You insult the intelligence of us both. Think, Katzhak. You are not made of stone. I know you. I am your wife. You cannot hide the truth about yourself from me. How much longer can you bear your burden alone? How many times will it take before you destroy yourself? You cheat me, Vladislev. You cheat me of the right to be a good wife to you. To love my husband and meet his needs. You rob me of my chance to be a woman. I am through. I will not allow myself to be shoved in the background, out of harm's way, while I watch a good man torture himself to death. I am more of a person than that, Katya. More of a woman, more of a wife. I will not sit in dumb agreement any longer. I will not give my loving, tacit approval to your death. I want no part in your self-destruction. I love you, Katya. But you must help me. I agreed to be a full partner in your life. I want to protect my interest in you. Do not think that you are heroically sparing me from unhappiness by denying me the truth, denying me my rights as your wife, as a woman, as a human being. You are making me miserable. Open a little to me, Katya. Let me fully love you as I used to. I know you will be surprised at what I can do."

Katzhak was caught off balance. He had not anticipated this long-pent-up tirade of emotion and hostility. He was totally stunned and silent. These were not the tantrums of a simple child, these were the eloquently outspoken feelings of a beautiful and complex woman. He had seen a side of her nature which he had not known before. She was articulate, intelligent, and direct. She was strong and logical. He was filled with a twin sense of new and deep respect for his wife, and shock at his own blindly callous treatment of her. She merited his best, his deepest confidence, his most profound love. He was choked with

19

admiration and appreciation of her in equal and abundant doses. For several moments he was silent, unable to speak. Finally he found his tongue.

"I am so sorry . . ." he began. "I did not realize. How I must have hurt you all of these years."

"All of these years are not nearly as important as the present, Katya. Can you be honest with me now?"

He looked away and paused.

"All right," he said. "What do you want to know?"

"As much of the truth as you can tell me. And do not feel sorry for me. It is I who have felt sorry for the way you have treated yourself."

His answer was a wan smile. She asked him questions now, in rapid succession.

"Did Tuskov know he would be killed?"

"I don't know."

"Do you know why he was killed?"

"No."

"Do you have any idea?"

"None. I think he was silenced. I know only that it is very big."

"Then, since you don't know what it was, you don't know if they are after others, perhaps yourself."

"That's right. But there is one way I might find out. There may be a clue here in Sovetsk."

"So you did come back at least partly for business."

"Have I done many things in the past few years that were not at least partly business?"

He had a point.

"How soon will you know?"

"Tomorrow morning."

"Where is this clue?"

"Here. In this house."

She stifled a shudder.

"Then why will you not know till morning?"

Without a word Katzhak stood and drew her to her feet. He looked into her eyes briefly and kissed her. He picked her up and carried her down the hallway and into their bedroom, grinning broadly. She giggled and quivered with amusement and excitement.

"Katya!" She trilled and continued laughing as he set her gently on the bed.

Although neither had made love for several months, it was clear that both had eagerly anticipated this heretofore unforeseen and yet anxiously awaited moment. It was passionate but not rough. Katzhak was as gentle as the breeze that rustled each of the thousands of leaves on the trees outside their window. Swaying gently back and forth and sighing deeply, like their branches. They floated easily on that breeze, buoyed up, carried higher and higher, drifting aimlessly through clouds, up, up, darting in and out between the stars, tumbled and whirled about in a tempest of thunder and flashing lightning, before returning and falling down as gently as the rain. It was beautiful and un-utterably fulfilling. Satisfied beyond expression, they lay in the quiet, peaceful stillness of their love. Home at last, with his head upon her breast, Katzhak was soon happy and asleep.

Natashye was puzzled, and although quiet and peaceful, she was inwardly anxious for her man and a little fearful for them both. She wondered about her husband as she cradled his head between her breasts and stroked his hair pensively. Why had he come back home? What had jarred him that he felt compelled to return home and repair his marriage, which had fallen into disrepair due to a lack of all but a token maintenance? What shock had shaken him to the roots of his being, caused him to feel a swift and powerful need for her? She could understand, empathize with his instinctive desire to return to his origin, to the strength and peace of their marriage union. She knew that the greater part of his desire to make love with her had rested on the fact that he wanted to merge, to be one with her. He wanted to be swallowed up in her body and spirit, to lose himself within her. He wanted to melt away, to feel only their common identity. What was he fleeing from, gathering strength for? He was obviously deeply troubled, and she did not know what private an-guish had caused him to want her so much, need her so badly. She felt like the mother of a frightened little boy, the way she held him close to her and dried his inner tears. He was not a boy. He was a tough, competent, self-assured man. What had caused him to doubt himself, question that inexhaustible strength and ability? What had renewed his love for her, his unspoken desire to remain home in his life with her and never return to Moscow? He had been ardent, passionate, loving. Yet he was not the least bit rough or inconsiderate. He had been so gentle, so tender, so good to her. Even so, he was strong, forceful, and not the least bit passive. She had never seen him like this, never felt so deeply and completely loved in her lifetime. She had never felt closer to her husband. A sobering thought struck her. He had savored each moment, lavished his love upon her so fully, lingered sweetly at so many points, he had made love to her as if it were the last time. As if there might not be any tomorrow. Was it the last time? She wondered. She prayed within her soul, in the way that only an atheist can, that tomorrow would never come. She had her man back. Her lover, her husband, her friend. She had her marriage, and for the first time in years, she had herself back. She was appalled at herself. She loved this man, loved their life together so dearly that she would never allow him to leave her again for very long. She felt him begin to stir from his repose, and lovingly kissed the top of his head, drawing him closer to her, holding him more tightly, snuggled against the much-missed warmth of his body in her arms. She sighed and smiled, waiting for him to awake.

Katzhak opened his eyes but did not move further for several moments. He kissed her breast in greeting, and propped himself up on an elbow, looking at her. Her beauty never ceased to amaze or attract him. She looked so peaceful, so deeply content lying there in love with him. He smiled at her. She smiled back. There was such warmth here, such serenity, he never wanted to leave. Suddenly he hated his job, hated Moscow, hated being apart from her, hated the hopeless feeling that collapse is inevitable, which had come with age, experience, and cynicism. She was decent and profoundly sane. Somehow she had remained uncorrupted, unspoiled, pure enough to be loved by a man who subjected everything to the harsh, glaring light of the truth.

Gradually he began to stroke, squeeze, kiss, and caress her from her head to her feet, arousing her again, and himself, in the process. With a love of such proportions, such a dimension that she could not recognize it as anything she had felt before, she reached for him and tenderly pulled him over and on top of her. Instantly she felt the welcome warmth of his body along her full length, the warmth and life of her other half, the second part of her nature, her being, a part without which she felt incomplete. These halves had to be in contact, connected, a united whole. She wanted his being to merge with hers, to be inside her, part of her. To move as one. To think and feel as one. To synchronize their rhythms, to become one creature. She guided them together, rejoiced in his warmth, felt gradually and gratefully filled by him. She was at last whole and content. She loved the feeling of absolute fullness and warmth in her whole body, mind, and spirit. His presence was everywhere. He was above, below, around, and within her, in a total sense that never failed to thrill, fulfill, and satisfy her, meet her deepest needs. She was lost in joy, and she hoped never, ever to be found again.

Katzhak stood, watching her as he dressed. She might have cried, had she not been asleep, to see the inexpressibly loving way he looked at her. His eyes traveled lightly over her, resting here and there in his favorite places. He traced her outlines, memorized her every curve and swell. It was the last time he would see all of her this way, he knew. Tears formed in his eyes and welled up until he shut them to keep them from falling. "Tash," he whispered. "Oh, Tash," he said again. "My little Natashye."

Slowly he crossed to the bed, and taking a last, lingering look at her full length, gently and with infinite care and affection pulled the covers over her. He nestled them warmly under her chin. She sighed and murmured in her sleep, snuggling in this new warmth. He watched her face as she slept, nearly overcome with emotion and love for her. He kissed her softly on her forehead, paused a moment in the doorway, and went out.

It was nearly morning. The scattered rays of the soft gray country dawn were diffused and radiated through an iridescent fog which covered everything in a light mist. The half-acre of vegetables planted behind their quaint but modest house was wet with fog and dew. Katzhak had shed his overcoat in favor of a lighter but still warm jacket. His ever-present cap, most frequently worn when he was not working, was in its accustomed spot atop his head, and it too was becoming damp on top and beginning

23

to glisten like white sugar granules whenever the light would catch it as he walked. He loved his country home in the morning. It reminded him of his parents' home, which he had emulated in selection and refurbishment of his own house. The air was deadly still, except for the songs of birds. He walked for perhaps fifty yards before arriving at his destination.

It was a weather-beaten wooden toolshed, which doubled as a work and storage area. It was no more than ten feet tall, with a flat roof and a window in back, complete with a large outdoor sill. The walls outside were almost completely devoid of paint. Glancing around him, he unlocked the rusting padlock, which fought him at first, swung open the latch, and stepped in, leaving the door open. He lit a small lantern on the shelf which served as his workbench, replaced the glass, and shut the door. Holding the lantern aloft, about a foot above his head, he began carefully to inspect his surroundings with keen eyes. He began with the floor. It was sawdust, and would instantly reveal the past presence of any but the most ingenious intruder. As he had hoped, the only prints he could see were Natashye's and his own. Free now to move his feet, Katzhak surveyed his workbench. Everything seemed to be much as he had left it. The coating of dust that covered all did not seem to have recently been disturbed. Satisfied, he sighed slightly with relief and set the lantern on the end of the bench nearest the door. In a few steps he was at the small homemade coop he had built for the pigeon. He was slightly gratified and mildly excited to see the bird in its place, although he knew its mere presence there did not necessarily dictate the promise of a note. He clucked softly to the bird as he unhooked the latch on its cage and reached inside.

He was even more excited, and possibly anxious, when he spied the tiny beige band around the ankle of the small creature. He picked up the bird, and trembling with anticipation, slipped off the message. Katzhak returned the pigeon to its cage and fastened the latch again. He then placed the message behind his ear and crossed to the door, opened it a crack, and peered outside. Confident that he was alone, Katzhak returned to the workbench and the light of the lantern. He pulled up a wooden stool, un-

24

raveled the note, and read. The handwriting was unmistakably Tuskov's. The message read: "Blitzkrieg—June 18, 1815—stop Cosmo—Comrade Malenkov," followed by the address of a flat in Moscow. It was signed "Do not fail me. Good-bye. Arn." Katzhak stared at the note. The last words of—and a request from—the closest thing Katzhak had had to a friend in his adult life. He bit his lip and shut his eyes tightly, shaking his head in a slow rocking motion from side to side. He dropped the message on the bench and held his head in his hands. Leaning forward, he raked his fingers through his hair before sitting upright again. He studied the message for another moment before lighting it and watching it burn. Then he ground the ashes into powder. He unlatched the cage and reached inside, extracting the bird. He broke its neck. If it were found here, it could implicate him, and that would be his death and Tash's. If he simply let it go, it would sooner or later return to Tuskov's. If the remains of the house were being watched, and Katzhak guessed that they were, the bird might circle or otherwise attract attention, might somehow be tracked on its return. Katzhak dismantled the cage, discarding the wire and contents, brought the rest into the house, and burned the pieces in the fireplace. He washed thoroughly in the kitchen before entering the bedroom to wake his wife. Sleepy-eyed, she blinked up at him, smiling.

"I must return at once to Moscow," he said.

The smile faded from her lips. She nodded, resigned and sympathetic.

"You found what you came for, then?"

"In every way, Natashye."

A slow smile crept over her features.

He wanted to reassure her and himself. "As soon as this is concluded, I will return to Sovetsk with all possible haste. I will not leave so soon again then."

They gazed into each other's eyes, both of them suspecting that this would prove to be a lie. It was necessary for them both to pretend, to try to believe, that they would be together again soon. They embraced suddenly, clinging tightly to each other. They kissed for a long time, which to them seemed like the briefest of moments.

"I will make your breakfast," she said.

He released her and allowed her to get up, tie a robe

around herself, and walk softly on bare feet to the kitchen. He watched her prepare their food, and his hand never left hers as they ate. At the doorway he looked at her for a long time. She was being very brave.

"Good-bye, Tash," he said, his heart heavy.

"Do not say . . . do not say that, Katya. Say only, 'I will see you soon.' I will see you soon," she repeated, trying to convince herself. Her lip quivered. He had better go before they both broke down. He kissed her deeply, pressing her against him, holding her tightly.

"You are a good wife, Natashye. The best a man could have. Thank you for this. The life you have made us, together." He was too choked to say much more.

"You are a good man, Katzhak. Take care of yourself, my husband. I will never forget this homecoming of yours. It was so kind of you, I . . ." She could not go on.

"You are such a good woman, Tash . . ." He faltered. His honesty and overwhelming desire to make her happy, somehow, to give her something which would mean something to her, encourage her, finally succeeded in making his excuses seem absurd.

"I love you, Tash," he said. It was crazy. She smiled; right in the middle of her tears, she smiled. Even as she was crying, she began to laugh. She was saying, "Oh . . . oh . . . oh," over and over again, interspersed with tears and laughter. She hugged him, pulled away to look at him, hugged him again.

"You have made me so complete!" she exclaimed. "Oh, come back, Katya. Please come back to me."

"I will do my best," he said.

He kissed her, took one last, lingering look, turned, and as she watched from the doorway, walked quickly down the stairs, up the path, and out the gate. He did not turn around.

6

On the train bound for Moscow, Katzhak sat staring, morose, and still. He watched the scenery drift slowly by before disappearing from his view. It occurred to him that the same thing happened in a man's life, was happening now in his—people and places, familiar and unfamiliar, new and old, beautiful and ugly, participants in a vast and lengthy panorama, paraded before his eyes, had their moment, and then slipped past him. A thought struck him, which, although it could not be proven, was nonetheless interesting. The scenery existed before he saw it, and, he had no doubt, after it vanished from his sight. Although he no longer perceived it, it was still there—real, tangible, constant. Frozen in time and space. Perhaps that was the way a man's life was. The people he knew existed before they appeared to take part in his life; maybe, like the scenery, they too existed in time and space after they were gone. The past and the future were perhaps parallel dimensions to that of the present. Connected, inseparable, and no less "real." He realized that he was merely grasping at straws in an effort to remain a part of, to preserve, to stay in, past worlds, even though he had to leave. No, his parents were gone. Tuskov was gone. Natashye was gone. Everything was gone. Or at least everything worthwhile. He was not sure he wanted to return to Moscow, to be a part of a world in which every good thing was dead or dying. He was a dinosaur. His contemporaries were all extinct. He was the last of the line. He asked himself if the reason he was so determined to unravel this mystery was not that Tuskov had been killed because of his involvement, and he hoped, secretly, to be retired to the past where he belonged. He shook the question off. He had not realized, unaccustomed as he was to introspection, that he was such a romantic. He did not know what it meant, but he suspected it was a dangerous luxury. It had been his experience that the people who were not one hundred percent behind staying alive usually weren't. He made a mental note to himself not to encourage such thoughts in the future by entertaining them.

Although he had succeeded in disciplining himself for the present, he still could not focus his attention on anything relevant. He rode for perhaps another half hour this way before mentally embarking on a course that was at least halfway productive. He then turned his mind to the message Tuskov had sent him, and carefully analyzed it to wring out any drop of evidence unobtrusively hidden in its folds.

The first word had been "Blitzkrieg." Why German? he wondered. Perhaps because he knew it would have a special, if terrible, impact on Katzhak, given his background. Yes, Tuskov was trying to reach him on a subconscious level, by arousing the suppressed traumatic fears of his childhood. The danger must be great, he must have wanted Katzhak to feel instinctively threatened as well. What did the word mean? It was a sort of compound formed by the connection of two German words. Literally, it meant "lightning war." Traditionally, a blitzkrieg was total, all-out, swift, and without warning. It was generally an action carried out against a smaller, weaker nation, and generally it was unprovoked. A date had followed (what was it?) —oh, yes, June 18, 1815. Although he combed his memory, he could come up with nothing regarding that date. Then what? Two words which did not make sense. "Stop Cosmo." This was the mission Arno had pleaded with him not to fail. But how could he succeed? He had not the vaguest inkling of who, or what, Cosmo was. He began to review in his mind the dozens of code words and signals filed in his brain, from military operations, dossiers, war games, passwords, and plans. He was almost certain it was a new one. He had drawn a blank here, too. Perhaps Cosmo was the name of a military operation he had not heard of. Tuskov's lightning war. It was probable, but he could not be certain. Who was going to launch the attack?

Against whom would it be made? How soon would it come? How did Tuskov expect him to prevent it? His mind spun. Tuskov was killed because he knew about Cosmo. He was killed by Soviets. That meant one of two things: either the Soviet Union was aware of a lightning war about to be conducted, one which it condoned and wished to be kept a secret until it was under way, or it was launching one. It was bigger than he had suspected in his wildest conjecture. It was awesome, and obviously vitally important. Why should Tuskov want to thwart the aims of his own country? Unless he knew something. Knew it might fail. That last was simply too much to swallow. Before he let himself get carried away any further, he questioned the authenticity of the note. It had definitely been Tuskov's handwriting. And there had been the reference only he and Tuskov or someone who was aware of their backgrounds would write. It was almost as if Tuskov had intended to validate the message by his choice of words. Had they learned of Tuskov's background through drugs or interrogation? Katzhak pictured the note once again in his mind. The handwriting had been steady. Not that of a man tortured or drugged. Perhaps the drug had worn off . . . or the note was forged? It was getting absurd. There wasn't time or evidence of anything but a routine assassination. Routine? The thought of assassinations being "routine" made him shudder slightly. This case was obviously not routine. No, the note had to be genuine. But that possibility was even more incredible. Perhaps Tuskov did not mean "war" in the literal or national sense. Perhaps he had meant a purge. It was possible, but highly unlikely. Politically, things had been running about as smoothly as one could hope for, given the Soviet system of government. Besides, large-scale liquidations were becoming a thing of the past. He hoped. His staff had turned up nothing as late as yesterday morning. Katzhak was under the impression, fantastic as it might seem, that Tuskov had meant exactly what he had said.

He turned to the remainder of the note. Who was Comrade Malenkov, and what was his connection with Arno Tuskov? Was Tuskov fingering his murderer from the grave? Katzhak doubted it. It was Cosmo he had been asked to stop, not Malenkov. Besides, Tuskov would have made it clearer, knowing that otherwise he was sending his friend into a trap. And Malenkov couldn't have arranged the auto wreck, the apartment and home fires, the silence of the papers and the government, as well as Tuskov's successor. If Malenkov were a Soviet official with enough power to do all of these things, and without attracting attention, it was highly unlikely that he could be found at odd hours in a Soviet apartment house. He examined what he had in summary. A sudden unprovoked and unheralded attack was going to occur (it appeared, relatively soon), which the government either was launching or wanted launched, and Tuskov had warned him not to fail in preventing it, in effect, setting Katzhak at odds with his own government. He was completely baffled, and he felt an ominous feeling of dread. He was agitated, anxious, puzzled, and afraid. Afraid of finding out the secret, discovering he must try to stop it, and the consequences it would have for them all. Yet he was determined, as he had been from the start, to get to the bottom of it all, learn the truth, and ride it out to its conclusion. He was not naive about what that might entail. And he wanted Tuskov's killers. Badly. He was far too restless to return to his paperwork, so he settled down in his seat and tried to relax for the remainder of his journey, to the vortex of a whirlpool from which he might never escape.

Katzhak was in his office a full hour and one-half before the bulk of his personal staff arrived at five A.M. He spent the time, as usual, in poring over papers and in careful study of the personal reports of his staff. This often served a dual purpose. First, it eliminated the necessity of his being subjected to a briefing by members of his own staff, and second, it kept his subordinates constantly alert, and more than a little in awe of him. Katzhak thought it prudent not only to keep up with his predominately younger underlings, but in addition, to create the illusion that he was somehow omniscient, and completely aware of their findings, almost before they were. He also made it a frequent practice to run down information he had assigned one of his own people to unearth, in order to impress them with the fact that he knew all, and that they were constantly under his critical scrutiny. In this way, he felt he elicited peak performance and efficiency from his people, while at the same time minimizing betrayals. Katzhak earned their respect and their fear; he was followed not only because his was the most efficient operation available, but also because it was foolhardy and probably injurious to do otherwise by aligning oneself with his enemies.

He had a special purpose this morning, however. He wanted private access to the computers in his section of the underground catacombs. Under normal circumstances he could have gained such access simply by ordering it. This was, however, a task usually relegated to subordinates, and Katzhak was doubly cautious not to give rise to the slightest shade of suspicion by varying his routine in dispatching the matter himself. This tiny deviance might go unnoticed entirely if he were to allow it, but he wanted no clue, however tenuous or slight, to remain fixed in the mind of any individual in whom suspicion might later be aroused. It would take only a matter of seconds.

Katzhak punched the keys quickly, his fingertips darting over a series of numbers, symbols, and raised Russian letters. He fed first the date Tuskov had given him, and then (a shot in the dark) the name Malenkov. The machinery hummed, whirred, and ticked. Katzhak had programmed it to give a printed readout instead of a punched card. Beside the numerical code which stood for his first inquiry was a blank spot signifying the failure of the computer to come up with anything regarding the date he had supplied it with. The second response was more encouraging. Along with a smattering of data on a small number of Malenkovs of various types was a Mikhail Malenkov. Beside his name were two symbols. One suggested that the interrogator might find additional supplemental information under some other heading, while the second denoted an interesting fact. Malenkov was a Jew. Excited, Katzhak knew instinctively that he was on to something. With the speed of a shark hot on the scent of fresh blood, Katzhak's fingers flurried all over the keyboard, reprogramming the machine to surrender all data stored in its memory banks relative to Mikhail Malenkov. This program was slightly more involved and took somewhat longer than the first procedure had. Even so, Katzhak had his answers in seconds.

Quickly his eyes scanned the small page, searching for pertinent information. Elated and mystified in equal proportions by what he had found, Katzhak glanced at his watch, realizing that he had better return to his office. He slipped the now folded printout into his coat, walked out, and shut the door behind him.

It was nearly two hours later when Katzhak first had the opportunity to be alone and devote himself to this morning's gleanings. Extracting the paper from his coat, he re-read the information he had studied previously, chiefly to verify to himself that he had indeed seen it. He gloated over his prize now, alone in his lair, and let his mind wander as to what it all could possibly mean.

Tuskov had given him only one lead. The name of a Jew. What possible connection could Tuskov have had with a Jew? How did a Jew figure into "Cosmo," and what part had he played in Arno Tuskov's death? Was Malenkov aware of Tuskov's background? Had they ever even met? How did Tuskov expect Katzhak to casually meet with this man, a member of an oppressed minority, especially when he had no idea as to this man's background or involvement? How could Katzhak be sure that this man, perhaps hostile to and resentful of him, would not betray him, assuming the meeting took place at all, barring his arrest for dealing with Malenkov? These problems were concern enough, were it not for what the printout revealed in addition to Malenkov's registration as a Jew. Mikhail Malenkov was a dissident. He had served eight years in a Soviet labor camp for participating in a ten-minute demonstration in Red Square, protesting the policies of then premier Nikita S. Khrushchev. He had been arrested on December 4, 1963, and freed in January 1972. Since then he had returned to Moscow, and although no new charges had been brought against him, he was suspected of continuing his "antistate" activities, possibly belonging to a militant faction of the Jewish underground synagogue as an organizer and contact in Moscow. Malenkov's actions were under investigation by a government office, an asterisk pointing to the number of that office. Katzhak glanced down. Apparently the affair had gone out of the regular channels and had been turned over to senior officers for study and hopeful infiltration and disintegration. He glanced back up the page, and crumpled it, prior to dropping it into the paper shredder beside his desk. He caught himself just in time. He leaned back in a sigh of relief.

He had almost overlooked a vital clue. He shook his head slightly in self-disgust. He had had it in his hands and had almost thrown it away, destroyed it by his own hand. Slowly he uncrumpled the piece of paper and laid it on his desk. He reached over to his right and leafed through a small red notebook that contained the names of all but the most highly classified departments, offices, and government agencies and their military classification numbers. When he found what he was looking for, he leaned forward, carefully comparing the number on the computer brief with that of a specific intelligence office. There was no question. The numbers matched. Katzhak leaned back, puzzled and deep in thought. He knew a man who worked in those offices. Arno Tuskov.

Of course. At last it all made sense. The task of investigating, infiltrating, and destroying the Moscow chapter of the underground Jewish synagogue had been given to the heads of the offices in which Tuskov worked. Tuskov had been assigned to infiltrate and destroy the organization, if possible. He must have learned that the militant faction of the underground was planning a series of violent strikes against government agencies or their personnel, code-named Cosmo. He was caught and killed by these people, but not before he had warned Katzhak and told him where Malenkov could be found and arrested. No, wait. Tuskov had been killed by the government. Tuskov was a Jew, once. Perhaps the underground had gotten to him, perhaps he was sympathetic, or a defector. No, if Tuskov had made or was considering the suicidal decision to defect, they would have discredited him, made an example of him, not buried him. Or perhaps he was preparing to "go over." Yes, and "Cosmo" was the code word for the lightning crackdown on the underground. Tuskov had wanted to warn Malenkov, had hoped Katzhak would be sympathetic, or clumsy enough to tip them off. It was possible, but Katzhak doubted it. He could not be sure until he found one more answer, at least. He had an idea. Quickly he set a piece of paper in his typewriter and began to type.

He made a list of perhaps fifty dates, all within the last three centuries. Among them was the date Tuskov had given him, June 18, 1815. Katzhak then pressed a button on his desk intercom, summoning his secretary. He sent her to locate a junior member of his staff. This functionary was to be given the list and told to take it to the university. Once there, he was to run the dates through the computer and to report directly to Katzhak with the printout. Katzhak explained that the dates were for historical records, and the charting of trends and cycles in nonsocialist societies. They would be used in the propaganda ministry.

The State University in Moscow is the oldest university in the Soviet Union, established in 1755. Katzhak hoped that the general information contained in its computers might hold the key that the essentially military memories of his own computers did not. He busied himself with other work until his messenger arrived. Katzhak thanked him without looking up, gesturing vaguely at a spot on his desk already piled with papers. He could not have appeared less concerned.

As soon as he heard the door close behind his runner,

Katzhak picked up the pages, hunting for the date which had necessitated the dozens of decoys. What he found did not make sense. According to the computers, June 18, 1815, was the date upon which Napoleon Bonaparte had been decisively defeated at the world-renowned battle at Waterloo. It was a blind alley. Katzhak rubbed his forehead with the fingertips of his left hand. He was tired, annoyed, and frustrated. He leaned backward in his chair, resting his head on its back. He laced his fingers together, pulled them apart, and laced them again, pondering. He must overcome his tendency to reject this enigma as impossible, and apply himself to solving it if it could be solved. If there was a solution, he would find it.

What was Waterloo? It was the beginning of Napoleon's demise. It was the story of the resounding defeat of a superpower . . . Katzhak smiled. Perhaps this was a vital clue after all. He rearranged the message in its translated form in his mind. It read: "Lightning war—massive defeat—stop Cosmo—contact underground Jewish synagogue —do not fail." Suddenly it all made terrifying, chilling sense. Although he knew it was purely speculation, without evidence, mere conjecture on his part, he began to piece together the parts of an apocalyptic fantasy so immense, so incredible, it defied description. As nearly as he could guess, a swift and terrible war, with genocidal overtones, was soon to be launched by an undefeatable superpower against a smaller, weaker nation. Somehow, by means as yet unknown, this attacking army would meet with total and certain defeat. The code name, the watchword for the attack, was Cosmo. Tuskov had known that, given Katzhak's background, personality, and position, he was the one man uniquely qualified, the one man who had any chance at all of unraveling the mystery in time, and stopping Cosmo. Tuskov's last words had begged him not to fail.

For all of this, he still did not know which of the superpowers was launching the attack, and against which tiny victim. It was a nightmare. Tiny victim? Nightmare? The words had special meaning for Katzhak, and they triggered his memory now. With awe and fascination, he recalled the nightmare he had seen on the train to Sovetsk.

How had it begun? It came back to him slowly, as if it

35

wished to impress him with its full significance. He had been alone, in much the same way in which he now found himself. He had witnessed the awful rise and growth of something monstrous, something evil. It was borne on the backs of many people. It had begun as a project, a joyful task in which nearly everyone participated. The burden of the people was light. But the monster which they had raised soon towered above them all. It had been dependent, small, weak. But their blood, and the sweat of their labor, and the tears which they cried, nurtured and fed it, till it became their master. The terrible weight of the thing threatened, in time, to crush the life out of them, as it had their freedoms, joy, and spirit. Then help was needed, and the leaders of the grotesque parade directed the enslavement of others to support the great beast.

It became fierce and impossibly tyrannical in its demands. It growled, threatened, and roared belligerently. It was always hungrily eyeing new prey, thirsting insatiably for the fresh blood of its helpless victims. Until the last sacrifice.

Katzhak remembered with horror the way in which the monster, the great and terrible beast, had fallen. It had been so sure of its tiny morsel. Its iron jaws had snapped down in full fury. And, then as now, he was the only one who guessed the danger. He had tried to warn them, tried to stop the holocaust.

Unexpectedly the mighty iron teeth had splintered without piercing; the claws, which so often seized and rent, had snapped like dry twigs. The hellish fires that burned within it had gone out in an instant, and the beast had turned to stone. It stood, then, a dumb idol, a monstrous statue, a massive monument to presumptuous foolhardiness, indecent, obscene.

And then it had begun to rain. Katzhak was not sure why, but he remembered, looking up at those clouds, massive and dark, that he had been afraid of the rain that would come from them. As soon as the first drops touched the head of the beast and ran down toward its feet, a trickle of blood had followed them, dribbling out from its mouth, staining it from head to foot. Then it was as if the dam had burst, and a terrible flood had been unleashed. The damning red tide overflowed from within the monster, spilled over, poured out, flowed all over the thing, splattering everyone who had touched it; rising, reaching, running streams rose up from beneath their feet, until they were splashing and wading in it. There had been an earthquake first, which had laid the almost unnoticed cracks across its feet. There was thunder, too, and lightning, and as the beast had begun to totter and fall, there were hailstones, large and heavy, beating it down, splitting the heads of its worshipers. It was being stoned to death from the sky, and the whole universe seemed to cooperate in its punishment.

There was no hope for the thing, no clemency, no reprieve. Katzhak was the only one who knew. It seemed as if he were the only one with eyes that saw and ears that heard. They had not been able to hear him. He had warned them; he had told them; but they were not listening.

Katzhak wondered at how closely the dream paralleled his present reality. The great beast had gobbled up many, like the giant superpowers. They were strong, undefeatable, tyrannical. Their eyes did not spare, no matter how small or weak their next target; and there was none that could deliver out of their hand. He knew that soon, like the beast of his dream, a great power would attack a much smaller enemy, a seemingly helpless enemy. But somehow this force would meet, would collide with, a power much greater than it had imagined. The iron jaws will not close around this morsel. This tiny land will not be swallowed up. All of nature would cooperate in its defense, as if it were all of one mind, or coordinated by some common will. Who would have believed it? Someone had better. Before it was too late. Who was this great beast, and who was its tiny enemy? Why had he been entrusted with this job? Who had granted him this vision of things to come?

Katzhak did not believe it could be the "God" of his little Hebrew boyhood. The master of fates, dreams, and men. He remembered as well as one could, after more than twenty-five years, apocalyptic visions, prophecies of some far-distant time. He could not recall their specifics at all, only that his parents and other Jewish families relied on their truth, on their fulfillment exactly as written, although they did not understand at the time what they meant or when they would come to pass. Sometimes, too, he recalled faintly, a single man was shown the destiny of a vast nation, might sometimes be sent to warn its people or leaders of its collision course with God's wrath. Funny, how all that legend and superstitious folklore persisted in his memory all those years. He smiled at himself for once taking part in that archaic way of thinking. Perhaps, in a world of harsh and often ugly reality, one needed a fantasy, a beautiful promise of a bright and better world. The road to a better world began with enlightenment. It took a man with no illusions, with belief in himself and his particular "vision," to change the world. The simple explanations of primitive peoples would not suffice to meet the needs of a complex and intelligent man. A man needed knowledge to dispel fears and to dare the heretofore impossible, not the irrational hope that some benevolent power would some-day rescue the world from the chaos of a man-made hell.

Katzhak frowned. What really made sense was the life he had back home with his wife. The love they shared was simple and fulfilling. He had left that beautiful woman and his house in the country to come back to this. He looked around his office. Underground, half-lit, cluttered with reports of lies, murders, betrayals, and wars. It was a real paradise. The regime's view was rhetoric, he knew. Yet he was divided, personally, on the issue. People were emotional beings, not inherently logical, or even rational. They needed hope, needed their dreams of a loving God, and an afterlife in a safe and beautiful world. All of this was necessary to keep functioning in a senseless, violent, chaotic world that offered a short and often unreasonably cruel existence. But hope, for him, had to be founded on a true basis in order to be effective, credible. He needed a good reason to expect that what he believed was true, in order to hope in the promise that it offered. Up till now he had not found that reason. A most peculiar thought struck him. Perhaps Arno Tuskov had. He wondered from what remote, intuitive part of his mind that thought had come. It struck him as profound, somehow, very close to the truth.

Katzhak thought about what Tuskov might have found that eventually caused his death. If Cosmo was going to fail, why was it so vital to prevent its launch? Despite his origin, Katzhak took Tuskov for a patriot. He was like

38

Katzhak. Whatever he had been before, he was a Russian now; he owed his life to that fact. Twisting and turning, try as he might, Katzhak could not escape the point to which all the evidence was leading. The beast in his vision, and the aggressor in the lightning war, was his own country. Tuskov would not have mourned the failure of an enemy of his land. He had wanted to prevent the ill-fated attack from ever being launched. He had been convinced of the disastrous outcome of such a move, and had sought to prevent the slaughter. His message had been all the more lyric, all the more potent because of his signature. He had said, "Do not fail me." It was obviously personal, close to his heart. He would not have felt this for an enemy. He had closed with "Good-bye. Arn." Tuskov had no doubt known he would be killed. The last words of a man who had nothing to lose carried a lot of weight. If Tuskov had discovered the plans of another superpower, he would most likely have been made a national hero, rather than murdered and erased. You don't silence a man who is trying to warn you, to save your life; you silence someone who might warn others about you. Tuskov must have become convinced of the disaster of Cosmo, while his government was not. Tuskov had been trying to prevent the loss of Soviet lives, Soviet power, Soviet prestige. But why had he been so convinced of tragedy? And why was he so sure of the danger, while his government did not seem aware that there was any?

Again, the conclusion was ludicrous. The Soviet Union commanded vast wealth and might, worldwide. It had at its disposal a gigantic military machine. Part of that machine was a network of spies, satellites, and a plethora of sophisticated electronic eyes and ears. Yet with all of this intelligence-gathering apparatus, and with highly trained men and women skilled in how to use it and interpret its findings, no one had as of now the slightest hint that there was anything amiss. Tuskov, on the other hand, with only a small portion of that resource at his disposal, was positive, not only of danger or risk, but of the absolute certainty that the attacking army would meet with doom.

It was evident, then, Katzhak mused, that the government and Arno Tuskov gathered from—or chose to believe —widely divergent sources of information. Katzhak knew whom the government believed, but whom or what did Tuskov believe? Why was he persuaded as he was? What was there in his experience that he trusted above the genius and science of his own military?

It was getting more farfetched all the time. Katzhak knew of only one thing that a man could put his faith in beyond the reach of every natural, physical force. The supernatural. Although it seemed ridiculous, Katzhak stuck with it, trying to understand the mind of Arno Tuskov and to reconstruct his last days and hours.

Perhaps the Jews had said or done something which had reached Arno. Possibly something half-remembered from his early training, having lain dormant all of these years, had suddenly sprung to life. Something had revitalized his interest, his ability to believe. What was it? Could he have been convinced by the Jews, or their teaching, that the attack would fail? Would that not logically mean that the Jews, in all probability, knew that the attack would be launched in the first place? How could they know? What could possibly make Tuskov believe them, if they had made such a contention, raised such a contingency? Unless . . . Katzhak began to see how it might have happened.

The Soviet government had been conducting surveillance on Mikhail Malenkov and others. They were aware of the presence of an underground Jewish synagogue, with at least one militant wing, a portion of which was active in Moscow. Determined to stop Malenkov and the underground, it was decided that capable operatives like Arno Tuskov should be assigned to investigation, infiltration, and destruction of the group. In Tuskov's case, however, the government had unwittingly assigned a Jew to betray and destroy Jews, and their church in exile. After a time, Tuskov began to become sympathetic to their cause, and so began to lend credence to their views. They had told Tuskov of an apocalyptic prophecy which they believed involved the Soviet Union. Tuskov must have come across something, by accident or design, which revealed the presence of such a plan. Tuskov believed that, just as the first portion of the prophecy had proved true, the second portion, the part pertaining to the outcome of the attack, must also be true. There must have been some other secondary evidence, perhaps some other prophecy fulfilled, as the weight of one coincidental discovery would be far too slight for a man like Tuskov. It was all coincidence, of course. Katzhak did not know how Arno had been deluded into thinking otherwise, but delusion was the most flattering term he could use and still be accurate. Katzhak was inquisitive, from the mere standpoint of curiosity, as to what had eventually gotten to Tuskov, but he did not even consider that the prophecies might be true. He still had the desire and the responsibility to find out about Cosmo and to ensure its safe execution.

The first and most valuable step in determining just what Tuskov knew, unfortunately, lay with the Jewish underground. He did not know just how he would go about it, but he must meet with this Malenkov, find out if Tuskov had told them anything. Compromising security on a project as big as Cosmo could very likely get a man killed. Tuskov's death was becoming less of a mystery all the time.

Still, the last words of Arno Tuskov nagged Katzhak, and he realized that he was fighting a losing battle with his mind, against reconsideration of his theories. Finally he surrendered.

Tuskov was hard and practical. He was not a mystic or an alarmist. He was not known for his deep metaphysical views on life. If Tuskov had indeed listened to the Jewish underground in their interpretation of the Scriptures, it had taken a lot of persuading and more than a little hard evidence. Yet, if Katzhak vindicated Tuskov's judgment and prudence in belief of the visions, he was by inference admitting their credibility. This was too much, too big a step for him to make at this juncture. He chided himself for being so willing to accept his earlier, pat conclusions. He reminded himself that if he was to get to the truth, his mind had to remain open, ready to consider any possibility, no matter how remote it might seem. Yes, he would meet with Malenkov, but he would keep his eyes and ears open. Arno Tuskov had died in his beliefs, whatever they were, and Katzhak owed him the most thorough and unbiased investigation possible.

Tired, Katzhak rubbed his eyes. It was slightly before noon on Thursday morning, October 31, but he had been up since two. He had already put in an eight-and-a-half-hour day. Deciding it was time for lunch, he locked his office, walked down the corridor and upstairs to the commissary. He lunched on black bread, cheese, borscht, and rich Georgian tea. The republic of Georgia was the only place in the Soviet Union where tea was cultivated, and Katzhak enjoyed it. He ate leisurely, savoring this brief respite from work and worry. He thought idly of this and that, nothing too heavy, and nothing too long. He found this a fair way to relax during the day, releasing his mind from intense concentration and his body from tension. He no longer smoked, having preferred to eliminate this danger to his health, and took vigorous physical exercise when he could, in order to stay fit. It was an effective routine for Katzhak, and all in all he was quite healthy. He remained over his lunch forty-five minutes before returning to his office.

Katzhak spent the remainder of the afternoon dictating reports and routine correspondence. He did an hour more of paperwork before giving last-minute instructions and criticisms to his staff. He left his office for the day about four P.M., chatting for perhaps ten minutes with another officer before wending his way toward the motor pool. Again Katzhak declined the offer of a driver, and drove slowly up and out of his cave. Emerging into the sunlight, he squinted and turned right.

Katzhak drove for half an hour before spotting his destination. He drove on for approximately a quarter of a mile, parked the car, and got out. He was wearing his nondescript cap and overcoat so as not to betray his occupation or rank. It took ten minutes for him to double back this way, and in that time he found himself in front of Mikhail Malenkov's apartment house. He paused for a long minute, staring up at the drab exterior, wondering if Tuskov had been here often, and what he might expect to find inside. Finally he went in. He took the stairs up to the third floor, pausing before he stepped into the hall to reach inside his overcoat and withdraw his gun, which he deposited in an outside pocket. He closed his coat and stepped into the corridor. His weapon was more accessible here than in his holster, and as he did not know what to expect, he thought this a wise move. Cautiously he approached the proper door, and, one hand on his gun in his

42

overcoat pocket, knocked and waited. There was no response. Anxious, he glanced both ways, and knocked again.

The door opened slightly and a woman's voice asked, "Who are you? What do you want?"

"I want to see Mikhail. I am a friend."

"We have no friends. Go away."

"Please," he said. "It's terribly important."

"It is always terribly important. Go away."

"If I could just speak to him for a moment . . ."

"My husband is not here. Please leave us alone."

"Mrs. Malenkov, I know about your husband's work. I may be able to help him."

"Help him?" There was bitter, ironic laughter from behind the door. "Of course, of course. Why don't you please come in, then, friend?"

The homemade chain was released, but the door did not open farther. Wary and alert, Katzhak stepped a little to one side and gently pushed upon the door. Quickly he glanced around the room, his eyes lighting on one lone woman seated on a window seat staring at the floor and rocking gently back and forth. He walked into the room, and he winced when he saw her better.

The entire right side of her face was bloated and purplish-red. Her lips were split and hopelessly swollen, as were her eyes. The right one was completely shut, and the left was little more than a slit. There was a cut above it. Her nose, although swollen, did not seem to be broken.

Katzhak backpedaled and shut the door after glancing again up and down the hallway. He refastened the chain and then advanced to where she was sitting. Katzhak shuddered inwardly, and the thought occurred to him that she had once been pretty. She looked up at him dully, never straightening her neck.

"Come to finish the job, eh?" she rasped through her dry, cracked lips. "Only take one big strong man like you to finish up. Not much of a threat anymore? Just a broken-down old woman. Not much," she said. "Not much anymore," she repeated.

Katzhak had to bend to catch her words. There was a sizable wad of rolled cotton along the teeth on the right side of her mouth, partially soaked with her blood. From similar strips in her clenched left hand on her lap, he

43

could see it had been changed several times. It appeared as if one of her teeth was missing; another was loose, and bleeding slowly. It must have hurt her terribly to speak, but she did not seem to notice. She was numb, probably in shock.

Horrified, Katzhak walked swiftly into the kitchen. He spied a rag, seized it, and ran cold water from the tap. Then he began pulling open cupboards and drawers, looking for a basin or large bowl. He ripped open the door of a large cupboard pantry, and was sickened with remorse and pity at what he saw. Inside the cupboard sat, hunched and cowering, a terrified little boy and girl. When he saw Katzhak, the little boy grimaced, as if preparing for a blow, and tried to cover and protect his little sister. His left arm was around her back, his right hand covered her mouth to stifle any sound. She made none, but a frightened whimper.

Gently Katzhak reached for the little girl.

"Easy, easy," he said in Russian. "It's all right now. No one is going to hurt you."

His tone was soothing to the scared children, and his conduct so opposite to what they had expected that it calmed them considerably, and they began to warm to Katzhak. Setting the little girl on the kitchen floor, Katzhak saw that she could not stand up. They must have cowered hidden in that cupboard all night. Their legs would be cramped and stiff. He picked both children up, trying to shield their mother from their sight, and carried them quickly into their parents' bedroom. The boy was perhaps twelve, the girl no more than ten. Katzhak rubbed, pinched, and patted their legs vigorously to restore their circulation, covered them, and returned to the woman in the living room.

He applied the cool cloth to the swollen side of her face, and she moaned softly. He returned repeatedly to the kitchen to cool the cloth. Gradually the swelling subsided somewhat, and the bleeding in her mouth seemed to stop. Katzhak noticed with alarm that aside from the dark mahogany hues of her wounds, she was unusually pale. The pain hurt her more now that she was coming out of her shock, and although he was ashamed, Katzhak felt obliged to ask questions.

"Mrs. Malenkov, who did this to you? Where is your husband?"

"Husband?" she croaked. "I have no husband. Not anymore. I don't have anything anymore, as you can see."

She was near hysteria.

"I am a widow," she continued. "I have been for years. I had a husband once, but they took him away. I'm really a widow today. An ugly old widow." She was crying, her head held low, her fingers twisting in her lap, the knuckles white.

"Are you police?" she asked.

"No," he lied.

"Yes, you are." She was still very much alive. "I want to tell you what went on here last night," she said listlessly. "Two men, secret police, came last night. Mikhail knew a secret policeman. He was a good man, so they murdered him. Why do you always destroy the good ones?" she asked him. "Mikhail was a good man. They took him away."

Katzhak was bursting with eagerness to find out what had happened to Malenkov, but he knew he dared not push this woman in her fragile condition. He surmised that the murdered secret policeman she spoke of had been Tuskov. His attention was riveted on her now, and she had his full sympathy.

"He told us, Mikhail and me, to watch. He said another man would come. He was a good man, he told us. He would learn to be our friend, too. They were friends, he said. He wouldn't let them arrest Mikhail. He was blond, sort of, and tall, this man, with blue eyes. He said we should wait for him. 'He'll come pretty soon,' he said. Last night I opened the door a little, and the men said they were police. One was big and he had blond hair, too. I couldn't see his eyes, but I let them in."

Katzhak shuddered. He could imagine the rest. Tuskov had told them that one day Katzhak would come asking for Mikhail. Tuskov had been intentionally vague, not wanting to give Katzhak's name, should Mikhail be arrested and interrogated. They had let two other KGB agents in, mistaking one for Katzhak. He guessed that Mikhail had not been home.

She continued. "They asked for Mikhail and I told them

45

he wasn't home. The big one hit me in the face with his fist and said I was a Jew bitch. He said I'd better tell them the truth or they'd take me too. I was kind of dizzy, and I said I didn't know where he was. Then they started hitting me and kicking me. They beat me for about five minutes. They know how to hurt women. I was in agony. Then Mikhail came in, and the big one kicked him real low. Mikhail screamed and doubled over. The other one spit on me and shouted not to break any bones, because he hadn't talked yet. The big one said he had just kicked Mikhail and that he wouldn't need anything where he was going anyway, damned Jew. I passed out, and when I woke up, Mikhail was gone. I know he's not coming back this time."

Her voice broke, and she sobbed uncontrollably, Katzhak rose.

"I'm not finished," she said through clenched teeth. Katzhak sat down again.

"I could not move for several hours," she went on. "Finally I crawled into the bathroom. I started bleeding in the place that women do, and vomiting. I was sick for an hour, and I bled all night. I still do. Do you know what else?" she asked, trembling and trying to bite her lip. "I was six weeks pregnant. I am glad for that child. That he will never come to this. I envy that child."

She collapsed into deep, shuddering, convulsive sobs, and Katzhak felt sick.

"Get out."

He felt helpless, torn between his duty, his compassion, and his obligation as a human being to follow whatever request she might make of him now.

"Get out of here! You make me sick."

Her words were filled with acid and bitter hatred. It was useless to try to explain. He dropped the cloth to the floor, stood up, and walked out on the broken widow of his only lead.

9

Stunned and shaken, Katzhak walked down the hall unseeing, stumbling down the stairs to the street. It had suddenly turned colder, although nothing at that moment could have matched his inner chill. The fuzzy gray rounded outlines of several large clouds drifted silently across the surface of a sea of others, passing, bumping, mingling, and merging in a thousand collisions without sound. The waning yellow sun pulled these shrouds of evil closer to its face, as if to shield itself from wind and cold. Ashamed to raise its head, it abandoned the world to wickedness and gross darkness. Alone, he shuffled through deserted streets. The winsome wind, like the homeless, transient spirit of a dead man, took up its haunting lament. It played over everything, picking up bits and pieces of paper and debris, whirling them in a graceful dance. It temporarily gave them life, before, sad and lonely, it tired of its sport, dropped reluctantly the illusion, and let them sink to their unmarked graves once again. For accompaniment it rattled leaves in eerie whispers and tuneless songs. On the street, vehicles without occupants rested, quiet, cold, and still. The winds blew through them. He cast his eyes over the tin millions. The windows, like glassy, eyes, fixed and unseeing, stared blankly upward. The doorways and alleys gaped like dumb open mouths, perpetually silent. In vain he searched for something he had lost, or something which had lost him.

Katzhak clutched absently at the collar of his overcoat, and squeezed it shut against the wind. He reached into his left pocket and extracted his gloves, which he now put on. He was tired, confused, and upset. He wanted very badly

47

to get away, to think, to reconsider, to regain control of himself again, to examine everything. Nothing made any sense anymore; he was becoming convinced of that. Everything was so senseless. He had run out of reasons; he was tired of explaining everything, of trying to figure things out that had no motive, no direction, no . . . Katzhak shook his head. He got into the car he had requisitioned, and pulled out from the curb. Putting all serious thoughts aside, he drove deliberately away from central Moscow and headed out of the city. Preoccupied as he was, he did not notice the ancient brown sedan which coincidentally happened to be traveling his way.

He was being followed along a straight road punctuated at intervals along its upward grade by gentle curves. The road afforded easily the space for two cars to drive side by side, for a fair distance. In one of his rare blind spots, Katzhak was open to pursuit and totally unaware of his pursuers. He was traveling at perhaps thirty-five miles per hour, and it was quite by accident that he noticed the other car.

He had routinely glanced in his rearview mirror for the first time in almost twenty minutes, and he had been quite startled to see the other vehicle, let alone to find it following his own so closely.

From what he could tell in that brief moment, it was an old brown Mercedes, battered and well-used. There was one, no, two young men in the front seat; he could not tell if there were any others in the car. The driver was dark, with short, shiny black hair and thick mustache; the passenger had curly brown hair. They wore the light, soiled clothes that identified them to Katzhak as manual laborers. He could not tell anything else. He did not have time to puzzle over it for very long. The events of the next few terrifying seconds were too quick and violent to allow him time to think.

Suddenly the driver of the brown Mercedes rammed the accelerator to the floor, simultaneously turning the car hard over to the left and veering quickly around Katzhak's rear. A heavy flood of black smoke shot out of the tailpipes as he did so. Katzhak's right hand flew from the wheel of his vehicle, diving into his right coat pocket in the familiar way and coming up with his gun. He stamped

48

the gas pedal hard as he did so, and this reaction might have been the one that bought him a split second of time, ultimately saving his life. As his gun hand came up, Katzhak began to twist in his seat, turning his head to the left, attempting to pull his gun across his body and into a position from which he could fire it. It was then, out of the corner of one eye, that he saw it.

Within the farthest reach of his peripheral vision, Katzhak could vaguely make out the front of the car fast pulling up beside him. From the front window on the side nearest to him, a thick, long black tubular silhouette was being slid out and leveled toward his car. Instinctively Katzhak ducked low, tucking, as he did, his face into the crook of his left arm, shielding it behind the door. Almost as an afterthought, although occurring in the same second, Katzhak realized with alarm that his gun hand was raised, and he violently jerked it down below the level of the window. He was only fractionally too late, though he had reacted as quickly as possible under the circumstances.

A deafening roar exploded from the barrel of the shotgun to his left, burning the air above and piercing his right hand with stabs of pain. Half the windshield disintegrated in front of him, and a blistering torrent of shattering glass zipped into the car, shredding the newly tattered car seat in a hundred places and covering Katzhak with glittering glass. His side and rearview mirrors were obliterated, and all three windows on the side opposite Katzhak were blown out. The roof above his head was hung with short tatters of fabric, and the light on the ceiling was no longer there. Katzhak had dropped and irretrievably lost his gun, and he watched it forlornly slide on the floor of the passenger side, well beyond his reach. He exclaimed an expression of surprise and pain, and followed it with a curse in the same breath. He cursed again as he tugged at the fingers of his glove with his teeth, gingerly releasing his bloodied hand. The car meanwhile swerved wildly, and Katzhak fought desperately for control with his left hand. The other car swayed wide to the left, eventually dropping back to avoid a collision with Katzhak's car. Unless Katzhak missed his guess, they had fired only one barrel, and the other had yet to be discharged. Suddenly he became aware of the danger of allowing them to get out in front of him and fire directly into the car. Yet he had to personally draw their fire in order to keep them from firing at the car and causing him to wreck it. Surveying his damaged hand, he realized he could still use it for shifting gears, and he slowed still more to draw them in.

Katzhak drove as slowly as he could without shifting gears, and much to his delight, his ploy seemed to be working. The Mercedes sped up and again pulled alongside. Katzhak kept the car veering erratically, in order to make the Mercedes keep its distance and prevent the unknown gunmen from firing down on him.

Suddenly the Mercedes leaped ahead, shooting out in front of Katzhak's car and taking him by surprise. He could hear clearly the thunderous thudding and hammering of an old engine pushed to its limit.

In another second or so the Mercedes would easily outdistance the nose of his vehicle, and he would be a dead man. All within the minutest fraction of a moment he saw that horrible funnel of death, a cannon at this range, flash like lightning and spit that searing, terrible cloud of flame, raining down on him a sadistic shower of molten metal. He could almost hear the roar, see the flash, smell and taste powder in his mouth and nostrils, striking and shredding, ripping and tearing, gouging and splitting, ruining the wholeness, the smooth symmetry and graceful intelligent perfection of his body. Then, all the billions of pieces that make up a man, the millions of thoughts, experiences, sensations, and perceptions, every feeling he ever had, his spirituality and insight, all the intricate and interlocking factors that made up his humanity and unique personal identity, all the things that separated him from an animal, would be gone. Blasted, cut down, lost in a single senseless burst of inhuman violence. Splattered all over the walls of a hurtling tin tomb, which too would be wrecked, twisted, crumpled, and destroyed once deprived of the guidance of its human master. All reduced to nothing in an instant. It was the height of ignorance and wanton waste.

But Katzhak had no time to ponder such profound and poignant ironies, to wonder at such pathetic blindness. Violence was like that. It left no time to think, no time to pity or love, no room for sentiment or compassion. It yielded only the briefest of moments to make a terrible decision: whether to die, or to inflict more pain, greater devastation and destruction, more telling wounds, more swift and terrible death than the danger which threatens at the moment. Violence hides the truth about ourselves, hides the truth about life and death, and distorts reality and the landmarks of the soul, where it does not cover or ignore them completely. It shrouds the mind in fear, so that the eyes cannot see, the ears cannot hear, and the heart cannot understand the simplest truths. Man lives in darkness and fear because of evil; it is like a deep pit from which he can never climb out, escape, or save himself. His mind and spirit are prisoners in this way, starving for a drop of the truth, a ray of light, pure wisdom, not muffled, distorted, indirect, or diffused. All but a fraction never know or understand this truth. (Because of this, it has taken on the nature of a secret.) And it is for this reason that most are so crippled spiritually, so twisted and warped as human beings, so shriveled, pitiful, underdeveloped, and pathetic as people.

Even Katzhak did not know these things, though he was both intelligent and observant. Perhaps he sensed them, or was beginning to in some dim way, in his subconscious mind, though he as yet did not know what he needed. Whether he was aware of it consciously or not, he still searched for the light in his personal darkness, in his honesty, in his constant sharp questions, in his critical examination of himself, his society, his relationships with others, his whole world. He burned with the desire to know, to find the secret, the answer, the key. He needed one fundamental piece of the puzzle that would make all the rest understandable. If he had this one piece, though he did not know what it was, or how or even where to start looking for it, he knew instinctively that all the others would fall into place. He could look at that completed puzzle, study that whole picture, and perhaps understand himself, who and what and why he was, and what would be to everyone else the mysteries of his world.

He wished to understand life and death, good and evil, light and dark. He wanted to explore the physical and metaphysical, to know and reconcile the body, mind, and spirit of man. To understand sex, power, gestation and birth,

51

women and men, strength and weakness, east and west. He knew that art, science, literature, missiles, moon shots, drunks, whores, and junkies all had some purpose, some meaning. He knew that architecture and fashion, weapons, and tools were all symbolic manifestations of basic elements, but what were they, why do they proliferate, why does no one human being understand it all?

The world was far too complex to be grasped by the assimilation of surface detail except in the tiny microcosm of one's own insignificant environment. Yet, he wanted to know, needed to know and understand it all, and felt somehow that he was meant to. There must be some simple, general, literal truth, then, basic and fundamental, which, once learned, would give to him a broad framework, a rule, a method by which he might interpret and understand almost anything he wished.

He must become wise, not only knowledgeable. The accumulation of facts, figures, statistics, measures, and principles could go only so far. To know even several fields well was not enough, would be absurdly limited and illogical. Katzhak searched for a higher, truer, more real, and more lasting knowledge. He wanted the knowledge of truth. It was his passion, and his pastime. He looked for it everywhere, actively or passively, consciously or unconsciously. It gave him a good reason to live, and although he did not know it, it was the loftiest ambition, the most easily obtained, yet, paradoxically, the least often attained by men.

It would have been uncharacteristic of him to think about himself and his motivation to a level of this depth, but all the same, these things were true, and he knew it. He could not possibly have dwelt on any topic at present, but seeing his life pass before him in the last few instants did touch him to think about such things. He was surprised at his ability to review so much so quickly, especially while engaging all the energies of his conscious mind in trying to escape his present crisis.

Meanwhile, in seeming slow motion, the battered Mercedes inched forward, and Katzhak watched, paralyzed, as the barrel of the shotgun was again thrust out the window and swung backward toward the front of his car. He was, unfortunately, forced to wait to make his move until almost the instant that the trigger was pulled. Slumped low beneath the dash as he was, this crucial timing was rather difficult to judge.

The Mercedes, perhaps half a car length out front, was attempting to creep to its right a little more before firing, the would-be killers angling the car diagonally in hopes of spotting their target and getting off a better shot. Katzhak watched, waiting as the cars swayed gently to the right or left, for the right rear wheel to pass his window. It finally did just that.

Instantly Katzhak jerked the wheel of his black sedan hard over, making a rapid and very sharp left turn. As his car began to respond, the startled gunman squeezed the trigger of the shotgun, which exploded the seat to Katzhak's right, filling the air inside the car with flying tufts of upholstery and damaging the back window. The driver of the Mercedes did not have a chance to respond before Katzhak's car veered on squealing tires and crashed full force into the right rear of the Mercedes.

The fender crumpled, the trunk popped open, its catch sprung; the bumper, torn lose, trailed behind, shooting bright orange sparks. The tail of the Mercedes skidded, screaming in a thirty-degree hell-slide, and ramming the left rear of the car into the left-hand embankment of the road. It gouged out a huge swath of earth, pinching the left end of the car to match the right, and scattering the road with rocks, pebbles, and loose dirt.

The curly-headed assailant was swung forward and to the side, his head slammed into the doorjamb on his side, shattering his cheekbone. His forehead, having cleared the doorjamb, struck the windshield, starring it in a six-inch circle with his eye as center. The cracks quickly filled with blood, before the ruined face was violently jerked away by the impact of the left rear of the car with the hillside. The drivers of both vehicles fought desperately for control, Katzhak trying to avoid wrecking his car into the embankment, and the driver of the Mercedes to avoid losing control.

Finally the cars righted themselves again, and Katzhak began to take command of the situation for the first time.

The other driver was obviously shaken and scared to near-panic. His plan had failed. His partner was dead. He was matching wit and skills with a professional. He was completely outclassed. He knew it, too, and it terrified him. Somehow it had all gone hopelessly wrong, and he scrambled and clawed, cornered and fighting for his life. The hit-and-run murder had seemed so simple. Now it was horrible, and deadly. His helpless victim was no longer helpless. He was being stalked by his prey, and for the first time he realized how recklessly dangerous his plot had been. He had chased a lion, and lost his two spears. The other little boy would not join him in any further sport. He was suddenly sick inside with the knowledge that he would never see home again. There would be no hero's welcome for foolhardiness. It seemed ludicrous and suddenly insane to him now. Why had they ever done it? Violence did not discriminate. Death was not particular. Murder, somehow, was not as easy, not as slick and rewarding as he had fantasized, had feverently believed that it must be.

He wished he had never ridden off in haste, hurrying to meet his own doom. He was trapped in a dark and narrow alley, one which he knew instinctively was blind, blocked at one end. And bloody, screaming death, gory and grotesque, roared after him, right on his heels. He was near the end of that alley now; he could feel it. His heart sank, his knees went weak. His life would last but seconds longer, and would end in agony, in the dust of the street.

Katzhak was by far the better driver. He was a veteran of literally hundreds of fights and scrapes. He was used to defending himself against attack, defending his life with awesome and often brutal force. The other man was not emotionally equipped to handle the idea that another human being was trying to hurt or to kill him, could not accept the possibility of his own death. Katzhak was not hampered by naive surprise at another man's capacity for violence. And although it did not surprise him, he never failed to react with rage, to strike back as fully and completely as he possibly could, when another person had the arrogance and audacity to attempt to end his life.

The song of war pounded, pulsed through his heart, sang in his breath and blood. He loved this part of it—running, racing, and chasing. Trying to catch up, intercept, and overtake. He loved to match wit and skill, speed and nerve. He exulted in rushing, rising to meet challenge. To use all his resources in mortal combat with death. He was at his height when he had successfully deceived an enemy into underrating him, misjudging, underestimating his strength and skill. That was half the game. Allowing an opponent's own errors in judgment to destroy him. He prided himself on that. He never killed anyone in cold blood. Once attacked, he carefully tested, did not flaunt or display his prowess. His enemies, in true Communist or totalitarian tradition, were first lulled, then lured, then liquidated. Like hounds hot on the scent of death, of fear, of blood, they pursued him until he caught them. He would limp, like a weary and injured fox, into the shadows, into the darkness of the thicket. He would rest there, hide, and wait, alone among the briars, thorns, and brambles, until they came for him. Then they would rush in to take him, to take his life, to make the kill. Then he would spring up and out and into their eyes, slashing, biting, stinging like a striking snake, and always they knew that his bite was fatal, that they would surely die, were dying already, failing while he smiled and mocked and lived. Their sudden shock, their terrible surprise at his capacity for fierceness and telling viciousness, his power and speed, gratified and amused him. All the time he was being hunted, he had them carefully and clearly in his sights. The timing, the taking, were all his. When he was ready, when he was satisfied, and at his choice, he cut them down. Down like grass, before the cold winter wind. Blasted, dried up, withered in an instant, mown and left to lie, scattered across the earth, strewn in pieces atop the ground.

Katzhak's car accelerated rapidly now, Katzhak shifting gears freely with easy grace and accustomed finesse. He easily outmaneuvered the Mercedes, veering from behind to come up on its right side.

He was all confidence now as he peered at his opponent through squinted eyes, his teeth clenched to one side, his lips curled in anger and defiance. It was a critical gesture too. He was sizing up his enemy before making his move, the way a cat will watch, crouched and inscrutable, before pouncing. He surveyed him coolly, almost detached, deciding what kind of man he was, and how best to take him.

He stared this way, fixed on the eyes of the other man, while he mercilessly rammed his car through its paces.

The eyes always told the story. Were they calm, as placid pools, easy, graceful, and slow as a soaring bird? Did they cast about like the pricked ears of a dog, anxious, alert, and ready? Did they flutter and start, glancing everywhere, darting pell-mell like a deer in flight, frightened and reckless? Were they widened sponges, soaking up terror, desperate, wild with fear, like a trapped rabbit?

This man was terrified, not too experienced, and not too skillful. But far from rendering him harmless, these things only served to make him more dangerous. A frightened and desperate man was almost as hazardous to fight as a very strong and highly trained enemy. He would be fiercer; he would go all-out because his life was on the line. He was irrational, unpredictable, unreasonable. Katzhak had, he decided then, to work slowly, to avoid any sudden move which might panic him, to avoid revealing the man's imminent, inevitable death, until it was too late for him to strike blindly with terror.

Katzhak, now alongside the Mercedes and still staring at its driver, began to inch over and bump the other car. He started out slowly, almost gently, and gradually increased in frequency and intensity. He was toying with him, scaring him, wearing him out. He was ramming the car in earnest now, giving it hard, slamming, regular jolts. The driver of the Mercedes was scared to death, and helpless. As Katzhak had hoped, his eyes were fixed on Katzhak when they were not anxiously eyeing the damaged front end of his car after each hammering, wrecking collision. He was not watching the road ahead of him. Katzhak waited for two minutes more before he had his wish fulfilled. He smiled. On the one-third of the roadway to the left of the two cars was a truck bearing down from the opposite direction. As it was now, it would pass dangerously close to the Mercedes. With luck, Katzhak could reduce that margin significantly.

His timing had to be perfect in order to hide the danger from the other driver until it was too late for him to respond. Katzhak veered to his right slightly in order to draw the Mercedes over to the right, thus clearing the left half of the road and keeping the truck driver from becoming alarmed and alerting the Mercedes with his horn. As it loomed larger, Katzhak stepped up his grinding assault, trying to keep the Mercedes busy and all its attention riveted on him. With unexpected suddenness he rammed the Mercedes as hard as he could, the other driver weaving wide to the left and skidding briefly as he did so.

Instantly the air was filled between molecules with the blaring blast of the heavy truck horn. The startled driver of the Mercedes jerked his frightened face front, and then wildly in Katzhak's direction. Katzhak had him pinned between the speeding truck and the stone wall of the embankment. He dropped speed, hoping to fall behind and veer to his right, letting the truck pass. Katzhak, anticipating his move, did the same. The huge hurtling wall of steel that was the nose of the truck would crush them in a second, but Katzhak could not veer off a moment too soon or the trapped Mercedes would have a chance to escape. The man's eyes were three-quarters open, and Katzhak could plainly see the wide, rolling, terrified whites. His look was pleading, plaintive now. He was crowding Katzhak, but Katzhak would not budge. He was pounding on the dash and steering wheel now, flailing his right arm, gesturing wildly at Katzhak, cursing, yelling something, screaming. Die, you bastard, thought Katzhak. You go straight to hell, you murdering son of a bitch. Katzhak watched him with cold, merciless eyes, ramming the Mercedes harder than ever in the last split second. The passenger in the truck was already throwing his arms up, crossing the forearms in front of his face. The driver of the Mercedes let out a strangled yell. Now! thought Katzhak to himself, and he tore the wheel to the right as hard as he could, yanking up his left arm to cover his face, while tons of grinding death roared past his windows.

The Mercedes climbed the embankment in desperation, the amateurish driver losing control and dumping the car on its roof at the foot of the incline. It rolled over again, the metal sighing, before lurching onto its top once more and sliding to a grating stop. The wheels spun, and were still. The Mercedes was dead.

Katzhak's car, meanwhile, did not quite escape the barreling truck, which had veered toward it somewhat to avoid the Mercedes, which was more directly in its path.

57

It was struck a glancing blow near the end of the left rear fender. The whole automobile shuddered and shivered, straining every rivet and seam with the impact. The rear trunk panel separated, the bumper was sheared off clean. Katzhak's car skidded blindly, the front end fishtailing and slamming into the tail of the speeding truck. The now totaled government car spun in wide-sweeping circles, doing three and a half neat revolutions before coming to rest in a thick cloud of smoke, still pouring off the now smooth tires, and a barrage of settling dust. The truck continued onward down the hill, but neither warrior stirred in his crumpled chariot.

10

Borky Zharuffkin gazed sharply over the entire scene as his car slowed down and finally stopped. He opened the door on his side and slowly stood up, leaning on the roof and open door of the car, one foot resting on the door-jamb.

"Wait," he said to the driver, and walked around the door and up the road, leaving the door open. He picked his way with care between the bits of glass and other debris, arriving first at the vehicle of the two would-be murderers. Pausing briefly by the passenger side, he stooped over and then quickly straightened up. The man was obviously dead. He walked around the front of the car, after noting and patting with his hands the battered overturned right side of the auto. Again he stooped and peered inside, squinted, and then knelt down. The upside-down driver did not seem to be so obviously damaged, aside from his almost diagonal legs-over position in the car. The mouth was slack but closed, and the nose was bleeding slightly.

Gently Zharuffkin reached in and touched the man, turning his head sideways, toward him. Zharuffkin's eyes widened. He frowned, sighed, and released his gentle grip on the man's head. Blood was trickling from one ear, and then Zharuffkin watched it spill out over the lips. He sat on his heels for a moment, thinking. His face grave, Zharuffkin reached over and took the man's hand, pressing two fingers against one of the lenses of his sunglasses. He dropped the wrist and stood up. He walked around the car slowly, making mental notes, pausing at each crumpled area of the vehicle and looking back down the road occasionally, past his driver, who was smoking, his back against the car. Reaching the other man finally, he lifted his hand and took prints of it, as well. He stood again and looked hard at Katzhak's car.

Unhurried, he strolled over and looked in the window. The entire car was riddled with dents and small holes; what remained of the glass and upholstery bore similar scars. The shotgun they had found miles away must have been used on him. Zharuffkin's lip curled. He hated agents. They were violent, largely unprincipled, clumsy, devious. Zharuffkin was a bureaucrat, methodical, careful, slow. A man of brains, not brawn. They were always wasting manpower and material in open confrontation of force. It was not subtle or refined. He always was left to pick up the pieces, of broken men and machines, was always cleaning up, sweeping and sifting through the aftermath. He took the motionless head, which lay slumped over the steering wheel, by the hair and lifted it roughly. A few cuts—probably it was the impact of the forehead with the steering wheel that had caused death. One corner of the mouth bled slowly. Zharuffkin let go, and the head dropped like deadweight. Bored, he gingerly applied two fingers to the neck of the body. Surprised, he hesitated, and felt for a better grip. This one was alive. He didn't much care. He pulled at the man through the window, struggled, opened the door and tried again, then leaned him back on the seat. Katzhak's overcoat fell open, revealing his uniform and his rank of colonel.

Zharuffkin's eyes narrowed. This could prove to be important. Quickly he rifled Katzhak's pockets for his papers. His breath came faster as he read. So this was Colonel

Katzhak, renowned for his toughness, efficiency, and integrity. Zharuffkin studied the face, and continued reading and memorizing. He replaced the papers and then motioned to his driver. The driver jogged over, and together they carefuly lifted and dragged Katzhak out of the car. The driver took over from there, his large muscular body easily handling Katzhak's weight as he slung him over his shoulder and carried him to the car. Zharuffkin, meanwhile, climbed into the car and extracted Katzhak's gun. Standing a short distance away, he fired it again and again into the gas tank, the third or fourth shot faithfully blowing the car to hell.

Calmly he walked over to the end of a widening pool of gasoline slowly draining from the Mercedes. Zharuffkin pulled the cigarette from his driver's mouth and flicked it into the fuel. In an instant the Mercedes was engulfed in flames, and Zharuffkin watched for a moment as the cars burned. He motioned to his driver. Both men got in the car, and it drove away, heading back to Moscow.

11

Zharuffkin was a short man with coppery-red hair, which he wore at medium length and which he was typically brushing out of his eyes, where it often fell. He was five feet, nine inches tall and weighed close to two hundred pounds. His skin was very fair, but not freckled. Although portly, he was still handsome, with a clean jaw that jutted slightly, and small green, very intense and piercing eyes. He was perpetually squinting, which lent his eyes an even smaller appearance, and his calm, impassive countenance and demeanor made him quite inscrutable, a quality which he valued as a great asset in his job.

Zharuffkin had a sense, a faculty for being in the right place at the right time. He always seemed to know, intuitively, when something was breaking, when something was being hidden. He knew when dirt was under a rug just by walking on it, and he never stopped until he had laid the foundations bare and had uncovered and revealed all that lay underneath.

Zharuffkin was cool and unruffled. Methodical and systematic. One step at a time, he searched with candles, his nose to the earth, his body bent close to his work. He rooted with his snout and tiny eyes through all kinds of mud and muck and mire until he dug up the truth, tossing the superfluous and the irrelevant over his back, piling up the dirt in front of him as he went. He reveled in it, wallowed in his accomplishments, joyed in splattering those above him with their own filth and burying them in it, dragging them down beneath him, trampling them under his feet.

To many, he appeared lazy, lumbering, and slow. He looked almost sleepy at times, but he never missed a trick. He had the well-earned confidence of a winner, but he was slowly sliding toward the abyss of his own pride. Although he was not athletic, was even a little fragile physically, he had an air of authority with most men, and a quiet arrogance and unstated superiority that he was barely able to keep in check. It was his feeling that his mental resources more than compensated for his other weaknesses. He was unobtrusive and easily overlooked or ignored as a potential threat. This factor, when coupled with his mental acuity and patient methodicism, was the secret of his success.

This morning he was dressed in a light brown, almost tan suit, with white shirt, dark tie, and black shoes. Ulev, his driver and part-time muscle when the situation called for it, was tall and blond, with broad back and shoulders and long arms that terminated in large bony hands. The latter was dressed in a cheap black ill-fitting suit, white shirt, and black shoes and tie. Everything somehow seemed much too small for him.

Ulev accounted for half of a team of strong-arms, the right and left hands of Borky Zharuffkin. These men were responsible for much of Borky's legwork, and all of his

61

dirty work. They did the waiting, the surveillances, the murders, threats, and extortions. Zharuffkin, however, always delivered the coup de grace. Had they been brighter, they might have realized the dangerousness of their precarious positions. They were always expendable, in the event of a mistake or an accident, as a short list before them had all been expendable. Eventually they muffed an assignment, or inevitably they knew too much. Zharuffkin was always quick to take credit, but he had never, never taken any falls, not even his own. He was due for one, past due, and he knew it. He had had far more than his share of "luck." Even so, this thought never really bothered him. He had something on almost everybody by this time, and if he could not buy, threaten, blackmail, or extort his way out of debt, he could drag more than a few others down with him. He was pleased and somehow comforted by that knowledge. His demise would shake the foundations of several glass houses, and a good many others would topple with him in that day.

It had been Ulev and Andrei who had paid the call on the Malenkovs the night before. It had been fairly routine. The tortured death of a man and his unborn son, and the brutal, slow, and deliberate beating of his helpless wife. Neither man knew that to Borky they had just lost their usefulness. The next time there was danger, they would get in the way, with tragic results.

Zharuffkin had a sense about this case. Some undeniable, indefinable intuition told him that this one was different. Bigger. More explosive than any he had handled before in his life. He was getting older. He would tackle this one himself. It felt like the biggest event in his career. The prize, he knew, was enormous. He was irresistibly drawn toward it, like a con man taking the last impossible swindle. His mind was made up. He would do it.

Gradually Zharuffkin's mind turned toward the body of the unconscious Katzhak, which lay on the rear seat of the car. He reached into his pants pocket and came up with a small penknife.

Reaching back between the seats, he lifted Katzhak's right wrist and carefully pulled it through the opening, laying the damaged hand palm upward on his lap. Zharuffkin studied it closely for a moment, and then began prying and popping out the small pieces of shot embedded in the surface of the hand. He worked gently and precisely, but even so, Katzhak moaned a little in his involuntary sleep when Zharuffkin extracted some of the more deeply entrenched particles lodged in the injured skin. Zharuffkin smiled to himself when this happened, and he took it as a good sign that Katzhak responded to the pain. He was in better shape than he had first thought.

Removal of the pieces had caused the hand to bleed in many places, and Zharuffkin wrapped it well in the clean white folds of the handkerchief he always carried. Satisfied, he lightly rested the hand across the stunned Katzhak's body and resumed his thoughts, gazing out the windshield, but watching only the images in his mind.

What to do now was the obvious question he posed to himself. He wanted a chance to determine the identities of the not-so-fortunate pair he had last seen burning in the wrecked remains of their ruined auto. It was crucial that he obtain this knowledge. He had to know whether or not to arrest Katzhak. If he did arrest him, and he was wrong, Katzhak could ruin him, perhaps get him killed or deported. If he failed to arrest him but should have, someone else would steal his shot at what promised to be one of the biggest coups of his career. He had to have the first crack at Katzhak himself. If there were only some way to determine the extent of his injuries, and whether or not these required treatment. If there were only some way to interrogate Katzhak first. But how would he handle him if such an opportunity were to present itself? Would Katzhak yield any information without the pressure of pain and torture? Zharuffkin did not think so. If half of what he had heard was true, he would probably have to kill him first, or damn near. If, that is, he was not dying already. Katzhak was a hard man, one of the few truly tough men. He was used to being extorted for the ransom of loved ones. Used to enduring pain. It was said that he never responded to this kind of pressure, even if it meant the most agonizing death or hellish half-life to those closest to him. In effect he protected himself and them in this way. He shut his eyes and ears to their sufferings and to his own inner ones. Everyone knew it was useless, and so they did not even try anymore. Besides, there were no

63

people who were close to him, except his wife, whom few knew about. Those that did were not certain whether or not he had any feeling for her anyway. He lived his job, solitary, alone. There was only Katzhak. He could not be seduced, because he remained faithful to his legal wife, regardless of the state of his marriage. That was the kind of man he was. He could not be bought, and worst of all, he had no fear of his own death or disfigurement. He was strong, efficient, and with a long memory for wrongs and a policy of swift retribution for debts and dues.

When attacked or threatened, he was like a turtle. He withdrew into himself, behind the stony exterior shell that had been formed, scarred up, and hardened through years of the roughest abuse. If he had a stone heart, it was the heart the Zharuffkins gave him, and the one wall they could not penetrate or breach with more of the same. He had been inoculated over the years, given the disease in small doses. He had developed effective resistance, become immune. No germ like Borky and his parasitic colleagues could ever hurt him now, and they had only themselves to blame. The only way to get at the meat, the soft belly of a man like Katzhak, was to try to boil him in oil, in which case the heat might roast them all, or to wait, and hope that somehow, someday, he would forget or grow weary and stick his neck out just a little too far.

Time, however, was not on Zharuffkin's side. Soon the cars and bodies would be discovered. Katzhak's car would be identified. Katzhak himself would be missing. There would be searches, questions, explanations. He simply had to turn him in soon. But first he must wash his hands. He had to find a plausible explanation for the tragic "accident" that had taken place on the road from Moscow. An explanation that covered his transportation of Katzhak, his late reporting of the accident. An explanation that had nothing, absolutely nothing whatever, to do with shotguns and assassins. An explanation that would keep Katzhak free from detainment, interrogation, and observation. An explanation that left Borky free to watch, and to wait.

At length Zharuffkin decided to take him directly to a minimum-security facility for treatment and interrogation.

Although he was not unaccustomed to lies, it had been his experience that the less he fabricated in order to deceive, the safer and better off he would be and the more likely the chances of his stories being viewed as credible. He resolved, then, to stick roughly to the truth, omitting all mention of the apparent ambush. He reasoned, not without precedent, that it was foolish for him to risk himself when he still had nothing to go on. Instinct told him that uncommon caution and unusual prudence and discretion must be followed and rigorously employed in this case. He ordered his driver to make all haste in reaching this point of temporary surrender.

Once at his destination, Zharuffkin was careful to discharge scrupulously the normal duties that now fell to him. Once his driver had deposited the still-unconscious Katzhak in a treatment room, Zharuffkin posted him at the door as sentinel and went off down the hall to phone authorities more closely attached to the military arm of the secret police. This accomplished, Zharuffkin returned to the room and sent his man to procure a doctor and treatment. He then kept watch himself, hoping that this hardly angelic vigil at Katzhak's bedside might prove productive. As yet, he had informed no one as to the identity of his unfortunate discovery.

Katzhak lay stretched along the length of a narrow diagnostic table or couch, Zharuffkin seated on the only other piece of furniture in the room, which was a small stool, pulled to perhaps two feet from the couch on which Katzhak lay motionless. The upholstery of the narrow bier was worn but clean, the stuffing protruding in a few places through splits or holes in the pale green vinyl. The room itself was likewise a dull greenish-gray, lit only by a large round lamp positioned directly over the table. This produced only lopsided lighting at best, there being no windows in this basement chamber, the corners of which were almost dark. Only the body of Katzhak and the impassive face of Zharuffkin were fully illuminated. The latter did not stir on his pedestal, but like a gargoyle, his face distorted and somewhat grotesque by the light of the overhead lamp, he stood watch, waiting to pounce on the slightest word or whisper of a word. He was completely attentive, ready to catch the softest murmur, the most

65

obscure gesture. He watched this way, frozen and stoic as a statue, for perhaps ten minutes before a doctor arrived, but Katzhak made no sign.

Reluctantly Zharuffkin broke his concentration and stood up, motioning with his right hand for Ulev to return to his post and shut the door. The doctor worked quickly, checking heartbeat, respiration, pulse. Satisfied for the present with the apparent stability of vital signs, he began to look at other things. He looked into Katzhak's eyes and ears for possible skull fracture. Then he gingerly felt along Katzhak's chest and stomach, working slower now, checking for signs of obvious internal injury. Again, apparently reassured, he turned his attention to Katzhak's injured hand, shooting a disdainful look at the bloodied handkerchief and then at Zharuffkin. The latter shrugged and took up a position about three feet beyond the end of the bed.

At length the somewhat terse and slightly bored doctor had finished his cursory examination, and brushing past the ill-esteemed bureaucrat, he stepped into the hall and conversed briefly in low tones with an orderly, who then nodded and walked unhurriedly down the corridor. This casual manner and easy gait both reassured and exasperated the now impatient Borky, who, although frequently treated with well-deserved contempt, found it increasingly difficult to tolerate. As his age and successes mounted, so did his pride, at first suppressed by youth and prudence, but lately expanding at a rate almost more than equal to his accomplishments. Indeed, an uncharacteristically careless attitude was beginning to manifest itself. As the years fled away, and uselessness and death drew nearer relentlessly, Borky found himself less and less content to remain in the shadows. Ego demanded greater and greater personal participation in his intrigues and plots, a larger share of his thoughts, time, and energy. He wanted to be known in his own name, take credit and fear in his own right. He was unwittingly beginning to compromise his own effectiveness by his growing desire to shed the very anonymity that had protected and hidden him over the years. The tight rein and close discipline he had imposed upon himself for his own defense was cracking and crumbling in places. There were holes in the wall, chinks in the armor, through which a well-placed dart or thorn might penetrate, strike home. His ballooning ego was fed, pumped up, by the hot air of defiance and belligerence. As it swelled out, bigger and brighter, it was much easier to bruise or to puncture. It became nearly impossible to avoid dealing it some blow, either real or imagined, and it was, with each day that passed, much more likely to explode.

Zharuffkin was gradually losing control, becoming more emotional, more prone to error and poor judgment. And this increasing torrent of new and wild feelings, flooding for the first time into his consciousness, brought with it an even more dangerous demon than pride—self-indulgence. Borky was beginning to allow room in his designs for one of the most self-destructive of passions, that of personal vengeance. It seemed the quite natural result of his self-deification that he should immediately begin judging those around him for their imagined slights and their absence from worship at his altar, and that he should enthusiastically pursue the destruction of the infidels. He searched diligently, his own best apostle, for converts in everyone he encountered, thus fostering their contempt and his own frustration. As with all new religions, there existed a multitude of unbelievers, steadfastly refusing to bend the knee, and an alarming lack of disciples. Zharuffkin nonetheless continued undaunted, determined to cause these blind and misguided unfortunates to see the light, and, by his magnanimous grace, to become his devoted followers. For reasons beyond the short, overweight, and myopic new god, the work did not seem to be progressing at quite the rate he had anticipated, and he was forced to spend much time in the righteous condemnation of his recalcitrant subjects, and the punishing execution of his judgments against the host who were, mysteriously, unrepentant.

Among such men who denied and voluntarily exiled their emotions rather than learning to master and control them, this pattern was common. No vacuum can exist for long, not even a spiritual one, and when that sea of unharnessed, raging waters wells up and rises sufficiently, as inevitably it does, and that dammed-up tide vents itself on a childish, undeveloped being, he has no chance, no

67

cultivated strength to channel off or resist, but instead is swept helplessly away. He is rushed, swirled and buffeted, battered, to and fro. Carried quickly out to sea, dumped into oblivion, transported as quickly and easily as a fleck of foam on the wind, blown over the edge, drowned in the dark abyss.

The mechanic, then, of broken and run-down human machinery, at length returned to Zharuffkin, who inquired, by an inclination of his eyebrows, what the doctor had learned. The latter, with elaborate patience quite overdone, explained to Borky in a subdued voice that the unknown's injuries did not appear to be serious, but that X rays would have to be taken of the head and internal organs to determine the extent of any internal injury. He guessed that Katzhak had suffered a concussion at least—how severe, he did not know at present. The orderly would soon return with a colleague and a gurney with which to transport the injured man. He would then be stripped, bathed, and X-rayed, his hand meanwhile stitched and bandaged where required.

Zharuffkin's anger mounted as this doctor, so weary of trying to piece back together the ruined bodies and hopes and wasted potentials of an endless stream of men and women, treated him as the child so lacking in understanding that he really was. This anger was only just barely checked by Zharuffkin's desire to placate the doctor, in order to learn from him and his patient all that he possibly could. Finally the doctor went too far.

"I did not find his papers when I examined him. I wonder," said the doctor, staring straight into Zharuffkin's eyes, "what could have become of them?"

The accusation in his voice was clear. Zharuffkin stared a dull look into the gray eyes of the doctor, so cold and deadly that the skin of the latter grayed to match the eyes and hair.

"You do not look well, comrade," was the only reply, the words delivered slowly, like well-placed punches, for their full effect. "A rest period might do you good. A change of climate, perhaps?" uttered Zharuffkin without altering his expression or once taking his eyes off the doctor's. "I have a little authority; be assured, I could arrange it. I would see that no one disturbed you until you were completely recovered."

A slight smile or perhaps a sneer curled the lip at one corner of Zharuffkin's mouth. The doctor was ashen, and his complexion as dull and colorless as his head and beard. He managed a fragment of a smile, which at once vanished, not finding a reflection in Zharuffkin's face. Satisfied with the intimidation produced by the assertion of his power, Zharuffkin turned on his heel and made for the door. But he had not reckoned on the tenacity of the courageous little pest. Through bloodless lips he croaked yet another, daring taunt.

"I did not hear your name spoken either, sir," the doctor stammered.

Surprised, Zharuffkin turned once more, his eyes narrowing. Coolly he surveyed the trembling little man again. He was even shorter and certainly slighter than Zharuffkin. Still squinting, Zharuffkin's eyes returned to the man's opposite him, his countenance full of unmistakable menace. Borky's labored breathing, his sweating red face darkening, his flaring nostrils, all belied the calm delivery of his seemingly unrelated words.

"Your people are skilled in autopsy, are they not?"

The doctor's voice was a hoarse whisper, scarcely audible. "Yes, comrade." Realizing his peril and repenting his foolhardiness, he had already elevated Zharuffkin to his level. "Yes, they are." He hesitated; then: "Why do you ask?"

Feigning thoughtfulness, Zharuffkin pivoted his gaze to the diagnostic bed before replying.

"It would satisfy my curiosity immensely," came the chilling reply. Confused, the doctor was at a loss.

"But the inspector is aware . . ." the doctor rattled, his heart bursting his eardrums, his face as faded as sun-bleached newspaper, elevating Zharuffkin still further to flatter and make amends. "The inspector is aware that autopsies are performed only upon the dead."

At the sound of his word "dead," Zharuffkin swung his eyes like a twin cannon directly into the doctor's face.

"Precisely," he hissed.

Impossible as it seemed, the doctor paled still further, his scalp crawled, his hair stood on end. He was filled with

69

sudden terror on realizing that the prostrated victim had not been a factor in their conversation and that Zharuffkin had been speaking of him all along. The latter waited until the acknowledgment of this horror registered in the startled and vacant eyes of the little man squirming in front of him before delivering the final blow. The last stroke, the fatal plunge, always had to be the lightest touch to Borky. As if he conquered by the breath of his nostrils. He smiled. A hideous baring of the teeth, more a grimace than a grin. This last devastated the doctor and left him a wet, quivering pulp. Filled with self-satisfaction, Zharuffkin again turned and went out, leaving the doctor staring after him and contemplating his brush with death.

12

Ulev was left with instructions to follow Katzhak's body and to keep it in sight at all times. He was to allow no one to interrogate him should he regain consciousness, and Borky was to be called the moment he did so. The cleanup, X ray, and stitching requiring perhaps the better part of an hour, Zharuffkin decided not to spend it idly. In the ensuing forty-five minutes he drove to his own department, dropped off the sunglasses imprinted at the scene of the "accident," and left word that he should be called at the medical facility as soon as his staff had something to report. Before departing his own offices once more, Zharuffkin telephoned twice. The first inquiry was to Andrei, his man at the apartment of Mikhail Malenkov. It had been his job to remain and continue to keep watch while Zharuffkin and Ulev followed the tall man who had visited Gallina Malenkov that afternoon, some hours ago. As Zharuffkin's surveillance of the apartment had netted no new information in that interval, he was satisfied that he was on top of the action at present. He gave his man some additional words and hung up.

His second call was to the medical facility to be sure that Katzhak had not yet regained consciousness. Confident on that point, Zharuffkin returned to the hospital. As he drove in the darkness, he began to reflect on the last several hours, recalling events and musing on each in its turn. In the somewhat less than seventy-two hours since he had been ordered to arrest Mikhail Malenkov, Zharuffkin's career had taken a surprising turn, one which, it was quite evident, would either solidly establish or ruin him. He comforted himself that at present, at least, he held information which no one else did. It was his hope that to some degree this information would protect him. He was bolstered in this belief by the magnitude of what he held, quite literally, in his pocket. What was a colonel, especially Colonel Katzhak, renowned for his caution and knowledge of almost every happening in Moscow, secret or otherwise, doing at that flat? At the apartment of a convicted dissident Jew. At the house of a suspected organizer for a religious underground, doubly illegal because of its militant terrorist factions.

Zharuffkin had enough to put an ordinary man away, get him deported, exiled, even killed. But this Katzhak was not an ordinary man. Still, it would be a real coup, not only in terms of decisive and satisfying victory in the interagency squabbles of the two rival services, but . . . That was another thing. Katzhak was military intelligence. This was clearly a matter of internal affairs, domestic intelligence. Katzhak's department was not concerned, so what was he doing there? Was he acting on his own? That would almost certainly make him a traitor. Why was he leaving Moscow? Where was he going? What would induce a man like the stone Katzhak to defect, to betray his own country, to risk everything he had built, his career, his freedom, his reputation, and his wife?

What connection did he have with Malenkov, and thus with the underground? Was he supplying them with intelligence, support, protection, arms? Who else was involved with him? How high did this conspiracy go? How much higher could it go? He did not need evidence to destroy Katzhak, innuendos were already knotted in a circumstantial noose around his neck. But he would need information to implicate the others. How would he get it? He doubted that Colonel Katzhak was likely to give it to him, no matter what threats or duress he employed. Not directly, that is. Katzhak must be freed. He must not be suspected. Further, he must not know that Zharuffkin suspected, if that were possible. This was an absolute imperative. The rat must be free to run to his companions, or Zharuffkin would be forever lost in the maze.

Zharuffkin leaned back a little in the seat and smiled to himself. He could hardly think of it; Katzhak was practically an institution, a legend. To bring him down would be a double triumph for Borky. Katzhak was everything Borky wished he was but wasn't. He had everything Zharuffkin wanted and could never have. At this moment Zharuffkin's pride was mating with his deep jealousy. He was rotten with it. This pitiful couple soon gave birth to a monstrous, growing offspring—hate.

Katzhak was respected; Borky was despised. Katzhak was admired for his strength and integrity; Borky was held in the greatest possible contempt and mistrust. Katzhak was feared; Borky was laughed at behind his back. Katzhak was an important man in his own name; almost everyone of any consequence in the secret services knew that name or had heard it. Borky lived in the dark slime of corners and alleys. Katzhak was tall, lean, and athletic; Zharuffkin was short, fat, and nearsighted. He wanted to nail Katzhak, not only for the prestige, but because it was rapidly becoming a personal thing. He would take great pleasure in hanging this man, burning down the house he had built, grinding his shattered triumphs in the dust, and scattering his name on the wind.

Zharuffkin was no gladiator, no front-line soldier, like Katzhak. He never fought in the open, in the bright naked light of day. He was an assassin. Firing from the shadows, existing in the darkness, where the harsh light would not hurt his squinting little rodent's eyes. He was a mercenary, fighting in his own causes, when the price was right. If there were enough personal satisfaction, enough glory, enough suffering involved, he would deliver anyone's head to prison or death or worse. He was totally without ethics, without scruples, without guilt or shame or compunction of any sort. He was a little dwarfish personage, a nothing, a worm. Short and misshapen, he had no part in the world of men. They did not even seem to see him. No matter how high he jumped and clamored and screamed and kicked at their shins, they never noticed him. He was like soiled laundry, soured milk, spoiled food, moldy, rank, disgusting, and repulsive. They loathed him, and laughed at him, and stepped over him, brushed him aside like a blood-sucking pest or parasite.

He hated women even more. It was worse with women. They avoided him and washed themselves thoroughly after the slightest chance contact with him or something that he touched. They thought he was dirty, crawly, and a freak. He swore he could hear them laugh behind his back, to his face, with other men. He hated them. They were even weaker and stupider than the men who chased after them. That was why Borky loved to debase and embarrass and humiliate them to the limits of his power. He really got gratification out of that. Out of watching them squirm and writhe and beg him, plead with him, for mercy, for salvation, while he stood over them. He liked to give them false hope and then take it away, to watch them cry and sob and prostrate themselves before him. He liked it best when they offered themselves, their gratitude for his mercy. It gave him a real thrill when they obliged him by degrading themselves in front of him like that. He would at first seem interested, but at the right moment he would just laugh cruelly or hurt or spit on them. Zharuffkin had the makings of a first-class rapist; but he was too low, too boyish, too immature, too pitiful and underdeveloped in every way even for that. So he contented himself with making their interrogations as painful and as humiliating as possible, while at the same time, of course, giving his men free rein.

That was why it gave Borky such pleasure to topple those people who others thought were important and whom men looked up to. He debased, embarrassed, and dragged them down as horribly as he possibly could. He was proficient enough at this, and was to this extent valuable to his superiors. Not only was he a useful tool for uncovering the plots and conspiracies of enemies of the state, he was also a frequently implemented device in use against the personal foes of his betters. For all of this, he was not any more well received by his masters than he was by those he spied upon. Zharuffkin was no more than an intelligent form of mold. He and his kind dirtied and covered the earth in decay. Worst of all, he was typical. This plague had infected and swept the earth, a dying earth. Its victims exhibited similar symptoms the world over: hatred, racism, bigotry, lust, conceit, selfishness, pride, vengefulness, greed. It threatened, in this century more than any other, to make a hell of the entire face of the earth, and people like Borky were its hosts, its carriers. They were its willing, if unwitting, servants. There had been outbreaks in the past, but nothing to equal the current epidemic. Darkness, like Borky's darkness, had almost swallowed up the world, an unprepared, unsuspecting, chaotic world, a world that did not even begin to guess the danger.

Suddenly Zharuffkin's heart was frozen with fear. What if this man were not Katzhak at all? What if he had been sent to test him? After all, he had not reported to anyone the injured man's identity. Ridiculous. The ambush was a rather expensive way to check his devotion. Was he duped into the arrest of Malenkov? If Colonel Katzhak had been on official business at the apartment that afternoon, perhaps Zharuffkin had arrested and exposed an undercover agent of his own government. If that were true, he was lost, because Mrs. Malenkov was beaten up rather badly, and her husband had been killed or at least was permanently insensible by now. He simply had to find out what Katzhak was doing there, why he was there and on whose behalf. It was a must that he be free of detainment and confinement, at least for a while. Zharuffkin needed him alive and free. Katzhak was a shrewd man. Zharuffkin did not want to make him feel threatened in any way, did not want to force him underground. Katzhak could cover his tracks well, and as he had demonstrated just that day, he was perfectly capable of defending himself with finality against those who challenged him.

Zharuffkin's cogitations were at length disrupted by his arrival at the hospital. He parked the car and flipped up the collar of his overcoat against the wind, at the same time jamming his hands in his pockets for warmth. He bounded up the stairs and up a concrete ramp that led to the basement door. Once downstairs again, he was informed that his man was upstairs in a bed on the second floor. Finally Zharuffkin arrived in the corridor and perceived Ulev conversing with a man Zharuffkin had never seen before. He knew that whenever his underlings talked, it was trouble. Angrily he strode up to within five yards of the two men and slowed down, listening.

He beheld a distinguished, ominous, and important-looking man talking to his hireling. He was six feet tall, with heavily grayed black hair combed straight back from the face. Somewhere in his mid-fifties, the man was barrel-chested and of an imposing carriage that spoke of power and arrogance. This air of command denoted a man used to giving orders.

As Borky approached, he expected the two men to stop talking and acknowledge his presence. They did not. Seeing this, he stepped up and almost between them. This time he could not be ignored.

"Yes?" said the stranger imperiously, obviously piqued by Borky's rudeness.

"Excuse me," said Borky in an apologetic manner, "I thought perhaps I could be of more help to you than this man."

The stranger's eyes were cold, his words icy. "You were mistaken," he hissed with mounting irritation. "He is doing just fine." The stranger behaved as if he would ignore Borky, and turning toward Ulev, might resume his interrupted dialogue.

"If you will permit me, I might offer my services."

The stranger, appalled at this fresh impertinence, turned slowly and regarded Borky with disdain. "Ah," he said with recognition and a hint of boredom, more to himself than to Borky, "you must be Zharuffkin."

Zharuffkin frowned slightly at the knowledge that it was the irritation he had caused this man which had identified him to the stranger. He also realized that someone must have taken great care to describe him this way. He wondered if Ulev had given descriptions of him in minute detail, and unflattering ones at that.

"Yes, sir," said Zharuffkin, unconsciously calling this

man by a term of respect, much as a dog responds to a commanding tone regardless of who gives it.

The unknown continued to appraise and reproach Zharuffkin with his eyes.

"You may go. Thank you," he said to Ulev, who gave a nod that was almost a bow and walked back down the corridor. "Come inside, comrade. I want to talk to you."

Obediently Zharuffkin followed the stranger into Katzhak's room, identical to the examining room with the exception of the substitution of a bed for the couch. The two men stood like two anxious doctors consulting in a corner in hushed tones over the status of their patient.

"I am Alexei Bulgarin," the stranger began, "military intelligence. I want you to tell me exactly the circumstances by which Colonel Katzhak came into your hands." Seeing Zharuffkin's surprise, Bulgarin continued, "Yes, I know who he is. That is why I came."

"Comrade Bulgarin, I thought—"

"Did you?" Bulgarin broke in. "I hope you have evidence to support that assertion. I must confess, comrade, your reasoning escapes me."

"I only felt that—" Borky resumed.

"My God! I think the fool intends to continue! Perhaps you do not understand me. Spare me your excuses. A man listens to enough lies in a day without asking for them. I doubt very much if you have anything original to offer me as it is. Do not persist in tiring me this way; I am too busy. Now, give me the truth, without any casual omissions this time, I warn you! Bear in mind that every word you speak will be checked and thoroughly investigated."

Zharuffkin was taken by complete surprise, his usually quick mind and glib tongue temporarily paralyzed. How in hell had Bulgarin known that he had Katzhak? His mind worked feverishly. In seconds it gave him the answer. The doctor that Zharuffkin had ground under his heel earlier. Yes, that cursed doctor! He must have notified military intelligence that a colonel had been brought in, perhaps had described him. In the meantime, they must have found Katzhak's car, identified and traced it back to Katzhak. But why, why had military intelligence taken such interest in it? This Bulgarin was obviously a very important man, a bright star in the dark void of military

76

spying. Yet he had come himself, and come immediately, although it must have appeared to be only an auto wreck. How could he have known it was anything else?

Borky's eyes began to function again, and he used them, once they regained their movement, to read, like a map, the inner feelings on his interrogator's face. He was tense, agitated, impatient to know exactly what Zharuffkin knew, and what, precisely, had transpired. He read also contempt for his person and his intelligence, and he decided that reinforcement of these feelings in his judge might be the most successful and advantageous route to follow. Damn. He did not have any idea what Ulev had said. Zharuffkin did not believe that Comrade Bulgarin was a man who, in his present frame of mind, would tolerate the least discrepancy. Borky did not think Ulev bright or ambitious enough to try to do him any ill turn, and so he resolved to reassure himself of Ulev's fear-induced faithfulness, and to proceed on the assumption that he had said nothing whatsoever that was of any consequence. He began to give the very omissions he had just been cautioned to avoid.

"This afternoon on the outskirts of the city, my driver and I came upon the scene of an accident involving this man"—Zharuffkin gestured toward the bed—"and I stopped to investigate." Zharuffkin paused.

"And to abduct, and to conceal, and to threaten the staff of this hospital," added Bulgarin helpfully.

"Comrade, I am confident that I can explain these mysteries of my behavior."

"Go on, then, by all means. There is no reason why we should both be skeptical. I hope you will pardon me, but I do not share this confidence of yours."

Zharuffkin flinched. Bulgarin had not softened a single degree. He would get nothing past him without great effort.

"I investigated at once," he repeated. "I ran first to Colonel Katzhak's automobile and perceived that he was still alive. I yelled for my driver, and together we pulled the colonel to safety. This was fortunate, because just after we dragged him a few meters away, the car burst into flames."

77

"Yes," commented Bulgarin. "I can see that it was quite fortunate."

Embarrassed, Zharuffkin resumed. "Quickly, after ascertaining that Colonel Katzhak was beyond any skill which I might have to assist him, I left Ulev—he is my driver—with the officer and ran to rescue the driver of the other vehicle, which was already engulfed in flames."

"There were two men in that car," corrected Bulgarin with suspicion.

"Ah, well, that is so much the better, then!"

Bulgarin was at a loss to comprehend. "Fool!" he roared. "What in the hell are you talking about now?"

"Why, nothing, comrade."

"Nothing? My God! You exasperate me! Explain yourself at once!"

"Certainly! Certainly! Only, first, calm yourself. I am not making sense, I admit, but surely, sir, you can perceive that you yourself already know twice as much as I do!"

"Indeed, you make me believe so," retorted Bulgarin in a fit.

"Two men, two men in the car, and not one! Yes, that's twice as much! Twice as much, exactly! Yes, that's good." And Zharuffkin chuckled to himself in an aside, as if quite swept away with mirth at his joke.

"I warn you again! Do not make me do so a third time. I want a clear explanation, and I want it now." Bulgarin glowered menacingly.

"I'm sorry. I'm sorry. Please forgive me. I apologize. Please excuse me." Elaborately Zharuffkin fought for control of himself. His perfectly moderated bravado was fading. This performance was quite demanding for the guts it required.

"I beg you, please accept my apologies. I indulge myself too much at times, I know." Zharuffkin shot a glance at Bulgarin out of the corner of one eye; he was ready to explode. He had succeeded in carefully arousing his inquisitor's anger to a fever pitch now; he was at last ready to exploit it.

"As I began to say before, the second car was burning, and the flames drove any thought of rescue from my mind. It was impossible. Carefully my man and I lifted the

78

officer and drove directly here. I was very cautious to observe the best possible discretion. Colonel Katzhak was examined, and while treatment was being procured for him as fast as possible, I was quick to call your people to inform them of this accident, in accordance with my duty and my desire to keep nothing secret."

"Nevertheless," countered Bulgarin, "you did keep his identity secret from his department and superiors. Was this also in accordance with your duty—to withhold evidence and information?"

"No, sir. No, sir, of course not. But perhaps Comrade Bulgarin will see that over the telephone, to persons with whom I was not well acquainted, discretion was my only decision." There was a moment of silence. "Apparently it was prudent of me after all, as a man such as yourself came with such haste, and I can plainly see from your agitation, if you will forgive the observation, that this is not an unimportant matter."

The lined, dour face, with its pouched eyes, drew itself up and hardened perceptibly. Zharuffkin hoped he had not pushed too far in his desire to learn something, anything, about what had brought Bulgarin out into the light. His last insight had been somewhat out of character, had belied the dull, simple image he had just striven to create. He hoped that this would go unnoticed by Bulgarin in the wake of being put on the defensive. If Bulgarin let nothing else slip at all, his fleeting expression had told Zharuffkin all he needed to know, and had confirmed his suspicions fully. It was Bulgarin's turn to be embarrassed.

"On the contrary. Nothing could be more routine. It is fortunate that my business carried me into the area."

"Yes. How fortunate," replied Zharuffkin in a tone that clearly stated that this lie had failed to deceive him.

Bulgarin shot Zharuffkin a quick glance of acknowledgment, as if to say "touché." Instantly the stone facade reasserted itself, and icy, assumed indifference took its place.

"You retain his papers, I think," said Bulgarin accusingly.

"Oh, yes, I turn them over to you."

"You would do well to offer your cooperation along

with them. The investigation of this incident is already under way, and all parties concerned report directly to me."

"Why do you concern yourself with an out-of-the-way accident, if I may inquire?"

"Accident?" Bulgarin stared hard at Zharuffkin, who nodded. Bulgarin laughed out loud, a harsh, bitter laugh, at once cruel, tired, and cynical.

"Come now, Zharuffkin, you amaze me. Whom do you think you are talking to? What do you take me for, anyway?" He laughed again, grimly and without mirth. "Even you must have seen the skid marks and debris. It was two miles long."

Zharuffkin stared in disbelief as Bulgarin laughed again, insidiously. He was shaking his head and looked quite crestfallen, as if he did not understand some joke that had been played on him, as if his pride had suffered a great blow. Bulgarin's laughter was mocking and derisive now.

"Do you mean to say, comrade, that it was not an accident that Colonel Katzhak was involved in at all? What could it be, then?"

Instantly Bulgarin stopped laughing, and his intimidating face melted and reformed in an expression of complete fatigue, boredom, and sudden viciousness.

"Idiot!" he exclaimed. "Ass!" He spat the words with vehemence and force. "I think Comrade Katzhak killed them both. I also think you knew about it. In any case, if you want to save your head, you'll get off your fat, lethargic ass and find out why. Who were these men? Where was he going? Who attacked whom? Follow him everywhere. Find me these answers, and above all, above all, Zharuffkin, be certain I never lay eyes on you again. Do I make myself clear?"

Zharuffkin was beside himself. Without asking for it, he had obtained permission, indeed, had been ordered to pursue this mystery to its ultimate conclusion. It had, of course, been his intention from the start, but Zharuffkin behaved as if charged with a grave and somewhat repugnant task, a solemn duty which he was obliged to perform for the good of the state. Humble, and obedient to the end, he bowed in mute submission.

"If that is your wish, comrade. As you will concede that this is an unusual case, have I your permission to use what men and materials I require to complete my commission?"

"Yes. Yes. Take whatever you need. Use my office if necessary. It will open some doors that might otherwise be closed in your face. It will also get you more and better manpower and equipment, quickly and without questions."

"There is just one more thing, Comrade Bulgarin, which we must discuss. Colonel Katzhak is a man much esteemed. He has a certain apparatus, a formidable hand, a long arm, a sharp eye. If he should suspect, will you and your department, your superiors, support me; do I have your assurances? Forgive me, I do not wish to seem frightened or weak, but I have heard many things about this man, have seen many opposing stars fall from the sky. Stars much higher than mine—a few as bright as your own. You must understand my reluctance to spy, to challenge a man like that. He must be handled more delicately, not to threaten or alarm him, not to alert him until it is past too late. If I prove that he is guilty of antistate activities, will you cooperate in his arrest? What can you give me as security, in case you or your superiors decide that this operation is no longer a cause which you can support? I must have this weapon in reserve, in case I must use it. Without it, you may withdraw, and Katzhak will stretch my hide in the sun to dry; from inside the walls of the Lubyanka he could reach me. As you see, I have a certain respect for his abilities. I am sure that with care and patience, even the loftiest head can be made to fall. They squeezed Comrade Khrushchev, didn't they? I want some concrete assurance of protection, if this Katzhak tweaks my nose. Last of all, I must inquire, please, indulge me, but I must ask you, we must understand each other, without mistake. If the light of my investigation should illuminate some well-guarded, hidden secret, if some path emerges which appears to climb higher than the colonel, as I fear it may, curse the thought, will I have the authority, which is to say, will you give it to me or obtain it from wherever it must come, to continue my investigations wherever they may lead, implicate or incriminate wherever the truth may burn? Answer me now, clearly, fully, irrevocably. May I pursue this affair to its conclusion, come what may? What is your answer, yes or no?"

"Zharuffkin, I want the answers. Get them for me. Do what you have to do, but spare me the details. I don't want to know. You have my assurance of support on any project you complete. But if you are discovered, if Katzhak comes after you before you have found something potent enough for me to act upon or to extend myself for, I will say I never knew you. I will leave you where the wolves may fight over you, and tear you in pieces, and I will not look back. Do you understand? If you succeed, I will aid and even protect you. If you fail . . . well, you fail alone. Find out everything you can. I authorize you to go wherever your findings lead you"—he paused—"no matter how farfetched the possibilities might seem. There may be great advances, recognition, gratitude in this affair for you, Zharuffkin. But these things can only come if we do not share this mystery too soon, or with too many. Let us be prudent, then, Zharuffkin. Prudent and discreet. You must report only to me; you must explain yourself and your inquiries to no one. Is that clear? No one. If news leaks to me that you have violated this trust I have placed in you, this solemn confidence between us, this mission which I have imparted to you, charged you with, I will take your ears, Zharuffkin. As to the 'concrete assurance' which you spoke of, let me see . . . yes, I will draw up a blank warrant for you; you can fill in the names, and I will also leave empty the number of persons. You have only to have it sealed at my office at the appropriate time. I will have it drawn up, and I will sign it. You can pick it up tomorrow at the Bureau of Military Intelligence, but this order is to remain secret. It is yours, I give it to you. If you should have no need of it, keep it. It may be of use to you in the future. Is that all?"

"That should be quite sufficient, comrade, thank you."

"See to him yourself, then," said Bulgarin, gesturing toward Katzhak. "That is all I can do. If he wakes, he would not tell me anything, anyway. I will contact you when I want you. Good-bye, Zharuffkin."

"Good-bye, Comrade Bulgarin." Bulgarin looked once at Katzhak and then went out. Zharuffkin wondered fleetingly if the doctor had remarked the type of indentations made by the shot in Katzhak's hand, and if he had mentioned them to Bulgarin. He dismissed it, and breaking his distant gaze out the doorway, he turned mentally and physically toward Katzhak. He would have to deal with that doctor later. He owed him.

As he stood deep in thought, the massive form of Ulev appeared in the doorway. He remained there, obedient servant that he was, until Zharuffkin was ready to speak to him. In a moment Zharuffkin looked up, and Ulev entered, respectfully slowing his gait to match his master's mood. Bowing his head slightly, the giant imparted to Borky the news that his staff was ringing him in the hallway. Zharuffkin flicked an index finger toward the bed and walked quickly out of the room and into the corridor. Ulev, having immediately interpreted this gesture, nodded, and assuming an air of the most sober vigilance, posted himself at the foot of the bed as sentinel.

Outside, Zharuffkin listened eagerly. After the space of about two minutes he broke into a broad grin; he nodded and barked questions excitedly, smiling after each response. With a look of puzzlement, but otherwise complete satisfaction, he hung up the receiver and stood thinking. The news was better than he had expected. It was also much more confusing than he might have wished. There was even an element of possible danger to himself. Like an archaeologist jubilantly turning a new find over and over again in his hands, so Zharuffkin turned the phone call over and over in his mind.

Three of the four prints he had taken from the hands of Katzhak's two unfortunate attackers were in good enough shape to be used for purposes of identification. The fourth was only a smear that Zharuffkin had made himself in handling the glasses on which they were taken. What the three good prints had revealed was startling, although it was precious little.

The prints belonged to two young men who shared at least one thing in common. They were Jews. Both had been recently demoted to the lowest positions of manual labor at the factory where they worked, because they were behind in their "ideological education."

They had been under fairly close scrutiny by the KGB since their two-minute conversational "dispute" with their supervisor some months earlier. (This "close scrutiny" had brought a smile to Zharuffkin's lips. Where had they gotten the gun?) Surprisingly, there was more. A fragmentary or partial print lifted at the scene of a recent militant terrorist "crime" was connected to the prints of one of the men, although it was in no way conclusive. The secret police had opted for a surveillance like the one that had netted Katzhak, in the hopes of uncovering the persons and activities of others. This surveillance was not continuous and had been a fairly recent development. That was all they knew. The car which Zharuffkin had described was being run down, as was the approximate time Colonel Katzhak had departed his building. That completed Zharuffkin's inquiries to his staff. He charged them, naturally, to repeat his inquiries and their findings to no one, under any circumstances, and to destroy all materials relevant to his requests.

What did it all mean? Colonel Katzhak had been at the home of an organizer for the militant Jewish underground. The two men who encountered him on the road were, Zharuffkin had no doubt, members of this same group. What was Katzhak's involvement, then? If he had not been a traitor, or at least a sympathizer, why had he stayed so long at Malenkov's, apparently doing the survivors no harm? What was there that he or his staff could not have found out by some other means, perhaps even from Borky himself? If he had infiltrated their group, how had he obtained his interview with Malenkov? And why had he worn his uniform? If he had come to arrest him, why had he come alone?

If Katzhak were a traitor, why had the underground tried to kill him? To try to shotgun to death on the open road a man like Katzhak, and a colonel, with his record, they must have been very angry, or very desperate. Or had that been the plan all along, interrupted by the arrest? To lure him and kill him? Katzhak was not an idiot. He would not have come alone. He was cautious, and he certainly did not need the arrest of Malenkov, would not have sought it on his own, not without at least taking the precaution of watching the house for a few hours before he walked in. In a sense, it added up. If they had intended to kill him, they could not have, would not have dared to assassinate him in Moscow, just outside their fallen leader's watched house. Not unless they were fools. Perhaps they had not known who Katzhak was, had had no idea. Then why had they tried to kill him? They must have blamed him for Malenkov's arrest. Perhaps they had been watching the house too, had seen Katzhak enter, remain, and finally leave. Did Mrs. Malenkov have some way of communicating, of coordinating the assault? No. She was not in any shape to avail herself of any such device. Yes, the underground must have been watching, must have struck blindly at Katzhak. Instinct told Borky he was on the right track. Had they mistaken him for Ulev, one of the men who had hustled Malenkov away the night before?

Mentally Borky compared the two men. Tall, athletic, blond, wearing overcoats. It could be. Well, it was of no consequence. Suddenly Zharuffkin's mind filled and swelled with real respect and admiration for Katzhak's poise and toughness. Surprised, and disarmed before he could react, and wounded in the process, Katzhak had defended himself, disarmed his attackers and killed them both. Zharuffkin's eyes narrowed with the recognition of another insight into Katzhak's character. He might have merely escaped. The shotgun, miles from the scene, was evidence that for the majority of the contest the young attackers were weaponless. Katzhak had chosen to kill them rather than to escape or stop the probably terrified and newly penitent men. He might even have gotten ahead and recovered his gun. This would certainly have been a much safer method of revenge—and a superior one—for Katzhak. Zharuffkin imagined him filled with rage and defiance, fighting against these hatchet men who had naively dared to challenge him and had made the mistake of not doing so openly, of trying to murder him from behind. Katzhak, it was clear, had no respect for men like that. Did not, perhaps, see them as men at all. If Katzhak were not always fair, he was always open. He mistrusted and disregarded men who were not. He was possessed by a determination to see justice done that was often poetic, dramatic, and final. That was why he chose the cars.

Once he had gained the advantage by disarming his opponents, he wanted to repay evil for evil. He created a chilling climate of fear by invading their space, forcing them out of their league, forcing them to fight on his terrain. He raced the cars until his superior skill was frighteningly evident. He bashed, pounded, crashed, and skidded them together without mercy. He played the part of the enraged madman; the portrait of an animal out of control had terrified them.

He surprised them, scared them, let them feel the sensation that he was returning to them just what they gave him. He had risked his life to do it just this way. This Katzhak was an interesting, challenging, dangerous man. He was willing to risk his life, to stake everything for honor, for principle. Everything he did was a statement.

This old-school genre of thought and action was a weakness, which, if exploited properly, might be very effective. If one could only learn his principles, study him, find out the workings of his heart and mind, his own rules of conduct could so entangle each other that they would be certain to trip him up in a snare of absolutes. If one could learn this code of ethics, which was so obligingly clear and overt, open to all, could bind and paralyze him in his own rigidity and unwillingness to change, bend, or compromise, he would be helpless. If the tenets of his philosophy, the foundations of his being, could be manipulated into opposition with each other, he would fall. He would be immobilized by confusion, trying to choose between ideals, motives, and courses of action that were equal to him. This strong, decisive man would only gnash his teeth in turmoil, torn between ideas of equal merit, unable to dispense with something he thought was right, unwilling to alter his word or his character a single fraction of one degree.

There was at least one more weed in the garden. Katzhak had strength, integrity, and self-respect. He also had pride in his strength. That was a necessity. If nurtured and fed with care, it would overshadow that strength, that accomplishment. It was difficult to have integrity in a lying, deceitful, and duplistic world. Especially in Katzhak's line of work. It was hard to keep his word, to be consistent, to keep from betraying people's heads for another promotion, for one more hour of life. It was an accomplishment to be proud of. If extolled loudly enough, it would obsess him. He had well-earned self-respect. He respected himself and others too much to stoop to some things. If this self-respect could be changed to self-love, and then into self-worship, it would destroy him.

Zharuffkin smiled to himself at that thought, staring, as he was, at the foot of the bed. He nodded, too, in self-satisfaction for having solved the puzzle of a man who had defied the best attempts at discovering who he was and how to deal with him. His reflections were abruptly cut off by the anxious tapping on his shoulder made by the giant Ulev. Zharuffkin turned, and Ulev nodded toward the bed. Katzhak's eyelids fluttered. He was waking.

Zharuffkin snapped his fingers, and Ulev left the room, closing the door behind him. At this sound, Katzhak's eyes opened, and he started. He cast his eyes around the room quickly, started to lift his head, thought better of it, and let it sink back the inch or two he had raised it. Turning toward the foot of the bed, he saw Zharuffkin and froze. The two men stared into each other's faces, neither willing to speak or move. Gingerly Katzhak moved his legs, first one and then the other, ever so slightly, his face still riveted. He lifted, then, his bandaged right hand, raising it perhaps a quarter of an inch above the bed, never taking his eyes off Zharuffkin. Satisfied that he was not too badly damaged, he stared Zharuffkin down, almost making him wonder which of them was really in trouble. Grinning finally in triumph and sarcastic mocking, Zharuffkin spoke in a quiet and falsely solicitous tone that could only be interpreted as threatening.

"Do you know where you are?" he asked.

Katzhak shook his head slowly, watching Zharuffkin intently for a clue to his mood and the depth of his own predicament. He said nothing. Zharuffkin decided to withhold this information in hopes of intimidatng Katzhak by fear and pretending to know much more than he did.

"Your hand has been stitched and bandaged, and all the shot removed. The damage was not severe. You are fortunate." He paused. "In that way." Zharuffkin was doing his best, and although he did not see the reflection of doubt and uneasiness in Katzhak's eyes that he had hoped for, he knew that it was there. Katzhak was not disappointing him. He was pleased but did not show it.

Katzhak did not move. He watched and waited—for

what, he did not know. But he was disturbed and suspicious of the unexpectedly considerate treatment he was receiving at the hands of the equally inscrutable Zharuffkin.

"I thought you might like to know," said Zharuffkin, leaning forward, looking around, and lowering his voice conspiratorially, "that the two men who tried to kill you are dead. You got them both before we could get to you. We picked up the shotgun also, miles back. You never got a chance to fire your weapon, did you? I congratulate you. The NKVD was quite surprised at the reports of the investigation. It is a shame, but . . . Well, what can be done?" Zharuffkin shrugged and made a face, accompanied by an appropriate gesture of resignation. He straightened up, as if he had just paid his last respects to a fallen heroic enemy. He sat back and lit a cigarette, glancing toward the window, apparently unconcerned with the dead. He grasped an ankle comfortably and blew smoke, watching it rise in wisps to the ceiling.

Meanwhile, Katzhak's mind raced. This man was in possession of a lot of information that he should not have known. But how much did he know, and where did he learn it? Wait. How much did he really know for a certainty? What had he said? They found the shotgun. They knew two men had tried to kill him. His gun had not been fired. The whole incident was under investigation. All this stranger had were a few facts that anyone arriving at the scene after the wreck might have found. These were loosely connected with guesses, threats, and a possible lie or two. None of which required much thought. The chances were considerable that this unknown was trying to intimidate Katzhak for blackmail or to get him to betray information his interrogator had no access to.

His best defense was to keep silent and try to find out where he was. He glanced around the room vainly, trying to catch a glimpse of something that would tell him where he was. Nothing. His eyes darted out the window for some landmark or familiar sight. It was too dark, and a tree obscured his view. He guessed it had just turned dark, or that doctors or visitors were not allowed in his room, because the blinds had not been drawn. He decided at length to play the same game with his interrogator that was being played on him. He knew that if the man who sat beside him so disinterested and at ease had not yet gotten what he wanted to know, he would have to begin again, and soon. Other people would miss him, ask questions. The importance of the stranger would be a good indicator of how little he knew, and how important that missing information was to him. As a last effort, Katzhak strained his ears to the sounds of the place where he was and to those of the street outside his window. Again he drew a blank.

Exhaling, Zharuffkin frowned slightly, let his leg fall to the floor, and stabbed out his cigarette. Katzhak smiled inwardly. Already he was ready to resume. Zharuffkin shifted his bulk toward him and bent closer; his face hardened perceptibly from its earlier tone, and his mood presumably was following suit.

Zharuffkin's problem was aggravated by the fact that if his hunch was correct, Katzhak did not have any idea as to the identities of the men who attacked him. At this point he did not wish to furnish him with any clues, any leads that he might use to protect himself or to further his clandestine aims and activities. He elected, then, to tell him nothing about what he had uncovered. Round two began in earnest.

"Colonel Katzhak," he began in an offhand manner, edged with irritation, "a full disclosure of the events of this day will be forthcoming, I am certain, but I would prefer to hear the story from your own lips. Come, now, what happened?"

"I would be happy to cooperate, Comrade . . . ?" Zharuffkin did not offer his name, but continued to stare hard at Katzhak, as if looking at something distasteful through a microscope. "But you seem well enough informed to me. I seriously doubt that there is anything I could add. I'm sorry." Katzhak smiled a broad, innocent grin which showed his two neat rows of teeth, like a hungry fox. This display of cherubic innocence did not deceive Zharuffkin for a moment, and was not intended to. Katzhak was defending his ground with ease, and without a sign of weakness or fatigue. This physical resilience was oftentimes the most valuable of assets. This was where the rigorous conditioning and unrelenting discipline paid big dividends. He could drive his body, mind, and spirit when he wanted to, and he could always rely on them to perform for him when he needed them the most. He drove himself now, characteristically, did not give ground, and overall showed no sign that he was anywhere but at the peak of his powers.

"To kill two men in daylight on the outskirts of the capital of your state is a serious crime, which you seem to take quite lightly, Colonel." Katzhak had had enough needling from this amateurish dog. He was determined to assert himself, and to put up with nothing further until the man at least identified himself.

"Crime? Crime!" he rasped. "I am a colonel of military intelligence, for twenty-five years a distinguished servant of the state you keep talking about. It would behoove you to spend less time instructing me about my duty. And I will continue, comrade"—he spat the word at Zharuffkin—"to commit the 'crime' of defending myself against the assassins and murderers who are the enemies of myself and the work which I do on behalf of the party. All the enemies of the Union of Soviet Socialist Republics, and its peoples and agencies, whoever they may be. Do I make myself clear?"

Zharuffkin's ears bent back. "Of course, but—"

Katzhak, sensing his advantage, broke in. "Then it should also be clear that the treatment I have received from you has been contemptible. Unless you identify yourself, we have nothing further to say. Although you are fluent in the use of my name, it is obvious that you are illiterate as to its meaning. Be careful how you use it, comrade. Now, drag your tail out of here; I find the sight of you offensive."

Zharuffkin glared at Katzhak for a long moment. His usually pale face was flushed with rage. In a tightly controlled voice, barely audible, Zharuffkin spoke. "As you wish, Colonel. We will meet again, I think. I hope for your sake that you are half the man you think you are."

"Thank you, comrade. I feel certain that *you* are."

Zharuffkin winced as if he had just received a vicious slap. He nodded, staring, and walked out. Katzhak closed his eyes and pursed his lips. He had won, at least for the moment; but victory was fleeting over worms, dogs, and children, and not satisfying. Zharuffkin was all of these. Katzhak was aware that he had gained nothing but a temporary reprieve—and a vicious, sniveling enemy. He could look forward to some unexpected stab in the back, some "accidental" shot in the darkness. He would have to be very careful, perhaps forever, or at least until a more final contest could eliminate this danger more surely. Suddenly weary, he sighed, shook his head, and retreated along some dim alley into sleep.

13

Katzhak sat at his desk alone in the early hours of the morning, working with uninterest on a stack of papers. There was a knock at the door, and he rose to answer it. He opened it to find a messenger, dumb and grave as death, in a gray uniform, young and somehow almost inhuman in aspect. In complete silence he held out to Katzhak a small envelope. Stunned and shaken, Katzhak had stared at the note, wondering whether or not to take it, when, insistently, it was not withdrawn but held until, trembling, he reached out for it. Somewhere a bell began to toll faintly, solemn and mournful. As his hand closed around the envelope, a tremendous clap and peal of thunder split the air, and Katzhak jerked his head toward the sound. The rain suddenly poured from the sky, and he heard the thudding and staccato racket of hailstones. Turning back once again toward the doorway, Katzhak was frozen with fear. In the spot where the messenger had stood, there was only a puddle of water, dotted in a few places with small drops of blood. There was no one in the hallway. From the ceiling, from the walls, came the pitiful crying of a young woman, sobbing and weeping without hope of consolation or surcease. Soon there was another older woman wailing and moaning. An old woman joined the chorus, then a little girl, then another, and another, and another.

As Katzhak watched in horror, the grotesquely battered and beaten form of Mrs. Malenkov appeared. Her face was still bloated and bruised purplish-red, swollen, cut, and streaked with tears. She shuffled along the hallway slowly, knocking weakly on doors which were finally opened by men who hid back in the darkness. Only the bloody hands showed on the knobs. She would ask, "Where is my husband?" or "Have you seen my baby boy? Where is my little son?" Some doors were slammed in her face. Some men laughed or shook their heads in innocence or cruelty. Some kicked her with their heavy boots or spit on her. They showed her their bloody hands and shrugged their massive shoulders. Some men offered her bundles wrapped in blankets. She would smile and look up with gratitude. Timidly she would unwrap the blankets, and inside, she found a gun, or a snake, or a scorpion, or a golden bear. Terrified, she threw the monstrous things from her hands. Hanging her head, she trudged on. Finally she sobbed and sank to her knees in a doorway. "Oh, God, where is my husband?" she shrieked in prayer. "Where is my child? Oh, God, where is my face?" She had lost all control. "God, who will love me and kiss me with his mouth? Who will sleep with me and share the warmth of his body? Who will want me and fill my womb with life? Who will give me babies and comfort me in my toothless old age? Why have you abandoned me?" At length she fell prostrate on the floor, hysterical.

Katzhak stared in shock and disbelief. All at once the wall of the corridor before him dissolved, and he beheld a sea of sobbing Russian women. Some touched their lips, some their breasts, some between their legs. All heads were bowed, their faces contorted in anguish. Each wore stenciled on her garments above the heart a number which stood for the husband or brothers or father or sons or grandfathers she had lost. Katzhak scanned their terrible faces and froze. On the right, toward the front, stood

Tash, bent and weeping uncontrollably. Soon the wind came up and whipped at the hair and clothing of the bereft and destitute women. There was thunder and lightning, and horses neighed. Men shouted and the women sobbed louder. The rain fell and drenched their bodies. Katzhak stumbled backward and into his office. He leaned on his desk and slammed the door shut. Abruptly the tumult ceased. Katzhak sat collecting himself. At last he opened the note. In small but highly legible print at the top of a single page it said in black type: "They have killed me, you know. It is too late for me. They will kill you too. It is up to you now." Then, in the middle of the page, in large, thick, dark type: "STOP COSMO." "Do not fail," it said at the bottom in the same size lettering as the top. "Everything depends on it."

Shuddering, Katzhak saw in his mind's eye the violent death of Arno Tuskov. Saw him terrified and driving in a car. Saw him pursued, saw his car riddled and chopped with row after row upon row of bullets and shotgun blasts. Saw his friend hit again and again. Saw him faint, saw him skid, saw him crash and burn. Saw his face, saw him beckon. Saw his face, and then a skull, alternating a dozen times within a second. Saw the face of Tash, bowed and weeping, Tash begging him not to go. He cried, himself, and reluctantly moved toward the door. He opened it, and his eyes, at the same time. His room was dark and still. He was sweating and shivering at once. His neck and arms were covered with gooseflesh and his hair was raised a little all over. He had to admit to an awesome, chilling terror and weakness. He felt dizzy and his heart raced. He tried to calm himself, and called for a doctor. His yells echoed throughout the empty corridors.

14

At eleven o'clock the next morning, Katzhak was given a short psychiatric exam. At noon he was released. His doctor had wanted to detain him for a day or so for observation. He had settled instead for a lengthy lecture on the gravity of any concussion or blow to the head and had extorted promises from Katzhak to avoid strenuous physical activity or reinjury.

His head split with pain, which occasionally affected his vision or made him nauseous in waves and rolls that swept over him at intervals. His hand throbbed, and he was obliged to keep it raised to control the pain and bleeding. Pale as the concrete stairs of the hospital beneath him, he felt weak and stopped several times to keep from fainting and falling down the steps.

He hated that bastard, whoever he was, that had brought him in. Already they were dividing up the carcass. Yes, he was exactly like a buzzard. He was a dirty, loathsome, and disgusting scavenger, trying to rip his limbs apart and feed on the raw flesh between the bones. Katzhak smiled wanly. This was one meal he was not going to get. Not yet.

Stopping at the car he had had them call for him, he leaned on his left arm, which lay across the roof, to rest. Feeling sick and choked, and suddenly wildly claustrophobic, he did not want to get in. He finally did so, however, if only because his knees were beginning to buckle beneath him. In a voice that was little more than a muffled croak he told the driver where to take him, and let his head slump back onto the rear seat. He really was too sick to move, but he drove himself, experience teaching that the slightest delay might be critical to survival. His insides retched and he felt fitful. They were finally somehow there, and by sheer force of will Katzhak dragged himself through the corridors to his office. He collapsed into a small field cot and lay panting in the security of his office. In moments he was asleep, and remained that way until three o'clock.

At last Katzhak opened his bloodshot eyes and blinked several times. Slowly, and with the utmost respect for his battered head, he propped himself up on an elbow and then raised himself to a sitting position. Gingerly he massaged the back of his neck with his good hand and then sat for half a minute thinking.

Leaning on the edge of his desk and then the arm of his chair, he sat down, paused a moment longer, and reached out for the intercom. "Tatiana, send a girl in here; I have some work to do."

"Yes, Comrade Colonel," came the usual crisp and efficient reply. Still, they had worked together for years, and Katzhak could have sworn that he detected some uneasiness in the voice of his personal secretary.

The door opened and then closed again. Katzhak finished reading and looked up. His eyes widened and his scalp slid back. Before him stood one of the most beautiful and attractive women he had ever seen. Black hair tumbled loosely to her shoulders. Large, dark eyes, wide with sultry innocence, lips long and pink and moist and full. Her breasts were medium-sized, high, pert, and well-shaped. She had a narrow waist, and hips that curved in a not-too-wide but obviously feminine way. The legs were long, perfect, and parted slightly, one foot demurely placed in front of the other. Katzhak was impressed. Someone had guessed his tastes quite well, considering. With long, loose hair, dressed in starched blouse and pleated skirt, she was very feminine, very much a woman. But her appeal was not blatant, it was subtle, although deliberately alluring. She was modestly dressed, pretty, clean, fresh, innocent. She was well shaped, but not overdone. She had a nice figure and body, but she was not a whorish sex machine. She was a lady, not an animal in heat. She was attracted to him, yes. But not overwhelming or pretentious. She was beautiful, but capable of giving and receiv-

95

ing on many levels. Yet she was aware of her body and his. She was not pure in the naive, pristine way of a child. Katzhak pretended not to notice the fact that he had never seen her before and that she obviously had been generously added to his staff during his unfortunate illness and convalescence.

The creature smiled at him. Not knowing what else to do, Katzhak smiled back. She blushed and smiled again. Katzhak did the same. At length he motioned her to a chair beside his desk and began to dictate a meaningless report. She stole occasional furtive glances at him while she worked, but was on the whole silent otherwise.

Suddenly, as the woman sensed the report and her audience coming to an end, the stenographer's pencil flipped from her hand and rolled a short distance from under her chair. She smiled, flustered, tugged at her skirt, and reached down for it over the arm. The skirt rose up, nonetheless, to reveal several bruises on the inside of her thighs and upper legs. They were dark combinations of blue and yellow, blue and green, and an occasional purplish-red. Her blouse had fallen open slightly, being pulled and strained somewhat from its original location, exposing at least one other cruel wound and the softly rising, rounded swells of two very beautiful feminine attributes.

Katzhak's eyes narrowed and snapped back in a wince that was checked before it was begun. The corners of his mouth, which ordinarily would have tugged his lips into a grimace, did not move. His body registered no other response to what he had seen. Katzhak examined his mind to see if it could match his body for discipline and control. With a sharp blade he mowed to the ground his sprouting feelings of protectiveness and outrage, and cut back to the roots the tiny new blades of tenderness for her. Confident that he had resumed full command, he made certain that everything was battened down and securely lashed to the deck, in the event of the most piercing storm, before he at length attempted to again take up his course. With these obstructions out of his view, he might see her more clearly.

Although his outward appearance wore an impregnable mask of mute and patient indulgence, his eyes were all over her, everywhere at once, scanning, surveying, studying, searching. He did not gaze at any place too long, examine, dissect too minutely. His practiced glances through the magnifying lens which he held up to her would focus his intense energies, would sear her, cause her pain, alert her. He poked, prodded, sifted, separated, probed with his eyes.

The creature sat up once more, demurely rearranging her garments. She shot him a tortured glance of recognition, which was at once scolding and pleading. Oh, her performance was not yet concluded. Katzhak could see that there was much more to come. In the momentary pause which she had allowed herself between acts, he wondered how her blouse had fallen open so far, like the skin of over-ripe fruit. In his mind's eye he rolled the tape. There had been a knock at the door. It had opened; she stepped in. Stop. Freeze that frame. Yes! It had been buttoned almost to the throat. Quickly he compared his mental image to the one his eyes now reported. He counted; the pictures did not match. Slowly he restarted the projector and combed the film, frame by frame. Nothing; that fourth button must have naturally unfastened as she had leaned over. He was almost at the end of the reel. She was about to drop her pencil. Any moment now, there! Wait. Rewind. Slowly he watched again, fascinated. As he looked on, the Katzhak on the screen had leaned on his elbow, rubbed his forehead, trying to expunge the ache, and now! He had rubbed his closed eyes with both hands. The head straightened up, the hands came down, and there it was. As the eyes opened, the pencil was in midair, the blouse was buttoned one notch lower. He watched again, freezing the action just before he closed his eyes and just before the girl moved to retrieve her implement. He placed the still pictures side by side. It had happened while his eyes were closed. He smiled in triumph and self-satisfaction, and returned to the present. All of this had occurred in an instant of time.

Wordlessly Katzhak rose from his chair, a masterfully painted portrait of tenderness and tightly controlled emotion. He stood next to her and placed a warm, gentle, firm hand on her shoulder. Her lips trembled; her chin quivered; her hands shook; and she made fists to control them. A soft tremor went through her body, and her face dis-

97

solved. She cried in a paroxysm of quiet agony and hot, blushing shame. To see her humbled and broken this way, disconsolate and pitiful, had a powerful and compelling effect on Katzhak. He forced himself to see her gloating over his dead body, the ugly, aging, laughing harlot she was. Ready to lie down on his grave if the price were right. She was not a woman. Women he respected, loved, almost reverenced, adored. She was totally different, an alien creature. She was a whore. She was nothing like Tash. There could be no connection. This weeping wanton had been hired and paid, sight unseen, to deliver him to death. She was trying right now to bypass the legendary mind, to win his heart so that she would have something to sell. In his heart, Katzhak turned away. He cried and gnashed his teeth, and could not look at her. To see a woman—a beautiful creature with the power to make a baby in her body, to deliver a life into the world, to feed that child from her heart—degrade her sex, pervert her nature, abuse and twist and misuse her unique destiny and purpose and privilege this way. It always disturbed him profoundly. It was immoral, monstrous, evil, and unforgivable. No. No, it was horribly wrong. That was not the way it was intended. Women were . . . He groped for the word, but could not find it. Twenty-five years ago he might have said "blessed." They were—sacred?—somehow, they were almost . . . His heart longed to say "holy"; but his mind, and the state and his years, choked on the word. Strangled it before it could even be formed, submerged it below the surface of the deep and fathomless pool that was his consciousness. Unutterably sad and helpless, he watched his hope, his decency and goodness and true nature, sink with that word. Wept bitterly within his soul as it vanished from his sight beneath the depths. He lifted his head when he heard the sound.

The woman sat on a purple-and-scarlet throne on the bank opposite him. Her legs were wide apart. A cup, a chalice, she swung in her hand and drank from. The cup was silver and studded with precious stones. Her lips were wet, red, and grapy. When she drank, the wine trickled down her chin and rolled down her front. The cup tilted and Katzhak realized it was filled with blood. She was obscene, and called out to him. Her talk and her laughter were filthy, lewd. She leered and beckoned and teased. Her imitation of womanhood was shocking, disgusting, a mockery. She reeled with drunkenness. Katzhak saw his leaders, saw his enemies, saw the heads of many nations snort and stamp and paw the earth, climb upon her, pay homage to her, deck her with jewels and presents. They killed men for her pleasure. Her body was sweet and sticky, and smeared with blood.

Katzhak watched Arno Tuskov crawl up from the side and look under her throne. There were dead men's bones and rottenness, like the inside of a tomb. A foul smell poured out, and the skeletons of the men and the women and the children cried out. The important men were frightened and pointed to him.

The woman laughed and turned her head down toward him. He looked up, and she laughed again; at the same time, she swung her arm down and slammed the heavy chalice into the side of his head. He was knocked flat, and the woman turned back to her men, only she paused to drink again from her cup amid their laughter. Dogs came and licked timidly at his blood. He must not, dare not, forget who she was.

Suddenly he hated her. He was choked with an inexpressible fury and rage. He wanted to tear her to pieces, to shut her lying mouth forever.

Just as suddenly, his mind changed. She was not so evil, perhaps, not so demonic. She was totally ignorant of her nature, her being. She had no inkling of what she was composed of. She did not know what she was doing, what she was tampering with. She could not begin to guess the kind of creature she was. She blindly abused and debased them both. And the people who sent her were doubtless just as ignorant and in the dark. He sighed within himself. He looked at her with compassion. He was sad; he loved her as a fellow creature, and he pitied her for the darkness in her soul, for the veil over her mind, which prevented her from guessing the truth about herself and her world.

Katzhak took her hands and pulled her to her feet. He held her shaking form while sobs racked her body and she cried into his chest. As a precaution for himself, he led her to the cot against the wall of his office and coaxed her to lie down. Katzhak squatted on his heels beside her and stroked her hair and forehead soothingly. "You need a doctor," he said. Her face went white. She yanked herself up by her stomach muscles and begged him, "No. Please. My husband would kill me. I'm all right. It was an accident. I'm fine." Katzhak was silent.

"Did your husband do this to you?"

"No. No, of course not."

"Why did he do it?"

"He didn't."

"You're lying."

"I know."

"Tell me why your husband beats you. Gives you bruises where they won't show."

"No." She shook her head.

"Why? Why won't you let me help you?"

"Because I want us both to live. And if you feel the way I do, you'll forget about my problems. Besides, what do I want with another man?"

This was the timid refusal of an offer he had not made. She was cunning and subtle.

"I'll take you home in my car," he said.

"That won't be necessary, Comrade Colonel." Her words were meant to rebuke his sudden familiarity.

"Nonetheless, I will. I feel obliged to aid you in some way."

"Don't. If you value your happiness, don't bother." She sat up.

"Come on" was all he would say. She shook her head in disbelief. "You'll be sorry," she promised.

They walked through the corridors in silence. "Colonel, wait. You are very kind. Too kind. I'm indebted to you, really. But you don't owe me the time of day. Run home before you get hurt."

Katzhak just looked at her as she stood by one of the dark sedans in the motor pool.

"Why do you insist on being a fool? I told you to let me go."

"Where do you live?" he persisted.

"My dear husband and I were separated as of this morning. I have no place to go. Pull in your ego and sexist pride and leave me alone. I implore you for the last time."

"Get in the car," he commanded. Without further hesitation she obeyed. She sat in the corner against the door like a sullen, recalcitrant child. Katzhak gestured for a driver and gave him his instructions. The heavily set young man with black hair and a pale, clean complexion leaped into the car, and the three of them took off slowly in the direction of Katzhak's flat.

Abruptly she turned her head from its perpetual gaze out the window and regarded Katzhak appraisingly. Timidly she reached out and took his hand, turning it over and over in her own. A tear fell silently on the back of one of them. She looked up and smiled before snuggling her head on his shoulder for the remainder of the ride. Her hand was on his chest, clinging to him, hiding in his manhood, in his strength. With her nose and chin she nuzzled his neck softly, and gently stroked his bristly cheek. Soon Katzhak could tell by the measured regularity of her breathing and the evenness with which her breasts rose and fell that she was asleep. He smelled the clean sweet perfume of her hair and skin and closed his eyes. He wished that it was all somehow real, and that somehow he held Tash in his arms. Wished that it was she who clung to him, she who found rest and comfort on his chest. He rode motionlessly, until finally the car lurched to a stop in front of his apartment.

He sighed and shook her gently to wake her. She murmured and nuzzled deeper into his coat. He shook her again, and she opened her eyes, blinking at him and at her surroundings. Katzhak opened the door and climbed out, holding it for her as he lifted and pulled her into the cold night air. The driver looked away discreetly, and had soon disappeared, leaving the two of them in the street. They looked at each other for a long moment, before Katzhak slowly took off his coat and wrapped her grateful body in it. Turning with his arm around her, Katzhak led the way up the stairways and into his flat. He made coffee for her and left her sitting alone while he ran water for her bath in his small lavatory. Once thus warmed in so many ways, she consented with great emotion to his concern for her. He said nothing at all now as he began slowly to undress her. Their eyes held, locked, as their bodies longed to be, separating only while he looked at her body, absorbing its

101

full-length beauty, enjoying the feelings it stirred in him. This interlude was ten times more touching for its tenderness, and the absence of words went quite unnoticed and unmourned. She stood before him naked now, wondering at his awesome strength and disarming, paradoxical gentleness. He touched lightly with his hands the injured parts of her body, touched each mark and bruise as if he felt much more pain than these had ever given her. Sweetly he kissed her forehead and guided her to the tub.

A wave of tremendous warmth and satisfaction swept over her as she stretched out and lay back in the hot, steaming water. The tub was short, and she drew her knees up in provocative innocence to compensate. Katzhak massaged her neck and shoulders. Caressed her breasts and their terrible impressions. Manipulated gently the skin of her soft thighs and long legs. She purred like a kitten, becoming obviously more aroused as the moments floated by. Easily Katzhak questioned her.

"Tell me about your husband. What kind of man is he?"

She seemed to stiffen in his hands, her body shifting uneasily in the warm water. "What would you like to know? Why he beats his wife and shames and humiliates her? I don't know. He is a jealous man. Bad-tempered when he drinks, but nice enough when he's sober. When he drinks, like last night, he gets ideas."

"What kind of ideas?"

"The usual kind. He becomes positive that I am unfaithful to him. He beat me last night because I denied it. I was not lying, if it makes any difference. Next time, I think I'll confess. He's dangerous. He has humiliated me so many times with his yelling, and I'm sure it makes noise when he hurts me. He accuses other men of lying with me. Right in front of them; they probably think that I put him up to it. That I am neurotic, that I fantasize, that I want them. Sometimes I am so furious and hurt and ashamed of him, and somehow of myself, that I could . . ." She let her voice trail off, leaving the thought unfinished.

"Why don't you divorce him? Or leave him?"

"Because he is my husband, and he can be decent at times."

"Do you love him?"

"He is my husband. When I am ready to leave him, he

is good to me and I lose my will. I suppose so. I used to."
She tilted her head and looked at him askance. "You're
curious, aren't you? And persistent. Do you always get
what you want?" Her knees parted a fraction, and she
turned closer to him in the water.

"Sometimes," he said.

"Honest, too? You are strong and fearless. I like that.
It excites me, somehow, makes my skin tingle all over.
Have you ever had that feeling?"

Katzhak smiled and took her hands, raising her to her
feet and surveying her beautiful nude body. She was alive
and exciting, a luscious female animal. All sex now, and
all his. Without a word he led her, wrapped in her towel,
to the light switch in the entry of his apartment. Slowly he
turned off the switch and reached for her in the darkness.
The towel fell when she raised her arms, and slid to the
floor with powerful eroticism. Gently but firmly Katzhak
opened the door and shoved her out, wet and naked, into
the freezing corridor.

"Katya! What are you doing?"

"Say hello to your husband for me, darling."

"What? I don't understand!"

"Tell whoever sent you that I want an apology. He's in-
sulted my intelligence and my taste. Only an amateur or a
fool would pull a stunt like this against a professional.
Take care, honey. And thank you. It's been a wonderful
evening."

"Oooh," she hissed. "Now, you listen here, you little
bastard, you open this door! You impotent son of a
whoring bitch, give me back my clothes!" The steady
stream of obscenities and expletives continued unabated
until, kicking, shouting, and cursing, she succeeded in
drawing attention to herself. There was a knock at his
door. Katzhak opened it a ways and beheld the apartment
managers and a uniformed guard clustered around the
shivering girl, who was livid and purple with rage, shaking and red with shame. Obviously embarrassed, they
spoke rapidly to Katzhak. He looked suddenly contrite,
and a triumphant smile passed over the woman's lips. She
waited with confidence and reinstated pride for him to
speak. "I've never seen her before in my life," he said,
smiling. The managers perceived their error in confronting

him, guilty or not, and they were quite ready to accept his word and back off. The woman screamed and clawed and spat at him before being carried away, cursing and struggling, down the hall. Katzhak laughed as he looked after her, shook his head, and returned to his apartment. He sat for a moment thinking, smiled again, and prepared for bed. He slept uneasily till the morning.

15

Katzhak was up at 4:15. The morning was cold and gray and heavily overcast. His head still pounded, but soon it would subside into a dull ache. In spite of the Moscow cold he knew he would find outside, he splashed his face with cold water. He inspected his lip in the mirror and combed his short military cut. He treated himself to coffee while he dressed, and in another five minutes he was on his way to work.

Katzhak took a taxi after his harrowing ride of just a few days before, and he enjoyed the second course of his breakfast in his office by five A.M. This consisted of tea and the early-morning rushes furnished by his staff. He refreshed his memory, kept sharp, alert, and abreast of the news, both foreign and internal, and planned his day's activities and itinerary. Informed, and keyed up for his day, he settled in to work. "Tatiana, send down to ID and get me someone who does sketches, good ones. I want someone tight who owes me an inside. When he's gone, I want a technician in here who can set up the computers and make these faces. Also, get me someone older, experienced, from vehicle identification. Someone who knows what's been hot for a while back. Try to get Raseilei Tamarzov. Jump on it; I'm in a hurry."

"At once, Colonel," came the dutiful reply. Within ten minutes Katzhak was signaled that his first request had just arrived. Katzhak opened the door himself, leaving strict instructions that he must not be disturbed. The two men were closeted for nearly two hours. The artist was a horn-rim-bespectacled young man of about twenty-eight, with very short chestnut-colored hair. He carried two large volumes which contained, in horizontal rows, hundreds and hundreds of sketches of different eyes, brows, noses, lips, chins, foreheads. It was up to Katzhak to select the individual features most closely related to those of his assailants. The artist combined and blended, under Katzhak's watchful eye, attempting to construct a good composite. When at length they had finished, Katzhak dismissed the artist and made two photocopy duplications of the likenesses. These he sent out, accompanied by two of his junior staff members (ambitious young men, content for the moment with doing someone else's legwork), to all the morgues and hospitals where the young would-be killers might have been taken. One was injured, he knew. Pretty badly, he thought. He could not guess or remember whether or not the other had met a similar fate.

It was 7:15. Without taking a break, Katzhak again ensconced himself in his office with his second visitor, a short, portly blond technician of perhaps forty years of age. In moments the men came out and walked briskly down to one of many computer tie-in points, where they might have some privacy. The first priority was to seclude and seal off the work they were doing from anyone who might be "watching" electronically. The second was to tap the computers for the tiniest scrap of knowledge concerning the two men. This was a difficult and time-consuming task, relatively speaking, since all the programmer had to work with were imperfect sketches and hazy physical descriptions. They were searching for a blade of grass, which they could not describe, in a three-acre meadow. Nevertheless, the technician worked diligently, Katzhak looking on with interest as he plied his craft. Finally, after several intricate programs had been assembled, tried, and discarded as failures, the men caught a flicker, just the faintest glimmer of hope. A symbol flashed on the screen indicating a possible affirmative response on microfilm. The file number and code were printed out as well. More programming. Suddenly the flickering, erratic image of a type of newsreel appeared on the screen. It was a government film of protesters in an almost momentary demonstration, broken up by the police with fire hoses and heavy truncheons.

The men watched with the eyes of predatory beasts—open, alert, and ready to pounce. Though they watched the film again and again, however, they saw nothing. Finally Katzhak asked if the speed of the film could be slowed down. The technician made another adjustment, and the film began again in slow motion.

"There! Stop! Run it again. Good. Now, get ready to freeze it when I say."

Silently, as the film ran backward this time, the clubs of the police bounced off heads and were put away. People lying on the ground or being dragged in the hands of others leaped into the air and back onto their feet. The whole procession magically reassembled and filed backward up the street and around the corner. "Now!" shouted Katzhak, and the marchers froze. "Forward this time, as slow as you can. Hold it."

Before the two men was a small black-and-white still picture of a man who resembled one of the suspected killers. The hair was a different length. The picture was at least a year old, and not of high quality. There was absolutely no way to be certain. "What kind of protest was this?"

The other man's only response was to put in a short new program. In seconds the machine ejected a brief printout. "These are dissident Jews protesting Soviet involvement in the Middle East."

"Dig in there and find me the arrests and their sentences." More programming. Katzhak wet his lips. Pictures, images of people, some still bloodied, began appearing on the screen. There were some fifty who took part. Two died and three were hospitalized when they "fell" fleeing from the police in their club-swinging attempts to disperse the crowd. This was not unusual, even though the so-called demonstration was more a parade than a protest. Some of the quicker and more resourceful ones escaped. In all, about thirty were arrested. Katzhak watched, bored, while the sentences for these antistate crimes were flashed across the images of the demonstrators. Most were sent to labor camps, two to asylums, one to prison. These last few must have either been the leaders and organizers or perhaps had resisted arrest. Katzhak's man was not among them. "Is that all?" he asked. The technician nodded. "Make reprints of that picture and have them circulated to the survivors. Offer them conditionally reduced terms for any information that can be verified."

"Yes, Comrade Colonel. Is that all, sir?"

"Not quite. Forget this, or I'll have you shot."

The technician believed him, convinced by the look on his face. Katzhak accepted the man's frightened nod as a binding contract. He too nodded, and looked once into the room before turning on his heel and striding out, leaving the technician to complete his assignments. When he returned to his office, the man from vehicle identification was waiting for him. Katzhak ushered him in and shut the door behind them. Moments later, Tamarzov emerged, puffing through his ruddy cheeks like a steamship forging through rough seas toward its destination.

In their interview, Katzhak had asked about and described the Mercedes that had borne his attackers just days before. He explained that he wanted it found, gone over minutely by Raseilei personally, and then destroyed. He wanted it traced at all costs, the reports to be delivered only to him. Tamarzov was to answer no questions from anyone concerning his inquiries. His second assignment was to ferret out the truck that Katzhak had pressed into service as his death weapon against his assailants. Katzhak himself was not certain whether or not the truck had hit the Mercedes, but he believed that he himself had collided with it just before he crashed. Apparently the truck was large enough to survive the impact and had continued on its way without stopping. Yet there must have been paint transfers at least, which would leave a fairly easily traced residue on his vehicle. Raseilei, then, was not the only person looking for the truck. At least he might have a temporary edge, since he knew it was a truck and Katzhak had caught a close-up view of its operators. As a final precaution, Katzhak ordered Raseilei to draft two low-level agents to accompany him. Katzhak took no chances. He wanted the information he had asked for, and Raseilei, if possible, in one piece. The escort would also prove useful in apprehending the driver and his passenger. Katzhak wanted them both for leaving him to die, like an injured animal, on the highway. He would have to instill an appreciation of roadside etiquette.

Finally, Raseilei and Katzhak consulted maps, in order to give the former a general area in which to concentrate his efforts. Katzhak was not very helpful in the description of the condition of the vehicles when he left them, as he had no idea ultimately of what had happened or of how he had survived. With that, Raseilei left him. Thoughtfully, Tatiana brought him tea when he was done, and gave him some information that brought a mysterious smile to his lips. His secretary told him that the new junior steno girl who had worked with him yesterday had been recalled while he was out. Katzhak laughed in obvious amusement, leaving his chief secretary to wonder why this announcement should cause him so much mirth.

"Whom did you speak to? What was his name?"

"I've forgotten, comrade."

Katzhak frowned and shrugged. "But I wrote it down." He looked up, smiling. This woman was as efficient and clever as any he had ever seen. She rarely failed him, and never without more than ample excuse.

"Give it to me when you go out, then."

"Yes, Colonel." He had great respect for this woman. And she loved to show her respect for him. She went out and closed the door. His intercom buzzed. "Padzgorin," she said. Katzhak reflected. An alias, he had no doubt. But he would have it checked out, nonetheless. His morning exhausted, and part of the afternoon, he decided to break for lunch. It would be the first time he had eaten since his breakfast at the hospital the day before. As a small reward for his work and as an opportunity to clear his head in advance of the demands of the afternoon, he opted to lunch in the subcommissary. He locked his office, and soon had his lunch and a seat by the window. A steady stream of workers from all levels filed past his table, and he ate alone, chewing the morning's events in his mind. For a long time he stared out the window, rehashing the week's happenings, before turning back to his lunch. On his tray had appeared a plain folded manila card. Quickly he glanced up to see who had dropped it there. His eyes met only a small sea of faces, backs, fronts, and hands. It could have been any one of two dozen people. Rapidly he glanced around the room to see if anyone was watching him, trying to spot someone with an obvious interest in the note. He saw nothing. Unobtrusively, then, he opened it. The message instructed him to walk to a nearby park and to sit on the bench facing the street at three o'clock. There was nothing else.

As much as he wanted to keep the note and examine it, Katzhak realized that he had better destroy it at once. If he were being watched, he could be arrested or even killed as a conspirator, and the damning evidence would be found in his pocket. It might even have been placed in front of him by an enemy in his own government who wished to trap him. Worse still, perhaps he would be taken or assassinated at the rendezvous point and implicated far more deeply in some traitorous intrigue against the state. Too, it might simply have been placed there by the same people who had tried to kill him just two days ago. They would want revenge, or at least to complete their assignment. He paused, debating an instant longer, and then set fire to the note. He crushed the ashes with his fork and left the table. Katzhak was on his way to the rendezvous the note had hoped to establish.

The whole thing was tortuous, diabolical. This note might be his only solid lead. There was a slim possibility that it would bear fruit. More likely, it would yield a harvest of danger, or death. Who was hunting heads, and why? Katzhak wondered if Arno Tuskov had received his own little note. Maybe these were get-acquainted greetings from Tuskov's killers. Wait a minute. What if there was a killer KGB, inside the KGB? He had heard rumors, once or twice in his career, of an assassination bureau. A special supersecret branch inside the regular, working espionage and counterespionage agencies. It was their job solely to kill. To liquidate by murder the traitors, the double agents, the bungling, the old, the inefficient, the potentially embarrassing. These agents were not known even to their own co-workers, but only to the few men, perhaps three, who were the unseen heads and coordinators of the whole network. Katzhak had suspected, had reasoned that it had taken just such power and authorization, just such a setup, to liquidate Arno Tuskov. Maybe the killers were after him now. Maybe the people he probably killed the day before were agents of his own government, acting on official instructions. Patriotic men. Not traitors. Only following their orders. Maybe the word was out on him already, or soon would be. There was no one he could trust anymore. That girl he had humiliated the day before. That phony secretary! She might have been one of them! Tatiana, anyone. If the whole service, the entire government were mobilized against him, there was no place he could go. He was already dead, only nobody had told him yet. Katzhak felt a nauseating wave of terror and revulsion sweep over him. He was suffocating, clawing, choking on the fear. Trying to swallow it, send it back inside, get on top of it again. Wait. There had to be a reason. A reason for these men, however brutal or cold they might be, to kill their own people. What could it possibly be? What did Tuskov know? Or rather, what did they think he knew? What did he and Katzhak have in common? What did this insidious bureau think they did? Cosmo. It had to be Cosmo. But what was Cosmo?

Maybe Tuskov had uncovered the existence of the bureau. Or some plan of the bureau's. Some plot, some murders, some purge. Maybe he became a threat. Suddenly Katzhak froze with fear. He had sent men out to find and investigate the men who had tried to kill him. If they were from the bureau, if they were unsure about him, he had probably tipped the scales forever and made his own death a regrettable necessity.

No. Katzhak had a hunch there was more. Much more. There must be an assassination bureau, all right. And they had certainly killed Tuskov. But it was because of something else he knew. Something big. Something terrible. Something no one, not even the most trusted senior officers, was allowed to know. If they were after him, if they had wanted him, they'd have had him. He would never have escaped the hospital, or the girl, or his office. No, he was not their assignment yet. And he might not be. If he didn't make waves. If he didn't touch any sensitive areas, if he never said the wrong word to the wrong person. That would be tough. That would be damn near impossible. He didn't know what Cosmo was or who was behind it, so he didn't have the slightest idea of what to avoid. Or whom. How efficient were they? How big were they? Whom could he trust not to be a willing or unwilling informer? Apparently his rank and position in the intelligence community or the government did not even make them hesitate. Cosmo was big. It was worth the lives of anybody and everybody who got in its way. In order to keep out of the way, he would have to talk to no one, stop using channels, go it completely alone. He was scared as hell.

16

Borky Zharuffkin sat muffled, deep and warm, in overcoat, scarf, and gloves; but he was bareheaded against the cold. The wind was bringing the temperature of everything lower and lower, and nearer to zero. He sipped hot coffee from a small cup that also helped to warm the fingers of both hands. He squinted and sat up. Quickly he patted the arm of Ulev and passed him the cup, exchanging it for the small pair of field glasses on the seat between them. They were down the street a ways, on the other side of Katzhak's huge stone edifice. He had just emerged from a street-level exit and was walking quickly away, toward one of Moscow's small parks. Hurriedly Zharuffkin spun the small knob, attempting to focus his artificial eyes. He watched for an instant before Ulev tapped his arm and pointed to the exit from which Katzhak had just come. Lowering the binoculars, Zharuffkin looked over and caught the image of Andrei, who hung back in the alcove, signaled to Zharuffkin, and waited. The latter shook his head. Andrei nodded and shifted from foot to foot, as if trying to keep warm. Flipping his cigarette from him, he

111

turned and walked south, in the opposite direction from Katzhak. Zharuffkin pocketed the field glasses, and he and Ulev got out of the car, following Katzhak at a good distance. He turned suddenly and trotted across the street. Zharuffkin and Ulev hustled to do the same.

Within five minutes Katzhak arrived at the park, all but deserted now, in early November. He glanced around with quick, darting, suspicious eyes, then quite naturally turned and sat down on the appointed bench. He thrust his hands deep into his pockets, and felt reassured by the heavy, cold, solid feel of the handle of the automatic pistol nestled in his right coat pocket. A light snow was beginning to fall, and it descended and settled in white icy flakes on Katzhak's jacket. He longed to withdraw his warm black folded lamb's-wool cap from his left coat pocket, but he was unwilling, out in the open as he was, to release the gun. So he shivered in silence and looked up. Zharuffkin and Ulev were not to be seen, and Katzhak did not know that they were there. On seeing him stop, Zharuffkin and Ulev had waved Andrei forward. He had picked them up in Zharuffkin's car, and now the three of them sat undetected half a block away.

Katzhak watched people and cars, the windows, doorways, and alleys of buildings across the street, even tree trunks. He saw nothing. Zharuffkin was equally puzzled. Katzhak was obviously waiting for someone or something. He had gone there to meet someone, but whom? Zharuffkin knew he was on to something, but had no idea what it was. Suddenly he leaned forward, squeezing the last ounce of precision out of his field glasses. "What the . . . Damn!" he roared explosively. His head snapped back over his shoulder, and he barked orders to Andrei, who sat in the rear seat of the car. "Get out there and walk past on the sidewalk. See what they're saying." Hesitating, Andrei shot a glance of confusion to Ulev, who reflected it right back. Neither man had seen anyone approach, and Katzhak had not moved from his spot. The trees were too thin to hide behind, and there was not even a dog to carry a radio receiver. Worst of all, they guessed that Katzhak was armed, hostile, and very nervous. "Dammit, get out there!" Zharuffkin shot an arm over the seat and shoved Andrei closer to the door. He frowned and climbed out,

112

walking briskly at first and then slowing down. Zharuffkin, obviously miffed, returned to watch the strange spectacle that unfolded before the glass screens that he again held to his eyes. Colonel Katzhak was sitting on a bench in a deserted park in the snow, talking to himself. He had been sitting there waiting, when he was startled by a high, tiny falsetto voice that came from nowhere. It echoed strangely and sounded somehow distant, even though he felt that the speaker was quite close.

"Good afternoon, Colonel. How nice of you to come." Katzhak was mystified, but as the voice continued, his scalp slid back, and his eyes darted to a space in the road, some six feet directly in front of him.

"Don't speak, don't move, and don't look down, please. Stare straight ahead, and I promise you, you won't be hurt. Raise your hand to your mouth and cough if you can hear me." Katzhak did as the disembodied voice commanded. There was a long pause. "Good. Is there anyone nearby? Rub your hands. Fine.

"We are the friends of Mikhail Malenkov. Two of our people, hotheads, went out to kill you two days ago. They have not returned."

"No, and they won't, either."

"Look to your left, Colonel. Do you see the man on the sidewalk near the corner?"

"Yes."

"And the gentleman on the roof above him?" Katzhak looked up. "Please don't speak again, Colonel. You can never tell who might be watching." The voice continued, and Katzhak realized that it emanated from the manhole cover on his side of the street. It was a well-chosen location, impossible to watch or to effectively pursue. "Those men were younger and braver than they were smart. I believe that they met with an accident. Did you kill them?"

"Yeah, I think so. Listen, there's somebody coming."

The voice was silent. Soon Andrei passed, reluctantly. "Okay," Katzhak said.

"I'll come to the point, Colonel. We heard, after your accident, what you did for Gallina, Mikhail's widow. Is she a widow, Colonel Katzhak?" There was obvious bitterness in the voice, obvious hostility and contempt. "Pretend your teeth are chattering."

Katzhak obliged. "I don't know. From the way she talked—"

"Well, that can be of no consequence now. We believe you were not involved in what happened to Mikhail's family."

"I wasn't." A car passed.

"Be careful, Colonel. Does the name Arno mean anything to you?"

"He was my friend. I've known him all my life."

"And he was yours. Fortunately for you, he was also ours."

"Did you shotgun him, too?"

"Don't talk to us about brutality, about violence, Colonel. Arno seemed to think he was in danger from his own side. It seems that you aren't very discriminating about whom you kill, if you even shoot your friends. We know who our enemies are." It was both a perceptive comment and a derisive taunt.

"I don't know anything about that. Was he helping you?"

"He was trying to help you. Would you like to know what he was working on? He seemed to think you would know what to do."

"Yes. Yes, very much."

"For Gallina, then. And for Tuskov. He thought you were worth it. Good-bye, Colonel."

"What? Wait a minute! How will I contact you?"

"I'll be in touch, Colonel."

"But . . ." Katzhak looked up. The man on the rooftop was gone. The street was clear.

"Christ . . ." he said, not dreaming the significance of that seldom-used expletive. He was alone in the street amidst the gently whirling snow.

17

That same afternoon, in an austere but comfortable subterranean office, a sinister meeting was taking place. Alexei Bulgarin recounted, in painstaking detail, every episode, shade, and nuance that had transpired since the death of Arno Tuskov. He sat in a large tufted chair upholstered in black leather. It was one of two chairs that sat facing a large and handsomely appointed dark wooden desk. Beside the desk stood the flag of the Union of Soviet Socialist Republics on the right, the flag of the NKVD to the left. The walls were a sort of dusty olive; the carpeting, in dramatic contrast, was red. On the wall directly behind the desk was the seal of the NKVD, flanked by two portraits where windows might have been, several stories higher up. One was a representation of the god of the revolution, Lenin. The other was a portrait of the first secretary of the Communist party, the current prophet of the Red messiah and leader of his people in the ongoing revolutionary effort. The picture of the president of the Soviet Union was not in evidence. A rich, lighted map of the world, marking the areas of Soviet Communist domination, covered most of one wall. The whole was illuminated by overhead lighting and a small red-shaded desk lamp trimmed with gold.

The only other piece of furniture in the room was a blood-colored overstuffed leather chair. In it sat a large, impressive man of fifty-two. He wore a dark suit, with silk shirt and tie, very expensive and very tasteful. With dark curly hair and massive black brooding eyebrows, he appeared quite foreboding and vigorous. His eyes were coal black, his upper lip thin, his lower lip thick and rub-

115

bery and slightly protruding in a perpetually scowling, angry pout. His whole appearance and that of his office was rich, elegant, awesome. His countenance was dark and turbulent. Emotions blew over the surface of his features in capricious gusts—violent, unpredictable, rapidly shifting, changing, alternating between light and dark. The eyes flashed, snapped, and crackled with electricity. Placed in the middle of his carefully controlled, moderated, and subdued office, he looked like a storm in the sky. Bulgarin huddled now in the tiny island of security that his position afforded him. He spoke calmly into the strange, evil eye of that hurricane, always testing the wind. Outside the sanctity and peace of this temporarily extended audience, outside the grace of the haven that this powerful man offered for a time, lay the deadly whirlwind of violence, anarchy, war, and bloodshed. The loudest shout would have no chance of penetration, and anyone in its path would be destroyed.

Bulgarin whispered in quiet solemnity in the face of such a man. There was an eerie, chilling peace in his presence. It was too quiet. Too still. The air was heavy, and each moment thickened with anxiousness and anticipation. Where he pointed, the lightning struck and men's souls fled from their weak knees and faint hearts.

Although he sat impassively, Bulgarin heard the rolling thunder and knew that in contrast to his appearance, he listened intently to his every word, and that each syllable was carefully weighed, tested, and scrutinized. Bulgarin had no idea why he had been singled out, commanded to step forward and speak before the red throne of this dragon. He obeyed, nonetheless, without question or hesitation, his unearthly summons.

Apparently this mysterious case was hotter than he had been led to believe when he had received his instructions a short time ago. His superiors were intentionally vague about his assignment and their goals. He was charged with a very great responsibility, he knew. He was valued, and chosen for his obedience and discretion, and for the fact that he never asked questions in the wrong places. He had been assigned to watch, but not to see. He was to prevent, at all costs, an event that he had not been told about. Yet he had picked up the strong message that it must

116

never, ever see the light of day. And he knew instinctively that if he himself were to learn of it, even by accident, his life would be forfeit. He had hoped to place that annoying idiot Zharuffkin between himself and merciless death. If Zharuffkin stumbled upon the mine, uncovered the deadly secret, surely they would know; surely they would eliminate him. Bulgarin would complete his assignment and still escape the devastation, if there was any escaping it. This afternoon he had been called to give an account of his methods and progress so far. He told the complete, unvarnished truth. He had no idea what to hold back, what facts to avoid, and he felt convinced that if he did not disclose everything just as it was, he would have no hope of survival. The creature who sat across from him, omniscient, omnipotent, would know without doubt, and its wrath and revenge would be terrible and without mercy. He was frightened, but too experienced and too clever to show it. He knew his best defense was nonchalance, the proof of innocence and ignorance. But what was the use? The dragon knew his thoughts, read them in his face, felt his fear, smelled it in the air. There was no defense against him, so he offered none.

While he spoke, the other man occasionally asked questions in a calm, quiet tone, which thrilled Bulgarin with fantastic terror, so evil and so malevolent did it seem. The other's eyes gleamed yellow, weird, and unnatural, the lids hot, sultry, and half-closed, like those of a huge beast of prey.

"Two days ago, at evening, I received a telephone call from Dr. E. Radislov, at a security medical facility thirty kilometers from here. He was extremely agitated, by the sound of his voice, and obviously fearful of what he was doing, and its repercussions. The comrade doctor informed me that he had urgent matters to communicate with me. I determined that he had given my staff nothing and compelled him to hold while I switched to a scramble line. Then, in confidence, he told me some very disturbing news. According to him, at dusk a man was brought in by a comrade, Borky Zharuffkin." The listening beast raised its eyebrows in mute interrogation.

"Some functionary," Bulgarin explained, "an agent, a bureaucrat." The dragon tilted its steamy head in another

117

unuttered question. "Forensics, pathology," Bulgarin answered.

"What sort of man is he?" The question was soft in tone, but probing. The soft-spoken manner of the beast was all the more terrifying for its calmness, which belied the deadly power it commanded with a whisper.

"A swine," came the swift and accurate reply. "He skulks in alleys in the darkness, and slides through gutters. Zharuffkin came from the sewers, and somehow, he escaped from under the streets."

The other man nodded in comprehension and approval. Bulgarin had correctly guessed that his interviewer never asked needless questions and had directly requested an overlay, a general sensory perspective view of the man under discussion, based on Bulgarin's firsthand experience. The facts, which Bulgarin sensed the omnipresent, omniscient creature before him somehow already possessed, could only follow this initial scouting report.

"He deals chiefly in extortion, blackmail, murder, and interagency intrigue. He is an opportunist, with allegiance to no one. He is untrustworthy to his enemies and current employers alike, and thus can never be relied on—only intelligently and carefully handled and managed. Zharuffkin is sadistic and dislikes field agents and bureaucrats. He is ambitious but has only jealousy, bitterness, and the utmost contempt for those superior to him. Information supplied by him has already ruined many and tipped the balance in several power struggles. He would seem to be motivated solely by personal gain, although he does take pleasure in the fall of those whose activities he exposes. Zharuffkin will accept gladly the dirtiest assignments, and his freedom and existence are testament to his success. A list of those whom he is believed to have been instrumental in removing is on your desk, I believe . . . yes, and you will perhaps note that more than once he has destroyed both his assignment and the man he has received it from.

"In summary, one may infer from these things that Zharuffkin is dangerous, duplistic, arrogant. He feels superior, both to those who use him and to those he is used against. The truth of these statements, I am confident,

118

will become completely apparent as I continue to recount recent events."

Bulgarin paused, took a breath, and waited. The beast nodded slowly, apprehending and digesting by bits the portrait his subordinate had drawn him at his request. The eerie creature, in its chilling mockery of human form, settled back on its throne to ponder, lifting its chin and lacing its digits together as it did so. It sat like a machine at rest, lifeless and strangely inanimate. The still body of the man sat staring into space, at some point well beyond the ceiling, past the earth, even, into blackness. The eyes of the beast remained open in a vacant, trancelike stare, as if transmitting all of this information and awaiting new instructions.

Transfixed, Bulgarin watched this uncanny spectacle with primitive superstitious fear. The air was thick with the supernatural, stifling his mortal lungs and making it difficult for him to breathe. The room bristled with cool electricity, prickling his skin and raising the hair on his arms and neck.

At length, communication was broken; power levels went up; life seeped back into the body; and the creature began to stir. Gradually the head descended, the eyes lowered, the fingers disentangled themselves, and the beast assumed the appearance of a man once more, sitting forward in his chair and regarding the human with penetrating eyes, conscious of what Bulgarin had seen transpiring.

Bulgarin felt that his quivering essence was clearly seen by the beast and that his thoughts were under close inspection. The intensity of the weird creature's gaze dissected his rude being into all of its component parts, each one curiously and thoroughly examined before reassembly.

"Please continue, comrade," the creature commanded him with a deadly authority that belied the polite prefacing and soft-spoken delivery. At this word, "comrade," Bulgarin's blood froze and turned to ice in his veins. He felt no comradeship with the thing behind the desk. The term was ironic, if not comical, though it caused him not the slightest mirth. They were different creatures entirely, with natures completely diverse and pertaining to the unique realm of each. Somehow it was clear that they inhabited different planes of existence and the turbulent

119

intersection of their two worlds in that man and that room were frightening beyond expression. It was difficult for Bulgarin to face the creature, so great was his dread that the true appearance of the being across from him, only thinly disguised, might be revealed to him, stopping his heart and revealing his destiny. Still, he knew intuitively that they both belonged to the same kingdom, both served a common will. This notion had surfaced periodically in certain of his meetings with his superiors, but never as with this man, in this unearthly bastion. He shrank from that awful realization, from that ultimate truth, fought it, denied it, ignored it with his might. But the apparition haunted him increasingly with age, was much more difficult to shake off. It burdened and chased him, tired him, hastened his death and his face-to-face meeting with unutterable, irreversible fate. He did not know what he feared, or why, or how he knew it was real, but he did not doubt, could not escape the reality of his vision. He wanted to run or weep bitterly and plead for mercy. There was no mercy, no hope; only pursuing his inevitable course to its conclusion. He had seen other men hounded too by what they knew. Some went mad, some panicked and rushed to their deaths, others recklessly abandoned themselves and chased it, rising to great power until it suddenly turned on them, larger than their minds could comprehend, taking them, it seemed, in an instant; they vanished from the earth without a trace. Their strong statues in stone and severe portraits in oils were grotesque mockeries of their weaknesses and frailties, desperate attempts at permanence for those whose misfortune it was to stay behind listening to fools repeat the ancient rhetoric contrived to preserve the sanity of the great ones, who, like Bulgarin, had somehow seen through to the ugliness and ashes.

Bulgarin continued as ordered. "Zharuffkin brought in a man whose papers were not on his person. The doctor recognized at once the uniform of a colonel of military intelligence. From the insignia and various other decorations on the uniform, the doctor concluded that this man was possibly very important. According to him, he questioned Zharuffkin about the colonel's papers, which Zharuffkin declined to produce. Still, he did not notify the authorities, for fear of Comrade Zharuffkin's threats. Here is the intriguing part: the victim was unconscious when he arrived at the ward, and remained so throughout the examination and preliminary treatment. He was suffering from a concussion, a potentially serious one, as the result of a direct, forceful impact delivered across the forehead. If it had been a little lower, say, just above the eyes, it would have fractured the skull or killed him. As it was, the blow was somewhat more distributed. There were numerous bruises, slivers and cuts from which glass was extracted, and one more thing. The right hand. The right hand was peppered with indentations varying in depth, from which the small particles that made the entrance wounds had been removed. The removal was not done with surgical instruments or procedures and would have caused a lot of damage on their own, had the particles entrenched themselves any deeper.

"Now, the significant part. Minuscule amounts of some black substance, just the most minute shreds, were gleaned from the wound prior to a more thorough cleaning and stitching. This dark material turned out to be tiny shards of leather. It is the doctor's belief that the colonel was wearing gloves at the time when the wounds were made. And yet, there were no gloves, either on the body or among the personal effects. This would strongly suggest a deliberate attempt to conceal some crucial facts on the part of Zharuffkin or someone else who might have had access to the body. Further, the entrance wounds, although partially obliterated by the clumsy removal of the particles that made them, appeared, under close examination, to be roughly round in shape and of fairly consistent size. This would suggest a weapon, probably a shotgun, as opposed to some sort of accidental occurrence. Finally, the whole of the thumb, the base of the hand, and the top surfaces of the fingers were pierced in a uniform manner, indicating that the colonel was most probably holding something in his hand at the time of the injury.

"Zharuffkin contends that, passing along the road, he came upon an auto accident and rescued the colonel just before his vehicle and the other were engulfed in flames. He is unclear about various details, and maintains that due to the identity of the individual involved, he retained

121

possession of his papers, as well as private knowledge of what they contained."

"And what was the identity of the colonel?" the soft voice demanded.

"Katzhak was his name, sir. Vladislev Tovarish Katzhak."

"Katzhak! You're certain?"

"I've seen him."

"I see." There was a pause, as if the other man were digesting bad news. He appeared genuinely disappointed, as though he had heard of an ailing friend or colleague who had taken a turn for the worse, and would probably die. "Please continue, comrade."

"There was another car involved; both had exploded and burned by the time investigators arrived. We found no weapons except Colonel Katzhak's burned revolver at the scene. There were two men in the other vehicle, numerous skid marks and littered pieces of both cars along a long section of the roadway. An investigation into all aspects of the case is, of course, continuing, and Colonel Katzhak has been released without surveillance. Until we have had a chance to go over those cars and to identify the other two men, that's all we have. Zharuffkin has not been disciplined, because he is useful to me now and because I also want to watch him. He reports to me and no one else."

The other man nodded, his probing eyes once again penetrating Bulgarin's features. "What do you think?"

Bulgarin drew in his breath and wrinkled his forehead, frowning a little as he did so. "I think that two men tried to ambush Colonel Katzhak with a shotgun. He successfully resisted and killed them both. I think Zharuffkin was following Katzhak at a great distance at the time of the ambush. For reasons which I do not at the present time understand, Zharuffkin wished to make the whole affair look like an accident, because he hopes to gain something by casting the light away from Katzhak. Just what that something is, I regret, I cannot say."

The creature regarded him coldly. "Thank you, Comrade Bulgarin. As usual, you have acted with wisdom and discretion. I hope that with continued success you may go far in the service of your state and your party."

122

"Thank you very much, sir. Do you have any further instructions for me at this time?"

"Yes, Comrade Bulgarin. Here is what I want you to do. Watch Zharuffkin closely. If he does anything out of line, please contact me at once. Do not fear him. I promise you, at the close of this affair he will say nothing to anyone. Rely on my protection. He can do you no harm."

"Yes, sir. Thank you, sir. You've been more than kind to me." Bulgarin rose and turned to go.

"Comrade . . ." Bulgarin froze and refraced his steps in answer to his summons. "Comrade. There is one more thing. A small thing, but I would appreciate your indulgence in a small favor. I am a very busy man, as you may be able to understand, and unfortunately, I am not always able to extricate myself immediately from my obligations. Even in my position, the demands and pressures . . . Well, I'm sure you're well acquainted. They cannot easily be escaped. I am never sure from day to day when my schedule will allow a personal interview, even when the business is very urgent. So if you would not mind, accept this envelope and carry it with you.

"As I have said before, I want you to keep a close eye on events, particularly those involving Colonel Katzhak. I regret that I cannot share with you the reasons for my concern for the colonel, but I'm sure you understand. Even in this office, that is not one of my privileges. You don't believe me? It's true. I assure you. It's foolish for men to aspire to great heights. Don't you agree? If I were you, I would not do it.

"Colonel Katzhak is an important man. Any information regarding him cannot be trusted to delays and schedules. So, in that small envelope which you hold in your hand is a telephone number. Listen carefully. If Colonel Katzhak should be in some danger, or involved in some intrigue, or if you should suspect him of committing some crime, please do this immediately: open the envelope and call that number. Give the colonel's name, including rank, and hang up. That is all you have to do. I have already instructed the persons at that number as to what their responsibilities are in the event that you should dial that number. Don't open the envelope unless you have suspicions, and don't hesitate to open it if you do. I'm sorry

I can't tell you more, comrade. This door is closed to you. Don't try to open or peek under it. Do you understand all that I have said to you?"

"Yes, sir. Completely."

"Good. Good day, comrade. Thank you for your co-operation." The audience was clearly ended, at last. Bulgarin nodded and withdrew, closing the big polished olive-wood doors behind him as he made his grateful and obedient exit.

Bulgarin could not be certain, as he walked down the shiny tiled corridor to the elevator and his black limousine, just what the number in his coat pocket portended for his future, but he knew what it meant for Katzhak. No doubt he would call the number, and while he listened to a ringing sound, his call would travel through secret relays to its actual destination in some distant scramble line. Katzhak's name was merely to identify Bulgarin, to verify that the dialing of those numbers was not an accident or done by the hostile or the curious. The man or woman at the opposite end would listen, and then, like a radar-guided missile, armed by the dialing alone, proceed to the predetermined target. Whoever this Katzhak was, whatever he was involved in, he was in a hell of a lot of trouble. The assassination bureau had been alerted and instructed to kill him on the slightest ill breeze of suspicion. Katzhak's position was roughly like that of a tightrope walker doing cartwheels on a rotting rope that was frayed at both ends. Bulgarin was enormously relieved that he was apparently on much sounder footing than the unfortunate Katzhak. Even if he should survive his own death, his career, now tainted with suspicion, was obviously much curtailed, or perhaps, as was more likely, judging by the gravity of his superior's demeanor, was utterly ruined and at an end entirely. Bulgarin stiffened with the sobering thought that for the time being at least, and for the foreseeable future, he too was working without a net.

18

It was bitterly cold on a windy Moscow street ten kilometers away, a street steeped in snow and already darkened by enormous blackening, billowing snow clouds. The three men turning onto that street were curiously unaware of the strangeness of it all. Here tiny, almost identical beings crawled over the surface of a small chunk of rock, hurtling through the icy blackness of space. The light of a distant star illuminated and warmed their planet, allowed blotches of vegetation to crop up, which the minuscule creatures consumed, cut down, and cut up, to be stacked into little dwellings or pressed into thin sheets or burned for fuel. They bored holes and dug tunnels, drilling, drilling, for minerals and fossil fuels, the decomposed bodies of the creatures and plants before them. They were always unaware of the weirdness of radical changes in climate, of their sphere's revolutions around the star, of the blackness of half of their days and the odd dormance of their bodies when they lay still, and almost dead, their secret minds in control.

They built minute vehicles to carry their heavy forms from place to place, daring towers, like stubble, covering their globe, all connected by a maze of trails and roads scratched along the surface of their world. Above them, great clouds of frozen gases migrated over the planet, releasing liquids or solids or blocking the light and sending them all scurrying inside their little shelters for warmth. An occasional electrical storm lashed them, frightened them, drove them into hiding. Sometimes the detached plates that formed the tiny crust of rock that straddled the hot, molten core would move, or split, or collide, shaking the ground violently or spewing fire from the fissures.

The microscopic creatures meanwhile exaggerated their unobservable differences beyond imagination, with terrible results to their ephemeral shelves. They created weapons of great devastation and unleashed unspeakable horror frequently and tragically on one another. They consumed voraciously the finite little pockets and belts of matter which they used for fuel or wore or displayed, killing each other without thought in endless battles for control of the dwindling substances.

Great millions starved to death, while millions of others struggled for personal power, or wasted in boredom and unconcern, or were rewarded for not cultivating or for destroying their crops. They built vast storehouses which contained the cumulative knowledge of millions upon millions of their ancestors, relentlessly instructing and educating their young, and yet, if any of them were wise, they were not in control of the little colonies, and every new idea was like another plague, because it was inevitably perverted for destruction or subjugation.

There were so very many billions existing at one time, and yet they never unified or cooperated or used their common wealth and being to make peace or to help different bands coalesce for the health and safety of the whole planet. They destroyed and polluted their environment, and scarred their planet as thoughtlessly as they slaughtered their own kind.

And privately they raped and beat and terrorized and murdered and maimed and trapped and enslaved each other daily. Never realizing that, as they did so, they doomed themselves to hopelessness and utter futility.

It was nearly four o'clock. Raseilei Tamarzov and the two agents sent by Katzhak for his security and legwork had just pulled up across the street from Moscow's main security vehicle-impound facility. It was here that anything from Katzhak's demolished Volga sedan to a subway car was taken for examination by the NKVD or KGB under security conditions ranging from the relatively loose to the most stringent in the nation. Having already visited the crash site and turned up nothing missed by the authorities, the three men had come here seeking answers. They had parked across the street from the huge building, and they crossed, beginning to make their way up a wide alley or driveway that was the vehicle entrance to the compound. Raseilei marched in front, the other men keeping a slow, steady pace behind him.

As the three approached, they were met by a very stern man of about forty-five years of age, emerging from the small galvanized guardhouse. He stopped and lowered his Soviet AK-47 at the line formed by Raseilei's belt. All four men stood still. From each of the two doors on the right-and left-hand sides of the guardhouse a tall, heavyset man stepped out, the right hand of each invisible beneath his overcoat, tucked with obvious meaning and menace below his left arm. The guard advanced; so did Tamarzov. The two men stopped, the barrel of the weapon held inches from Raseilei's belly. They spoke rapidly in low tones.

"Who are they?" Raseilei asked, vaguely alarmed and gesturing toward the grim sentinels who remained motionless in their original positions.

"Who are they?" responded the guard sarcastically, glancing in the direction of Raseilei's escorts.

Tamarzov shrugged, trying hard to maintain nonchalance. "My superiors feel that this is important and they want to discourage trouble."

"Mine, too," said the man with the gun, without relaxing. "What do you want?"

Puzzled and unruffled in the face of apparent hostility, Raseilei told him, playing down the significance of his requests.

"I want to see the cars, Yuri. I'm running down some pretty routine stuff, but it's for a very important man. Name's Katzhak. Colonel of NKVD Katzhak. Seems he smashed up his car and one other yesterday or the day before. He says he thinks maybe someone tried to scare him, maybe kill him. Anyway, I'm supposed to check it out. I guess he was too banged up to notice what shape the vehicles were in. He's so shook-up he doesn't even know for sure what happened. What have you got on an old brown Mercedes? I'm not sure about the year. I also need to see the colonel's Volga. Our friends can entertain each other while we look 'em over. Also, anything you have on a pale green closed-cab truck, possibly a sixty-four or sixty-five." Smoothly, without giving the guard time to protest, Tamarzov waved his men forward as if he expected the guard to shoulder his weapon and lead the way inside.

"No" was his only reply.

Raseilei played dumb, stalling for time. "Nothing at all on the truck? No transfers, anything?" As he said this, the guard edged nervously, gripping his rifle tighter and shooting a glance at Tamarzov which indicated that his waving ahead of his men had been both dangerous and unfair.

"Back off, Ras, before you get us both killed," he hissed, frightened and angry.

"Dammit, Yuri! What the hell's the matter with you?"

"Listen to me. Just shut up and listen. I have orders and I have to carry 'em out. That's what those two are for. Get out, Ras. Get out now; get out from under Katzhak, today. Run from this thing, run for your life. Now, go, and take those kids with you."

"Okay, okay, but Christ, think of me, will ya? I can't take that back to him. Jesus! How long do you think that shit'd go over? 'They wouldn't let me in at the big impound building downtown.' Hell, Yuri, somebody tried to blow his head off. I come up empty now, and he'll have both our asses by tomorrow morning."

"All right." Yuri sighed deeply. Roughly he shoved at Raseilei with the muzzle of his weapon, Tamarzov stepping back in a show of being run off by the guard's hard line. "Look, there's no way I can let you close to those cars. Fall down," Yuri ordered, jamming the barrel into Raseilei's stomach. The latter obliged, landing in the snow at the edge of the alley.

"Same percentage?" Raseilei asked.

"God, no! Please! Don't give me anything. Don't come near here till this thing is over. The cars were burned. Totaled. So, see, no paint transfers, no make on the truck you want. Two men died in the Mercedes. That's all I know."

Tamarzov was getting up, brushing his coat and cursing loudly for effect, now pointing as if arguing with the guard.

"Convenient. I'd sure like to know who the hell owned that car. Why is this damn thing so hot, anyway?"

"You tell me. You carrying a gun?"

128

"Yeah. Why?"

"Go for it."

"What?"

"Go for it. Now."

"Oh, come on, Yuri. Is that really necessary? I'm getting a little too old for—"

"Goddammit, Ras! Do what I tell you! I'm trying to save your life."

Reluctantly Raseilei's right hand dived into his overcoat, scrambling for his gun. With sudden brutal force Yuri slammed the upended butt of his rifle squarely into Tamarzov's face, snapping the head backward. The savage thrust nearly lifted the short man off his feet, driving him down hard and backward onto the icy concrete. Simultaneously, shots rang out behind the pair as the two backup guards fired once each into the concrete, halting Raseilei's startled men.

Instantly Yuri brought the butt of his rifle down on Tamarzov's right hand, kicking the gun from the helpless fingers and sending it skidding several feet away on the ice.

"I'm sorry," he said as he passed the moaning form of Tamarzov. He walked slowly, retrieving the gun and methodically turning the cylinder, allowing the bullets to slide out and fall into the snow. He retraced his steps, dropping the empty gun on Tamarzov's overcoated ribs, adding insult to injury. Going a few steps farther, he looked up and froze internally, forcing his sudden-leaded feet to continue toward the guardhouse. His heart pounded. Next to the left side of the guardhouse stood three men. One was tall and blond, one was of medium height and dark, and the third was rather heavy, short, and fair, with squinting, stony eyes.

The red-haired one tossed his head in a silent command to Yuri to finish what he had started. The latter obeyed, again unslinging his automatic rifle and turning toward Tamarzov's escort. He led the two men back to their fallen comrade and out of earshot. He stood guard over the three of them as they spoke to Tamarzov and attempted to bring him to his feet.

"Are you badly hurt, sir?" one of them asked.

"I lost some teeth. Find my teeth! Jesus! Give me your handkerchief." Vainly Tamarzov mopped at his face with the wadded handkerchief, trying to stanch the blood. He drew himself up on one elbow and turned to look toward his right. "Christ! Look at my hand! Look at it! Shit! It's ruined. God, I must have broken every bone."

"Be grateful it's only your hand, Ras."

"Shut up, goddamn you, Yuri!"

"It could have been a lot worse."

"Yeah, I guess you're right. You could have killed me!"

"You don't know them. Did you want these kids blown away? Two more steps and they'd have cut 'em down. And if your shoes so much as squeaked, they'd have wasted you too; and I would have had to help 'em."

"Oh, forgive me for misunderstanding you! How could I have misjudged you? How could I have overlooked your obvious kindness, you son of a bitch? You did this for me! You're a noble bastard, aren't you? Yeah, you're a goddamn prince!"

"Dammit, Ras, don't push me!" Yuri's grip tightened on the weapon, Tamarzov's men certain of disaster and helpless to draw their own guns.

"Push you? Push you? I'm not only gonna push your little ass around; I'm gonna kick it till it gives milk. I'm gonna have it stuffed and hung on my goddamn office wall!"

The second of Tamarzov's two nervous attendants whipped out his handkerchief, preparing to wrap the two or three bloody white teeth he had gleaned from the snow in it.

"No," Yuri said, "it should be wet. Soak it in the snow." Then, turning to Tamarzov he said, "Maybe Katzhak would be interested in this."

Raseilei, still fuming, glanced up in contempt. Yuri dropped a torn piece of heavy cloth surreptitiously on the snow. "Wrap it in the handkerchief," he ordered. "I don't know what it means, but a few days ago they brought in a major. KGB. I didn't get any kind of look at the body, it was pretty messed up, but there wasn't enough blood in the car, you know?"

Tamarzov nodded, becoming interested.

"The car was in the parking gear, and one more thing. I found that piece of material in the doorjamb. On the passenger side. The door was locked, and the torn threads

130

were to the outside. It's a piece of his overcoat. He was hit, Ras. Set up. Assassinated outside the car and then dumped in. Then they shoved the car off the road. Our own people are covering it up. Get outta here while you still got your life, Ras. Now, please go."

Tamarzov nodded and his two men helped him to stand, supported by their shoulders.

"Thanks, Yuri," he said. Both men were suddenly seized by the gravity and the grim reality of the danger they had passed, and the knowledge that this deadly mystery would only get worse, perhaps suck them all up, take both their lives.

"Watch yourself, Ras."

"Good luck." Tamarzov was aware, as he spoke these words to his longtime acquaintance, that Yuri's luck had hopelessly run out. Yuri lingered for a moment, his eyes clearly communicating the bleakness of his situation and a terrified and lonely plea for help and human contact that he knew must go unheeded. Tamarzov looked down and shrugged, a signal that he was ready to leave. The two young men bore him away. Yuri watched his limping half-friend for a moment, as if seeing to it that the intruders had gone, and drawing a deep breath, his last free breath, he turned and trudged toward his own death on weary feet.

19

Borky Zharuffkin gestured to the two men who had been in the guardhouse with Yuri to come forward. When they did so, he thanked them, charged them to say nothing of what they had seen, on Comrade Bulgarin's orders, and dismissed them to their usual office and activities. Inwardly he applauded himself, as was increasingly becoming his custom, for his foresight in recruiting and dispatching these men. He had judged Katzhak's quickness correctly, and this further gratified him. The worst of the threat now passed, Andrei and Ulev could assume control over the gateway temporarily while he adjusted this matter of the regular gatekeeper.

"Sergeant? Sergeant Yuri Gregorivich?"

Yuri nodded.

"Sergeant, is there someplace we could talk privately?"

"Well," Yuri stammered, "there is my quarters . . ." He knew now that he was in serious trouble, and resented having to entertain his executioner in his own home before the slaying.

"Fine, Sergeant. That's just fine. Will you lead the way, then?"

Yuri clicked his heels in mute assent and strode off up the driveway to a small low one-story building similar to a barrack in appearance, with thick walls and high windows of textured, wire-reinforced glass. It was arranged like a duplex, with Yuri sharing his home-away-from-home with visitors or specialists during important investigations. It was vital that he be on duty twenty-four hours a day, if necessary, so that he often had to spend months at a time away from home.

"Oh, yes. It looks quite comfortable. I suppose it's not like home, though, eh?"

Yuri was somewhat put at ease by this relaxed pleasantry and was suddenly wildly maudlin and homesick for his private life.

"No, sir," he said.

"Is this your family, I take it, then?" Zharuffkin reached for the photo on the scarred, neat desktop. Yuri wanted to say, "Don't touch it," but of course he could not. He dreaded that touch, that handling of one of his most sacred ties with his heart and home, as if, with the likenesses of his loved ones, the fat, ugly man held their fates in his hands as well. He did not enjoy this defilement of things the gross and insidious stranger had no right to come near. He wished that this odious visitor would leave his family alone and go.

"You have a charming wife, Comrade Gregorivich."

132

Yuri gritted his teeth. In one breath, both his name and his wife had been violated, fouled.

"And I see you have three boys."

"Four, sir. One is grown now. He's in the army." Yuri bit his lip.

"I'll come straight to the point, Yuri."

Thank God, Yuri thought, though he shuddered somehow at the use of his first name.

"I saw what happened out there just now. All of it."

"Yes, sir?"

"I said all of it, Sergeant Gregorivich. That was Raseilei Tamarzov you were speaking to, wasn't it?"

"I don't know, sir."

"You're lying, Yuri."

"No, sir."

"Aren't you? Isn't it true that Comrade Tamarzov has dealt with you many times in the past when he wanted secret information?"

"No, sir."

"Isn't it also true that he paid you for this antistate activity from funds he received from important bosses? Illegal funds for a bribe, to seduce you from your duty as a functionary of this state? That he has paid you thousands of rubles for years for your perjury and treason, isn't that also true, Sergeant?"

"I don't . . . I don't know what you're talking about, sir."

"Don't you? Don't you indeed! Then perhaps you could explain what this was doing in your mattress?"

"No, sir. I've never seen it before."

"Isn't it rather odd that I should find almost three thousand rubles in your mattress? Answer me, Sergeant!"

"I can't explain it, sir."

"Then perhaps you could explain how it is that I found five hundred rubles in cash in your overcoat pocket after your accomplice departed."

"That's a lie, sir."

"What did you say, Sergeant?"

"I said that's not true, sir."

"I think it is." Zharuffkin pulled the notes from his own pocket. "Here, do you see; here is the unfortunate evidence."

133

Yuri paled as he began to understand.

"You see, if I say you took a bribe this afternoon, then it is just as I said, is it not?" Yuri hung his head. "Let us be sensible, comrade. I have the money. Your money. We searched your room while much of that drama took place out there. Do you still deny its source?"

Yuri stood silent, thinking.

"Oh, come now, Yuri. I admit it would take a little more time to prove, but we've got you. What did you tell Raseilei Tamarzov just now, Yuri?"

"Nothing."

"What do you take me for, Sergeant? Five people saw you speak to him, for several minutes. And then there's this nasty business about the money. I want to help you, Yuri, and your family."

"My family?" Yuri was becoming alarmed.

"Yes. Your family. That's where the money went, wasn't it, Yuri? To Yolanda and the boys. Especially little Igor? Well, it's obvious. You don't have anything nice for yourself, not a thing after . . . how many years here?"

"Twelve, sir. Twelve years."

"There, don't you see? Isn't it just as I said? Twelve years, and nothing to show for it. Nothing like you deserve. All for someone else, for Yolanda and the boys. It's almost impossible for you to see another woman, for months. You rush right home to your wife as soon as you get liberty. You've always been faithful to your wife, haven't you, Yuri? All these years, never once straying. Isn't that so?"

"Yes, sir. Yes, it is."

"You love your wife very much, don't you, Yuri?"

"Yes. Yes. Yes, I do."

"And your children, too?"

"Yes. My boys . . . my little sons."

"You don't drink much, do you, Yuri?"

"Sir?"

"Drink. Your commanding officer says that the bottle in your top drawer is the same one you've had all winter. Is that true?"

"Yes, sir. I guess so. If you say so."

"How cold does it get in here at night, Yuri? In the winter, without your wife, without Yolanda beside you?"

"Sir, I don't see the point."

"The point, Yuri, is that I can see that you're a fine man. You've always done the right thing for those you love so very much, haven't you? For those who depend on you."

"Sir, I still can't see——"

"Yuri, I like you. I respect you, and I respect what you've done, the sacrifices that you've made for years, without asking anything for yourself. And I want to help you. I want to help you protect Yolanda and the boys. Can't you see?"

"Protect them from what?" he cried, frightened and bitter.

"I don't want to see them charge in and make a lot of arrests."

"Arrests?"

"Yes, arrests. Somehow this treason has to be paid for, Yuri. I understand why you did it. I admire you for it. But I can't guarantee that my colleagues out there will be nearly so sympathetic. Treason is, after all, a capital offense, Yuri. But I'm sure you weighed the risks carefully when you began this undertaking. I don't want to see Yolanda in prison, exiled, or executed. Your oldest boy destroyed, his career and freedom snatched away for accepting a bribe, the price of secrets which your own government entrusted to your care, for their protection and safety. It would be a sad thing. A tragedy, Yuri. And it breaks my heart to think of your boys, especially the youngest, being ripped from their mother's arms and becoming wards of the state, or worse, perhaps, the labor camps. It just doesn't seem fair, Yuri, after all you've done for them. All you've done to ensure their happiness and safety. Your life, after all, has been one sacrifice after another for them. How ironic and terrible to see it all go for nothing, and the man who gave his life for them disgraced, perhaps publicly executed. How dreadful if that scandal, if the taint of treason, should touch them, scar them, mark them, Yuri. I want to prevent all that. I want to help you protect them, Yuri, if you're willing. If you're the man I think you are!"

Yuri sank into a chair behind the desk on which Zha-

135

ruffkin sat. His chin rested on his chest. His eyes by this time had closed.

"What do you want to keep this from her?"

"What did you say?"

"How much? What do you want?"

"I knew you were a compassionate man, Yuri. I could tell."

"Get to the point!"

"I want to know who sent Tamarzov to you today."

"Couldn't you find that out yourself?"

"Indeed. I already know."

"Then why are you asking me?"

"All right," Zharuffkin said, rising. "I'm sorry, Yuri. I really am . . . but you leave me no alternative." He turned.

"Wait! Wait, please. Don't go. Don't do that. It's just that . . . I can't betray him."

"Tamarzov?" Yuri nodded.

"I'm sorry. I didn't know you were friends."

"Neither did I."

"What?"

Yuri shook his head in signal he had said nothing.

"It was Colonel Katzhak, wasn't it?"

Yuri nodded. "It was Colonel Katzhak."

"What did you tell the colonel's man, Yuri? Answer me, Sergeant!"

"I said he couldn't see the cars."

"The Mercedes and the Volga?"

"Yes."

"What else did he ask you?"

"About the truck."

"I can't hear you, Sergeant, what . . . ?"

"A truck. He said there was a truck, sir."

Zharuffkin's mind turned back the hours, and once again he saw the pale green vehicle hurtle past his car as he followed Katzhak days before.

"Oh, yes. Anything else?"

"No."

"You did not, then, I take it, mention to him anything about his inquiries at all, nothing about any other officer who may have been brought in?"

The man was a demon.

136

"Officer, sir? No, I didn't . . ."

Zharuffkin gathered up the money and turned to the telephone on the desk.

"Stop it!" Yuri grabbed his hand and forced the receiver back onto the cradle. "There was another car. A major. KGB. I think he was murdered. I think he was killed outside the car. That's what I told Tamarzov, and that's all! I swear it! Oh, God help you now, Ras."

"Tuskov! Arno Tuskov."

"Who's Tuskov?"

"I don't know what you're talking about."

"You said a name. Tuskov. Arno Tuskov. Who is he?"

"I don't know. Tell me how Tamarzov asked about him. What were his exact words?"

"He didn't ask about him."

"What do you mean? Why did you tell him, then?"

"I thought it might help. It seemed just as hot as the cars he was asking about. He seemed interested."

"Thank you, Yuri. You've been very helpful. And now I'm going to help you."

Zharuffkin reached into his overcoat and pulled out a small, large-caliber pistol and a handkerchief. Slowly he began to wipe the weapon clean.

"You mean you're going to kill me?" Yuri asked, staring in disbelief. "After all this? I've told you everything. I swear, I've told you every damned thing!"

"Yuri, calm down," Zharuffkin said in a quiet tone, at the same time both patronizing and deadly. "Of course I'm not going to kill you." He set the weapon on the desk. "I'm just going to sit outside for a few minutes and smoke a cigarette while you get a few of your things together. And while you do, I want you to think about Yolanda and the children. Your children, Yuri, and their father's memory. I want you to reflect on your years of sacrifice and self-denial for them. Then I want you to think about the cost of treason, the high cost of treason on the innocent little ones. I want you to think of little four-year-old Igor's face when they take his mother away. When they split his family apart . . ."

Yuri's head shook slowly from side to side. "No," he said. "I won't do it. I won't do it for you."

"If that's your decision, Yuri. What a waste. I'll phone the KGB while you pack."

"Oh, my God . . ." His voice trailed off, and he sank his head in his hands. "My God," he said again. "Get out! Get out and leave me alone!"

"Of course. Of course, my friend. I can see I was right about you all along. I knew that once I explained it to you, you would want to do the right thing. For Yolanda. And for the boys. They look like fine boys. Well, I'll leave you, then, to . . . prepare for your journey. Such a lovely family."

Zharuffkin put a hand on Yuri's shoulder and walked toward the door. He turned. "Of course, I won't turn in the money, so no one need ever know. I'm sorry, but I wouldn't want to jeopardize your wife and children with substantial evidence such as this. You understand, I'm sure." He could never resist the coup de grace. Turning once more, he stepped out into the fading sunlight and walked a short distance before leaning against the wall of the building and methodically lighting a cigarette. Perhaps a minute had gone by before he heard the explosive roar of a gun discharged several feet away. He took one final drag on his cigarette and flipped it away from him, smiling slightly, as it was snuffed out in the snow. He pushed himself away from the wall with his foot, and placing one hand in his overcoat pocket, walked slowly down the alley toward the gatehouse. Andrei and Ulev were jogging anxiously up the driveway toward him and smiled when they caught sight of him. With a wave of his hand he motioned them toward the car, and they piled in, driving down the slippery alley and turning out onto the street.

20

Five-fifteen. Katzhak, somewhat anxious about Tamarzov's progress and his findings, was nonetheless preparing to go home for the evening and resume his vigil there. He had locked all his paperwork safely away, electing to leave his job behind him tonight and to take an all-too-rare holiday from his work.

He had just turned out the light and was locking the door when a light flashed on one of his desk phones. He flicked the light switch back on again, and glancing in the hallway, shut and locked the door.

"Tamarzov, Colonel," the voice said. "I had them patch me in to you direct."

"Very good, comrade. Switch to a scramble line, please. Thank you." There was a pause. "Go ahead, Ras."

"Bad news, Colonel. Very bad news. I'm pretty friendly with the regular man over at the impound facility, the main one."

"Yes."

"The cars are there, sir. Both of them. No sign of the truck. My man was pretty scared, but he said the cars were burned. They removed two bodies, males, from the wreckage of that Mercedes. No way now to make any positive ID."

"You said," he said, "the cars were burned?"

"Yes, sir, that's right. He wouldn't let me near them. He wouldn't take a kopeck from me, either. There were two new soldiers sort of inspiring him to be diligent. They fired warning shots at the men you gave me. Everybody was touchy as hell down there. I lost some teeth. Got my right hand pretty badly smashed up. Guard seemed to think we were lucky to get out at all. He didn't know your name until I mentioned it, but he seemed to have a strong hunch it's gonna become a dirty word real soon. This is hot, Colonel, hotter than you realize. I think you're heating up right along with it. Be careful you don't get too close, you might get burned."

"Thanks for the information."

"We're even now, sir."

"Yeah, sure, Ras. We're even."

"One more thing, since I won't be talking to you again. Yuri gave me something he thought you might be interested in about a major they brought in almost a week ago. KGB. Yuri thinks he was assassinated. Do you want it? . . .

"Colonel! Colonel Katzhak! Are you still there?"

"Yes. Yes, I'm still here."

"Okay. He doesn't know his name, but he's pretty sure he was murdered."

"How? How does he know?"

"A piece of his overcoat was found locked in the doorjamb on the passenger side. Yes, that's right. The passenger side. But he was found slumped across the front seat. The torn threads were to the outside. Meaning that he was outside the car when it was ripped off. . . . Colonel?"

"Yes."

"There's more."

"Go ahead."

"The car was found in the parking gear, and Yuri says there's no chance that the body he saw was killed inside that car. There simply wasn't enough blood. Say, listen, why do our own people want this covered up?"

"I don't know. . . . And I don't wanna know. . . . Thanks, Ras. I owe you. This means a lot to me. Do you want protection?"

"I can take care of myself, sir. I'd like to keep clear of this thing if I can. I hope you understand."

"Sure. Have it your own way, then. Call me sometime, Ras. I pay my debts."

"I don't know if you should plan too far in advance, Colonel. . . . Colonel?"

"Yes?"

"There is one thing, if you're serious about squaring things, I mean."

"I'm listening."

"Could you check on Yuri Gregorivich? I'd appreciate it. If you could just make it known that you're interested in him. I'm not worried about you, but, well . . . while I was there, a red-haired bureaucrat and two of his stooges came up. I couldn't see him too well, but if . . . I mean, just in case it was that assassin Zharuffkin . . ."

"Who?"

"Borky Zharuffkin. Our paths have crossed before. Wherever he is, you can expect misery and suffering too. And if he's got his eye on Yuri, well, sir, I'm concerned. I had to leave him alone with the five of them."

"Consider it done. I'll make arrangements tomorrow, first thing in the morning."

"No, sir, you don't understand. If that pig is with Yuri right now . . ."

Pig? Katzhak thought. "Describe this Zharuffkin. What does he look like? Is he heavyset, light-skinned, kind of squinty eyes?"

"You've met him, then!"

"I'd lay money on it. Listen, Ras, I've got to go now. I'll take care of Yuri right now, tonight. I'm sorry about what happened."

"Yes, sir. Thank you, sir. It was worth it if you can pull Yuri out."

"I'll do what I can, Ras. Forget all this. I'll let you know."

"Okay. This major. Did you know him?"

"Yeah, Ras. I knew him. Thanks."

"Glad to be of help, sir. Good luck."

"Good-bye."

Katzhak sat in silence for several moments, holding the receiver in both hands and resting his chin on it. Then, shaking himself from his thoughts, he leafed through a government directory and dialed the number of the vehicle impound himself. The gatehouse telephone buzzed.

"Let me speak with Yuri Gregorivich, please." Katzhak read the name he had written down during his conversation with Tamarzov.

"Ah, one . . . one . . . one moment, please."

Katzhak waited; there was much shuffling, muffled voices.

141

"Who is calling, please?"

"This is . . . Borky Zharuffkin."

More waiting. A different voice this time.

"Comrade Zharuffkin? Terrible news, terrible. Sergeant Gregorivich is dead. Shot himself through the head just after you left. Must have known you had him. It happened just after you left to get the warrant for his arrest. We heard a shot and we came on the run, but I'm afraid we were too late. I'm awfully sorry. I still can't believe it. You tell Comrade Bulgarin that we cooperated fully with your investigation. If Yuri Gregorivich took bribes or conspired with traitors as you said, I assure you that he stood alone in what he did. Tell Bulgarin that. And say also that we welcome a broader investigation. We welcome it. And if any one of my men does not cooperate fully, or is found to be disloyal, I will shun him as I did Yuri Gregorivich and I will turn him over to you at once. Without hesitation. What does he think, comrade? Does he believe any further investigation is warranted? It's gone far enough, hasn't it? Comrade? Are you there? Who is this?"

The guard cupped a hand over the telephone. "Corporal! Trace this line."

Katzhak hung up, his mind spinning with dizzying speed. He sat hunched forward on the edge of his chair, his right hand still on the receiver of the telephone in front of him. Stunned, his dazed eyes stared wide and vacant and he drew in a long, deep breath as he leaned backward, releasing it slowly as he sat upright, allowing it to escape by bits through clenched teeth. He sat erect and still for several moments before at length leaning on an elbow and bringing his left hand to his face. He slid that hand across his eyes and forehead, eventually sliding it back and forth through his sandy hair, causing his ever-present cap to slip backward on his head.

He was reeling from the blow, his brain scrambling to make sense of things for him once more. He had it all now. Tuskov was definitely deliberately murdered. Set up and assassinated as he stood beside the car. Katzhak had little doubt that it had been the assassination bureau that had done it. He wanted the killers, all right, but more important right now was not who pulled the trigger, but who

142

ordered his execution in the first place, and why. That guy from the impound complex had mentioned Bulgarin. Katzhak knew that name. Bulgarin was big, but Katzhak doubted he was that big. That he had given the order. Bulgarin couldn't have pulled all the necessary strings so vital to the smooth erasure of Major Tuskov. Not the successor, the state snub, the party propaganda organs, the apartment fire. Not all of that. No, he was obviously working for somebody, but whom?

Katzhak was agitated, beginning to sweat. This went higher than Bulgarin. Had to. There wasn't much room left at the top, not of his agency, anyway, for the finger to point to. God! He wished he'd never gotten into this thing—whatever it was. Oh, it was worse, much worse than he thought. He shrank from the knowledge that his worst fears were probably not far off; most of them were already justified. His heart pounded; his blood raced.

My God, this thing was dirty! They killed that guard just to rattle him. Just because he came near it! Christ! He obviously had no idea what was going on; he was no threat to anybody. Jesus! Just blew him away! Just like that! Oh, oh, no. No. They were crazy. Somebody was . . . mad. They had to be. Katzhak knew more than that luckless sergeant did. He knew too much. He even knew Tuskov. How long till they found that out? How many hours till somebody added it up and set loose the head-hunters? This was a total war. A war of attrition. They would stop at nothing now. There was no turning back. But hell! Nobody even knew who these people were! The members of the bureau were given their assignments secretly. They never saw or spoke with each other, with anyone except the highest echelons. It could be anybody—Tamarzov, Tatiana, anybody. Whom should he look out for, how could he guard himself? Whom could he trust, where was he safe? Was anywhere safe?

Wait. Katzhak forced himself to slow down. Gradually the wildfire of fear which had raced through the tinder of his thoughts was subdued and brought under control. He must think logically; his mind must be clear if he was to see a way out of his dilemma. What else had he got? Oh, yes. Borky Zharuffkin. How did he figure in all this? What was he doing down there this afternoon, and what really happened? In his mind's eye Katzhak set up the scenario. Silently he watched it play, changing actors or their lines until he believed he had it as it must have happened.

Tuskov had stumbled on something—whether in the course of his work or not, he could not be certain. Someone high up had something, some secret that he wanted to protect at all costs. Tuskov uncovered it, or came too close, and he was killed for it. Not only assassinated, erased. They wanted no clues left behind, so they fired his house and purged his name. Arno knew the magnitude of what he had, or had a glimpse of it. He was sure they would catch up with him, certain he would be killed. Why was he so sure? It must be black, black. Arno had begged the only man he trusted to bring it to the light of day or die trying. He had stressed that the highest stakes were involved. Had he spoken as a Soviet, a Jew, or a friend? Perhaps all three? Katzhak was uncertain.

Meanwhile, someone connected with Mikhail Malenkov, the lead Tuskov had given him, thinking that Katzhak was responsible for Malenkov's disappearance, opened fire on him just outside the city. Katzhak had killed them, or disabled their vehicle and his own, and had been picked up, unconscious, by Zharuffkin. It had to have been Zharuffkin. He was on the scene too quickly, had backed off his interrogation too easily. Unless . . . it was Zharuffkin who had hired the two would-be killers in the first place? No. The friends of Mikhail Malenkov had exploded that theory already. Zharuffkin had kept working on him. Sending that file clerk to seduce him as soon as he had been released.

Further, Zharuffkin had astutely guessed Katzhak's uncertainty about the outcome of the accident and had anticipated his investigation of the vehicles involved. Zharuffkin was a little man, yet he had an army waiting to greet Tamarzov when he arrived, eager to do his bidding. Where had he gotten them? When Katzhak had telephoned the facility himself, the officer in charge made it clear that Zharuffkin was working for Bulgarin. At least he had been told so by Zharuffkin.

That fit. But somehow Zharuffkin had squeezed the gatekeeper so hard that he had blown his own head off,

144

saving Borky the trouble. Obviously Zharuffkin was not interested in subtlety or discreet investigation. Why was it necessary to liquidate Yuri Gregorivich? Katzhak's next thought chilled him, thrilled him with terror. It was not necessary. It was not at all necessary. The implication was awful. Zharuffkin had killed him to scare Katzhak, and probably because it gave him gratification to do so. He was obviously ruthless. Insane. He was a butcher, preferring to slaughter everything and burn the forest than to stalk his prey in stealth and skill. Yet he was cunning and bold in the way he flaunted his contempt and conceit. This combination of shrewd acumen and apparent recklessness was confusing and effective in its efforts to keep an adversary off-balance. Like a shark, Borky floated easily, almost lazily along, with half-closed, sleepy, scavenger's eyes, turning suddenly in vicious attack, frenzied at the smell of fresh blood, darkening and churning the water around him in defiant challenge.

But how was Katzhak to avoid poking his nose in the wrong places? That was the real question. He must not underestimate Zharuffkin in his contempt for him and his early successes in dealing with him. He must not mistake a few pawns, expended as a ruse, for weakness and play into his hands.

Katzhak buzzed a relief secretary, noting that Tatiana, off duty since five, had gone home.

"Get me a dossier on a KGB agent, Borky Zharuffkin. . . . I'm not positive—like it sounds. And check microfilm. I want every scrap on him. Have it on my desk in fifteen minutes. Go."

"At once, Colonel," came the crisp reply.

Katzhak got up and extracted a bottle and a small glass, which he half-filled with vodka, before taking two or three deep swallows and leaning against a filing cabinet. His mind was traveling to a small village a couple of hundred kilometers away.

He thought of his home. The gate first, the yard with the walkway made of stones, the trees, the house with the porch swing and the storm windows. Most keenly missed was Tash, the object of his thoughts at present and the center of his concern. Tash. If Zharuffkin found out about her, there was no telling what he might do.

Katzhak's face changed and the glow left his eyes at this thought. He must conclude this affair quickly, and finally. Zharuffkin, he knew, would not take captives. It was all or nothing with him. The lines on Katzhak's face deepened, and his whole aspect seemed to darken with the acknowledgment of a brutal fact of life. It was impossible to show mercy to one who never does. Somehow, soon, Zharuffkin would have to be put away—for good. He could not let him live now, if he wanted to, which, fortunately, he did not. Wounded animals were dangerous, and if Katzhak merely bested him, the sadistic revenge he would inevitably plot defied imagination. His conscience did not trouble him much. He was certain Zharuffkin would make the first move when the time came. But Tash. At the next incident, at the very next move by Zharuffkin, he would have to expose himself and warn her. She must get out and at least be prepared, until the matter was settled.

On the desk a light blinked on and Katzhak's intercom buzzed. Quickly he set down the glass and stepped to his desk.

"Yes?"

"Comrade Colonel, I am sorry. The papers you requested are gone."

"Gone! How?" Katzhak held his breath.

"They were removed for inspection yesterday by a member of Comrade Bulgarin's staff on orders of the comrade himself."

"You're certain?"

"I am positive, sir."

"I see. All right. Thank you, comrade."

Katzhak was frozen. Zharuffkin was definitely under Bulgarin's umbrella, apparently with sweeping powers. He was already covering his tracks. Katzhak was beginning to get leery of automobiles. He elected to take the metro home. He would have a better chance in a crowd than he would by himself. If Zharuffkin had wanted to put him on the defensive, he had done it. From now on Colonel Katzhak would be a very careful man.

21

Vladislev Katzhak walked the short distance to the access point near his building for the Soviet subway. He was about to board one of the cars as a crowd of people emerging from one of the trains swarmed over him. As he was jostled and bumped by the little human squall, he was suddenly elbowed hard just beneath his breastbone. Katzhak's hands flew out of his pockets in surprise, and he choked, gasping for breath. Instantly a folded envelope was thrust into his right hand, and his fingers jammed over it. A bespectacled figure in a black peak hat and gray overcoat pushed and shoved quickly away, losing himself in the crowd. Katzhak was terrified. He wondered what incriminating evidence had just been placed in his hand, now that he was being hit, and he was sure that he was. Desperately he fought to suck in enough air to find his voice and cry out. God, they were clever! The rush of shielding people was dwindling fast, and still he had barely managed a muffled croak. Transferring the envelope to his left hand, he shoved his right into his overcoat pocket, slipping it over the butt of his pistol. Katzhak glanced rapidly from side to side, trying to figure from where the shots might come. Seeing nothing, he whirled around and looked behind him. There was no one there. Nothing. He stood panting for a moment, his head lowered, his body full of adrenaline.

Relaxing a little, he opened his left hand, allowing the envelope to unfold. Lifting the flap, he found inside a single ticket to a home performance of the Bolshoi ballet. Katzhak balled the envelope and the contents in his gloved hands and prepared to throw them away. He checked himself and stood thinking. Someone who had wanted to kill him would have done so where he stood, helpless. Someone who wished to set him up at the Bolshoi Theater had no guarantee that he would come at all, let alone without an armed escort.

Katzhak guessed that this unorthodox method of contact (he frowned at the pun) must be the work of the friends of Mikhail Malenkov.

It was expedient that he be contacted in public, in a place with multiple exits and maximum anonymity. The metro, the conservatory, the Bolshoi Theater—these were all choices he might have made. It was apparent that the two young hotheads who had ambushed him days before were the exceptions, not the rule, in Malenkov's circle. Still, he would be taking an intolerable risk. He doubted that it mattered much. He guessed that time was running out, and a few hours either way made little difference. What he could not have guessed, however, was that fifteen or twenty kilometers away, another man held a ticket of some significance in his hand. It was a red-haired, fair-skinned man with squinting, small pig's eyes. He was taking a journey to the country, and he smiled as he rode the train.

22

Warily Katzhak stepped into a small cubicle that served as a washroom and freshened his appearance as best he could. In minutes he was rerouted toward his destination and some of the most beautiful buildings in the capital. He was not really noticing the pride of his city on this night. He dreamed awake of what awaited him in his appointed chair, of all the terrible things that had happened. He dreamed too of Cosmo, the small word with the devastating power, upon whose altar at least five lives had already been sacrificed, and he mused on the possibility that out there, somewhere, lurked the high priest who would earmark him as the next offering, the latest lamb to bleat and bleed. His heart was heavy and frozen within him, as the tightening circle of fear and apprehension constricted and choked him, like thick and stifling clouds blotting out the sun. He stared out a window dully, a condemned man on his last ride. Katzhak hoped sincerely that there was no God, no judge, no eternity. He wanted to rest. Rest and surrender to sleep, to be lost forever in peace, to melt into the darkness and quiet of oblivion.

Abruptly his thoughts were jolted as the train lurched to a halt. On the street again, Katzhak was able to hail a cab and continue to the theater. Outside it snowed, and the icy November wind blasted him as he stepped from the cab and walked briskly into the theater. It was bitterly cold, and the warm, well-lighted interior was the most compelling of contrasts. Katzhak surveyed the lobby crowd with hard-bitten haste and skill. Nothing seemed amiss on the surface. He asked an usher where to find his seat and refused the offer to be guided there personally.

Half an hour passed. Three-quarters. The house lights dimmed and murmurs died away. The stage lights came up, and once again the red-and-gold richness of the famous center could be discerned. The music, which started in a subdued, smooth tempo, soon quickened into a lively, stirring, markedly martial beat. This performance was patriotic, and oddly for him, struck him as droll and ironic. As he watched the initial movements, superlatively performed, as usual, he felt detached. For the moment, he was not a Soviet, not a Communist, not a military man, but a truly objective observer, like a visitor from another world, infinitely curious, but lacking any kinship in time or space, any common experience. For an instant a fragment of a dream he once had was called to mind, cued by his present emotions.

Katzhak strained, trying hard to recall it. It was gone. It had sunk too deeply to be retrieved. Yet it seemed important. What was it? Where was he and what was he doing? Oh, yes. Now he remembered. It was a street. He was standing in the street. It was dark, and cloudy, and . . . yes! This was the dream of the great stone bear, the nightmare he had had on the train to Sovetsk. The exultant military music had brought it back to him. He had been an outsider that day, too. The people shouted and sang songs of praise. Their might and their power were limitless, unbreakable, until the rain. When the rain began to fall, great cracks appeared in the foundation, in the feet of the idol of the beast. Blood had spilled out of its lifeless mouth, and the triumphant multitudes had perished when it fell, crushed by its deadweight. The people were definitely Russian in his vision, yet he was not one of them. He had not raised his voice with theirs in tumultuous, hollow rejoicing. Hollow. That was how he felt and how the prestigious National Ballet Company seemed to him tonight. Silent mimics, puppets on strings, acting with ludicrous grace an obscene and macabre mockery.

Katzhak rubbed his eyes. God, he was tired. It was getting to the point where he almost didn't care anymore who showed up to meet him. The strain of these last few days was really beginning to catch up with him. If only . . .

"Good evening, Colonel Katzhak. Don't move, and don't turn your head. That's right; now, lower your hands slowly, please. Thank you; that's just fine."

Startled, Katzhak did as he was told.

"Who are you?"

"Listen carefully, Colonel. Tomorrow morning a few of us are getting together to pray in the southern forest, near the old mill road on the outskirts of the city, about twenty-five kilometers from here. Do you know it?"

"Yes. I think so. But—"

"Sunrise. Be there. Alone."

The man who sat beside him rose on nimble feet and walked quickly up the ramp on the extreme left wall of the theater. Katzhak turned his head just in time to see him vanish. He snapped his eyes to the front and sank down into his seat, exhaling, and lifted a trembling hand to his forehead, already damp with tiny beads of perspiration. He sat still for a long time, afraid to move.

Dammit! What was their game? What had Tuskov got himself involved in? Meeting with these people would be close to treason, especially if he were ever closely connected

150

to Arno Tuskov. He had better make certain that he made no more moves until he found out what kind of trouble he might be in if he were apprehended with these people. Tomorrow would be the last time. He was not that bad off, not yet. Maybe if he just stopped being so curious all the time . . .

Yeah. Sure. Maybe if he ignored it, it would all go away. The two killers in that Mercedes could not be ignored. Tuskov and Yuri and Mikhail Malenkov would have liked to ignore it. Maybe if he ignored the bullets, they would bounce off. Katzhak had to get a good grip on himself.

These people were lunatics; they had to be. Telling the NKVD where and when their next subversive rally would be held. It didn't make sense. Unless . . . unless they were sincere. Did they really expect him to be so obliging, so honest, so naive, as to go off in the woods somewhere, alone, when they had tried already to kill him? What was to stop him from bringing the third army along, just for company?

On the other hand, what if, aware of everything that had transpired, the assassination bureau had contacted him, had been meeting him all along? Yes! To get him out of Moscow, alone, without witnesses, as they must have done with Tuskov. No, perhaps the ambush would not take place there at all, but by the roadside en route, where he would be unprepared and his numerical advantage badly negated by the terrain. It made no difference. If he was already being hunted, he was lost; all was lost. As was becoming the frightening pattern of events, as usual, he had only one real option. Play along. Wearily he pushed himself up from his seat and trudged up the ramp toward his bed and a few precious hours of sleep before the sun.

23

It had finally stopped snowing. Through his small window Katzhak could see the glimmering black bodies of two government sedans slide to a slippery halt in front of his apartment building. From this height he could just make out the droplets of water, which had once been snowflakes, glistening on the hoods of the cars. Fully dressed, he sat in silence, in overcoat and cap, smoking a cigarette and watching. As he had requested, the driver of the second car emerged, climbed into the front seat of the first car, and shut the door. It then returned to Moscow, leaving Katzhak with a vehicle with which to make his rendezvous. The sun would be up in half an hour. Somehow he was not in a hurry to begin this day. True, he had no real idea what it held in store for him.

But he had faced death or prison or worse before without a hint of the apprehension and trepidation that made him hesitate this particular morning. Elusive as quicksilver, he could neither isolate nor identify the feeling, the almost precognitive notion he held, with waking, that today was a day full of trouble, chaos, destiny, and death. He did not know how he knew, but yet he knew, without doubt, without equivocation, before the sun rose on another day, he would have Cosmo, or Cosmo would have him. With the grim determination of a scarred and battered gladiator he stared through his window across the arena of time and space and sized up his opponent with experience and the knowledge that he would probably fight his last battle today. He saw it clearly for the first time in the soft gray light of the coming dawn. Saw the essence of the beast, its evil, its ugliness, its power and menace. He could almost sense the supernatural aura, the unearthly malevolence of the thing. Tugging on the visor of his cap from his corner in the darkness, he adjusted the visor of his helmet. Then he buttoned his coat, his shield against the slashing wind and icy frozen barbs, from the blows he would have to take in minutes. He smoothed the leather of first one boot and then the other, as if lacing up for battle, all the while never taking his eyes off his nemesis. Finally he took out his weapon and weighed it carefully in both hands, sliding his hand along the shaft of it, like a warrior's lance. At last he was ready. Katzhak tossed his crushed cigarette from him like a cup of bitter wine, took one last glance outside, and swung open the door, stepping out into the long and lonely corridor, a man to the end.

He drove with set face and resolute will. He would see this thing through, no matter what the cost. Although reasonably alert, he saw nothing that struck him as unusual. The tiny November sun did not have the strength to pierce the ominous gray clouds, yet it was clear that it had indeed come up over the horizon and had climbed by inches for perhaps five minutes. Katzhak pulled the car off the road and let it coast to a stop between two trees. Locking the door, he set out for a deep bowl-like depression just over a small rise, perhaps one hundred meters away. The snow was deep and soft, and he was soon panting for breath. Nothing like advertising his coming. Continuing to trudge through the heavy drifts, Katzhak at last reached the edge of the protective wall of the natural bowl, and not yet wishing to be seen, threw himself down on his stomach. Crawling to the rim, he peered downward into the depression.

Katzhak's eyes came to rest on a small group of perhaps ten men and three or four women. One man, the oldest and one of the tallest of the little band, held a small sheet or scroll from which he appeared to read. The others, meanwhile, stood silent, listening, and a few knelt in the middle of the semicircle to pray.

Katzhak, too, listened, even more intently than the worshipers. His keen eyes scanned the forest and the white expanse before him in search of a hint of color or the slightest flicker of movement. Reasonably satisfied, he pushed himself up and started down the side of the decline toward the group. However casual he may have appeared, his fingers were tense in his coat pocket, and his gun was gripped tightly in his right hand.

Abruptly the reading ceased, although the praying continued. All except those who knelt in the snow turned and looked at Katzhak, mute. He halted at a spot five meters from those who stood staring at him. Besides a slight breeze, all was still. No one moved, and Katzhak waited.

"My name is Katzhak. Are you the friends of Mikhail Malenkov?" No one spoke or moved or gave any sign that they had heard him at all.

"Did you know Arno Tuskov? I was his friend." Again nothing.

"Two of you tried to kill me last week. I'm sorry about what happened. There was no other way. I'm sorry about what they did to Gallina, too. I had nothing to do with that, believe me. Please." Katzhak glanced nervously around him.

"Look. We're wasting time. One of my men got hurt trying to find out what's going on. Now, you've been contacting me. I'm in a lot of trouble because of you, and I want to know why. Why have you been contacting me? Why was Malenkov arrested? Why was Tuskov murdered? Why do they want me?" Katzhak beheld a sea of stone faces, blank and expressionless except for the eyes, which regarded him coldly.

"If I wanted to have you picked up, I would. I've come alone. Why did you send for me?"

Almost as one the pairs of eyes blinked and looked upward behind Katzhak. Disconcerted, Katzhak listened and could just make out dim sounds in the distance behind him. Suddenly the air was split with the staccato roar of first one, then another and still another motorcycle flying briefly off the edge of the depression and landing in the snow behind him. The man in the sidecar of the first machine held a policeman's baton in his right hand, and before Katzhak had even turned to face the sound, rose up and cracked him across the back of the head with it, before speeding on toward the huddling enclave, which made no move to flee.

Katzhak's head exploded with pain and color and light,

154

and he fell facedown in the snow, senseless. The marauding riders tore into the splintering, cringing group, swinging, kicking, and steering directly at the knots of cowering people. With maximum effort Katzhak clawed out two handfuls of snow and ground it into his face. He had to get up. Dragging his elbows up under him and lifting his head, he watched in disbelief as the worshipers did not resist their beating, did not fight back at all. He had never seen anything like it.

At once Katzhak was on his feet. He could not let this brutal, one-sided slaughter continue for a moment longer, regardless of who was involved. Watching the spectacle before him made him sick and ashamed, made him feel more kinship with these daring Jews than with his own police. Something inside him snapped.

In a kind of running stagger which exactly paralleled that of his soul, Katzhak hobbled into the center of the fray. One of the motorcyclists just to his left had clubbed a praying woman, still kneeling, to the snowy ground. The bike wheeled and prepared to return, perhaps to ride roughshod over the unconscious body. Frenzied, Katzhak glanced wildly for a branch that might give him enough reach. In a blur he grabbed at it, stood it upright, and snapped off the frozen twigs from the base, making a gnarled and knotty pole, or war club. With no time left, he grasped it with his might and swung it full force into the back of the head of the driver of the passing motorcycle.

Eyes and ears from everywhere jerked to the spot and were riveted as, with a tremendous crack, the helmet sailed up and away, somersaulting through the air and landing in a clattering skid across the ice and into the cushioning snow. Its rider, too, was lifted from his seat, flipping forward, over the handlebars, and thudded to earth, like a duffel bag full of wet towels, as his snarling machine hurtled past him, spinning out of control and smashing sideways into a tree trunk. The rider in the sidecar was thrown clear; tossed like a rag doll, he cartwheeled into a snowbank.

For a moment everything was still as the surprised invaders, suddenly decreased in number by a third, together with the worshipers, stared at Katzhak in stunned silence.

No one could believe what they had just seen; most startled of all, perhaps, was Katzhak. But shocked amazement soon gave way to renewed resolve as the remaining two cyclists dug in their heels, peeled back the throttles of their hungry steel steeds, and roared off straight at Katzhak at full tilt. Katzhak's mind whirled and spun, trying desperately to recall a technique for unarmed combat he had been taught and had not used since World War II. They would be upon him any second.

Grasping the long pole of wood in the middle, his hands a foot apart, Katzhak held the bar vertically at his right side. The riders were almost there. Turning his body sharply, he snapped the pole to the horizontal at the throat level of the converging riders, braced himself, and remembered both to duck the rebounding bar and to let go of it as it passed. Though both of the men tried to veer, only one of them tried to duck. The fortunate one caught it across the forehead of the helmet and escaped serious injury. The other was struck in the throat. Both men, caught off guard, were knocked from their saddles, unintentionally throwing the throttles of their machines wide open as their hands left the steering grips. The bikes leaped forward and overturned, churning up snow, each sputtering to a lifeless halt.

Katzhak got up slowly and turned, surveying the battlefield, now strewn with moaning bodies and broken machines. The Jews tended to their wounded, except for the old man, who stood in the midst of the misery and stared at Katzhak, as if fearful that he would disappear and the whole scene dissolve into a dream. His sides heaving, Katzhak stared back, wondering what was on the old man's mind. The latter shut his eyes, and raising his hands and face to heaven, gave thanks to God. Katzhak thought he was crazy, and himself likewise. He shook his head in disbelief at what he had just done.

Suddenly a leaden fist slammed into the small of Katzhak's back, and a swift kick swept his feet out from under him and dumped him down hard on the ground. Four hands gripped his arms like talons and dragged him to his feet. Quickly his overcoat was yanked down over his shoulders, pinning his arms. Two more kicks spread his legs in preparation for a third, much more painful one.

One of the motorcycle drivers was up, ready to avenge his hurt pride and aching head. Two of the sidecar riders held his victim. Katzhak prepared for excruciating pain and sweated, waiting.

All at once the snow sprang up in a dozen places near their feet as a spray of bullets from an automatic weapon danced across the surface of the ground in an even line. The men froze. On the ridge, a man beckoned. A kneeling soldier, poised to fire, sat beside him.

Reluctantly the motorcycle driver lowered his upraised fist and cursed Katzhak. He nodded to the men who held him, and they released their grip, still standing with their backs to the man who stood on the crest of the hill. Quick and brutal, the driver brought up his foot and kicked Katzhak in disappointed rage and defiance, causing him to double over and go to his knees on the ground. The driver gestured to his lackeys, and they returned with him, dragging their fallen comrades up the hill. Terrified of Katzhak's anger, the apparent leader of the group sifted through the heavy snow to where Katzhak knelt, struggling for control over his agony.

"Colonel Katzhak. Please forgive me, comrade. I only just now heard your name and was told that you were conducting an investigation for Comrade Bulgarin himself. I know I have compromised your position here, jeopardized your work. . . . If there were any way to recompense you for inconvenience . . . Shall I arrest these traitors, now that I have exposed you? I can at least do that."

"No," Katzhak croaked, trying to get his breath. "No. Leave now, at once. Wait . . . How did you know who I was? How did you know I would be here? Who told you I work for Bulgarin?"

"You were followed from your apartment. Another man, a red-haired man, told me who you were, and whom you were working for. It was his man who followed you here and called us. His boss met us after my men charged you."

Zharuffkin! The big blond had been left on his doorstep as a lookout. Katzhak wondered why Zharuffkin had not harassed him in almost twenty-four hours. Apparently he had been gone somewhere and had just got back. The overzealous KGB had probably given him heart failure,

157

attacking Katzhak and ruining his chances of doing the job himself for personal gain.

"Where is the comrade now? I want to talk to him."

"He has returned to Moscow, leaving me instructions to release you unharmed and to do whatever you asked."

"You and your people clear out and I will forget this misunderstanding. Say nothing to anyone if you value your life and position. Get going."

"Yes, Comrade Colonel. At once, sir."

The embarrassed officer waved his men on.

"We will return later for the motorcycles. Are you all right? Can we take you or one of the others to a hospital?"

"Just go now."

The officer saluted and was gone, trudging back up the hill and out of sight. Katzhak waited until he heard the sound of engines starting, and fading out in the distance. He looked up and saw the old man standing over him.

"Colonel Katzhak?" Katzhak stared dully back up into the face framed by grayish-white hair.

"Why did you do this? What made you do it?"

"Somebody had to," Katzhak muttered in disgust. The old man smiled broadly, as if Katzhak had given the perfect answer.

"Are you badly hurt?" Katzhak shook his head, closing his eyes. "Striking a policeman carries a mandatory prison term of three to five years. It is for this reason that we could not help you. I hope you understand. We did not dare to. Until now, there has been no one to protect us. No friendly ally to champion our cause."

Katzhak shook his head in a gesture of disapproving affirmation.

"Not until now," the Jew repeated. Katzhak looked up again, puzzled.

"Are you familiar with the second book of Moses, Chapter Two, Colonel?" Katzhak did not answer. "I know it by heart:

"And it came to pass in those days, when Moses was grown, that he went out unto his brethren, and looked on their burdens: and he spied an Egyptian beating a Hebrew, one of his people. And he looked

158

this way and that way, and when he saw that no one watched him, he struck the Egyptian, and he died."

"You people," Katzhak said, "you're all insane. This meeting is illegal and it constitutes treason. Only one thing will save you all from the labor camps."

"And what is that?"

"Tell me quickly what I want to know."

"We must serve God. He commands us to remember him."

"I command you to forget him, and to remember the penalty for antistate activities and subversion."

"Who madest thou a prince and a judge over us? Do you intend to kill me, as you killed the Egyptian?"

Katzhak held the gaze of the courageous fanatic in front of him. Slowly he got to his feet.

"Tell me about Arno Tuskov."

"Indeed, Colonel Katzhak, indeed. Only, we must leave this place. We are in grave danger because of what you have done for us."

"No. No more stalling. Give it to me now or you're all under arrest."

"Arrest us if you must, Colonel. But you heard them say yourself that they would be returning shortly. Do you want to be here for that?"

"Where do you want me to meet you?"

"Drive on the Stolbovaya road until you come to the asylum. Far behind the camp there is a clearing, perhaps twenty meters into the trees. Unless you see a pickup truck in the midst of the clearing, do not approach. We will meet you there at two o'clock. We must tend to the wounded first, from this morning's encounter. When Arno became our friend, he told us much about you. We were eager to learn all we could. I am pleased to report that the things he said appear to be true, just as he told us. Until this afternoon, thank you, Colonel, and may God bless you for what you have risked, and continue to risk, in our behalf. Shalom."

"I've given you a bargain; make sure you keep your end. If you try to cheat me after I've been beaten and almost killed and ruined, I will not leave a single forest standing in the state for you to hide in."

159

The old man bowed his head in mute assent, although nothing in his bearing suggested that this had been a servile gesture. Katzhak imparted to him a final glance of warning and started back up the hill behind him. The elder man stood watching the retreating figure with sad and wizened eyes, as if somehow aware of his future, and conscious that his life would not be a long one. At last, he too turned and picked his way up through the powdery crystals.

" '. . . may God bless you for what you have risked, and continue to risk, in our behalf. Shalom.' "

" 'I've given you a bargain; make sure you keep your end. If you try to cheat me after I've been beaten and almost killed and ruined, I will not leave a single forest standing in the state for you to hide in.' "

"Oh, Katzhak, you melodramatic fool. I've got you. I've got you!" Zharuffkin lowered the binoculars. "You're certain that's all he said?"

"Yes, comrade."

"I never thought it would be this easy." Zharuffkin spoke to the lip reader whom he had gotten out of bed to accompany him in his further surveillances of Katzhak, not wishing any precious conversation to elude him, as it had yesterday afternoon at the park. The disciplined side of his nature struggled for control over premature elation and self-congratulation.

"Do you recall what the old man said to him before and after Katzhak turned his head? About the location?"

" 'Drive on the Stolbovaya road . . . twenty meters into the trees. Unless you see a pickup truck in the midst of the clearing, do not approach. We will meet you there at two o'clock . . .' "

"Ah, yes. That memory of yours. Phenomenal. Do you remember every word you saw?" The older, spectacled man nodded proudly. "I'm sure, with that talent, you'll never have to worry about your future." Zharuffkin rolled over on his back on the snowbank behind a screen of trees that had been his place of concealment to watch the dialogue below. "Oh-h-h-h," he complained, "I hardly slept on the train. A clearing, twenty meters into the trees, on the Stolbovaya road. . . . There is one place, only one place.

160

The asylum. Let's go. I want to find the place and pick a spot, long before the colonel and his friends arrive. Hm, perhaps that's where they will send him after his arrest. Come on." With that, Zharuffkin and his admiring entourage bounded toward his car through the snow.

24

Vladislev Katzhak drove his weary and aching body furiously back to his offices. He had so little time. He must get Zharuffkin soon—tonight, if possible. Where would they have records besides his official dossier? Promotions? His name in a registry of KGB employees? An enemy? No. No. No. A photograph. Katzhak needed one so that Zharuffkin could be picked up without mistakes. But where was he to get one on such short notice? Of course! Every agent on the KGB payroll had to have passed some form of security clearance somewhere along the line. His identification papers, something that had photographs, existed somewhere. The officer had said that Zharuffkin had returned to Moscow. He would have him arrested—no, detained—this afternoon, and held until this thing was over. Zharuffkin had been a thorn in his side long enough. Besides, he was clever, persistent, and totally ruthless. This affair would go much more smoothly with his elimination.

Zharuffkin could have lied for Katzhak's release for only one reason. He wanted to make the arrest himself, and he would act quickly. Damn, damn, damn! Everything was happening so fast, and he had so little time to think. Tamarzov had been right. Katzhak was getting hotter and hotter by the minute. He doubted seriously that he had more than a day or two left in which to unravel this thing and save himself. He shuddered to think of the brutal gang beating

161

he had narrowly escaped this morning. It could only get worse from here. And those policemen! A couple of them had to be critical, or dead. He was pretty certain that he had hit that first one much too hard. He had destroyed government property, interfered directly with the KGB in the performance of their official duties, met and conspired with the contacts of convicted subversives, sent men to bribe the guards at the state-security vehicle impound . . . Katzhak had no choice now. He had to discover the secret of Cosmo and use it, somehow, trade it for his life, or he was a dead man.

Katzhak had one ace in the hole, though. Zharuffkin also had acted illegally every step of the way—from his subterfuge at the hospital after the "accident" to the beating of Tamarzov and the suicide of Yuri Gregorivich. Just today he had released Katzhak and a handful of activists. If they were traitors, then so was Borky. But . . . but Zharuffkin was under the protective umbrella of Comrade Bulgarin. What a weird alliance! No. Katzhak's one and only hope for survival lay with the Jews and the awful secret they would tell him this afternoon, behind, appropriately, an insane asylum.

Katzhak parked his car, and once inside the building, strode quickly down the polished corridor to one of the doors of the main computer room at that level. Even though he was on the offensive, his footsteps echoed in his ears like those of a creature in flight. He tapped one of the technicians on the shoulder with obvious meaning, the man looking quickly at Katzhak and then surrendering his seat at once. The technician saluted briskly and stood at attention, eyes staring straight ahead.

Katzhak's fingers darted over the keyboard like a robin plucking at worms, requesting a projection on his monitor as opposed to a printed readout. In seconds a picture of Borky Zharuffkin stared blankly up at him from his television screen. Katzhak punched more buttons, freezing the image in place, and then signaled the machine to begin making photostatic copies of the picture in front of him. Instantly, in a bin some three feet away, the pictures fluttered out, one after another. Katzhak ordered it to make twenty-five copies before getting up to retrieve them, and at the same time relinquishing the inquisitor's chair to its customary occupant.

Satisfied, Katzhak left the room and walked down toward his office. Once inside, he called together his lieutenants and distributed the pictures, five to each.

"This man is Comrade Borky Zharuffkin. He is KGB. I want him found, but not picked up. Do not pick him up or alert him in any way, is that clear?"

"Yes, Comrade Colonel."

"I will reward the first man who calls in with information regarding his whereabouts. But if you find him, under no circumstances let him out of your sight. His dossier has been stolen under the direction of Comrade Bulgarin, so you won't find anything there. Some of you might be wise to watch Bulgarin's headquarters. Zharuffkin was last seen an hour ago on the outskirts of the city, and was reported returning to central Moscow immediately. He has two men who travel with him almost constantly. One is Ulev, sixtwo, two hundred and ten, two hundred and twenty pounds, and the other is five-eight, a hundred and fifty-five to a hundred and sixty-five pounds. The tall one has blond hair, very short, with blue eyes, and the other has dark hair, beard, and mustache. I want Zharuffkin today. I don't care about the other two. Don't come back without him. Get out on the street. That's all."

Without a word the five men closed their notepads and pocketed the pictures, exiting one by one out the door, each filled with the quiet determination to return in triumph as Katzhak's number one. Katzhak watched them go and then shut his office door himself. Returning to his desk, he withdrew his gun, placed there after this morning's events, and two full leather pouches of ammunition, which he threaded onto his belt. Carefully he opened the cylinder, revolved it under close scrutiny, and locked it back into place. He placed it in the handsome black holster of his uniform this time, snapping and unsnapping the flap once or twice, just to test it. Then, ready as he ever would be for such a day, he turned out the light, slipped on his heavy overcoat and cap, and locked the door.

In another part of the city, meanwhile, a short darkhaired man with beard and mustache bounded up the stairs

163

to the elevator. He pressed the button and waited with urgency and impatience. Soon the doors opened and swallowed the little man up, carrying him upstairs to his destination on one of the building's highest levels. It spit him out again, and he followed the signs to Comrade Bulgarin's office.

A secretary-receptionist asked his name and his errand, but quickly buzzed Bulgarin when the official order carried by the messenger was flashed under her nose. The little man smiled arrogantly when he was immediately ushered into the imposing office and presence of the man whose signature and sanction he sought.

"My name is Andrei Kretschevik. Comrade Zharuffkin sent me to you with this order to have it sealed and officially completed."

"Yes, Andrei. Here, let me see that, would you? Thank you. Yes, it's my order. For how many persons shall I stipulate on the warrant?"

"Ten. With power to exceed if there are others."

"Ten? I'm supposed to sanction the arrest of ten persons without a word? He didn't even come in person!"

"Possibly more, sir. There was a meeting of antistate activists this morning, several policemen were involved. Some were injured. One or two seriously."

"I see. Where is Comrade Zharuffkin now? I gave him explicit instructions that there were to be no"—he looked at Andrei with disdain—"go-betweens."

"He is at a second meeting site, sir; it is there where he plans to make the arrests."

"I see," he said again. "And are there any principals involved, er, Andrei?"

"Yes, sir. Comrade Zharuffkin specifically asked you to mention Colonel Katzhak."

"Katzhak! He told you to ask me for Katzhak? On what grounds, did he say? What proof does he have?"

"It was Katzhak who assaulted the policemen in defense of the activists."

"You're not serious!"

"But I am. That is one of the charges."

"One of the charges! I might have known. Why should he do that? Why would he expose himself, meeting with these people?"

164

Andrei shrugged. "If the comrade pleases, I am in a hurry to return."

"Yes, of course." Bulgarin wrote hastily, his brow wrinkled and deeply furrowed, folded the paper once, twice, three times, and affixed the personal seal of his office. "That should be all he needs. I wonder . . ." Bulgarin paused for a moment, deep in thought. With the painful weight of a life-or-death decision, he reached into a drawer and extracted a small envelope. "If something should . . . something should . . . go wrong this afternoon, give Comrade Zharuffkin this envelope. Tell him under any circumstances to call this telephone number in the event the colonel eludes him. He must call this number, is that clear? Tell him to say the colonel's rank and name, and to hang up. Have you got it?"

"Yes, sir."

"Here you are. Guard that letter and that number with your life, because it's your life and Zharuffkin's as well if you fail. Good day, Andrei. And tell Comrade Zharuffkin to see me as soon as his situation has stabilized."

"Yes, sir." Smiling, Andrei accepted the missives and went out, closing the doors behind him. Alexei Bulgarin stood, having dared to disobey in order to possibly save his life and career, wondering desperately if he had done the right thing. Well, he sighed to himself, it's done. There's no stopping it now. In his heart he hoped that Katzhak would not survive. That would be the only salvation of them all.

25

Katzhak's car ground to a crunching halt in the icy snow. Behind him in the gray distance loomed the oppressive walls of Stolbovaya, prison of the deranged and the unpopular, doomed alike to share a shadowy hell on the edge of the abyss. Even at this range it was anachronistic, ugly, and distorted. The hideous thing littered the landscape, marred it like some grotesque, unnatural growth, sinister and insidious. Even Katzhak quailed at its sight, shrank from it, turned finally and drew away. It was an omen.

He ventured a few steps farther, toward the edge of the dark, foreboding forest. Suddenly a huge black bird shrieked and flapped away, like a grim harbinger gone mad at his own message, leaving Katzhak alone to face the danger. Recovered, he trudged on over the mantle of snow, under the curtain of darkness. Another few meters . . . There! Only, the truck stood empty, like ghostly bait, to lure him from cover. Katzhak watched and waited. For ten minutes there was no movement, no sound but his own heartbeat. With great determination he unsnapped the flap on his holster and stepped out into the clearing, into the center of the large circle of light that surrounded the truck.

At once the old white-haired man he had seen earlier stepped out, facing him. Simultaneously two younger men approached, one from each side. Katzhak stood still, not daring to breathe.

"Katzhak, you have come, then, eh? And alone?"

Katzhak made no reply as the man on his right advanced and took his weapon. All three of the strangers

166

stepped in close and stood next to Katzhak, more or less in a line, so that they could lean against the truck. This was perfect for the watchers on the hill, deaf but for the man who read words in the wisps of frosty vapor that emanated from the mouths of the figures below.

The old man spoke for his group, the other two men serving as lookouts.

"We are the friends of Mikhail Malenkov."

"And of Arno Tuskov?"

"Yes. We knew Arno. For a short time."

"Until you killed him."

"We had nothing to do with it. Do you think we are terrorists, murderers?"

"Two of you tried to kill me."

"Boys, Colonel. Two boys who went out in sickness and outrage at what they had seen. They had no clear idea of what they meant to do. We pity you for what you had to do. It must weigh heavily upon you."

"Where did they get the gun? From Malenkov?"

"Mikhail hated guns. The young men made it piece by piece from scraps of metal, parts accumulated for months. We pleaded with them not to go out."

"Why?"

"We feared for their safety. Now they are dead. We are not killers. No, Colonel. We hate violence, most of us, more than we hate our immoral and unjust detainment in your country. We, being the victims, the targets through the centuries, the scapegoats, the prisoners, the orphans, the widows, we know violence best and we hate it. It is a plague to us, it brings only blood and death and sorrow. There are violent men in any struggle, but to take up arms, to murder unawares, it is a shame. The synagogue in exile would never lay hands upon you. You need have no fear of that."

Katzhak threw back his head and laughed, hard and bitter.

"Tell me what you are laughing at, sir, and we will laugh together."

Katzhak laughed again. "You're no terrorists. No murderers. Malenkov was not the leader of any revolutionary cell. There's no plot. No treason. Just a bunch of idiots cowering together to pray in the snow. His crime was ideo-

167

logical deviance. He refused to be reeducated, enlightened; he clung to reactionary myths. Is that why Tuskov was killed? What is everybody so afraid of? Surely a martyr is worse than an insignificant subversive?"

The old man stared at Katzhak with sad and weary eyes.

"Arno Tuskov was killed for quite a different reason, Colonel. One which he found far less a cause for amusement. We know that when he came to us, it was as a spy, to infiltrate and destroy the underground churches of which our synagogue is part. Yes, we are in cooperation with Christians for support and aid. Many of our beliefs and sacred writings are the same, and to a point, we worship the same god. We await the promised deliverance; they believe they have found theirs."

"Why didn't Arno's God deliver him? It seems that his sincerity led him to the grave, the same one we all must face sooner or later."

"Who can search the infinite mind of the Almighty? As the Scripture says, 'His wisdom is unsearchable.' Very possibly, Katzhak, to bring you here to us. For your sake, perhaps. Perhaps for ours. I believe that, in any case, when you have heard what I have to say, you will know, and your course will become clear for you. We have all prayed for this."

"I have risked death more than once to know. Was Tuskov . . . ? I mean, did he . . . ? He was born a Jew. Tell me this first. Did he die one?"

An enigmatic smile crossed the old man's lips, and a visible peace flowed over him. He soaked up the comfort from the unseen springs like a sponge.

"He was truly a Jew."

Katzhak thought for a moment, nodded. Whatever Tuskov had found changed his life drastically. He had renewed his boyhood faith in the closing moments of his life. Inexplicably, Katzhak was glad, and somehow in a mood of anticipation.

"Arno was obviously not one of us, but we tolerated his presence as best we could. He listened to our teachings over the months, and actually absorbed some of it, in the performance of his duty. He informed and watched us only part of the time. As you are probably aware, his major interest was computer systems and how to make them more secure. Arno found a way to 'dial in' to some of the most airtight data banks in the nation. He picked out bits and pieces of highly classified material, like a game, gradually building evidence for a shocking exposé of current security measures safeguarding our most sensitive information. Please understand he told us this in retrospect, we have no other way of knowing any of this. At last, one day, he cracked the most highly classified military bank in all the Kremlin and learned a terrifying secret. If he had not been killed, I am convinced that his knowledge would have torn him apart."

"What was the secret?"

"Shut up. Shhh. I saw something move up there on the slope. A man." This from the young man on Katzhak's right.

"All right, whatever you do, don't fire that thing. If you shoot, they'll kill you. You saw Gallina Malenkov, and what they did this morning. They're trained, you're not. Did you get a good look at him? How was he dressed?"

"Overcoat. He was bareheaded, I think."

"Are they your men, Colonel?" the old man inquired.

"No. No one knows I'm here."

"Were you followed, then?"

"Impossible."

"That's him! I saw him at Mikhail's! Murdering son of a bitch! I owe you." The man raised the weapon.

"Noooo!" Katzhak's frantic yell echoed through the forest, cut off by the roar of the gun. Katzhak delivered a hard, roundhouse kick that sent the youth flying to the ground near the front end of the truck and the gun out of his hands and into the snow. Katzhak dived for it, rolled back, and yanked the old man, who had frozen in disbelief, down off his feet and into the snow near the center of the truck. "Get down! Get behind the truck!" Katzhak scrambled underneath to the other side, dragging the frightened old man with him. The man who had fired the shot crawled around the front of the truck while the other one leaped full-length into the bed of the truck, seeking shelter behind the steel sidewall.

The returning Andrei shrugged an apology and a question in the direction of Zharuffkin. He responded by drawing his own weapon. Zharuffkin's hatchet men exchanged an approving sadistic glance of pleasure and prepared to go to work. Andrei fired first, pumping round after round into the truck covering Ulev's advance down the slope. Glass flew everywhere, as did great hunks of paint and metal, chipping and flying helter-skelter, like a flock of frightened birds taking flight. The air above their heads zipped and hummed.

Katzhak knew he had little time. It would be only seconds before the gas tank would be hit and exploded; in less time than that the man in the truck bed would certainly be killed. The bullets tore through the body of the truck like paper. He sprang up and fired blind in the direction of the shots. A hail of bullets chased his head back where it had come from, beat him back.

Suddenly a second deadly fusillade poured fire into the hood and beneath the truck. These shots were much closer and seemed to Katzhak to come from a different direction —lower, and to the right of the first salvos. Had the shooter moved? The second gun resumed firing in answer to his question. There were at least two then. Soon they would be caught in a crossfire. He had to get a bead on one of them. Katzhak popped up to fire again, this time near the front wheel. He barely caught a glimpse as he was buttoned down a second time. How would he get a shot? Unless he did, they were all dead men.

As quietly as he could, Katzhak pried the hubcap off the wheel nearest him with the hammer of his gun. He dared not try to handle them both, since he had not seen either of them. Looking around, he saw nothing useful, and at length decided on his cap, which he threw to the young man behind the truck with him.

"When I give the signal, I want you to toss this up in the air as high as you can from the back of the truck! Get ready. Now!" In a split second the boy let the cap fly high and away; at the same time, from the opposite end of the truck, Katzhak sent the hubcap rolling and flashing in the sunlight.

The original gunman, startled and trying to protect himself, opened up on the clay pigeon, squeezing off three or four quick shots, all of them wild misses. The second man, distracted by the flying cap and frightened gunfire, jerked his eyes back toward his own action, firing in amazingly accurate reflex, nailing the shiny hubcap and sending it flipping into the snow. While it was still in the air, Katzhak popped up over the hood and squeezed off two shots, one of which slammed his target with the force of a mule kick, taking him squarely in the chest and knocking him flat, backward, and sprawled spread-eagled in the snow. Ulev was dead.

The startled Andrei realized with dismay that his partner would not be getting up, and in all probability could not be relied on to supply a lot of covering firepower in the future. No time to worry about that now. At least he still had Zharuffkin. Why hadn't he fired, so that he could take cover? Ulev's untimely departure had left him rather dangerously exposed. Andrei glanced partway up the hill once or twice, too nervous to fully take his eyes off the truck.

Katzhak inched upward, nudging his slightly inclined head just far enough to . . . Andrei's gun boomed and Katzhak ducked, barely in time. Another shot, this one near his feet. Katzhak jerked. Another, just centimeters away, and another.

"Oh, shit!" Katzhak cursed as he huddled behind a wheel, génuinely afraid. He popped up again near the rear wheel. He saw nothing, but felt the wind of a shot that had passed close enough to his eye to singe the lashes. Falling backward, he was again narrowly missed. He grunted a terrified sound of fear, deeper and more instinctive than words. "Jesus," he added to calm himself.

High up on the hill above him, Katzhak heard the loud report of a single shot echo through the woods. What the hell? Damn! Damn! They must have reinforcements, he thought. Cautiously, he peeped out over the rear end of the truck, just in time to see a short, heavy red-haired man scrambling up the crest of the hill. Gun in hand, he was retreating from the field, abandoning his comrades. In the trough between two snowdrifts, Katzhak could just make out the head and shoulders, the outstretched arms of a man who had obviously been the recipient of the fleeing figure's single shot. Facedown in the snow, he had apparently been shot from behind as he witnessed the drama below. Katzhak's eyes swung back to his man as, outraged and scared to death, he fired futilely at the fat man who leaped to safety on the opposite side of the slope. This last volley loosened still further the heavy blanket of snow that covered the boughs above his head, and it fell, scaring and blinding him in white. Katzhak sprang up like a striking snake, extending his arm to its full reach and emptying his gun. Andrei's anguished cry died on the hollow, haunting wind.

After such a fast and furious storm of man-made thunder and deadly lightning, the stillness and the sudden quiet seemed unreal, dreamlike. Time was frozen, its progress halted and crystallized. No one moved for an eternity, and only the whispering wind through the trees betrayed any sign of life. Slowly Katzhak stood up, gradually straightening and holstering his weapon while staring straight ahead. No one else stirred.

Walking as if in a trance, he approached the body of Andrei and stood looking down at it. Gently, with the toe of his boot, he nudged and rolled the body over on its back so that he could see the face. Katzhak's face did not change, and he remained impassive as he walked the distance to the second dead man. As he had guessed, it was Ulev, the tall blond of the hospital, and the Malenkovs'. He broke his gaze and began to climb up the slope toward the third unfortunate.

These two were Zharuffkin's men. No doubt it was that fat pig that had murdered the third man and left Andrei to fend for himself. Katzhak knew that this meant the worst for him. Andrei and Ulev were just tools to Zharuffkin. The fact that he was through with them, that he no longer needed them, was clear evidence that his job was finished. Having exhausted his pawns, Zharuffkin had willingly expended a superfluous knight or two, now that he was ready to complete the game. Katzhak was in check, a former king stripped of his power, with no moves left to make. He had not even seen the jaws closing, the noose tightening. Zharuffkin was a good player, skillful and energetic, despite his laconic, lethargic exterior. He had worked hard, been everywhere at once, and now he was certain of victory.

When would he make his move? Katzhak could not guess.

He stopped beside the body of the third man, knelt, and

rolled him over. Katzhak did not recognize the face at all. Puzzled, he searched his pockets and found his papers. He worked for the KGB. A speech pathologist? What was a man of his training doing up here; what was he needed for? Katzhak saw the black knob of the object almost buried in the snow by the weight of the man's fall.

He tugged and pulled out a pair of high-powered binoculars. Brushing off the snow, he lifted them to his face and looked through. Down below, at the riddled, windowless truck, stood the three Jews, talking, examining, and brushing each other off. The mechanical eyes were much too powerful for the needs of the situation. Although he tried, Katzhak could not get any more than the head and shoulders of any one of the men in his field of view at one time. For another thing, he was close enough to observe the men below with his unaided eyes. These binoculars were completely useless for anything besides reading lips at this range. He smiled at his little joke and lowered the field glasses. Suddenly he raised them again and trained them on one of the faces of the three men who stood below, apparently praying. Intently Katzhak watched the old man's mouth, here and there picking out a word. Of course! Katzhak lowered the glasses to his knees. Of course! It all made sense now. That's how Zharuffkin had discovered the location and precise time of their second meeting. How he had come early and selected a hiding place. Not by coincidence or sorcery, but by taking shrewd advantage of Katzhak's carelessness. He was watching, catching everything as they had spoken in the forest this morning. Just as he had watched and knew all of what had passed this afternoon. Zharuffkin had made a fool of him. It had not even been a challenge. Andrei, Ulev, and the lip reader had all been executed, having served their purpose. Far from misfortune, everything had gone today precisely as planned. Katzhak had even lived up to Borky's expectations beautifully as the instrument of death for two of Zharuffkin's loose ends, meanwhile digging himself in deeper and deeper. He had to move fast now if he was to save all of their lives.

Katzhak ran down the hill, tossing the binoculars away as he did so.

"Get in the truck. Let's go! We've got to get out of

173

here!" The three men only stood and stared at their David, slayer of two deadly Goliaths.

"Get in, dammit, and let's get out of here! The police will be here any second! Stolbovaya is right over there!"

The men bolted for the truck, one climbing into the back, the old man, the one who had spotted Andrei, and Katzhak all piling into the cab. Katzhak slammed the riddled door and pulled out the choke, trying the starter. He pumped the gas savagely and tried again and again. Nothing. Katzhak knew that Zharuffkin would be back in minutes with the police; possibly they would block the road up ahead, their only escape route. Frantic, he opened the door and climbed down, walked to the pierced hood, and fumbled for the catch. Raising the hood, Katzhak frowned and sighed.

Numerous wires, lines, and engine parts were bent or damaged and hung loose. One belt was almost sheared in two. There was an exit hole in the back of the radiator as big as the face of his watch, and beneath this, in the snow, was a good-sized puddle of antifreeze.

"We'll have to take my car," he said through the window. "Come on, everybody out."

"Won't they be looking for it?" one of the younger men inquired.

"Not for a while yet," he said wearily. "Besides, there's nothing else we can do. This truck's had it."

"Do as he says." This from the old man. "Where is your car, Colonel, and where are we going?"

"We're going to your flat. That's where you usually meet in the city, isn't it? And you're going to tell me everything you know. It's that, or the police station. It's up to you."

"We'll go with you."

"I thought you might. This way." Katzhak trudged off in the direction of his vehicle, the other men falling in behind, nervous and in haste.

Unknown to Katzhak, Zharuffkin had not rushed to Stolbovaya for help. Nor had he returned to the city to negotiate for his arrest, knowing that the bullets in the bodies of his two henchmen could easily be linked to Katzhak's gun. Instead, like a rat, he watched with squinting eyes from the darkness. Now he scurried off toward his own car, hoping to follow Katzhak's vehicle back to Moscow and arrest the whole nest of conspirators there. Holstering his gun, he froze at the sight of blood on his glove. He had shot the lip reader from extremely close range and had not noticed the blood on his hand before in the excitement. Scooping up some snow, he washed his hands, and smiling with eagerness and anticipation, trotted lazily toward his own auto.

The sky darkened; the clouds became darker, blacker. The swirling wind circled and recircled, dropping the already low temperatures still further by the minute. Tiny shavings of icy snow began to filter down, drifting and wafting about on the increasing wind, finally followed by bigger, more substantial flakes of snow. It was through this stormy buildup that Katzhak drove, his own thoughts stirring and whirling about, tiny bits of electricity ricocheting and combining their energy, coalescing into increasingly turbulent and violent feelings that served as a powerful interference, a heavy, radiating static to the pattern of his reflections.

"Colonel, who were those men?" the old man interrupted. "You seemed to recognize them."

"They worked for Borky Zharuffkin. He's a psychopath. Works for the KGB in Moscow. The bearded one and the other one, Ulev, are the ones who beat Gallina Malenkov. They were watching us this morning. The third man was shot by Zharuffkin. He was there to read our lips."

"Why did this Zharuffkin murder him?"

"He found out what he wanted to know, I guess. All he needs to arrest us. He doesn't like anyone to share the pedestal. He knew I could probably defend myself against his two men; he wanted them to die. If I had been killed or wounded instead, he was still there to fix things. Nobody had any real chance back there. Everything went exactly as planned."

"You said if something had gone wrong, Zharuffkin was still there. I never saw him."

"He went over the hill, and the bearded one finally figured out that Zharuffkin was leaving him there to die. He fired at Zharuffkin, and that's when I took him."

"Then Zharuffkin was there this afternoon all along, and he escaped to get reinforcements."

175

"Zharuffkin was there, all right, but he didn't escape, and there won't be any police."

"What do you mean? I thought you said that you saw him scramble to safety. Surely he will go for help."

"No, he won't. Zharuffkin has already killed several men in order to avoid sharing the credit for our arrests. Besides, he left five or ten minutes before we did. If he had gone to Stolbovaya to get help, why have we seen no police, no cars at all? Why wasn't the road that leads from the forest to the asylum blocked? It was our only possible route of escape."

"I see your point. But if he did not go for help, where did he go?"

"Nowhere. Zharuffkin has watched us everywhere, had me followed for a week now, every minute. I have never been out of the sight of him or one of his men since he became interested in observing me."

"But that means, with his two men dead, that—"

"Exactly. He is following us himself, right now."

"You have seen him!" said the startled old man, beginning to be alarmed.

"No. Don't turn around. But I know he is there. I can do nothing right now, but once we're inside the city proper, I'll lose him."

"Then," said the old man sadly, "we have very little time."

"I'm afraid that's true. I'm not sure whether Zharuffkin started watching me because of you, or watching you because of me. In any case, I'm sorry that you and your people got in the way, and for what it has cost you."

"Colonel, I appeal to that regret. Let us go and turn away from our dwelling. Save yourself and us. Our beliefs are the only thing that many of us have to live for. We cannot worship openly; they have sought to deprive us of God's word; we cannot emigrate . . . Have pity on us. If you cannot do this in God's name, do it in your own. I want you to know what Tuskov feared; I want desperately for you to know, but don't do this, not for my sake, but for the others, some of the innocent children you have already seen, don't bring a plague upon us by leading him to our house. When it is safe, it will be our pleasure and our duty to welcome you into our homes."

The other men slid forward in the backseat and regarded Katzhak with anxious, imploring eyes. He looked at the three desperate faces of the men for a moment, futilely trying to find a way to soften the truth, speak it a little more gently than was his usual custom.

"It's too late for that now. Don't you see that? They'll come for you, and they'll find you, too. Do you think that after this morning, after this afternoon, after my connection with Arno, they are going to let any one of us out? They will kick in every door in Russia to find us."

Mentally Katzhak tallied the sacrifices. First there was Tuskov, then Mikhail Malenkov, then the two Jews in the abortive ambush attempt. Next was Yuri Gregorivich, then Ulev, the bearded one, and the lip reader. So far, at least eight people had been killed in the name of Cosmo, by actual count. This was not including Mrs. Malenkov's miscarried fetus, the attempt on his own life, and any Jews or police who had died as a result of this morning's affair in the forest. Oh, yes, and Tamarzov, too, had been beaten, as had Mrs. Malenkov. In all, twelve human beings had been brutalized in the past week, not counting the police and the Jews injured this morning. How many more had died or been threatened; how many more would be before this thing was over? A score of casualties in six days. It was incredible, and worst of all, nobody knew anything except Tuskov. They were trying to exterminate all the possible carriers of a noncontagious disease. It was insane. Oh, how he wanted that Zharuffkin and that bastard Bulgarin. He must figure out a way to get both of them. Whenever disaster struck, good old Borky was always there.

"Look. A dozen people have been killed inside a week, perhaps a dozen more injured. They are going to pursue this thing until we're all buried, and your synagogue and your families too. Your only chance is to take me to your flat, tell me what you know, and hope that it's enough to hang the people above the killers. That's our only weapon, our only hope. If you don't, we won't last till morning. Now, where do you live, exactly?"

The old man tried to think, debated for a moment whether or not to tell him, whether or not to trust him.

"My staff can have the answer for me in an hour. If you don't tell me, I'll find out anyway, and when I find you—"

"That won't be necessary, Colonel. I live at . . ."

They were soon reasonably confident that Zharuffkin would not be able to follow them, and minutes after that, reached their destination in safety. The car came to a halt in front of an apartment house about a block long and a few stories high. The old man lived below street level, so Katzhak had to walk downstairs in order to gain entry to the flat. He approached the door with understandable caution, allowing the others to enter first; taking a last look to reassure himself that Zharuffkin had not been able to follow, he shut the door behind him. The central room was sparsely furnished and had the swept-clean look that bare rooms often do. Katzhak's eyes scanned every detail he could take in, and settled finally on his host. The other two men had exited the room through the door on the right-hand side. This door was blackened with fingermarks and so stood out to Katzhak's trained eyes as an obvious sign that the house was used by many more persons than the fastidious owner. The old man spoke as the two stood facing each other.

"Where were we, Colonel, when we were interrupted this morning?"

"You were telling me about some information that Arno stole from Kremlin computers. What was the information?"

"I don't know. I wish I did."

"What is this? Don't you realize that there is absolutely no point in arguing about this? No point in lying? I could take your head off, right now." Katzhak drew his gun and pointed it at the old man's forehead.

"That won't help you. A gun can't make me tell you what I don't know."

"You know what Tuskov got out of those computers."

"No. But I think I may have figured it out. In any case, I have the number he dialed, so that you can find out for yourself."

"Where is the number?" Katzhak tightened his grip on the pistol menacingly.

"Here," the old man said simply, and unbuttoning his

178

sleeve, pulled it back to reveal a long number tattooed on his forearm.

Nonplussed by the man's calm and lack of any sign of fear, Katzhak lowered the weapon and looked at the outstretched limb.

"This is a Nazi stamp, isn't it? I don't understand."

"My family and I escaped Hitler and thus the marking. The two men whose lives you saved today are my sons. They would not let me go alone, and no one else trusted you."

"But you're a Jew. You're not Orthodox?"

The old man nodded.

"Then how can you tattoo yourself; wasn't there an ancient prohibition against making any marks or cuttings on your flesh?"

"You have an excellent memory for all these years, considering your life's work. Yes, that is quite true."

"Then why did you do it?"

"We felt that no place else would be safe. The number was too valuable to trust to seizure or theft or loss or search. We came up with the idea to disguise it as a number from the concentration camps. Some of this is superfluous, and only I know which numbers are part of the index, and which are not. I took the mark, in the form of a mark of suffering and death, allowed the symbol of satanic madness to be cut and burned into my flesh, that it might survive and be a mark of life, a symbol to avert a second holocaust and slaughter. Besides, I was the logical one to receive the mark, since I am free from the taboos and ritual constraints of the ancient law."

"But what does this mean? If you say you are a Jew, how can you fail to keep the letter of the ancient rites and observances?"

"I have found liberty; though I am under the law, I am no longer living by the law, nor judged by the law. I am free from the damning bondage of the law, free from sin and death. I live now under God's grace, and am a slave now only to his will. There is no longer any need for rituals and taboos, as the law has been crucified for us in the flesh. He who is dead to sin and dead to the law which convicted him of sin is no longer under the law, but is alive to grace. So there is no longer any condemnation.

We can approach the father with confidence, then, since we are not under the law, but under his marvelous grace. When he looks at us, he does not see our sins and imperfections as revealed by the law, in which case his only judgment could be death; instead, he sees only his perfect love for us. His grace, then, is a blanket, or a shielding umbrella, which protects us from the wrath and condemnation of the unjust. Seeing in us the perfect reflection of his perfect self, his perfect love and mercy, he pronounces upon us life, and that life, eternal."

"Are you saying that . . ."

"That I am a Christian? Yes."

"Then how can you, I mean, why do they . . . ?"

"Still follow me, and my leadership?"

Embarrassed, Katzhak nodded.

"They are changing slowly. They have looked up to me, relied on my experience and judgment for a long time now. I have told them the way I feel, shared my new convictions with them honestly. Most were confused at first. Many of the older traditionalists were hostile, and openly opposed me and my 'heresy.' A few have left us, but most remain, at least for now, tolerating as best they can, understanding where it is possible. They are good people, and we pray for each other. The Jews have always respected the right of others to believe and to worship as they please. It is the rest of the world which has refused to tolerate us, to allow us to live. Is it so strange that we continue to care for each other, although each of us believes the other to be failing to grasp the truth? Should we not both continue to search for it, and intensify our efforts to help each other discover for himself the meaning and purpose of life? What purpose would it serve, whom would it benefit, for us to separate now, except those who wish to discourage faith in every form?"

"I see your point. I understand that they accept or at least tolerate you, but I am somewhat curious. Why do you stay where you're not wanted? Why don't you seek out men who believe as you do?"

"I belong here, among my people. Among God's people. My mission is not to teach or to proselytize, or to self-righteously pity. My mission is to love and to help God's

180

people, whoever and wherever they are. In Christ there is no difference."

"What did Arno Tuskov believe?"

"Arno? I'm not sure. I am certain of only one thing—that he wanted to point the way for you. He wanted you to follow; what he found may surprise even you. I think that his secret was bigger than he realized, and that is enormous—bigger than any of us dreamed. We are both renegades, Colonel. Bastards and outlaws, traitors to our worlds, but with one important similarity—we are both true to ourselves and to our convictions. You have risked all by coming to me. Your search for the truth has led you into grave danger. You deserve the answers to your questions, and you shall have them. Do you want to know your destiny? Few men have that courage. Very well. I see you are determined." The old man smiled warmly. Suddenly a shadow passed over his face, his features darkened, and his eyes welled with tears.

"Apparently Arno worked on his surveillance of us and on his own secret computer study concurrently. One day we studied chapters from the book called Ezekiel. We were examining prophecies given to him by our Lord in the form of visions and direct revelation. He pretended to be sincere at all times, of course, but I could tell that in spite of himself he often listened to some of our words."

"I fail to see the relevance, comrade, of this type of dialogue. Is it your wish, perhaps, to influence me as well? I warn you—"

"Save your threats, Colonel. I have no fear of you. I am old and my heart would not withstand prison or torture. If you truly wish to learn wisdom, learn patience, as the saying goes. As I began to tell you before, Arno listened to this prophecy and must have retained some of it."

"What kind of prophecy? What did it concern?"

"Israel, for one thing, and many other nations. Arno came to our secret meeting less than two weeks ago. He was late, and knocked quietly, but not in the way that was our signal. I opened the door while the others prayed, and I was afraid that that night was the night he had chosen to arrest us. He had a deeply troubled and guilty look, ashamed to meet my eyes. 'Arno,' I asked, 'have you come to betray us?'

"He gave me the most tortured and agonized look of pain and inner suffering that I have ever seen on a human face. 'No,' he said, 'I have come to save you and my people. I have betrayed only myself!' He looked awful, pale and feverish, almost delirious. For several moments he could not speak at all. I led him into my bedroom, through that door there, and he fell to his knees on the floor. 'My God,' he said. 'What have I done? What have I done? What have we all done? Father,' he said, 'have mercy on me. My God,' he sobbed, 'forgive me. Forgive me.' Then he buried his face in his hands and wept. Finally, when he had regained control over himself, he told me that he had a confession to make, that although he had been born a Jew many years ago, he had come to us as a spy. 'I have sinned against you, and against God,' he told me. Then he asked me to pray for him, because he knew he was about to die. I asked him how he knew this, and he said, 'Because I know. Because I know their secret; I found it out! It is a horrible, unspeakable crime, a foul, damnable, vile thing. They know I found it, and they will certainly kill me now. They can't let me live. If it ever came to light, the world would be thrown into war, and no one would survive.'

"I shook my head in disbelief at his fantastic claims. 'But what is this secret?' I asked. 'Whom does it belong to and what does it contain?' His eyes bulged, and he became pale as death. He shook his head slowly, and tears rolled from his cheeks. 'Don't you know?' he asked me. 'How could I possibly know?' I asked him. 'I learned it first from you,' he said, 'but I would not believe it.' He laughed at this—short, bitter, ironic laughter. I thought he was near hysteria. 'It's true,' he cried, sinking down again. 'It's true; every word. Every damned word! The vision! The prophecies from Ezekiel! They are all true! It's happening now! We've got to stop them. We've got to! We've got to stop it before it's too late! It's too late already,' he said. He wept again. 'Too late,' he sobbed over and over, 'too late.' In a moment I realized that he had fallen asleep or had fainted. The strain was terrible for him."

"Dammit! What were the prophecies? What did he say? What was the secret?"

"I'm trying to tell you! Just be patient one more minute and you'll have the answer.

"He woke in five minutes or so, half-mad and terribly frightened. He said he worked for the KGB or NKVD. That he had found that our computers were not safe, that he had picked their brains for classified information. He had found out a highly guarded piece of information of the most sensitive kind imaginable. He would not tell me what it was; he said he could trust that information to no one. That is, to no one but you. Tuskov said he would make plans for you to find us, leave clues so that you could find out the secret yourself. He seemed calmer with that thought, relieved, somehow. He said that you had the best chance of dealing with it. The only chance. He placed great confidence in you, in your integrity and your ability . . . and your patriotism. I think he was a good judge of character, from what I have seen of you, Colonel."

So, Katzhak thought, relieved, Tuskov was not a traitor, had leaked information to no one.

The old man continued. "He described you to us, but did not wish to jeopardize you by giving your name. Unfortunately, this resulted in tragedy at the Malenkovs' and near-death for you. We forged plans to safeguard the number and contact you. Since then, four of us have died, and many have been injured. Although I have the number, I am at a loss to know how you can use it."

"Why?"

"Arno said that although he had dialed in, and stolen the information successfully, the computer had one failsafe device he had not anticipated. From the sounds the computer was making over the phone, Tuskov could tell that the computer was somehow holding the line open and tracing his call to its location. He could not disconnect the circuit, and he knew that it was only a matter of days, perhaps hours, until someone checked the device, realized what had happened, and came for him. It was inevitable."

Katzhak's heart sank. "Then I cannot call the number from any place but an open, monitored line."

"That would appear to be the case, Colonel."

"Then, either way, I wind up as Tuskov did."

"There is one way. Tuskov said that the prophecies were borne out by what he found. If you study the prophecies,

183

you should be able to figure out, in substance at least, the main outline of what Tuskov found."

"We're wasting time. Read me the book."

"Of course. Please sit down, Colonel." The old man gestured. "Joseph! It's all right. Bring me the book." As Katzhak turned to look, his eyes widened. Behind the old patriarch's two sons were several others, among them Gallina Malenkov. Katzhak put their number at around twenty in all.

"Thank you, Joseph. I ask you all not to be alarmed. Colonel Katzhak is our guest and wants to learn about Arno. That is all he wants. He is not interested in us or in interrupting our worship; are you, Colonel?" Like hell! Katzhak thought. But then, realizing that the old man was offering him a trade—Arno's information for immunity from his harassment or arrest—he nodded his assent. "Shall we get started, then?"

"I believe the first pertinent information is to be found in the book of Ezekiel, Chapter Thirty-four. I will read, and comment where necessary. Listen carefully. This will take some time, but it is vitally important.

"And the word of the Lord came unto me, saying:
"Son of man, prophesy against the shepherds of Israel, prophesy, and say unto them, Thus says the Lord God unto the shepherds: Woe be to the shepherds of Israel that do feed themselves! Should not the shepherds feed the flocks?

"You eat the fat and clothe yourselves with the wool, you kill them that are fed, but you feed not the flocks. The diseased have you not strengthened, neither have you bound up that which was broken, neither have you brought again that which was driven away, neither have you sought that which was lost; but with force and with cruelty have you ruled them.

"And they were scattered, because there is no shepherd; and they became meat to all the beasts of the field when they were scattered. My sheep wandered through all the mountains, and upon every high hill: yes, my flock was scattered over all the face of the earth, and no one did search for them, or seek after them.

184

"Therefore, you shepherds hear the word of the Lord: As I live, says the Lord God, surely because my flock became a prey and my flock became meat to every beast of the field, because there is no shepherd, neither did my shepherds search for my flock, but the shepherds fed themselves and fed not my flock; Therefore, shepherds, hear the word of the Lord; Thus says the Lord God: Behold, I am against the shepherds, and I will require my flock at their hand, and cause them to cease from feeding the flock; neither shall the shepherds feed themselves anymore; for I will deliver my flock from their mouth, that they may not be meat for them."

Katzhak's hair began to bristle at the back of his neck as he recalled with an icy chill the terrifying dream he had had of the great bear. He saw again, in his mind's eye, the beast greedily eyeing the last tiny morsel, the sickness with fear that he felt, the feeling of dread, as it had picked it up and brought it to its lips. He recalled with horror how its teeth had snapped like brittle twigs, without penetrating, how the iron claws had crumbled, and the beast had tottered and fallen. He trembled as he said the words to himself in his mind: "I will deliver my flock from their mouth, that they may not be meat for them."

The old man continued:

"For thus says the Lord God: Behold I, yes I myself, will search for my sheep and seek them out. As a shepherd seeks out his sheep. When they are scattered, so will I seek out my sheep, and will deliver them out of all the places where they have been scattered in the cloudy and dark day."

An electric chill thrilled Katzhak's body and his arms broke out in gooseflesh: in the cloudy and dark day! The dream again! He remembered vividly the black profusion of clouds, the thick darkness, the diffused, smoky atmosphere of his vision. He sat up straighter in his chair and began to grip the armrests. He was terrified to hear more, but desperate to hear it all. He was locked in, helpless to break away.

"And I will bring them out from the people and gather them from the countries, and will bring them to their own land, and feed them upon the mountains of Israel. . . . I will feed them in a good pasture, upon the high mountains of Israel shall their fold be. . . . I will feed my flock, and I will cause them to lie down, says the Lord God.

"I will seek that which was lost, and bring back that which was driven away, and will build up that which was broken, and heal that which was sick: but I will destroy the fat and the strong; I will feed them with judgments."

Katzhak's heart quaked within him at the words "destroy the fat and the strong." He pictured in his memory the fat, powerful beast, saw its gorged belly, its incredible power. He saw also the blood spill from its lips, and judgment rained upon it. It froze his blood with fear and consternation to see how these ancient words meticulously outlined the dream he had had less than a week before. The parallel was uncanny.

"I am skipping repetitive or less pertinent parts, Colonel," the old man interjected before continuing.

"Therefore, I will save my flock, and they will no more be a prey . . . the tree of the field shall yield her fruit, and the earth shall yield her increase, and they shall be safe in their land, and shall know that I am the Lord, when I have broken their yoke of bondage and freed them from those who served themselves of them.

"They shall no more be a prey to the godless nations . . . they shall dwell safely. Thus shall they know that I, the Lord, their God, am with them, and they, even the house of Israel, are my people, says the Lord God. And you, my flock, the flock of my pasture, are men, and I am your God, says the Lord God.

"Well, Colonel? Are you intrigued? Would you like to hear more? The choice is yours." Katzhak nodded, spellbound, and the old man read on.

"Chapter Thirty-five is not nearly as well suited to a quick understanding as Chapter Thirty-six."

Katzhak waved, impatient and eager to proceed.

"Chapter Thirty-six, then:

". . . Because they have made you desolate, and swallowed you up on every side, that you might be a possession to the remainder of the ungodly and you are a joke and a derision on the lips of people, prophesy therefore, concerning the land of Israel, and say unto the mountains, and to the hills, and to the valleys, and to the rivers, thus says the Lord God: Behold I have spoken in my jealousy, and in my fury, because you have borne the contempt of the ungodly, therefore, thus says the Lord God: I have lifted up my hand, surely the ungodly nations shall be ashamed. But you, O mountains of Israel, you shall shoot forth branches and yield your fruit to my people of Israel, for they are ready to come. For behold, I am for you, and I will turn to you, and you will be tilled and sown. I will bring men upon your surface, the house of Israel, the cities will be reinhabited, and the desolate places rebuilt. I will do better for you than at your beginning, and you will know that I am the Lord.

"Yes, I will cause men to walk upon you, the house of Israel. They will possess you, and you will be their inheritance. You will no longer be a joke, and no longer shall the nations which live upon your surface fall.

"Moreover, the word of the Lord came to me, saying, Son of man, when the house of Israel dwelt in their own land, they defiled it by their own doings, and their way before me was disgusting, and unclean. So, I poured my fury out upon them for the blood that they had shed upon the land, and for their idols with which they had polluted it: and I scattered them among the ungodly and dispersed them through the countries: according to their way and according to their doings, I judged them.

"And when they went among the ungodly, they brought dishonor to my holy name, every time people

187

said: These are the people of the Lord, and they have been driven from his land.

"But I had pity for my holy name, which the house of Israel had dishonored when they were sent among the godless. Therefore say to the house of Israel, Thus says the Lord God: I am not doing this for your sake, O house of Israel, but for my holy name's sake, which you have dishonored wherever you went.

"I will sanctify my great name, which was dishonored among the ungodly, and they shall know that I am the Lord, says the Lord God, when I am sanctified in you before their eyes.

"For I will take you from among the ungodly, and gather you out of all countries, and will bring you into your own land. Then I will sprinkle clean water upon you, and you shall be clean from all your filthiness; and from all your idols will I cleanse you.

". . . You will dwell in the land that I gave to your fathers; and you will be my people, and I will be your God. I will save you from all your uncleanness, and I will call for the corn, and will increase it, and I will lay no famine upon you. And I will multiply the fruit of the tree and the increase of the field, that you shall receive no more reproach of famine from the ungodly.

"Then shall you remember your own evil ways, and your doings that were not good, and you shall loathe yourselves in your own sight for your iniquities, and for your abominations.

"Not for your sakes do I do this, says the Lord God, be it known to you: be ashamed and confounded for your own ways, O house of Israel.

"Thus says the Lord God: In the day that I shall have cleansed you from all your iniquities, I will also cause you to dwell in the cities, and the wastes shall be builded. And the desolate land shall be tilled, whereas it lay desolate in the sight of all who passed by. And they shall say, This land that was desolate has become like the garden of Eden; and the waste, and desolate, and ruined cities have become fenced and are inhabited. Then the ungodly that are left round about you shall know that I the Lord build the ruined places, and plant that which was desolate: I the Lord have spoken it; and I will do it. . . . I will increase them with men like a flock. As a holy flock, as the flock of Jerusalem in her solemn feasts; so shall the waste cities be filled with flocks of men: and they shall know that I am the Lord.

"I will pause briefly here, Colonel. I see you are puzzled by all this. Would you like me to explain what I have read?"

"Yes. Please. . . . It has been a long time since . . . since I studied these things. I do not understand the significance of these ancient legends."

"Call them what you wish, a name cannot belittle or detract from the truth. These 'legends,' as you call them, are prophecies, that is, God, who alone knows the future, sometimes reveals it to his servants and messengers for a specific purpose. It is a sort of 'history' of coming events, prewritten as warnings, forecasts, and so on, to help God's people know what he wants them to do, and how to be prepared for circumstances they themselves cannot see. In effect, God throws a spotlight on certain events which are hidden from us in the darkness of time, thus allowing us to avoid calamitous obstacles or to steer toward desirable goals."

"What is he doing in this case?"

"In this case, he begins with a look backward at how things were in the past, reviewing his dealings with us and laying a foundation for what he plans to do in the future. This is a general overview, which will now be sharpened and focused on specific attitudes and issues.

"In the first portion which I read to you, he began speaking metaphorically, almost poetically. He symbolically compares Israel to a flock of sheep, which, of course, rely on vigilant and loving leadership. He blasts the leaders of Israel, both in the church and in government, as well as all of those foreigners who have exploited and used his people. He says it is their selfishness and disregard for his people, the lack of strong guidance from those whom he chose to watch over his flock, that has

189

resulted in their wandering, their going astray and being scattered.

"He says he is against the 'shepherds' because of these things, and that he will remove them from power or having any more authority over his people. Instead, he promises to lead them himself from now on, to gather them together once again, 'in good pasture,' a reference to the promised land, as well as a figurative expression, and to personally seek out and return those who are lost or separated from the main body. He promises that after this they will not be dispersed or 'scattered' again, nor will others benefit from their 'wool' or use them for food, like a prey."

"But what has this to do with Tuskov?"

"Perhaps nothing, yet—perhaps everything. Tuskov, along with Soviet and other Jews who dwell in foreign lands, is one of the scattered flock of God's chosen people, Israel, whom the Lord is gathering right now to return to their original homeland in Palestine."

"Why? Why are they being gathered from exile to return to Israel? Why now? What's so important about it, presuming that, as I infer from listening to you, you believe these prophecies refer to the present?"

"I am sure of it, my dear Colonel Katzhak. And that is why it is so vitally important. Don't you realize yet what is happening here, all around us? How God is moving dramatically in our world?"

"Frankly, no. I do not. There is no God. If there were, the Nazis gassed him, or bulldozed him, or burned him in the ovens. What I saw in Stalingrad was not the face of God."

"Quite so, Colonel, and quite astute, also. What you saw was not the love of God, or the observance of his plan for mankind. What you saw was the graphic embodiment of the opposite of God. You saw hatred, genocide, chaos, madness; you saw the face, the true face of the devil. You saw the world he wishes to create for us all behind the gay deception, behind the bright promise of a world dominated by refined and civilized man. You had the rare opportunity to see a working model of the universe as it really is, the supernatural love of God, the peace, harmony, and safety of his spiritual kingdom, in black-and-white contrast to the nauseating stench of hell.

You survived that brief display; you of all men should clearly see through the feeble lies of the adversary, should have burned into your heart forever the blind terror of a world without God. And yet, you sit before me in the costume, in the shiny uniform of an instrument of just such a state. You, fearfully privileged above generations of others to have seen such horror completely exposed, instead of fleeing with your might from the yawning caverns of doom, embrace and support the enemies of God. You promote the very world which sickened you and causes you the loss of everything decent and valuable. Colonel Katzhak, the question of whom and what you serve and strive for is what we are studying here. What would you have, what would you give your life to? A cold, meaningless empire, an empty and transitory control over the dead and the dust of the earth, always under the shadow of impending destruction? Would you really trade your life for an hour in the Kremlin chair? Surely you are of more value than that, even to yourself; am I not correct? Nothing could be more relevant, Colonel. Can you not give yourself the chance to know some crucial answers, or is your time too valuable to spare before you take us all away? Shall I continue now, or have you heard enough to satisfy your curiosity?"

"You don't believe in letting up, do you?"

"My enemies never seem to."

Katzhak's eyes widened, and he regarded the old man appraisingly, marveling at his answer.

"Listen, then. We have so little time.

"As I told you earlier, God began in a general sense in Chapter Thirty-four, and gets much more specific in Chapter Thirty-six. In this section he says that the continued obstinance of Israel in ancient times, and their insistence on ignoring and disobeying him, brought judgment and punishment upon them. God judged them, sometimes allowing them to be taken into captivity by other nations, until finally pronouncing a more severe judgment.

"He said that Israel would be conquered and that the Jews would be scattered throughout the countries of the world for a long period of time, with no land to call their own. He said, however, that in due time he would have mercy on them and gather them back from exile throughout the godless countries and would reestablish their nationhood on their original land, the land he gave to the patriarchs. He would facilitate immigration, agriculture, population growth, land reclamation, religious and economic life, and generally rebuild and bless the new nation.

"This he has done in complete agreement with his word, and total fulfillment of his promises to us. After nineteen centuries! Think of it, Colonel. After two thousand years, God has begun to deal with his people again!

"As you know, after the war, thousands of Jews, thousands of thousands, immigrated to Palestine to the very land that God promised to Abraham and the patriarchs, and in 1948, in your lifetime, Colonel, in the fulfillment of these ancient promises, Israel was made a nation again on the original site. God has gathered, and continues to gather, his flock from every country of the world.

"Since 1948 we have reclaimed lands lost to marshes and deserts, reconstituted the Jordan, instituted massive reirrigation of arid lands, planted fruit trees and crops of every description, risen to a great enough height militarily to defend ourselves, although vastly outnumbered and ringed by hostile nations armed with the latest equipment. These miraculous achievements are God's work, Colonel, accomplished exactly as he said he would in the words which I have just finished reading you. These are too great to be coincidences, even for a world as skeptical as ours. But, I know, not enough for Katzhak, colonel of NKVD. Fortunately, Colonel, there is more. One piece of damning evidence, corroboration so convincing that it drove Arno Tuskov to delirium. Chapter Thirty-eight is the key to what we believe Arno Tuskov found, and is the reason for all of this murder and terror, for your persecution and ours. As I read this chapter to you, bear in mind one crucial fact.

"God has a purpose for all of this renewed activity, Colonel; you are quite right. The purpose is revealed in these words that I read in Chapter Thirty-six:

". . . But I had pity for my holy name, which the house of Israel had dishonored when they were sent among the godless. Therefore, say to the house of

192

Israel, Thus says the Lord God: I am not doing this for your sake, O house of Israel, but for my holy name's sake, which you have dishonored. . . .

"I will sanctify my great name . . . and they shall know that I am the Lord, when I am sanctified in you before their eyes.

"God makes it clear, stressing over and over again, that he is about to do monumental things which will elevate Israel in the eyes of all the world, but not for Israel, for the honor of his great name. Israel's behavior and attitudes toward God have not changed so radically throughout the centuries—there is no special merit of theirs which makes them worthy. No, all of the problems which have befallen them are quite the opposite; they have deserved it all, according to him.

"So, I poured my fury out upon them for the blood that they had shed upon the land, and for their idols with which they had polluted it . . . according to their way and according to their doings, I judged them."

"I still don't understand."

"I'm sorry. I forget sometimes that you are not familiar with most of this. It's very simple, really. God wants to restore honor to his name, yet he is conscious that most of the world by this time does not recognize him as God, or even remember that he exists at all. So he has a problem when he wants to reestablish respect for his name. How will he go about it? This is what he has decided to do:

"He caused it to be written and foretold centuries before its actual occurrence, so that when it happened, the people of the world would say, 'How can this be? Only a being who knew the future could predict it so far in advance with such complete accuracy.' This was the first step.

"Second, he could not establish anything through a people which was scattered in nearly every nation of the world. Step two was to gather his people and end nearly twenty centuries of wandering and abuse.

"Third, and this is closely connected to the second step, is to make Israel coalesce into a full-fledged nation again. The fortunes of a nation are much more easily recognized and evaluated than those of a dispersed minority of zealots.

"Before God could make an example of Israel, before he could expect the people of the world to see and recognize the things he would do there, he had to rebuild Israel, make it a tangible, visible actor on the world stage, and by its remarkable progress, bring it to world attention again. He outlined his plan, literally, thousands of years ago, and after a period of time has moved again, and fulfilled it exactly as stated, in our lifetime, Colonel, before our very eyes. Is that any clearer, or are you still confused?"

"No, I . . . I understand the foundation you're laying, but why? What is it leading up to? What could possibly happen that would convince the world that God exists—that he is alive and watches over the Jews, of all people?" Katzhak laughed in obvious disbelief, in spite of his efforts to control himself. Looking out on a sea of serious and anxious faces, staring intently at him, made him realize that his laughter was completely out of place, and somehow in macabre and very poor taste.

Katzhak was shaken to the roots of his being; the look of deep sorrow on the old man's face pierced and penetrated his skepticism. His troubled expression filled him with dread and apprehension.

"Do you really want to know?" he said in a hoarse whisper. Katzhak, his face darkened, nodded slowly. "I doubt that you know what you're asking, but I'll tell you.

"Chapter Thirty-eight is the last prophecy in this series. It says . . . it says that shortly after it becomes a nation again, a mighty military power will attack Israel. The attack will not be successful, however, because God himself will fight for Israel. This is the secret for which Arno Tuskov was murdered, for which Mikhail Malenkov died, and for which your life is in danger. The attacking army . . . belongs to the Union of Soviet Socialist Republics, and five-sixths of it will be destroyed unless you can stop it. This is the truth you have searched for, and the destiny you cannot escape."

"How do you know this, how can anyone possibly know?"

"Shall I read Chapter Thirty-eight? I think you'll be able to see for yourself!"

Katzhak nodded, his mind numb.

"And the word of the Lord came to me, saying, Son of man, set your face against Gog, the land of Magog, the chief prince of Meshech and Tubal—"

"Wait. What is that, 'Gog, the land of Magog'—what is all that?"

"Symbolic names, Colonel. Given to the descendants of the children of Noah's sons. The descendants of these sons of Noah, mentioned here, settled in Russia. In the Caucasus Mountains and elsewhere to the north and east. Moscow itself is a form of the plural of Meshech's descendants, Mosch or Moschi, from which we also get our word Moschivite or Moscovite. Tubal, Tobolsk . . . there are other similarities; I haven't the time to trace them all now with you, but I will furnish other, more quickly accepted evidence as I read.

". . . And say, Thus says the Lord God: Behold, I am against you, O Gog, the chief prince of Meshech and Tubal: and I will turn you back and put hooks into your jaws, and I will bring you forth, and all your army, horses and horsemen, all of them clothed with all sorts of armor, yes, a great company with bucklers and shields, all of them handling swords . . . and many people with you.

"Be prepared, and prepare yourself, you, and the company that is assembled unto you, and be a leader to them. After many days you shall be visited: in the latter years you will come into the land that is brought back from the sword, and is gathered out of many peoples, against the mountains of Israel, which have been wastelands, but now are brought back from out of the nations and dwell in safety.

"You will ascend and come up like a storm, you will cover the land like a cloud, you, and all your bands, and many people with you.

"Thus says the Lord God: it will come to pass, that at the same time [that Israel is reestablished] things will come into your mind, and you will think an evil thought: And you will say, I will go up to the land of unwalled villages; I will go to them that are at rest, that dwell in peace and safety, all of them living without walls, bars or gates, to take a spoil and to take a prey, to turn my hand upon the desolate places that are now inhabited, and upon the people that are gathered out of the nations, which prosper and dwell in their own land.

". . . Are you coming to take a spoil? Have you gathered your company to take a prey? To carry away silver and gold, cattle and goods, to take a great spoil?

"Therefore, Son of man, prophesy and say unto Gog, Thus says the Lord God: In that day when my people dwell in safety, won't you know it? And you will come from out of your place in the north parts, you, and many people with you, all of them riding upon horses, a great company, and a mighty army: And you shall come up against my people of Israel, like a cloud to cover the land; it shall be in the latter days, and I will bring thee against my land, that the godless may know me, when I am sanctified in you, O Gog, before their eyes.

"Thus says the Lord God: Are you he of whom I have spoken in ancient times by my servants, the prophets of Israel, which prophesied in those days that I would bring you against them? And it shall come to pass that when Gog comes up against the land of Israel, says the Lord God, my fury shall come up in my face. For in my jealousy and in the fire of my wrath have I spoken. Surely in that day there shall be a great shaking in the land of Israel; so that the fowls of the heaven, and the beasts of the field, and all creeping things that creep upon the earth, and all the men that are upon the face of the earth, shall shake at my presence, and the mountains shall be thrown down, and the steep places shall fall, and every wall shall fall to the ground.

"And I will call for a sword against him throughout all my mountains, saith the Lord God: every man's sword shall be against his brother.

"And I will plead against him with pestilence and with blood; and I will rain upon him, and upon his bands, and upon the many people that are with him, an overflowing rain, and great hailstones, fire and brimstone. Thus will I magnify myself, and sanctify myself; and I will be known in the eyes of many nations, and they shall know that I am the Lord.

"This is the unshakable truth which you were fated to discover, the unchangeable destiny and purpose for which you were born. In all the world, you and you alone, out of millions, billions even, you alone know, and can act on this terrible knowledge. You have been given the chance to succeed, the opportunity to convince your government to turn back. If it does not abandon its evil plan, if it does not cease to willingly participate in the execution of Satanic will, your nation will slide off the map into the pit of hell. You must try. If you do not, thousands, tens of thousands will die, and their blood will be on your hands, and the guilt for this upon your head. This is the reason for which you were created. It is one of the greatest privileges with which God has ever honored a man, and is also one of the gravest responsibilities. You dare not turn back or refuse to help us, Colonel. But, of course, the ultimate decision is up to you."

"Who told you all this, revealed all of this to you? Am I also to believe that you are divinely inspired, you old fool? The greatest evils to ever befall the world came from the minds of misguided half-wits, interpreting ancient fantasies as direct leading from 'God.' What makes you believe that a Soviet and a Communist has been chosen by your God, a God I have sworn to destroy and to eradicate for the benefit of the enlightened masses, to save the world for you Jews? I have been as patient as I can possibly be, but this flattering nonsense will not cloud my vision or gain you my protection or cooperation."

"Before you go, Colonel, I think you had better listen to this. It's from Ezekiel also, Chapter Thirty-three, just preceding the sections I have read to you."

197

Katzhak wanted to leave, but something held him. He felt compelled to hear.

"Again the word of the Lord came to me saying . . . When I bring the sword upon a land, if the people of that land take a man of their coasts, and set him for their watchman: If when he sees the sword come upon the land, he blows the trumpet, and warns the people; then whoever hears the sound of the trumpet, and takes not warning; if the sword comes and takes him away, his blood shall be upon his own head. He heard the sound of the trumpet and did not take warning; his blood shall be upon him. But he that takes warning will deliver himself.

"But if the watchman sees the sword come, and does not blow the trumpet, and the people be not warned; if the sword comes and takes any person from among them, he is taken away in his iniquity; but his blood will I require at the watchman's hand."

"That proves nothing. No one has chosen me. I'm not your lookout. I'm not your man. Thank you for your time, and for listening to Arno. I won't arrest you, but I can't protect you, either, if that's what you were after. Don't meet in this house again. Good night."

Katzhak rose, weary, and placed his cap back on his head. He turned and stepped toward the door.

"So thou, O son of man, I have appointed you a watchman unto the house of Israel [Katzhak halted, froze]; therefore you shall hear the word at my mouth, and warn them from me."

The room was still. Katzhak lifted his eyes and released a deep sigh. Then slowly, achingly, he turned and faced the old white-haired man. They stared at each other in silence for a long moment. Katzhak's hand crept up and removed his hat. He sat down and studied his boots.

"Joseph! Bring the colonel something to eat."

"What makes you so certain that we will attack, and that we will fail, that the weather will rebel against us?" Katzhak heard himself saying.

198

"Besides the tracing of generic and tribal words and names? Lots of little things. For instance, in the fifth chapter of Ezekiel God says: 'This is Jerusalem; I have set it in the midst of the nations and countries that are around about her.' This is true, Colonel, not only in a figurative sense, that God sees Israel as the central actor on the world stage, but also in a literal one. If you take a compass and set the point at Jerusalem, and then draw a circle large enough to include all of the landmasses of the earth, you will find that Jerusalem is the actual center of the earth. So directions given in the Bible, which have no clear reference point, are given relative to Jerusalem. Thus, when God says, 'You will come from your place in the north parts, to the uttermost north,' et cetera, he is speaking of the extreme north of Jerusalem. The only nation to the extreme north of Jerusalem, indeed the only nation north of Jerusalem at all, is the Soviet Union. God also tells us through the prophet Zechariah, 'My Spirit will be quieted in the north country.' It is a fact that your government constantly seeks to quench God's Holy Spirit, through destruction of Bibles, razing of churches, imprisonment, death and torture of ministers and believers, propaganda, its emigration policies, on and on. Arno Tuskov was sent here on just such a mission. No, I think you are described accurately enough. Even your intentions are recorded. But you will not succeed. On the contrary, God has chosen you to show the world that he still lives, and that he is the supernatural guardian of Israel. He will use your evil intent, your contemptible surprise attack, to be the instrument whereby he brings Israel and his holy name honor and glory. This amazing defeat of a vastly superior force will astound the world. By seeking to silence God in your country, and by laying bloody hands on his chosen people, living in the land which he gave to them forever, you will make God real to thousands of thousands. Judge for yourself, Katzhak; whose power is greater? Yours, which is able to make and carry out evil plans, or God's, who is able to turn your wicked intent into good, and to take you in your own trap?"

"How do you know we will lose? What makes you think that we will be destroyed?"

"God's word, of course, Colonel. He says so clearly and emphatically, and he tells us why it must be so."

"What does he say? I must know! I must hear it all. Now."

"Very well, Colonel. Chapter Thirty-nine. This portion is the last which I will read to you. It deals with the annihilation of an entire army. Only one-sixth survives to return home.

"Therefore, son of man, prophesy against Gog, and say, Thus says the Lord God: Behold, I am against thee, O Gog, the chief prince of Meshech and Tubal: and I will turn thee back, and leave but the sixth part of thee, and will cause thee to come up from the north parts, and will bring thee upon the mountains of Israel: and I will smite thy bow out of thy left hand, and will cause thine arrows to fall out of thy right hand. Thou shalt fall on the mountains of Israel, thou and all thy bands, and the people that are with thee: I will give thee unto the ravenous birds of every sort, and to the beasts of the field to be devoured. Thou shalt fall upon the open field: for I have spoken it, says the Lord God.

". . . So will I make my holy name known in the midst of my people Israel; and I will not let them pollute my holy name anymore: and the godless will know that I am the Lord, the Holy One in Israel. Behold it is come and it is done says the Lord God. This is the day whereof I have spoken.

"And they that dwell in the cities of Israel shall go forth, and shall set on fire and burn the weapons, both the shields and the bucklers, the bows and the arrows, and the handstaves, and the spears and they shall burn them with fire seven years. So that they shall take no wood out of the field, nor cut down any out of the forests; for they shall burn the weapons with fire: and they shall spoil those that spoiled them, and rob those that robbed them, says the Lord God.

"And it shall come to pass in that day, that I will give to Gog a place of graves there in Israel, the valley of the passengers on the east of the sea: it shall stop the noses of the passengers: and there shall they bury Gog and all his multitude: and they will call it the Valley of Hamon Gog.

"And seven months shall the house of Israel be burying of them, that they may cleanse the land. Yes, all the people of the land shall bury them; and it shall be to them a renown the day that I shall be glorified, says the Lord God. And they shall sever out men of continual employment, passing through the land with the passengers to bury those that remain upon the earth, to cleanse it: after the end of seven months shall they search.

"And the passengers that pass through the land, when any seeth a man's bone, then shall he set up a sign by it, till the buriers have buried it in the valley of Hamon Gog. And also the name of the city shall be Hamonah; thus shall they cleanse the land.

"And thou, son of man, thus says the Lord God: Speak unto every feathered fowl, and to every beast of the field. Assemble yourselves, and come; gather yourselves on every side to my sacrifice that I sacrifice for you, even a great sacrifice on the mountains of Israel, that ye may eat flesh, and drink blood.

"Ye shall eat the flesh of the mighty, and drink the blood of the princes of the earth. . . .

". . . And you shall eat fat till ye be full, and drink blood till ye be drunken, of my sacrifice which I have sacrificed for you. Thus shall ye be filled at my table with horses and chariots, with mighty men and with all men of war, says the Lord God. And I will set my glory among the godless, and all the unbelievers shall see my judgment which I have executed, and my hand that I have laid upon them.

"So the house of Israel shall know that I am their God from that day and forward. And the godless shall know that the house of Israel went into captivity for their iniquity: because they trespassed against me, therefore I hid my face from them, and gave them into the hand of their enemies: so fell they all by the sword. According to their uncleanness and according to their transgressions have I done unto them and hid my face from them.

"Therefore, thus says the Lord God: now will I

bring again the captivity of Jacob, and have mercy upon the whole house of Israel, and I will be jealous for my holy name; after they have borne their shame, and all their trespasses whereby they have trespassed against me, when they dwelt safely in their land, and none made them afraid. When I have brought them again from the people, and gathered them out of their enemies' lands, and am sanctified in them in the sight of many nations; Then shall they know that I am the Lord their God, which caused them to be led into captivity among the ungodly: but I have gathered them unto their own land, and have left none of them anymore there. Neither will I hide my face anymore from them for I have poured out my Spirit upon the house of Israel, says the Lord God.

"All of this, simply stated, is as follows: God wishes to catapult Israel into international prominence once more, and to restore honor to his name. He feels that Israel has brought shame to his name because all of those in the ancient world knew that Israel claimed to be God's chosen people, and hence must not have much of a God, if he has brought them to ruin. In order to accomplish this feat and to recapture the attention of the world after his long silence, he has decided to use one of history's mightiest war machines to attack Israel. This mighty and vast army will come to Israel in battle, but will never return home. More than eighty-three percent will die in Israel as a result of God's intervention through an earthquake, rain, hailstones, and so on. This 'act of God' will amaze the world, and his purpose will be accomplished. The slaughter will be so great that it will take full-time buriers and searchers more than seven months to bury the dead, and it will require another seven years for all of the weapons to be consumed. So you see, you must try to stop it. You have a moral obligation to do so. You must find out the date and time of the proposed attack and warn the world before it is too late. Otherwise, thousands, tens of thousands of your people will be destroyed. Now that you have heard it all, what do you think?"

"I'm sorry. It's all circumstantial. I can't help you. You

202

don't have one solid piece of evidence that what you say is true."

"But the number—"

"Worthless. I can't call it; you said so yourself. And without that number, well . . ." Katzhak shrugged. "Thank you for the meal, Joseph. I'm sorry you've wasted your time."

"You're sorry! You're sorry! You mean after everything that's happened, after today, that's the best you can do, say 'I'm sorry'?"

"Joseph!"

"My father risked his life twice today for you. We've been beaten and shot at for you. We gave up everything we had just to get in contact with you. And you're sorry?"

"Joseph, I said that's enough!"

"No, it's not enough. It's not nearly enough. I've had it with this arrogant bastard. Pompous ass! What does he want, anyway? Mikhail Malenkov was arrested and tortured to death for you, friend. Gallina Malenkov miscarried and nearly bled to death before we found her. You killed two of us personally, didn't you, Colonel? They were both my friends. And what about their wives? Did you think about them when you ran those men off the road? Did you? Did you know that one of the people that was beaten this morning is in a coma right now, and will probably die? Just so . . . just so we could meet you, you frigging cold son of a bitch! Nothing gets to you, does it? Nothing penetrates! Well, as long as you're leaving, take this with you!"

There was a flash as the small kitchen knife passed quickly under the startled Katzhak's arm and stabbed into his overcoat as he twisted away. Katzhak grimaced, and the boy spit in his face. With the side of his hand and watchband, Katzhak cuffed the youth across his right ear and spun him to the floor. Gingerly he pulled the bloodied instrument from the hole in his coat and flung it away from him.

The old man advanced toward Katzhak, who was reaching for a handkerchief from his coat to hold over the wound. Some of the group advanced toward the fallen Joseph, whose ear bled slightly from the watchband and the force of the blow.

"Leave him alone," ordered the old man. "When he's through lying there, he'll get up." He unbuttoned Katzhak's overcoat and slid it gently off the left arm. "Boris," he commanded quietly to his second son, "get me some water, some tape, and a clean handkerchief. Quickly!" The boy did as he was told.

Katzhak moved the handkerchief to expose the wound. It was a cut about two and one-half inches in length, and a quarter of an inch deep at its lowest point. He breathed heavily as blood seeped into the raw and painful channel along his ribs, over and over and over again. He was almost exhausted, and this latest insult to his battered and worn-out body was almost more than he could bear. His eyelids were half-closed over glazed and bloodshot eyes. Quickly the old man worked, blotting at the wound with a cool, wet cloth. Gradually the flow diminished to a trickle and finally to an occasional oozing drop. A fresh handkerchief was carefully folded and taped with strip after strip of adhesive to his injured side.

"I suppose I should thank you," said Katzhak, buttoning up his tunic with the right hand.

"Save your patronizing breath. You need stitches to close that gash and stop the bleeding. If you exert yourself or use your left arm, you'll start to bleed again. All I did was slow it down for a while."

"All the same . . . anyway, I won't press charges for this. You people have suffered enough for one week." He slid into his coat, assisted by the old man. All the while, he stared straight at the boy on the floor, whose bitter hatred and fierce expression had been replaced by the red flush of embarrassment and whose eyes stung with held-back tears. "Get Joseph paper and something to write with. He has something to write for me."

No one moved. All mouths were closed and all bodies paralyzed with pity and stifled rage. No charges, he had said. Then what was Joseph being ordered to write? Katzhak stared hard at the boy, and the boy returned his stare. He was frightened at first, and he wanted to throw himself at Katzhak's feet and beg for mercy or forgiveness. Soon, however, his face hardened and was filled with contempt and a kind of fearless pride. The father's eyes were pools of frustrated sadness, helpless and mute. As Katzhak continued to stare at the boy for a moment, after he had been handed the implements requested, the sadness seemed to drain somewhat, the hopelessness ease and break, the clouded brow lighten and clear up. The faintest shadow of a smile passed ever so briefly over the old man's lips, and his eyes held a peculiar, knowing expression, at once joyous and mysterious, as one might look who was witnessing a miracle, or a birth. The room was still. All eyes were on Katzhak, and all ears flinched in anticipation of the words he would pronounce. Joseph sat defiant, waiting.

"You are to write . . ." Katzhak paused, and no hearts beat, "the number which your father has tattooed on his forearm. I will take it with me. He'll tell you what it is. See to it yourselves."

Joseph's features softened, his father smiled in triumph, the assembly released its breath. Katzhak turned away, and the stunned and bewildered Joseph stared after him as his father advanced and hugged his son. The young man regained his wits and wrote quickly and legibly, tearing off the sheet and handing it to his father. The old man approached Katzhak as he might have a visitor from another world. Katzhak half-turned, and the old man pressed the note into his hand. The two men looked at each other for a moment.

"I have some questions."

"Of course, Colonel. Leave us, please. All of you! I must speak with Colonel Katzhak alone." The faces retreated into the darkened bedroom. "Now, Colonel, what would you like to know? Why I am a Christian? What makes me believe the attack will come soon?" Katzhak nodded.

"There are many more things in God's word than I told you, Colonel. Many more than you've ever heard. At first, Jews and Christians banded together for solidarity and common defense. It was in this sort of forced alliance that I first became exposed to the so-called 'other half' of the Bible, the 'New Testament,' if you will. I became amazed at how these 'misguided' teachings of a messiah who had already come seemed to fit into our own, like pieces of the same puzzle. The prophecies, the spirit, the theology of the Torah were all continued, shared, expanded naturally. The continuity, the hopes, the dealings of God with man in different ways were all one; it seemed that the desire of the two works was the same; the story it told was the same. But this growing revelation was not just intuition or merely basic agreement in style and message. There were the words.

"The words convinced me. The way that Jesus explained our own Scriptures, clarified our ancient laws, supported and cross-quoted the prophecies of ancient times. He correlated the whole law and tradition and used it to point beyond himself to God. He tried consistently to remove centuries of distortion from his commands and desires for us. Everything he said and did was in complete agreement with the Scriptures, and it had such an unmistakable ring of truth and inescapable authenticity. When I examined his words, I saw God, clearly and more fully, and in a newer dimension than I ever had before in a long lifetime of study of the Torah. The kingdom of God became a living reality, like a fresh and pure spring inside me, not merely a cherished and faraway hope.

"Finally, there are the other things. Carefully drawn portraits thousands of years old, of our world as it is at this moment, and its people. Trends, the changing climate of our philosophies and ideas. The deeper mystery, my dear Colonel, the larger and more spectacular secret, though, is yet to be revealed, but it is ready now. Everything has been meticulously prepared since the beginning of time, and now it is finally ready. His light is shining before him in the hallway, his footsteps are getting louder and nearer, and he is ready to burst through the doors after all this time. Any moment now we shall all see his face, the King of Kings, and Lord of Lords, come at last to take his rightful place. I missed his first visit, his humble and quiet arrival. But I will not miss his second, not his glory, not his reign. He's almost here, Colonel Katzhak! He's as good as here right now.

"You asked me a question, and I will give you an answer, but . . . briefly. Every moment is precious now, every second vital. Ever since the beginning, when the first man and woman rejected God's authority in favor of governing themselves, man has experienced nothing but disaster, ugliness, and despair. When he opted to try to bring himself happiness and peace and security, he did not take into account the very real evil forces bent on his destruction. He did not recognize his own imperfection and impotence, nor did he see the need for supernatural power to protect him and to safeguard his world. As a result, his spiritual vision has become so clouded and distorted that he has become totally blinded and in darkness. Adam and Eve knew that there was a spiritual world, and took it for granted, but man today is so blind and confused, he does not even recognize that a spiritual world exists and that he, too, has a spirit. How can man help himself, if he does not understand his own nature or the nature of his environment? He does not know his own makeup and is totally ignorant about the dangers he faces. This is why his every effort has been futile, and fragmented, his every plan blighted, his grandest creations inevitably brought to crumbling ruins. Man is so corrupt and violent today that there is no turning back anymore. He is like a pitiful puppet on a string, pushed and pulled, jerked and manipulated, by evil spiritual forces he has chosen to ignore. He fulfills the ghastly desires of his mad puppeteer, not even realizing that he is just a puppet, dragged toward peace and accomplishment, only to be yanked away at the last second, before he has the chance to swallow the good life he has just tasted. Man exchanged his freedom in Eden for the cords that shackle his wrists and ankles now.

"Forcing man to be obedient in Eden would not have answered any questions or fulfilled the greatest desire of man's creator—that man should be free and at peace, and that, free of any kind of force, he might choose fellowship with God, willingly and intelligently. Man's will and his intelligence were both created to be used and exercised. This is the purpose of all human history—that man be allowed to try every conceivable form of government, every means of providing, from the industrial revolution, to the technology of the present day, every social movement and form of human relations and politics, and that he decide for himself whose rule is better, God's or his own. Over the centuries, man's dismal failure to bring peace and any real security has been abundantly clear, and overly documented to understate the case. Today, after the best and most determined efforts, man is no closer to peace

207

than he ever was, in fact, he is even farther away, if anything. I do not have to tell you, Colonel, that our world is more violent, unstable, unjust, and unhealthy than it has ever been before. Most of the world lives in misery so wretched and abject as to make even the most optimistic humanist want to put a gun to his head.

"God, the just and loving maker of mankind in his own likeness, has every reason to be filled with loathing and disgust, every reason to turn his back on us and our self-inflicted destruction. We rejected him, can we expect better treatment from him? God's word gives a resounding yes! It is written in the so-called 'New Testament,' the 'new agreement,' if you will: 'The Father's great love for us is clearly revealed in that, while we were still sinners, Christ died for us.' God's love is so great, so overwhelming, that he sent his only son, Jesus, that whoever recognized him and believed his words should not perish, but have life which lasts forever. These are the words which draw me to the view that the New Testament is God's word. His coming was foretold for centuries; his name, his birthplace, his ministry, and his personality all were spelled out. The account in Psalms of the messiah's death fits Christ's to the smallest detail: his words from the cross, the gambling for his garments, the quoted chants of the mocking crowd, the vinegar for his thirst, the piercing of his hands and feet, and so on. There is still more.

"The prophet Daniel wrote about a vision which he had seen of an angel while he prayed one day. The angel told him that from the day that the decree became law which said that the Jews should be allowed to return home from their captivity in Babylon, to the day that the messiah should be crucified would be sixty-nine weeks of years, or four hundred and eighty-three years. Four hundred and eighty-three years after a Persian king issued that decree, Jesus was crucified in the place and manner foretold. But I don't believe because of any of this.

"I believe because of the words—the words are true. Jesus' words of love, of the Father's love for us, have such an unmistakable ring of truth and the authority that comes with confidence in the unshakable veracity of what he is saying. When he speaks of God, his hopes for us, his dreams, his mercy, it is clear that only someone who had close personal knowledge of him, had seen him, lived with him, could speak with such insight and force. The way Jesus spoke drew me, but what he said convinced me. The new birth he spoke of, when he told Nicodemus that he must be born again, spiritually and mentally; the way he pierced through to the heart of the needs and spiritual weaknesses of his would-be followers, always asking something different of them, searching their souls for the greatest stumbling block to their faith. He didn't try to convert, or to gain followers; he turned many away who wanted to attach themselves to him for the wrong reasons. He never asked for contributions, espoused any causes, condemned any person or group, held any office, or refused to pay taxes. He had friends among the poor, the rich, the lettered and the illiterate, the old, the young, civic leaders and public outcasts, believers and nonbelievers. One man who never sought his own. Intrigued?

"Listen to these words of Jesus:

"Be careful, so that no one deceives you. Many will come saying, I am the savior of the world, and they shall fool many people. You will hear of wars, and rumors of wars; see that these do not trouble you, because all of these things must happen, but this is not the end.

"Nation will rise against nation, and kingdom against kingdom; there will be famines, and epidemics and great earthquakes in many different places. All of these are the beginning of sorrows.

"Many phony 'spokesmen from God' will come on the scene and fool many. And because lawlessness and evil will abound, the love of many people will grow cold, wither, and die. Whoever manages to keep his faith in me will be saved. The gospel of my kingdom will be preached all over the world, for a witness to all nations, and then the end will come.

"There will be great tribulation at that time, such as has never been seen, since the beginning of the world.

". . . Just as it was in the days of Noah's time, so shall it be in the days of my second coming. Just as in the days just before the flood, they ate and drank, married and gave in marriage, until the day that Noah went into the ark, and they did not know what was going to happen until the flood came and took them all away, it will be at the time of my return. Be ready then, because at the time when no one expects it, I will return.

"Think about the trees for a moment. When you see that the branches are tender and budding, and they finally put forth leaves, you know that summer is near. By the same things that I have just told you about, coming to pass, you will know that my second coming is near, even at the doors. And I'm telling you the truth when I say that this generation will not pass, until all of these things happen.

"These are the words of Jesus, Colonel. Do you hear what he is saying? He says that at the time of his second coming there will be a series of occurrences which mark the beginning of the end of the status quo and the birth of a new world, a new order of things. The signs are unmistakable, Colonel. He says that wars and rumors of wars will be everywhere—"

"There have always been wars. War is man's most effective and frequently used tool for settling disputes."

"Precisely so, Colonel! Precisely! He says not to be too disturbed by these wars, because man is always fighting wars. He cautions us to be alert for something new and different which will clearly distinguish the time of his coming from any other: 'Nation will rise against nation, and kingdom against kingdom.' Simultaneously! He's talking about world war, Colonel. In all of history we had none, and in this century, two. Two, within twenty-five years of each other! Persons who were born at the turn of the century and who lived through the world's first global conflict saw the second one, and are still alive today. They are that recent, that they happened in one lifetime, in one generation. Remember his words: the generation which sees these things shall not pass until all is fulfilled? The remnant of the generation which witnessed these things is old and sick, and rapidly dwindling, Colonel. Someone born in time to see the First World War would have to be nearly seventy today.

"Famines. The world's population is greater at this point than at any time in its history, and is doubling almost by the decade. You're a realist, Colonel, aren't you? How long do you think we can sustain the masses on the surface of our planet? Does our food productivity double by the decade? Come now, you're a bright boy—figure it out. What happens in an energy and resource shortage, anyway, hmm? Have you thought about what it means to the production of food? What happens when there is no electricity to regulate irrigation, drive the fans, the pumps, the generators, the machines, light the hothouses? What happens when there is no petroleum for fertilizer production, for fuel for the burners, and tractors, and reapers, and trucks, and ships, and airplanes? What will a desperate nation with billions of hungry people do to prevent wholesale starvation and sweeping plagues? What will an industrial nation with a failing economy do, when faced with the specter of war or slow strangulation? Didn't the American Secretary of State and the American President breathe threats of war, invasion, and takeover during the recent Arab oil embargo? Aren't the oil suppliers drowning in wealth in return for what no one else has or is ready to market? Are the Soviets or the Americans insulated against the recurrence of the embargo, or are they just as vulnerable as ever? Tens of millions of people died last year, Colonel Katzhak, tens of millions, directly as a result of not having enough food to eat. This does not include those who succumbed to disease or accidents due to weakness. Add to this terrorism and a disillusioned, restless climate of bitterness and frustration. Many nations are collapsing economically, lawlessness is increasing with population, and finally, weapons. More and more and more nations are armed with nuclear weapons, and conventional weaponry is glutting every country that can afford to pay for it. Many nations now borrow money to buy arms. Think of it, my dear Colonel Katzhak, a volatile, desperate world, choked with overpopulation, starved for food, energy, and resources, and armed to the teeth with weapons capable of laying waste to the entire planet. Not just the race—the fish, birds, animals, plants, water, air . . . everything. You and I are debating on the rim of calamity, on the edge of disaster, and second by second our world

211

rolls and totters on the brink of the abyss. How long can the leaders of the world maintain their pathetic and macabre charade? They know how close we are to chaos, how little it would really take to plunge the world into war. That is a secret desperately guarded.

"As to the matter of strong earthquakes all over the world, consider these recent quakes: Anchorage, Alaska; Lima, Peru; Managua, Nicaragua; Tangshan and Peking, China; Italy; Pakistan; the Philippines; Iran; the Soviet Union; Romania; Central America; Mexico; and so on. . . ."

"What about the time being like Noah's time? What is meant by that? It doesn't make much sense that the world could be like it was thousands of years ago."

"Doesn't it? It looks different, certainly, but those externals are just props; the people are much the same. Listen to this passage from Christian Scripture:

"This know also, that in the last days perilous times will come. For men will be lovers of their own selves, covetous, boasters, proud, blasphemers, disobedient to parents, unthankful, unholy, without natural affection, trucebreakers, false accusers, incontinent, fierce, despisers of those who are good, traitors, heady, highminded, lovers of pleasure more than lovers of God, observing the form of godliness, but denying its real power.

"Look at our world, Colonel. Today man is so conceited and hedonistic, so proud, so ungrateful, so unholy, so fierce, that indeed he seems without natural affection, without any love whatsoever. You and I are in the winter of the world, Katzhak. We stand like mute stone statues while the cold wind blows and the snow whirls around us. The world is dead and frozen. All life, all beauty, all grace and reason have withered and fallen down under the ice. Dignity stands naked, and hope barren, stark, and black. Nature is poisoned and madmen desecrate the temples, the saints are cursed and executed, and we worship the dog, degrading ourselves while the snow piles deeper. There are no children anymore, Katzhak . . . when was the last time you heard someone laugh for joy? Eh?"

The old man's face shone with the earnestness of truth, and tears welled in the eyes which implored Katzhak, begged him for some sign of disagreement, some reason, however slight, to prove him wrong.

"There is a blindness, Colonel, a madness that pervades; man is acting out the thoughts, the words, the wishes of something from far beyond, something evil, something . . . cold. He moves like a robot, unseeing, unhearing, unfeeling. He is just a tool of the state he has built, but what are these states, really? Who designed them; whom do they serve? What is the meaning of all of this violence; what is it for? You've got to think for yourself, again, Colonel. You've got to open your eyes and resist the control, to come back to your senses . . . and your sensibilities. We all have. Now, today, and for the rest of our lives. We've got to slap our jaded minds and sting our glassy eyes before the world turns into a deep-frozen insane asylum where we'll torture each other endlessly 'for the good of the state.' "

The old man shook with the force of conviction. Tears rolled down his cheeks, and his nostrils flared in bitterness and an utter, inexpressible sadness.

Katzhak stood silent, moved.

"I'm sorry. Please do endeavor to forgive me the rantings of an old and somewhat tired man. Where was I before my last tirade? Oh, yes, the days of Noah. In order to see whether or not the present day is in any way comparable to the time of Noah, we must discover what his time was like. The Lord says in Genesis:

"And God saw that the wickedness of man was great in the earth and that every imagination of his heart was only evil continually. And it repented the Lord that he had made man on the earth, and it grieved him at his heart. The earth also was corrupt before God; and the world was filled with violence. And God looked upon the earth and behold, it was corrupt; for all flesh had corrupted his way upon the earth.

"The earth at the time of Noah was corrupt, wicked, and perhaps most of all, violent. If I had to choose a word

213

that described the earth today and the conditions that prevail here, I could not pick a more apt term than 'violent.' There is more, Katzhak. Much, much more. I do not have the time to tell you all that I know, but perhaps it is not important for you to understand it all now. I want to tell you this: all of my life I waited for the coming of the promised savior of my people, the 'messiah,' if you will. I know now, beyond the slightest shadow of a doubt, that Jesus, called Christ, is the one whom God sent. He has already been here and gone; the end of the world is at hand, and everything is ready for his return. There is no time left to philosophize, to debate with pious intellectuals old theological arguments! The Jews of Jesus' day could not accept the human, humble, almost obscure Jesus who came to suffer and die in man's place. They were looking for a grandiose king who would put down all earthly rule. They literally overlooked him, misunderstanding God's plan. Now Christ is ready to return at last, the way the Jews expected him to come at first, with power and supremacy.

"... The Son of Man shall come in his glory, and all the holy angels with him, then shall he sit upon the throne of his glory: and before him shall be gathered all nations, and he shall separate them from one another, as a shepherd separates his sheep from the goats.

"Then shall the King say, Come, you who are blessed by my Father, inherit the kingdom prepared for you from the foundation of the world. I was hungry and you gave me food, I was thirsty and you gave me a drink, I was a stranger and you took me in, naked, and you gave me clothes, sick, and in prison, and you visited me.

"And the righteous will answer, Lord, when did we see you hungry, or thirsty, or a foreigner, or naked, or sick or imprisoned?

"And the King will say to them, When you did these things for the most insignificant of persons, you did it to me. And to the others, he will say, Depart from me you who are under God's curse, into everlasting fire, prepared for the devil and his angels. I was hungry and you ignored me, I was thirsty and you turned your back, I was a stranger and you turned me out, I was naked and you sent me away, I was sick and in prison, and you forgot about me.

"They will say at that time, Lord, when did we see you and refuse to do anything for you? And he will answer, When you refused to help the lowliest human being, you refused to help me.

"That is why every man's rights are of vital concern to us, why no individual's life or needs are insignificant. That is also why we have risked our lives to contact and to inform you; because, as distasteful as this may sound to you, we believe that you are our brother, as valuable to us as our God, or as we are to each other. You see, we had no choice but to warn you, to help you avert the slaughter, if possible, even though you are our oppressor. We have warned you; the rest is up to you. Our responsibility has ended."

"And you expect me to believe all this?" Katzhak asked incredulously.

"It can make little difference to us whether you believe it or not. We know that the attack will take place eventually, exactly as the Lord has said."

"Then you don't believe it can be stopped?"

"On the contrary. God says, 'I take no pleasure in the death of the wicked,' and, '. . . the Lord, not wishing that any should perish, but that all should come to repentance.'"

"But this is preposterous!"

"Take my advice, Colonel. Herd as many of your people as you can into the ark while the doors are still open," he said flatly, his voice rising. "I think it's starting to rain."

Katzhak stared, confused, as the old man closed his eyes and began to pray: "Lord, now let your servant depart in peace, according to your word. For my eyes have seen your salvation, which you have prepared before all people. A light to bring light to the Gentiles and the glory of your people Israel."

As the old patriarch spoke, Katzhak buttoned his overcoat against the wintry chill and seated his cap upon his head, never taking his eyes off the upturned face, now strangely incandescent, with its complement of white hoary locks. Slowly he turned to go, and stepping up, crossed the entryway and opened the door. A cold wind greeted him with dancing flakes of snow, and in the street above, a streetlight shone brightly.

"Colonel . . ." the voice of the old man called out softly. Katzhak stopped but he did not turn around. "God be with you." The old man watched the back of the tall figure silhouetted in the doorway.

Katzhak crossed the threshold and stepped out into the night.

26

It was still now, and a light snow fell as Katzhak slowly climbed the stairs that led to the street above. He was tired and confused, and his side and hand and head all throbbed at once. He wanted to help, but it was all too fantastic. His spirits were at an extremely low ebb. He felt disgusted. Time had run out for him, and he was no closer to the answers than when he started. All this trouble and risk wasted. He was at a dead end; of that much he was certain. If he only had one good lead, just one. Katzhak's cap and part of his face appeared at the top of the stairs. A door opened in the black sedan parked just forty meters from the stairwell, and a heavyset man got hurriedly out, slamming the door behind him. Katzhak's shoulders and chest came into view as Katzhak neared the level of the street. The heavyset man walked briskly and purposefully in the direction of the preoccupied Katzhak, gaining ground zero just as he hopped up onto the sidewalk. As he passed under the streetlight, the heavyset man showed a head of reddish, coppery hair beneath his hat. The two men were only a few feet apart now. The heavy one was reaching into his coat. Still Katzhak had not looked up.

"Vladislev, my old friend! How are you?" The heavy one slapped Katzhak's shoulder gregariously and shoved him forward into his embrace. Startled, Katzhak jerked his head up. He saw the hand dart from inside the coat, saw the metal flash in the eerie light, grunted as the gun was jammed into his ribs. His heart froze and his eyes flung wide with sudden wild terror—that voice! Katzhak started to mouth a yell, "No, no, no . . ." but only the last hoarse whisper was audible. Katzhak stared into the face of a triumphant Borky Zharuffkin.

"Get into the car, Colonel," he hissed, "or I'll cut you in two right here on the street."

Katzhak's knees went weak, and Zharuffkin sidestepped to shove him into the car. There was the vague sound of car doors opening nearby, a sound which went wholly unnoticed by the two concentrating men.

Suddenly there were excited shouts. "Andrei! Victor! Comrades!" Katzhak was tripped from behind and fell to the pavement, while someone slapped the astounded Zharuffkin on the back. Powerful arms gripped and held Borky's to his sides, and then there were three or four muffled sounds, like loud knocks against a hollow door. Zharuffkin's weight collapsed beneath him, his eyes crossed, and he winced in pain. The smile faded from the cruel lips and he was supported and dragged to the waiting car, as was Katzhak. Zharuffkin was hustled to the curb and dumped across the rear floor of the car, like garbage. Katzhak was shoved in after him, and the car sped away down the street.

27

Momentarily relieved that he had escaped arrest or murder at the hands of Zharuffkin, Katzhak heaved a sigh cut short by the new terror that flooded his overheated brain. Who had kidnapped him? What did they want? They had probably murdered Zharuffkin and kidnapped a colonel of the secret service. They were bold, determined, and ruthless. He doubted that these men, having gone this far, would balk at taking his life.

Katzhak glanced at his surroundings. He sat on the backseat, sandwiched between two very large men in dark clothes. The men leaned backward, their heads in the roof corners, their faces in shadow. Two men sat in the front, silent, their eyes straight ahead. Katzhak had the eerie feeling that he rode in a hearse, and the presence of death was strong, obvious and oppressive. He steadied himself and stared down at the long, black, bloodied form of Zharuffkin. The black overcoat was drenched with blood and dotted with bits of gore, shining darkly. The body appeared to Katzhak almost to lie on a bier, as if in state. The eyes were closed as if in sleep, and Katzhak half-expected them to fly open and regard him coldly. The face, usually ruddy and freckled, was whiter than white, beyond pale; it was chalk or granite, as if the last drop of blood had drained from the head. Katzhak could not be certain whether Zharuffkin still clung to his life, although from the copious amounts of blood, he was surely more dead than alive.

The driver and apparent leader of Katzhak's abductors spoke rapidly in a foreign tongue that astonished Katzhak. He recognized it instantly as the language of his boyhood, the language he had been hearing all day—Hebrew. It had

218

been many years, and Katzhak did not understand all the words.

At the driver's command, the man to Katzhak's left slid forward on the seat and bent over Zharuffkin's body. Quickly he searched the pockets and waistband, extracting Zharuffkin's papers and two envelopes, one small and the other much larger. These he handed to the man who sat up front next to the driver, before matter-of-factly wiping his hands with his handkerchief.

"Him, too," Katzhak heard the driver say, and he watched his own papers being handed up front. The man seated next to the driver verified Zharuffkin's identity and emptied the contents of the large envelope in his lap, scanning them quickly.

"You know who this is, Colonel Katzhak?" the man asked in fluent Russian.

"Yes," Katzhak croaked, surprised at the weakness in his own voice.

"He had orders to arrest you, and to kill you if you offered resistance."

"On what charges?" Katzhak asked, alarmed at the realization of how close he had come to death, or prison.

"Treason," came the quick reply. Katzhak closed his eyes and shuddered, letting his head fall back to rest against the cushion.

It was over for him now—all over. His head had been sent for. Even if he escaped, his career was finished. Tash! He must get her out before he was apprehended. She must go to a place of safety. It was too late for him, but not yet too late for her. Tash. His beloved. The one thing in his life that was soft, warm, giving. She was his only comfort; she restored him, didn't drain him, didn't sap his strength. She was the only surface in his world that was not hard as granite, cold and unyielding. How could he get word to her, assuming he could manage to escape? Escape?

Katzhak threw back his head and laughed, short and harsh, and bitter—hard as the concrete street, sharp as broken glass.

There was no escape—no safety, no hiding, no sanctuary. He had spent his whole life plugging those holes. There was no way out. He had seen to that. Oh, yes, he had done his work well, all these years. It was funny. It

219

was all so funny, so ironic—surely they saw that, understood it. What a joke! What a colossal, hideous joke! His eyes rolled upward, and tears welled up, were forced out by the laughter and the violent tremors that convulsed him.

The man in the front seat turned around. "What's so funny?"

This question triggered the loudest laughter of all. He was bursting. "Don't you know?" Katzhak exploded. "Don't you see?"

The man did not move, but continued to stare at Katzhak, whom he presumed to be mad, chuckling, as he was, in Zharuffkin's tomb, squatting on the very corpse of his enemy.

"It's my wife!" Katzhak choked, struggling for control of himself. "She can't get out. I've spent my life ensuring that she can't." His laughter bubbled up and cascaded over the dam once more. "Now I can't either. None of us can." He snorted, still shaking. "Don't you see? We're all dead men, just like Zharuffkin, here. This thing is out of control, and nobody can escape it. It's like a whirlpool, and the closer you get to it, the stronger it pulls you and sucks you in. The more you fight it, the weaker you get. Do you think that you can just break free and swim away? All you did was shoot Zharuffkin on the way down. They've put out the order for my arrest, and the fact that you're here with me proves that you and I are right behind him. There's a madness, a bloody fiend, a slaughterer loose. We've stumbled into his closet, and I've spent my whole life locking the door behind us. Now I've pushed my Tash in there, and I . . . can't get her out. I know she needs me, I can hear her scream and plead for me to open the door, but I can't. I can't help her. I just can't get her out. No one can."

Katzhak stifled the impulse to sob like a maudlin drunk, nearly biting his tightly clenched fist in two. The other man watched him with mounting alarm and redoubled urgency.

"Colonel, Colonel. Colonel! Colonel Katzhak! Katzhak, there's one chance."

"No. There's no chance."

"The number!"

"Impossible."

"You call it, or we do."

"That would be most unwise."

"Why? The underground warned us of a possible surprise attack on Israel, but the old man you saw tonight wouldn't give it to anybody but you. And if you think for one minute that we wouldn't blow your face off for that information, then, mister, you're crazy."

"Who are you?"

"Mossad."

"I don't know how much that old man told you, but there's a fail-safe device on our top-secret computers. You call that number, and the machine can hold the line open even if you hang up. It will trace back the call to the source, and you'll wind up in an urn in the Kremlin wall just like Tuskov did."

"We've got to risk it. We have hard evidence of a first-stage alert on the frontier and a shift in the Mediterranean fleet toward our waters. It could be routine, but millions of lives are on the line if it's not."

"What else have you got?"

"Two of our people working on this have been lost. We know one was liquidated, and the other just dropped out of sight. We assume he was killed as well. I have a funny feeling that this is the big one."

"Don't be a fool." By now Katzhak had managed to tear the number in half, and he worked cautiously to tear it again.

"The one who was murdered worked on this affair for three months. In all that time, he got out only one word."

Katzhak was not listening. He was concentrating on trying to rip the paper in his pocket undetected, and on formulating a plan of action for escaping from his abductors. He stared out the window, trying to figure out where they were.

"He was sent in and set up five years ago; saved for an assignment just like this one. Five years, and only one word. At first we thought it was important, but it didn't correlate with anything we had already, or anything we learned in the field. Now we're not even sure it made sense. We actually had a man inside Stolbovaya for a time. That's the one who is missing. He found Ashlev dying in isolation, and pumped him full of stimulants to counteract the drugs

221

he had been given. He pushed him to the limit, and finally he says this one word and arrests, right there in his cell. That's the last time we heard from either of them. Cosmo. Does that mean anything to you, Colonel?"

Katzhak's heart stopped. His blood froze and would not allow him to move. An electric chill shot up his spine and bristled the hair on the back of his neck. His jaw dropped and his scalp crawled backward, widening his eyes in total, exploding revelation.

"What did you say?" he asked when he had found his tongue again.

"Cosmo. Do you recognize it?"

"How long have you had this information?"

"Ten days, no longer. It is important . . . isn't it?"

"Who signed the order for my arrest? Who authorized it?"

"Checking."

"Hurry up, man. My guess is we haven't a moment to lose."

"Here it is! Deputy Bulgarin."

"Bulgarin! Jesus!" Katzhak leaned forward and slapped Zharuffkin's doughy face. "Come on, you bastard! Come back! You've got to talk first! You've got to tell me!" Katzhak slapped him sharply again and again. "Come on, you son of a bitch!" Zharuffkin emitted a moan so low that no one but Kahzhak heard it. "That's it! That's it, goddammit! Come on!" Frantically trying to revive Zharuffkin, to pull him back before he sank all the way into death, Katzhak grabbed the lifeless head by the hair and shook it roughly. "Come on, you bastard!" Katzhak shoved the heavy legs apart and drove his knee up between them. Zharuffkin seemed to grunt. "Yeah! Yeah! Yeah! That's it!" He kneed him again. "That's it!" Zharuffkin groaned, and the doughy white face made what seemed like a grimace. Katzhak drove the knee up a third time. Zharuffkin moaned audibly, and his eyelids fluttered. "Yes! Yes!" Katzhak shouted, again filling his fist full of hair and shaking vigorously until the teeth rattled. "Come on, baby! Come on. Zharuffkin! Zharuffkin! Answer me, damn you."

He dropped the head on the floor and slapped the face again, now taking hold of Zharuffkin's lower jaw and shaking it.

222

Finally the eyes opened, at first crossed, but in a moment focusing reluctantly. Immediately upon reaching consciousness, Zharuffkin began to cough into the collar of his coat, which soon became spattered with blood and pink phlegm.

"Get me the cigarette lighter," Katzhak ordered.

"He's choking," a man next to Katzhak observed. "Turn his head or he'll die."

"Katzhak?" Zharuffkin croaked, staring hard at the face above him, trying to be sure.

"Yes, it's Katzhak. Why did you try to arrest me?"

"I had you," Zharuffkin wheezed. "You were dead. I beat you." He choked out a bitter chuckle of irony. "Now I'm dead. I'm killed. I'm killed," he said again. The eyelids drooped and closed, slowly opening again as Zharuffkin mumbled something.

"Dammit! Where's that lighter?" The cigarette lighter popped out on the dash and was yanked out and handed to the impatient Katzhak, who, without hesitation, upturned Zharuffkin's left hand and pressed it into the palm.

Zharuffkin's eyelids flew open and the eyes rolled downward into the more normal position.

"Let me go," Borky pleaded in a rasping, barely audible voice.

"Not yet, you stupid bastard! Not yet! Zharuffkin, they've blown your guts out. You're dying, get it?"

Zharuffkin's lids lowered and closed. Immediately Katzhak touched the lighter to his palm. Nothing.

"Christ! I think I'm losing him. Zharuffkin! Zharuffkin!" Desperate, Katzhak tugged back the collar of his inert witness and held the red-hot tip against his throat. Mercifully, Borky jerked back as if shocked by a live wire. Sputtering and choking, he cursed Katzhak by every name he could think of.

"Goddammit, listen to me!" Katzhak shouted, snarling, and bouncing the pleading head on the floorboards for emphasis. "You're dead. This is your last shot at making your life mean something. Why did Bulgarin send you to stiff me?"

Too weak and confused to answer or to concentrate, Zharuffkin only stared, and coughed again, allowing his head to roll to the side. Katzhak shook him with such vio-

223

lence and fierce determination that the others in the car were frightened of him for the first time.

"You talk! Talk!" Zharuffkin shook his head, signaling that this request was beyond his strength. He closed his eyes. Katzhak twisted one ear. This might have evoked a yell in a healthy man, but was hardly felt by the numb and dying Zharuffkin. Nevertheless, the eyes opened for a final time and regarded Katzhak in a way reminiscent of the old Zharuffkin, at the height of his powers. That look puzzled and chilled Katzhak with sudden, drowning fear, all the more terrifying because he could see no basis for it.

"Katzhak," Zharuffkin began weakly, "I want to tell you something. You haven't much time. You know that. They're coming for you; they'll hunt you, now that I'm dead. I've hated you. I still do. You're a fool. You deserve whatever you get. You have only one chance left now . . ." Zharuffkin coughed and choked in spasms now, finally turning his face into the carpet to retch. "In my coat. There is . . . Oh, Jesus Christ, I hurt! Oh, God! I can't breathe! There's a little envelope in my coat somewhere. Call that number. Shit! Call that number and tell them who you are. Just give your name and rank. They'll take care of you! You'll find out all you need to know. They'll give you an answer. Do as I say, or be damned. I'm finished with you."

"I will. I will."

"I knew you would." With that, the puffy, pale lids closed and the body lay still. The labored breathing, the great heaving of the massive sides, had stopped. As Katzhak stared at the ruined Zharuffkin, it appeared almost as if that hideous face was finally at peace. Katzhak had never seen it this way before. As macabre as it sounded, the lips appeared almost to smile at him, as if recording some final triumph, some last hidden joy. In Katzhak's throat, smothering terror without a name rose and nauseated him. Funny that the smile of this man in death still sent tremors through his body. Was it a premonition? Some intuition of woe to come? No. He was exhausted and frightened. He saw danger where none existed. Zharuffkin was dead, and it was certain he could do him no further harm.

It seemed to Katzhak that there was not enough strength left in him to blow out a match. Wearily he handed the

224

lighter up over the seat, which he now collapsed against, laying his head against the cold vinyl. He sat in silence for almost a minute, first staring at the lifeless and grotesque figure of Zharuffkin, then closing his eyes as if to shut out all reality. Katzhak did not think or formulate new plans in this private retreat, this inner sanctum; he only rested, refusing for a brief moment to go any further, to think any thought. Resigned, he opened his eyes with ultimate reluctance, his eyelids blinking slowly with his thoughts. When he spoke at last, it was with great effort—sullen, resolute, brief. Almost totally devoid of emotion, he intoned in a low voice, "About a week ago, I received a report that my friend . . . Arno Tuskov had died in an auto accident. Fearing the worst, I investigated, and found that his flat had been destroyed in a fire. Tuskov informed me that he knew he was about to be murdered, and that I should contact Mikhail Malenkov on a matter of the gravest importance. As soon as possible, I visited the Malenkovs, only to find that Mikhail Malenkov had been arrested and tortured the night before by the KGB. His wife was badly beaten also, but she is alive. Driving away from Malenkov's apartment, I was ambushed by two men who, I learned later, were militant Jewish dissidents who blamed me for Malenkov's arrest. I killed these two men.

"Since I had suffered some minor injuries, I was hospitalized and interrogated by Zharuffkin. From this point on, Zharuffkin was instructed to spy on me and to report all activities to Deputy Bulgarin.

"When I had recovered sufficiently to resume my work, I investigated certain clues which Tuskov had left behind. I also investigated the attack on my person and the circumstances surrounding Tuskov's death.

"I learned that Tuskov had definitely been murdered— by whom, I could not be certain. I have a contact who usually supplies me with all information regarding vehicles impounded for security inspection. This man could get no information from his informant. He was beaten and warned off by this informant. Zharuffkin was there, and within hours my contact's informant was dead.

"During this period I made contact with the Jewish underground. Our first meeting early this morning was broken up by the secret police. I took the side of the dissidents, and might have been killed, had it not been for the intervention of Zharuffkin. Believing Zharuffkin had left, I made plans to meet again with the underground after they had tended their wounded. These plans, of course, were observed by Zharuffkin. Zharuffkin obtained orders to arrest me, and returned to watch my second meeting with the underground. Zharuffkin's men engaged me in fire, and I shot both men dead. Zharuffkin escaped, but not without learning the location of the old man's flat. You know the rest."

"But what does it mean? What were the clues Tuskov left?"

"It means that in less than a week, lots of people have been rousted, arrested, busted up, or killed. It means that unless we can stop this thing, we're all dead men. It also means . . . it means . . ."

"The clues!"

"Tuskov begged me to stop something."

"Stop what?"

"Something called Cosmo."

"Oh, my God!" The driver exhaled slowly through his teeth.

"There was one more thing. He said 'Russia' and gave the date of the battle of Waterloo."

"Oh, no. You think he was talking about the annihilation of Israel?"

"No. Tuskov was convinced that the attack would be a disastrous failure. That's why he asked me to stop it. He asked me as a Soviet."

"Then who killed him? We didn't."

"I'm afraid that we did."

"Assassinated your own man? Why?"

"Because he knew about the goddamned plan, that's why!" Katzhak shouted in obvious anger and bitterness. "He knew something else, too. Some flaw. Some reason it couldn't possibly work. They butchered him before he got a chance to tell anybody what it was. I've got to find out what he was so afraid of. We've got to call the number now, before it's too late."

"Too late for whom? Why should we let you stop it if there is some mistake? I think you bloody bastards ought to be allowed to choke to death on it. We don't need you

226

anymore, either, Katzhak. Convince me not to dump you on the highway. I'm listening, Colonel."

"Call Tuskov's number, and you might get all your answers—but what if you don't? What about the number in Zharuffkin's coat?"

"We've got the number, comrade."

"They're expecting me. They won't give you a damned thing."

"I'm willing to bet they don't know what the hell you sound like, killer."

"And what are you going to do with the information once you get it? Blow the whistle, and you start a war, one way or the other. You can't get inside our war machine. I can. The question is, do I need you?"

"We're wasting time. Where's the safest place to call from, Colonel?"

"I don't trust my phones anymore. I can't be sure of my staff, either. The machine will trace, regardless of where we place the call from. An open line's as good as any. Damn."

"What is it?"

"Don't you see? They may have reprogrammed as a precaution. If they've changed the number somehow, we won't get more than a dial tone. There's another danger."

"What's that?"

"Look. They've been robbed once. They're expecting to be robbed again. If you want to catch all the thieves, you don't change the locks. You let them get in, and then you close the trap. Maybe they haven't changed the number. Maybe now they're just quicker on the draw than they were with Tuskov."

"We've got to try, no matter what."

Katzhak nodded. "I know. Pull over at the next public phone. I'll take one man in the booth with me. The others stand watch. If you see any trouble, honk once, then get out fast. We'll have to look after ourselves as best we can. Stop! There's one, on the right."

"Back up, mister. You're big stuff to your people, maybe, but you're on our turf now. I'll give the orders, if you don't mind."

Katzhak shrugged and laughed softly—ironic laughter. "You don't understand, do you? You still don't get it! We all have to move our asses together or we're doomed right now. Christ! We need a hundred more like you, just to survive till morning. To pull this thing off would take an army. Jesus! 'I'll give the orders, if you don't mind.' " He laughed again. "You've killed Bulgarin's man and kidnapped me. If that weren't enough, there's always Cosmo. I'm the only one in the world who has the slightest chance of getting any one of us out alive. Any chance. I know them. I've been in this business for twenty-five years, and if I don't know what I'm doing by now, we might as well give ourselves up right now. I promise you, we'd be better off."

The driver did not turn his head. "Go with him. Do what he tells you," he said to the man seated next to him in the front seat. The car slowed and stopped. The man in front got out, and Katzhak crawled out after him. It was bitterly, bitingly cold, and both men paused to raise their collars and adjust their overcoats. The snow had stopped and the starless sky was clear and darkest black.

Even so, Katzhak thought he could hear thunder and muted rumblings in the distance. He made for the phone booth, the other man edging backward nervously behind him. Katzhak stepped in and made to close the door, but the sentinel held it open a crack so as to listen, as well as to watch.

The entire posture of Katzhak's body drooped like a tired dog. His hand was paining him again, his head was splitting, and he realized with a curse that his riven side was bleeding again. In a whirl of violent emotions he reached into his overcoat and dragged out the heavy pieces of paper, piecing them together on the telephone in front of him. He hesitated for a moment, receiver in hand, before quickly dialing the long number. His heart pounded wildly, and his breathing seemed to deafen him. Katzhak listened as a series of clicks and mechanical tones sounded in his ear, and each digit locked into place. Nothing happened.

Suddenly a tick-pause-tick signaled renewed activity and a rapid-fire sequence of computer tones played their coded song in his ear. Then, in a flat and even monotone, a deadly litany began. The programmed voice spoke of plots and plans, and secret data on sensitive projects. Katzhak

228

found it easier to straighten up, and he let out his breath in a long sigh of relief. He lowered the receiver to his shoulder and closed his eyes. Instantly they flew open again, and the receiver bolted back up against his ear. First, there was the name. Cosmo was the code word for an ambitious and provocative plan for a surprise blitz attack. Target: (Katzhak bit his lip and shook his head for self-reassurance) Israel. His eyes slowly closed in confirmation of horror. They remained so, as details of the attack rolled out, one by one, outlining the plot, and lashing his brain. Katzhak's heart froze and stood still in his chest as the date of attack launch was generously provided. Tomorrow morning! He consulted his watch. They had five hours to stop the Soviet Union from going to war. Five hours, which would see him, or a vast army, dead.

Katzhak hung up the phone. The watcher turned around, and Katzhak nodded. He tore the pieces of the number to tiny bits and stood thinking. Remembering the trace in progress, he snapped out of his trance and asked the watcher for Zharuffkin's envelope with the number inside, which was the only lead he had gleaned from the dying man. Katzhak tore open the envelope and snatched out the number. He dialed quickly and waited. The phone was answered somewhere, but no one spoke. Following his instructions to the letter, Katzhak gave his name and rank and waited. The line went dead immediately. Puzzled and wildly alarmed, Katzhak dropped the receiver and fled the phone booth, the two men darting to the curb to be picked up.

"It's true," Katzhak confessed, once inside the car.

"How much time do we have? When does it take place? What kind of forces will be used?"

"Tomorrow morning," said Katzhak, still stunned. "It's an all-out conventional assault. Planes, ships, ground forces, all at once. I've got to try to stop it, but there's so little time left, so very little time."

"What are you going to do?"

"What can I do? I'm going to have to try to get inside the war room and cut off the attack from there."

"Aren't there any other channels? That sounds too risky. I don't like it. It could go either way."

"Like it or not, it's the only way to go from here. It's

too late for anything else at this stage. We have no options."

"Do you have clearance? If they're looking for you, you'll never get inside."

"If they're looking for me, I won't get near the building. We'll have to assume that the heat isn't that great yet, that the news hasn't circulated. If it died with Zharuffkin, we may have a chance. If we can keep the lid on for five or six hours, maybe we can bull our way in."

"What are the odds on that?"

"About as great as on Brezhnev's bar mitzvah, but it's all we've got. What do you say?"

"I hate you, you son of a bitch, but we're with you, of course."

"Wouldn't it be simpler just to go to the press?" one man piped up. "Surely world opinion . . . they wouldn't dare move after we blew the whistle on them."

"What press?" Katzhak inquired. "No newspaper would print it, no radio station would broadcast it, East or West. Not without corroboration or hard evidence, which you don't have. Even if you could get it out illegally before morning, which I doubt, who could pick it up? Who would believe it? We have one chance, and one chance only. We have to wade into the cobra's nest. Do we make plans?"

The others sat in stiff silence. Somewhere in the distance there was the deep muted thunder of a gathering storm.

"Tell us what to do."

"Maybe I haven't made myself entirely clear," Katzhak warned darkly. "This isn't an academy drill, no training exercise. This isn't just a tough assignment. This is a suicide mission, like the great kamikaze. I can almost promise you that if all goes according to plan, every one of you who comes with me will die. The men we will meet are the best we have, the best-trained, the most skilled, the most ruthless and resourceful. They will stop at nothing to stop *you*. If you are prepared to go with me, you must also be prepared to die. Think it over carefully. You have nothing to lose if the attack should fail." Katzhak looked at each man sternly, trying to impress on each one the certainty of the danger they faced, and to test their mettle and resolve in the face of almost certain defeat.

The men conferred briefly and rapidly in Hebrew, and in low voices.

"We are in your hands," the apparent leader of the men said simply.

Katzhak nodded, and all were silent in a solemn moment of reflection and requiem for themselves, and for each other. The men were resolved, and set their faces to the task in front of them.

Finally Katzhak broke the silence. "How many of you have weapons?" he asked. There were four murmurs of assent. "Good. Here's what we'll do: two of you will have to park on the street near the front entrance of the building. The other two will follow me inside. The men in the car will have to watch us go in. If you see anyone who even looks vaguely like he might be following us in, it will be your job to stop them—as quietly and quickly as possible. Don't use your guns unless you have to, and certainly not before we get inside. Under no circumstances, no circumstances whatsoever, will you let anyone into that building who looks like he might be following us; if we're going to have any chance at this at all, we've got to get inside the building safely and without drawing attention to ourselves. Use any means, any force necessary. We all depend on you. The other two will come inside with me to provide covering fire if the going gets rough. I'll explain the way the building is laid out in the morning, so it will be fresh in your minds. Any questions?"

"Yes. Once you are inside, if you get that far, how do you plan to head off the attack?"

Katzhak laughed softly. "If I get inside, they'll probably surrender."

"What will we do until morning?"

"Sleep," came the immediate reply.

28

Katzhak slept fitfully, his mind a whirl of gory and grotesque images, wild things, mutterings and voices. He saw Tuskov horror-struck, bloodied and pleading. Zharuff-kin's hideous corpse chased and tortured him repeatedly, always smiling sardonically in a way that chilled the blood, a loathsome, enigmatic mask of gloating triumph and wormy madness. He was haunted by the specters of the days just passed. Their disembodied faces paraded before him in ghostly review: Tuskov, Tash, the swollen, purpled face of Gallina Malenkov, the remembrance of her cowering children, and the roadside ambushers' terrified screams before they were forced up the rocky wall of the roadside embankment, pounding the steering wheel and begging to be released from grinding steel death. He saw Zharuffkin, the clever and composed prober at the hospital, saw him leaping to safety after feeding his two men to Katzhak's hungry bullets, savage bullets, leaping to safety after blowing a heartless red hole in the back of one of his servants, leaving him there with his face in the smothering snow, in the cold and unkind snow, and leaping, leaping up onto the concrete sidewalk, walking with an ugly gun in his bloody hands, and a misshapen smile on his deformed lips, walking to arrest, and to hunt, and to hurt and to kill, saw him pumped with bullets, saw him splattered with his own blood, saw him gag, saw him choke, saw him curse, saw him spit, saw him die—saw him smile. Katzhak was forced to watch again the morning's killer kicks and brutal blows, forced to hear again every thump, every crack, every snapping, every wound, every senseless moan and helpless gurgling in the snow. Tossing and turning, and squirming restlessly, he saw Ulev, giant and heavy, and solid as a statue, lifted clear off his feet and tossed backward in the snow, like a rag doll flipped away by an angry little girl. Andrei shivered, alone and desperate to avoid the shot he knew was coming, coming at his body, suddenly weak and fleshy and vulnerable as an egg, screamed in utter, bottomless despair, beseeching God or the devil or man. And Katzhak, arbiter and omnipotent judge of all humanity, pulled the iron trigger over and over and over again, guiding the sledgelike slugs with his keen eyes and his skillful hands, and sending them slamming certainly home.

Once again the old man's sad and searching eyes compelled him, transcended him, implored him, and ignored him. Once again the outraged boy with the tiny knife had lunged and plunged the cold steel cutter painfully into the tender flesh of his side, puncturing his body and slicing deep, only to rip and to gouge its way back out again. He felt the jagged pain as he watched the scene replayed an eternity of times. Now, one last fiend addressed him, one final horror visited his mind, to rob him of his rest and secure slumber: with unknown eyes he gaped at a colossus of power and appetite, virile, insatiable, and slavering over his food. Katzhak was dead to his roots as the huge bear scooped up the final scrap and greedily lifted the tiny prey to its lips. The jaws opened, the rows of iron teeth were poised. Slowly the jaws began to descend.

29

"Huh? Um-hm. Yeah. Thanks." Katzhak had just been shaken to life where his body had lain hunched all night against the door, and every muscle and nerve loudly protested this vigorously resented turn of events. He yawned

233

so deeply it was painful, and cradled his pounding head in his hands. "What time is it?" he asked, suddenly alarmed.

"Four-thirty."

Katzhak nodded in mute approval and forced his cramped body into a crouch, thus enabling him to see out the window. The car was on the outskirts of the city, heading toward the heart of the capital. He lowered himself to the floor and sat thinking, allowing time for his mental equipment to warm up. In ten seconds his heart was pounding and they were still an hour away from their task.

"You promised to explain the layout of the complex," the leader of the group of kidnappers prompted.

"That's right. Okay. There is a small lobby first, and a long counter. This counter is the place where orders, papers, and identities are checked. There is a hallway on each end of the counter. These hallways are flanked by interrogation, searching, and detainment areas. The halls open up into long rooms with banks and banks of secretaries and file clerks, with a few offices in behind. Just past the secretaries are more troops, military policemen, whose job it is to guard the entrance to huge elevators which lead to the sublevels. If the intruder alert is sounded before the elevator reaches its destination, it will stop automatically. The doors open into a long tunnel which branches out in all directions. If you go straight, about one kilometer, you will come to a corridor. If the alarm is sounded now, the steel doors will lock shut and the SM-70s will take over."

"SM-70s? What are those?"

"A new development, only recently deployed. These machine guns fire automatically. That is, they sweep an area in patterns without human guidance. There is also gas that causes unconsciousness, paralysis, or death, depending on the concentration inhaled."

"How long does it last?"

"Two minutes. Then it is dispersed by powerful fans. When it reaches a safe level, the doors automatically open again."

"What's beyond the corridor?"

"More police, and . . . the war room."

234

The men were silent, each one settling back to brood over his own private concerns. There was something nagging at the back of Katzhak's mind. It had troubled him all night, even as he slept. Suddenly it forced its way back, and intruded itself on his somber reflections. The call! The one he had made at Zharuffkin's insistence. They had listened while he gave his name and rank and then had hung up without a word. What did it mean? He tried to recall Zharuffkin's last words to him: "You haven't much time. . . . They're coming for you, they'll hunt you . . ." Hunt you, Katzhak thought, beginning to feel alarmed and sick. "They'll take care of you. . . . They'll give you an answer. Do as I say, or be damned," he had cursed. "I'm finished with you." Chilled, Katzhak recalled Zharuffkin's response to his promise to call the number: "I knew you would," and then that freezing smile . . . of triumph? Of satisfaction? "You're a fool," Zharuffkin was rasping over and over again in his mind, and he smiled that macabre smile.

Who was hunting him right now? Who had been ordered to take his head? What did they look like? How many would there be? Was he, like the fool Zharuffkin said he was, walking into the trap, wandering into the slaughterhouse like a sheep without a shepherd? Sheep? Shepherds? The words of the prophecies came flooding back. What was the sum total of it all? Where did he stand with the word?

The Jews had gathered and returned to their ancient lands as predicted. Israel had become a nation again after twenty centuries. The land was reclaimed and planted, the cities were rebuilt. Now a giant military machine from the north was leveling an attack on the reestablished nation. They were coming up like a whirlwind, like . . . "like a cloud to cover the land." They were "coming up out of their place in the north" . . . "against the land of unwalled villages, to take a spoil, and to take a prey." A massive military force was about to strike, and what did he think? He knew what Tuskov had thought. Tuskov had believed. Why did he care for Tuskov; why was he drawn to the white-haired old man? Integrity. Honesty. Either of these men was capable of error, but not of deliberately lying, of deception, of duplicity. These men had a sort of sense, a "feeling in their bones" about the world. They had always dealt in truth, and they seemed, as a result, to see it more clearly, and to recognize it more often than other men. Other men were not interested in the truth, not in learning, not in change. The truth avoided them, resting where it was welcomed and received. It was a natural law; light cannot cohabit or commune with darkness. Katzhak was battered and scarred and hunted for his pursuit of perfect knowledge at this moment. He was an outcast, a marked man, because of his thirst for the truth, his relentless searching for it; he would probably die because of his devotion to this ideal, because the gap between principle and practice was so narrow in his life. Did this not give him the right to know it? Did this not confer upon him, like a crown of laurel leaves, the honor of knowing it? It had always seemed that it should, that it would, that it did. He no longer thought so. Truth, it seemed to him now, was not a thing to be earned by sincerity and faithfulness. It could not be chased or uncovered. It was not a thing to be grasped. It was, strangely . . . alive, and all around him. It existed and it pervaded. One either embraced it or rejected it, but it breathed. Katzhak embraced its fresh, new, flesh-and-blood beauty, and he held his eyes shut tightly in deep, sweet communion. He felt an overwhelming calm, and something within him rested, lay down to sleep, was peaceful and content for the first time since he had breathed. Slowly he became aware of knowing all secrets, understanding all knowledge, of a mysterious oneness with Tuskov and with the old man. He seemed to himself to be, almost, recreated. Like a baby, he was just beginning to exist, he had just been born. His former self seemed as ugly and hollow, and lifeless and cold, as the body of Zharuffkin on the floor in front of him. He did not understand these feelings, but he felt no embarrassment, no wild terror that the knowledge would fade.

Something that the old man had said to him came slicing into his thoughts: "There is a blindness, Colonel, a madness that pervades; man is acting out the thoughts, the words, the wishes of something from far beyond, something evil, something . . . cold. . . . You've got to think for yourself again, Colonel. You've got to open your eyes

and resist the control, to come back to your senses. . . ."
Katzhak was committed to the total and utter destruction
of the plan. He would stop Cosmo, or Cosmo would stop
him.

"This is it!" Katzhak jerked his head up and looked out.
The national headquarters of all the vast armed services of
his country loomed ahead of them, up the block. His chest
tightened like leather thongs drying in the sun, and his
heart pounded in wild claustrophobia. The five men stared
in awe and trepidation at the immensity of the building
and their own undertaking. They were five ants about to
bite the heel of an unforgiving giant.

"Pull over and stop here," Katzhak commanded to the
one who had spoken. The driver complied at once. "Come
back here, with me," Katzhak ordered. "You drive," he
said to the man against the rear door, on the right-hand
side, nearest his elbow. Katzhak got out, and the men
switched places as ordered, the driver sliding over into the
middle so that Katzhak could sit against the door.

The car pulled back into traffic unusual for this area at
this hour of the morning. Katzhak checked his watch. A
few minutes after five.

"What about security?" the leader of the Israelis wanted
to know. "Won't they beef it up incredibly with an attack
in progress?"

"No. There are too many foreigners in this city, too
many foreign operatives, too many observers and satellites.
In the sublevels, yes. Aboveground, they won't want to
twitch in the wrong direction. Once the actual attack is
launched, air, sea, and ground forces shadowing our own
will know in an hour what our intentions are, and Western
intelligence will know shortly after that. There will be a
tense period of denial and debate while they wait for unmistakable evidence to confirm their suspicions. Then this
city will clamp shut like an iron gate, while the Kremlin
waits to see whether or not the world is at war. The
Americans and others must decide how far they want to
commit themselves, knowing, as they do, that by the time
they begin mobilization of their forces in this theater, it
will probably be too late to save the cause anyway. The
Kremlin must be confident of their position, and that of
our enemies, confident enough not to tip their hand. We

should have a good hour before all possibilities have been sealed off. However"—he paused for emphasis—"we may still face a serious threat before we get inside. Tuskov was murdered by someone working for our organization. That call to Zharuffkin's number last night may have set them on us. They could be waiting for us."

The car slowed to a stop about thirty meters from the broad concrete steps that led to the main entrance. Katzhak opened the door. "Be alert. Good luck," he said to them all.

"God be with you, Colonel," one of the men in the front seat called out after him as he stepped out of the car. Katzhak turned and looked back at the face of the man who had spoken, remembering the last words of the old man as he had left his flat. Slowly he lowered his eyes and then shut the door after the two men who would accompany him inside. Katzhak's eyes scanned the colonnades, corners, cars, and rooftops, quickly searched every face for a clue, every coat for a bulge, every hand for a weapon. Seeing nothing, he began to climb briskly up the steps of the building, flanked by his two guardians, making directly for the doors.

"Keep moving," he said under his breath. "Look straight ahead and don't turn around." The men were not aware of the three men seated waiting in a car across the street, which now pulled out and crossed over to the opposite side. On an apparent signal from their passenger, the two men seated in front got out and trotted quickly up the stairs toward Katzhak.

The Israelis hesitated for a moment before nodding to each other and starting the motor. Stepping on the accelerator, they were just able to jump the curb, and, honking in warning to Katzhak, slammed up a few low steps and bumped down the two men they suspected of following him. Pretending to be mortified and quite drunk, the two men opened the doors and lurched out, weaving with sloppy haste to "aid" the victims of their "accident." One man was partially pinned beneath a wheel on the driver's side, while his companion lay in front of the vehicle. The pinioned man moaned and struggled weakly, while his partner, shaken, and only slightly injured, cursed loudly and started to get up. Like lightning, the two tottering Israelis bent over to help the fallen pedestrians. Stooping

238

low, so that their open overcoats hung down to shield their movements from any onlookers, the Israelis quickly drew their guns, and placing the muzzles against the chests of the startled men, each fired two or three times. Sheathing his weapon, the driver stumbled back to the car and leaned on the horn, hoping to draw as much attention and police away from the building and Katzhak as possible. His partner meanwhile ran down the few steps to the street and, hand on the butt of his weapon, approached the auto from which the two slain men were seen to have emerged. Pretending to appeal for help, he drew his gun and threw open the rear door. Fully expecting to be shot, he positioned himself behind the flung-open door and prepared to fire without warning. The backseat was empty. Panicked, he whirled around and saw Katzhak and his companions turn from the accident and hurry up the last few steps and into the building. A large man with dark hair appeared to be in hot pursuit. The Israeli cursed briefly and for an instant entertained the idea of trying to shoot the fleeing figure. The man was by this time, however, nearing the top of the stairs, and police, both military and civilian, were converging from everywhere. Frustrated and defeated, he tossed his gun into the car and shut the door. Suddenly he spun around and looked back into the car. The keys were still inside! His partner was engulfed in a crowd of witnesses and police. There was nothing he could do for him now. If there was any possible way to aid Katzhak or his other companions already inside the building, it was his duty to save himself and get away. He had been trained to stay out of lost causes and to preserve his usefulness to his country. Up on the stairs, a woman was already starting to point toward him, and two policemen began descending the steps in his direction. Without hesitating further, he jumped in and slid over, taking the car. In the rearview mirror he could see the accusing fingers, and his partner being led away by the arms.

30

Katzhak and the other men walked straight up to the counter, and Katzhak presented his papers. He had told the two men with him that they would have to remain at the desk, as they did not have the credentials to go any farther. They were to wait and to watch for trouble. He had asked them to do nothing unless his detainment was certain, and to find the quietest possible way to free him, in order to avoid setting off an intruder alert and thus block his only routes to the sublevels. One of the men, on Katzhak's instructions, bought a package of charcoal-filled cigarettes. These he pretended to drop and then step on clumsily. Katzhak's papers now okayed, he complained of being slightly feverish, and the second Israeli, taking his cue, soaked his woolen scarf with water at a drinking fountain and brought it to Katzhak. The latter mopped his forehead and handed the scarf to the man with the crushed package of cigarettes. The Israelis sat down together in one corner and as quickly as possible poured the crushed charcoal into the waterlogged scarf. Katzhak had been cleared to proceed, and saying good-bye to the Israelis, accepted once again the carefully folded scarf.

Almost as quickly as Katzhak had left the lobby and entered one of the hallways, a large dark-haired man with a neatly trimmed mustache and a square jaw pushed his way into the lobby with obvious confidence, authority, and command. He was tall, rugged, and handsome, with the build and gait of a boxer or a vigorous outdoorsman. This great bear strode powerfully across the room, glancing rapidly at every face and piercing deep into every corner. His eyes narrowed suddenly at the sight of the two men he had seen enter the building with Katzhak. He motioned the two men over to his presence with one commanding swipe of his great paw. The men shuffled over, dragging their feet.

"Where is he?" he demanded with quiet menace. The men said nothing. "I can find him in ten minutes. Don't make me look for him. Now, where is he?"

The men did not have time to formulate a reply. In the hallway to the left, the secretaries were all sliding back their chairs and standing at attention as Katzhak passed. "Good morning, Colonel," the dark-haired man heard each voice saying. With only a glance backward at the two Israelis, he was off at a run across the lobby and into the hallway beyond it, to the left. Finally he spotted his man nearing the MPs at the elevator doors. "Katzhak!" he shouted, drawing his gun and planting his feet. Katzhak threw a glance backward over his shoulder and jerked sideways at the crucial moment. The bullet missed narrowly, and the guard to Katzhak's right was slammed against the steel door, and crumpled, like paper in a fireplace, to the floor. The second sentinel drew his weapon but did not fire it, hovering protectively instead over his fallen companion. Two or three of the women screamed, and the dark assassin prepared to fire again.

"Stop him!" Katzhak called out. "He wants to assassinate the premier!" As Katzhak bolted, the Israelis, having crossed the lobby, picked up Katzhak's accusatory shout. "Stop that man! He's an assassin!" they shouted. "Don't let him kill the premier!"

At this, bedlam broke loose; the secretaries flooded into the corridor between the shooter and his target, the MP advanced toward the gunman who was in plain clothes, and Katzhak kept running for daylight and the elevator. Suddenly the air was filled with sharp pencils, ball-point pens, and paperweights. Wastebaskets were rolled into the path of the dark assassin, causing him to trip in his pursuit and making him an easier target for the barrage of fire enthusiastically supplied by the secretaries. The assassin leaped up once or twice, trying to find a target above the sea of heads crowding around him. He sighted as best he could and fired, the missile tearing into the wall above the doors. He hopped up and fired again, hitting a woman in

241

the sid: of the head and killing her instantly. A secretary who had been splattered with blood shrieked and fainted, while the other women surrounded the assailant, kicking him with their pointed shoes and pummeling him with their elbows and fists. In pain and fierce frustration, the man twisted to break free of the snarling mob, desperate as Katzhak neared the doors. His protests unheard against the uproar, he threatened the women with a wave of his pistol, and thus backing them off momentarily, he squeezed off three fair last-ditch shots. The steel doors were closing as the bullets rained down on Katzhak. The first round ricocheted off the door and tore into the ceiling. The second volley flattened itself out much closer in, and only a foot from Katzhak. The third salvo blistered into the fleshy part of Katzhak's right side, just above the hip. He kept his feet and stumbled to the back of the elevator, leaning heavily on it for support as the doors slammed shut and the machine mercifully began its lurching descent. The motion and shock combined to dizzy and nauseate him. He fought the impulse to retch or to pass out.

The assassin had been disarmed and considerably roughed up by the secretaries and MPs. He was obviously furious over his capture and detainment, and he seemed very anxious to reveal his identity and to resume his pursuit of the NKVD officer. A security team wrestled him to the floor and pinned him there until someone grabbed his papers and endeavored to find out who he was.

The elevator continued to descend at a gradual acceleration. Katzhak sighed and wiped the perspiration off his forehead with his sleeve. Still no alarm. He held his breath. Dammit! The shallow gouge beneath his left arm which he had received the night before was starting to bleed again. He pleaded for strength, and was thankful that, typical of assassins, the caliber of his weapon had been relatively small, and had not killed Katzhak outright, or inflicted damage too massive and total to allow him to continue. My God! he thought to himself. Isn't this damned thing ever going to stop? He seemed to be locked into a bottomless journey into hell.

How much time before the fatigue and the loss of blood caught up with him? Enough, goddammit, he told himself, enough. He wanted to rest. Suddenly the floor was coming back up. Unbelievable as it seemed, the elevator had stopped falling and was beginning to slow. It jerked and held, and Katzhak drew in his breath to steel himself for what lay ahead. The doors split and rolled backward, and Katzhak pushed off from the wall, forcing himself to run.

On the surface level, security was startled and a little abashed as they read the papers of the man they held pinned on the floor. He was a government troubleshooter, and right now Katzhak was trouble. His credentials apparently gave him sweeping power and sanction, his jurisdiction was virtually limitless. There was one fact that was not so readily apparent, however. Unbeknownst to the security men and to almost everyone in the highest echelons of government, the man on the floor was the head of a supersecret infraorganization whose task it was to seek out and destroy enemies and potential enemies of the state. This unique bureau liquidated problem individuals who could not be handled by any other means. Aging operatives, defectors, leaders of splinter groups and satellites departing from the party line, traitors, spies, and of course loyal and patriotic individuals like Tuskov who occasionally stumbled onto something sensitive by accident. Once thus exposed to the dangerous plague, the assassination bureau exterminated the infected individuals for the good of all, thus stopping the spread of something deadly. Tuskov had fallen into this latter category, and his unfortunate termination had been a necessary evil.

The man on the floor had not known why, nor had he asked, nor had he wished to know, the reason for which Tuskov was to have been erased. He did know that it had been crucial to the top levels of his state, crucial perhaps to national security itself, that Tuskov be eliminated. And all his effects destroyed immediately. He knew this because he had been ordered to take the assignment himself, an event so singularly rare and significant that he had guessed at cataclysm from the start. His worst suspicions had been confirmed when he had been briefed on an unprecedented second personal sanction. Not only was Katzhak's name even bigger and more luminary than Tuskov's, but he had been warned that his target might show up here this very morning, if all went according to the most dismal scenario. Something tremendous was in the wind, and for Katzhak

243

to be who he was, where he was, when he was, was disaster incarnate. He was determined to destroy Katzhak if it cost his life. Katzhak had gotten past him, so perhaps it already had. If he were to save his life, Katzhak had to be stopped. He must make certain Katzhak was not successful in whatever it was he had come here to do.

He was losing time. If Katzhak had commandeered a jeep below, he might be anywhere right now, racing down any one of a dozen major tunnels. The security men were beginning to back up and to reconsider. The air of command and authority which the man possessed came to his aid once more as he shook off the loosening grip of the confused police and took advantage of their hesitation and indecision. Wresting back his gun and control of the situation at the same time, he jammed in a fresh clip and barked orders to the almost apologetic guards.

"All right," he thundered. "I want you to listen carefully. The officer who just went through those doors is a traitor and an enemy of the state. I was sent here to apprehend him before his plots against us were successful. You have cost me valuable time, and you have helped him to elude justice. He killed two of my men on his way in here! Now he is planning some coup, some sabotage, I don't know what, but he is an enemy of the people, and if you all don't start cooperating, you'll answer for it, I promise you. Clear this hallway, and call for an ambulance! Hold those two men"—he gestured toward the two Israelis—"they are part of the conspiracy. Interrogate them. Find out where Katzhak's gone. That's Colonel Katzhak. You men come with me. How long does it take the elevator to reach the lowest level?"

"Thirty seconds, give or take."

"Give us one minute and sound the alarm. Call security and get out an intruder alert. Make sure the fail-safe systems are tripped and operating. Better warn the war room as well; I think that's where he may be headed. Nobody enters or leaves this building except the medics and the wounded. Remember, one minute. Let's go."

The handsome chief of the elite assassins punched his clearance card into the machine next to the elevators, and the doors opened for him just as they had for Katzhak. He was elated to find blood inside the lift. Either Katzhak had

244

been injured, somehow, from the start, or he had hit his man after all. If chance was with him, perhaps his job would be a lot easier than he had anticipated, his failure, somewhat less glaring. It didn't matter how it had happened. The wound would make Katzhak weary, would slow him down, set him on edge. This assignment was as good as over with. On the other hand, Katzhak had a reputation for ability, resourcefulness, toughness, and tenacity. His wound might only serve to make him more dangerous, more unpredictable, more . . . savage. Caution and a clear head were indicated here. With proper handling, he would complete his contract, the mission would be saved.

Katzhak's jeep hurtled through the dark maze of tunnels in the bowels of the earth, in the guts of his country's military might. He pushed it, he honked, and he cursed, and he tried to stay awake, weaving around traffic that seemed to be motionless, narrowly avoiding a scrape here, a head-on collision there. The unshaded overhead lights flew faster and faster over his eyes, one by one throwing light on him, like tiny flares over a field of battle. He sped onward recklessly, headlong in his flight, as if pursued by demonic forces bent on his destruction. Suddenly, like a herald of doom, a mechanical harbinger took up its screaming, wailing lament. For a second or two the song was totally unheeded; like a sleeper unwilling to awaken, he had incorporated the sounds into his dream, and went on dreaming.

Finally an alarm went off in some part of his brain still willing to do battle; his mind thus awakened, the intruder alert exploded across his consciousness and shook him to life, like alcohol or lye dumped on a painful open wound.

"Jesus," he said aloud. Like the dream he had had, the vision imparted to him on the train to Sovetsk, he was in the street, in the darkness, the great bear was about to bite down on a tiny morsel, and he was mute, trying futilely to warn, to avert the judgment and the holocaust, and chased by the servants of the Monument, the god, to take his life, for his distasteful prophecies, and his refusal to join in praise and support of the beast. Jesus Christ, he had to get there! Had to be there on time, had to do something. He had to get to the last corridor before the doors shut, before it was too late. The alarm meant that they

245

were after him, probably right behind him, and he was
dead if he did not get inside the corridor. His one-way
street would instantly become a dead end, with death gal-
loping up the alley toward him.

There it was! The great steel cavern yawned dead ahead
of him. Damn, damn, damn! The doors were starting to
close! Slowly, a foot, then another, and another. Katzhak
slammed on the brakes, and the tires screamed and smoked.
There was hardly room for a truck to pass now. He was
a hundred feet away. Seventy-five. Fifty. Jesus! Would the
jeep make it? No, Christ! He was locked out! After all
this, it was over, over. He could hear the motor of the
assassin's jeep. He was standing on the brake. The jeep
skidded, and for an instant Katzhak thought that it would
flip. Instead, it pulled up sideways just as the assassin's
jeep came into view. There was less than three feet now
between the two doors. The assassin stood up to steady his
automatic rifle against the top of the windshield. Katzhak
leaped, twisting sideways as he did so. The assassin fired,
and bullets flew after Katzhak, who hit the ground just
inside the corridor as shots whistled above him and the
doors slammed shut, deflecting the remaining slugs like
hail on a tin roof. He had not been hit.

As soon as the doors were closed, Katzhak was on his
feet again, running. He was wounded, and had injured
his left knee in his leap from the jeep. Although his side
hurt from the injury he had received on the surface, and
he was limping painfully on that left leg, he had to get as
near to the far door of the corridor as he possibly could
before the machine guns and the gas prevented him from
getting any farther across. There was a click, like a machine
responding to an electronic signal, and suddenly the muzzles of the wall-mounted guns swiveled six or eight inches.
Katzhak dropped to the floor immediately, and lay flat,
hands on his thighs, heels together. He watched the guns,
chin to the floor. If he were correct in his guess, the guns
were synchronized and worked off the same system. If he
were wrong, he had no chance whatsoever. His only hope
lay in finding a pattern. If the guns fired randomly, he
was dead. He rolled just in time as two of the guns
teamed to strafe his former position. He crawled for a few
feet before noticing the entire right bank of guns drop

246

their barrels toward a low spot on the left wall. Desperately he rolled and tucked himself against the right wall, beneath the guns, which fired in deafening unison, raking the floor and the lower left wall.

Katzhak knew that in seconds he would be dead. Sooner or later he would make a wrong move, or a ricochet would catch him. He looked around wildly, in frantic search for some way to escape the deadly fire. Suddenly he stood up against the wall and leaped, or tried to, missing twice before catching hold of the rear part of one of the guns, away from the hot barrel. Agonizingly he managed to chin himself, and to swing his legs up and over the steel box, resting his pelvis on top of it. He grunted and made frightened anguished sounds with the effort of holding up his legs in this position. If he wasn't bleeding before, he certainly was now.

As he had reasoned, the guns were programmed not to fire on each other, and this position afforded him relative safety and protection. Katzhak was straining, his side throbbed, and his legs were starting to droop into the danger zone. The muscles in his stomach and arms were starting to rebel. Miraculously, there was peace. The noise had stopped, the guns had stopped. Katzhak let out a whoop of triumph and exultation that was very close to a laugh. He lowered his legs, using this momentum to drop the rest of his body to the floor. He smiled, and drawing his gun, began walking toward the door. Abruptly the smile faded and was replaced by an expression of terror and self-criticism. He had forgotten about the gas! It hissed loudly as it escaped from valves set in the walls at intervals. Dropping once more to the ground, he pressed his face into the crack formed by the meeting of floor and wall, and took several rapid deep breaths. He stored up as much oxygen as he could in his bloodstream, and held the last breath, trying to avoid both breathing the gas and hyperventilating and passing out. He held his nose and mouth in this crack for what seemed like eternity. His lungs were threatening to explode and burst his chest like an overripe melon. Carefully he released some pent-up breath in the hopes of taking some of the pressure off. This maneuver worked, and he exhaled still more, his chest contracting painfully and begging for air.

Scared to death he might lose consciousness and breathe in the gas deeply, Katzhak extracted from the soggy hip pocket of his uniform the makeshift filter mask he had made, consisting of the water-soaked scarf and the activated charcoal. This he pressed against his face as tightly as he could, exhaled in a rush of relief, and when he could hold out no longer, took his first tentative breath. He thought it best not to breathe too deeply, for fear of the effects of the gas, and thus he risked taking the shallow breaths slightly more often. In what seemed like five minutes but was really perhaps thirty seconds, he heard the powerful fans switch on and begin evacuating the gas.

Katzhak was tired, and the floor he rested upon was suddenly comfortable. The humming of the fans lulled him toward sleep, and the artificial winds thus created seemed to him but gentle breezes. He was beginning to lose his sense of urgency, and he could not quite recall the exact reason he was lying on the floor. He shifted his weight a little, and was jabbed by knifing pains in his side. Distractedly running his hand along his right side, he was shocked to find himself injured. He tried to muster enough mental effort to recall how he had come to be hurt, but this problem gave way to another, more pressing concern. He was having trouble breathing; he was coughing; and for some odd reason, he held a cloth tightly over his mouth, the fingers rigid and locked in place. His first impulse was to take this odd gag away from his face so that he could breathe easier. But something prevented him from acting on this impulse; something in his mind was saying no, and was refusing all directives to the contrary. It was too fatiguing for him to figure out. Perhaps, after he slept a bit, he would remember. Yes, he would . . . No! He wouldn't! He couldn't sleep. Not now. He must fight it. He must try to rem . . . Try to . . . try . . .

The gas! He must keep holding the cloth because of the gas! He mustn't . . . mustn't let go. Katzhak noticed his gun on the floor beside him. Why was his gun out? He looked down again. He had been shot! That was it! Now he remembered! He was being chased. He had to get up and get going. He had to get away. Wait. He listened for the sound of the gas. The fans had stopped. He dropped the scarf and reached out for his gun. His hand and arm

248

seemed to move with infinite slowness. His gun seemed to him to be riveted to the floor as if gravity had suddenly multiplied its pull. Then his heart froze with sudden fear as he remembered his mission there, and all came flooding back. Katzhak's pulse and respiration jumped off the scale, and adrenaline infused him with newfound strength. He was able finally to lift his gun up off the floor, and he slid his limbs under him, forcing first a crawl and then a sort of sitting position as he shuffled toward the steel doors, which were just beginning to show a crack of light between them.

Gathering all of his strength, Katzhak somehow got to his feet and began stumbling without any kind of speed or momentum toward the widening gap. The stone was gradually rolling away from the tomb, and he was emerging victorious. As he was presumed to have been most definitely and completely dead, his appearance at the mouth of the cave must have appeared to have indeed been a resurrection of sorts, or at least a frightening apparition. This surprise at his survival was a potent weapon which allowed Katzhak to at least make it partway into the war room alive. The few security men stationed at that entrance had expected a riddled corpse, not a gun-wielding intelligence officer.

Katzhak leveled the cavernous barrel of his hand cannon at the faces of the startled sentries. Assuming a very authentic appearance of a panic which he genuinely felt, he gestured with the big gun, thus ensuring himself of a monologue rather than a debate. Regardless of what the men thought about Katzhak's appearance, he had their united and undivided attention while he explained it. Their widened eyes shifted, as he spoke, between Katzhak and the muzzle of his pistol.

"My name is Katzhak," he rasped, breathless, holding out his identity card for them to read and then throwing it on the floor at their feet. "I'm a colonel, NKVD. I don't know what you've been told, but there's a killer loose down here. An assassin. He wants to kill the first secretary, who must be warned. Tell him he's got to get the hell out of here, now!"

It was not going well. The faces of the men were rigid with disbelief, their eyes narrowed accusingly. A small crowd was moving toward them from a distant part of the room. The assassin was surely only seconds away.

"Please," Katzhak begged, changing his tack, "he could be right behind me!"

Katzhak looked at the hardening ring of stony faces. They were glancing at Katzhak's wound and then back to his face, as if to say: Explain that.

"Do you think I did this myself?" he implored. He was frantic now. Another second, and shots would ring out; he would be dead, and with him, any hope of stopping Cosmo.

"Jesus," he spat, exasperated, "you can hold me till you catch him, but for Christ's sake, start looking for him, and guard the secretary."

They were still unconvinced, but the muscles softened in the hard faces, and the eyes wavered a fraction, did not seem so sure. Katzhak had dumped all of his ballast, but his ship was still sinking. What else did he have to cast out, to keep himself afloat? Katzhak lowered his gun before his logic had worn off the security detail. This gesture of defenselessness and submission, when coupled with his offer to remain in custody until the truth could be determined, had an effect—too small to win the men over perhaps, but big enough to register in their eyes, to Katzhak's satisfaction.

Suddenly footsteps pounded in the corridor from which Katzhak had emerged, their echoes coming closer and closer. The tall mustached man emerged, his gun held high in warning at the sight of his man, who was somehow alive, rescued by some miracle of a providence which did not exist. Katzhak whirled and fired, much faster than he might have blinked his eyes, blowing the assassin off his feet and hurling him backward through a plate-glass partition behind him, to his left.

One or two small pieces of glass fell from the frame and joined their contemporaries on the floor. The security team hesitated, unwilling to believe what their eyes had just seen. Katzhak took instant advantage by barking orders with the authority of a conquering David, quite reasonably asking for the head of slain Goliath to be kept as a souvenir.

"You! Get his papers. Search the body thoroughly. You three! Unsling your rifles and watch that entrance; he wasn't alone when he came down here. You, get on the phone and call security for reinforcements. You, come with me." Before they had had a chance to question him or even to think, Katzhak had trotted off with one of the guards. There was nothing left to do but to follow his orders.

Katzhak still did not know how to win the game. He knew only that to be caught or to stay too long in one place was to lose everything. In the gallery overhead, personal bodyguards had already thrown themselves over the premier and the first secretary, both of whom had turned out for the launch of Cosmo, for a once-in-a-lifetime look at history in the making. The fifteen-year-old son of the premier had been allowed the honor of attending this day of triumph and glory as well. Excited by the gunfire, he had slipped out of the protective custody of his father's bodyguards and had run down a flight of stairs toward the men whom Katzhak had positioned to guard the door. Katzhak recognized him at once as his ticket to freedom and as the leverage he needed to stop Cosmo. Edging toward him, Katzhak spotted one of the premier's men coming out of the stairwell. It was now or never.

As if on cue, the remainder of the assassin's security detail burst into the room, and the men Katzhak had stationed pulled back the bolts of their weapons, holding the surprised troop at bay. Katzhak had only seconds until the security detail betrayed the truth about him and the man who lay dead. The boy was his only chance. Having spotted the child, the bodyguard walked briskly after him. Katzhak walked even faster. The guard broke into a trot. Katzhak bolted. Already the assassin's posse was pointing at Katzhak, and the men whom he had commissioned were moving toward him. The bodyguard raced Katzhak, drawing his weapon, and the cluster of secret-service men dropped into firing postures. He was in their sights. With a sudden hobbling dash, Katzhak made a clumsy flying leap and tackled the unsuspecting boy. Katzhak fought to hang on, rolling with the boy to keep

251

them from firing, trying desperately to avoid losing his gun. He gave the terrified boy's arm a merciless twist, hoping that the boy's yell of pain would deter any heroics on the part of the onlookers. The cold floor felt good against his feverish body, and he held the youth's smarting limb in place while he nuzzled the mouth of his pistol into the nape of his captive's neck, where the spine and cord meet the skull.

"All right, back off. Back off! Get back. Get back, I said! All of you! I'm already hit, and I've come this far. You do exactly as I say, or I'll pop his balloon before you can spit. Right now. Right now! Okay. The guns. Now." The security people appealed to someone in the gallery, above and behind Katzhak. The guns were lowered onto the floor and kicked away, each man stepping backward a few paces. Newly arrived military police stood still but did not remove their guns. Plainclothes security men moved cautiously in an effort to get a clear shot. Katzhak shouted to the premier to call them off. He warned them away with a nod.

Working the boy skillfully, Katzhak shielded himself and inched nervously onto the main floor, no longer under the shadow of the gallery overhead. He commanded the bodyguards to stay behind and ordered the premier and the first secretary to come to the rail where he could see them. The confident face of the first secretary appeared almost immediately. He strode boldly up as if there were no danger, smiling broader than he ever had in public, as if the circumstances pleased him immensely, and Katzhak were a favorite guest. Leaning gently on the rail, he seemed at home, every inch a monarch. The secretary gestured, calling to the more cautious premier to come forward without further reluctance. "Come," he said, loud enough for Katzhak to hear, "Colonel Katzhak will not harm you. He did not come here to shoot either of us. Did you, Colonel? He is here on another . . . mission entirely, or perhaps I should say, a crusade? Am I right, Colonel?"

Katzhak's eyes widened and his scalp slid back at the mention of his name. The secretary knew who he was, what he was, and why he had come.

"If you know why I'm here, then you know what I want. Call it off."

"Call what off?" the premier inquired with pretended innocence.

"Shut up," Katzhak ordered without taking his eyes off the secretary. "I'm alive. And I know all about the goddamned plan. You blew it. It's over. Now, everybody's going to know. Call it off."

"I don't think that will be necessary."

"If you want this boy to live, it's necessary."

"Colonel, forgive me, but you yourself pointed out the fact that you are here. If you had told anyone anything at all, it would have been foolish of you to commit suicide down here. There would be no reason for you to risk it."

"Freeze," Katzhak said, jerking his head to the side to check the advance of a plainclothes security agent. The man backed off. "The fact remains that I have a gun to this boy's head. I'll kill him, for sure, and I'll probably have just enough time to put one right in the middle of your forehead, too. Now, pick up the phone and stop it. Call off the attack."

"I'm afraid that's impossible," the secretary replied tersely.

"You better make it possible," answered Katzhak, thumbing back the hammer of his gun, "or this boy's dead."

With the cocking of the pistol, the boy shut his eyes and bit his lip till blood came. The premier went white, and the knuckles of his hands were white also, as his fingers gripped the railing even tighter than before.

"You're too late. It has already begun. It has already started." The secretary smiled in triumph, and his face, in that weird, subterranean light, was full of shadows, angles, and highlights that lent it a terrifyingly inhuman character. Katzhak was stunned.

"You're lying. The attack isn't scheduled to take place for another hour."

"The main forces, yes. But the planes have farther to go. The first squadron took off more than ten minutes ago."

"Call them back. There's still time. You've got to call them back."

"They've scrambled, Katzhak. This is no drill. They won't respond to signals now."

"Then you'll have to talk to the pilots yourself."

"They'll ignore me. If even one plane turned back, the others would shoot it down."

Katzhak looked at the anxious face of the premier. "Is that true?" His only reply was to hang his head. Far across the huge expanse of men and machines, a prompter bell blared briefly, sounding much like a trumpet. The back-lit silhouette of the large party chief, far above him, reminded Katzhak of the vigorous and greedy bear of his dream. Fear was consuming him by inches, starting at his toes and gradually eating him alive.

"Wait," the premier implored. "There may still be a way. Yes, there is one way."

"How?"

"Not until you release my son."

"If I turn him loose, I won't live long enough for you to finish your sentence. Goddammit, you're stalling! You're wasting time, playing these horseshit games, and thousands of people . . . You are sending them to die! The attack will be a dismal failure, and most of the invasion forces will be slaughtered unless . . . unless you call it off. There has to be a way."

"There isn't any way."

"You don't understand! You haven't got a chance against . . . You don't know what you're up against! I tell you, it's not going to work! If those planes reach Israel, if one soldier sets foot on the land, it will be too late! Unless you abort this thing right now, those armies are doomed."

"Evidence, Katzhak. Information. Why are you so sure the attack is going to fail? Do you know of any sabotage or treason? Did you uncover some kind of conspiracy?"

"No, but—"

The premier once again cut him off. "Have the Jews been warned, somehow? Is there an ally who is prepared to go to war with us, right now, this morning, this instant, over Israel? Israel! Because, I'll tell you something, if there isn't, then we can't fail. I will be breakfasting in Tel Aviv before the American president and English prime minister and their Congress and their Parliament can decide where to meet to discuss it! Face it, Katzhak! You've failed. You and your subversives, your bought dogs—you are the ones who are doomed. I guarantee you that after this morning, the imperialists will pull in their lines all over the world, the West will shrink in upon itself like the pupil of an eye, and no one will ever again talk about the 'human rights' of dissidents and anti-Soviets, or try to dictate our internal affairs. They will be silent, because, deep down, they are more afraid of war than they are of us."

Tired and miserably depressed, Katzhak looked away toward the huge radar boards and satellite monitors. A fierce battle raged within him. How could he convince them? How could he make them see the danger, make them believe, as he had come to believe? What did he believe? He wasn't sure anymore. Perhaps they were right, and he was fantasizing this whole ridiculous fairy tale. What did he have, really? A group of fanatics, religious zealots, possibly terrorists, and a few coincidences. How could he convince these worldly men that God existed and that he was going to fight with them over Israel? They would say that he had lost his mind when he told them that this belief had led him to risk his life by placing himself in his present position. They would only laugh at his foolhardiness when he said that his search for whatever grain of truth might be found had caused him to run his life straight into the ground. If he only had something concrete, some way of demonstrating the danger before all hell broke loose. The monitors distracted him, tugged at his mind while he tried to think. As he watched, images appeared and disappeared, some flashed on and then off, while other shots were held, zoomed closer, pulled back, and examined from every angle. From some of the distant, overall views Katzhak could make out what appeared to be the coastline of Africa. Many of these long-range scans were difficult to identify because of a dense gray shroud, a milky covering which obscured the earth miles below. Vaguely alarmed, for reasons he could not guess, Katzhak watched now the radar screens, his eyes following the ray of light that swept the screen a few degrees at a time, before it made a full circle. A large dark mass seemed to be growing and slowly gaining momentum.

Katzhak watched it in horror, the tiny ray of light illuminating it over and over again. "What's that?"

"What is what?" the first secretary wanted to know.

"That"—Katzhak pointed—"on the radar boards. What is it?"

"Clouds," a controller said simply.

"What area is that?" Katzhak pursued.

"The target area. That's actually a composite of several sectors of the Middle East."

"Can you spotlight a single area?"

"Within certain limits."

"Can you isolate Israel?"

"Of course."

"Do it."

The controller looked sheepishly upward toward the first secretary, shrugged, and momentarily the huge mass grew smaller. It continued to move, however, and it was growing.

"Is that a storm of some kind?" Katzhak inquired.

"Well, technically, no. Right now it's just a series of sea squalls moving toward each other. They're being fanned by relatively moderate winds right now, but wind velocity is increasing, and we're keeping a close watch on it. The squalls may continue to move toward each other and coalesce, but they're just as likely to shift suddenly and move off in totally different directions. These things are hard to predict."

"What if they all combined and moved inland?"

"Then you'd have one hell of a storm on your hands. But the likelihood of that happening is almost nil. I can just about guarantee that—"

"Would there be lightning, thunder, torrential rain, things like that?"

"Well, as I said, the probability—"

"I'm not interested in probability. Answer the question."

"Well, naturally, whenever a huge storm like you're talking about blows across the sea and then moves inland, it has the potential of picking up pretty vast amounts of water. There's definitely something building, all right, but so far, it's well within normal, or what you might expect. It's certainly nothing to get excited about."

"Hail," Katzhak said weakly, feeling drained and near exhaustion.

"What?"

"Hail! Would there be hail from this type of front?"

"From a sea storm? No, sir. Generally not. Not this type."

"What about the clouds?"

"Which?"

"The clouds over land, aren't they moving inland?"

"Now you're talking about something a little bit unusual. They're massing, all right, and picking up speed, too. This amount of activity, if it keeps up—and it looks like it might—is really kind of rare. It's doing nothing right now, though, as far as precipitation or what you might call storm activity."

"Is it moving in any one direction in particular?" Katzhak looked away, biting the tip of his tongue.

"Well, yes. Right now, I'd say its bearing on the target area."

"Oh, my God." Katzhak shut his eyes tightly for a second. It's begun, he said to himself. It's already begun.

"That can change at any moment, though. That doesn't mean anything yet. Those clouds would have to move a hell of a lot faster than they are now in order to give our aircraft any trouble. They might eventually put our ground units in the dark, but that's about all we have to go on or to worry about at this stage."

Katzhak was bursting. It was all so obvious, so insidious. He felt that if no one saw it soon, he would go out of his mind. He glanced at their smug faces, split by smiles of pride and confidence. Suddenly a roughly patterned series of tiny blips appeared and moved with infinite slowness.

"What the hell is that," shouted Katzhak, "aircraft?"

"No, no, no. Flocks of birds, probably."

A tingling chill poured slowly down Katzhak's spine and flowed over his body. The word returned to him now:

> Thus says the Lord God: Speak unto every feathered fowl, and to every beast of the field. Assemble yourselves, and come; gather yourselves on every side

257

to my sacrifice that I sacrifice for you . . . a great sacrifice on the mountains of Israel, that ye may eat flesh, and drink blood.

Ye shall eat the flesh of the mighty, and drink the blood of the princes of the earth. . . .

Thus shall ye be filled at my table with horses and chariots, with mighty men and with all men of war. . . . And I will set my glory among the godless, and all the unbelievers shall see my judgment which I have executed, and my hand that I have laid upon them.

Katzhak turned. "The truth is . . . the truth is . . . that you have stretched out your hand over the people who belong to God, and the land which he gave to them to keep —forever. You cannot win, because God himself is going to fight against you, and he will destroy you. Thousands of years ago he said that this would happen, that we would live where we live, would rise to power, would call ourselves what we do, and that one day, one day, at the appointed time in history, we would attack his chosen people and try to take the land away from them that he gave to their fathers. He said he would make an example of us, that he would feed our armies to the birds in Israel."

"And how is this great God going to accomplish this feat? With a wave of his hand, perhaps? Or a breath from his nostrils? Or will he simply tilt the earth and slide us into the oceans?"

"With the weather. With torrential rains, and huge hailstones, with flooding and lightning and an earthquake. He says that this supernatural defense of a country not onetenth our size will prove to the world that he lives, that nothing has changed, that he is God and all men will face his judgment."

The first secretary chuckled. "Katzhak, you are mad. But it took real balls to come here. I admire your courage. Really. Now, release this boy and let's get this over with. Shooting him is not what you want, and it won't change anything; we both know that. I can promise you a trial before anything happens to you. Think it over."

"Beautiful. It's all so simple, isn't it? So uncomplicated. Silence thought, crush dissent, kill the critics. Destroy the opposition and there will be peace. Outlaw the truth and create your own reality. Debase everything. Admit nothing. Worship the lie. You wouldn't know the truth if it were written across the sky, if it . . . rained down on you from heaven. You can't hear me because you've closed your ears. You can't see what's right in front of you because you've shut your eyes. You're looking at your own destruction up there, written all over the walls. Read your fate in the face of the sky itself. Look at it," Katzhak yelled, twisting the arm of the frightened boy viciously, and causing him to cry out, as tears were wrenched from his eyes. "Look at it! There, there is your overflowing rain."

Katzhak panted, worn out and breathless. He felt weak and wondered if he could go on; his left knee buckled, and Katzhak fought to keep his feet, stumbling back a little and leaning heavily on the boy for support. To his relief, the leg righted itself once more, but gave no indication of how much longer it might be willing to support his weight. He had to hold together for a little while longer.

What was his next move? Where did he go from here? He was in a poor position, really, and the more time that elapsed, the more dangerous his position became. He was tired, and feverish, and in pain. He had no idea of how to do what he had come to do, of how he could get out of that room, out of the city, out of Russia, alive. Now that he had done all he could, had said what he wanted to, the boy was no longer of any use to him. Katzhak wanted to let him go; after all, he had had nothing to do with any of this. The boy could not be released, however, until Katzhak was ready to die. Ready to die? He was not ready, would never be ready to quit, to concede defeat, to . . . God, he was tired. There was always a way—if one were determined enough, if one were willing to open his mind and his eyes. Katzhak stared down on the back of the boy's head as his idea came to him in bits and pieces that gradually became a plan. The risk was insane, and even if he got away with it, the chances for success were ridiculously low. None of that mattered anyway, because any minute now he would faint and his collapsing body would be shot dead before it hit the ground.

"Tell them to get a helicopter ready. I want a pilot, too.

I want an interceptor fueled and waiting when we get to the base."

"What are you going to do with my son?" the premier asked stoically.

"I'm going to try to overtake our aircraft. If they listen to me, I may be able to head off the slaughter."

"And if they don't?"

"My transmitter will be going full blast to whatever nation might be listening. If I can't convince our people to turn back, maybe I can cause enough chaos to make them reconsider."

"You won't try to shoot down any of our planes? If you attack them, you'll have primary advantage, but this is combat, my son will be killed!"

"Then I'd say it's in your best interest to work with me and make that event unnecessary. How about that helicopter?"

"Standing by. Katzhak, be reasonable. You have no chance. Why commit suicide? It's not too late to turn back."

"It is too late. Clear the corridors to the elevator."

The orders were given, and Katzhak nudged the boy forward on stumbling feet. One by one, the men stepped aside, allowing Katzhak and his hostage to pass. At the mouth of hell, the opening of the corridor through which Katzhak had had to negotiate around the guns, lay the lifeless body of the slain lord of death. Katzhak had conquered the last enemy, had vanquished him most feared, had broken with his sharp sword, his power to destroy. Now he would ascend to the surface, return to the world of men, and then, in a whirlwind, would disappear into the clouds.

Katzhak bit his tongue as hard as he dared, to keep himself awake. The ride in the back of the jeep that raced for the elevators was lulling his weary body and brain perilously close to sleep. It seemed that they had traveled for eternity, and several times he had nodded off, only to jerk his head back up in pretended vigilance. He had finally fallen asleep completely when the jeep squealed to a stop at its destination, jolting him back to life. As a precaution, the jeep driver was ordered into the elevator first, and was also the first to disembark. The latter duty was one that caused him enormous fear and consternation, not knowing about the welcome that might await him on the other side of the steel doors. The trip was uneventful, however, and once again the curious, concerned faces parted for Katzhak, like the waters of the Red Sea.

One of Katzhak's errant disciples meanwhile had abandoned the auto he had stolen from the assassins and had walked back to a spot near the building he had seen Katzhak enter so long ago. What had become of him? Was he still alive, and if so, of what use might he be to him now? He was just about to leave the area when he heard it. A helicopter was starting up its engines in preparation to take off. The Israeli agent ran toward the sound, back between the buildings, till a fence halted him, but did not obstruct his view of the helipad. It was not possible. Could it be? It was! There was Katzhak working his way slowly out of the shadow of the buildings and limping toward the chopper. Something must have gone wrong. Damn! He had been hit in there, and he was bleeding like a bastard. With a wince, the Jew took note of the limp and of the stumbling, dazed gait of a man in shock and on the verge of total collapse. On the other hand, Katzhak was still alive, and he apparently had a hostage of some importance to exchange for his freedom.

Oh, my God, he thought. There they were. Suddenly sharpshooters quietly took up positions and were aiming with infinite care at the struggling Katzhak. Dammit! Dammit, dammit, dammit! They were going to try to pick him off before he reached the chopper. Shit! He had to do it. He had to. The Israeli prayed silently and drew his own gun. He picked a sniper at random and fired, one, two, three, hitting twice. The man flipped his gun away as if he meant to, and spun off the rooftop. Katzhak's head jerked sideways in fear and surprise, his body whirled one hundred and eighty degrees, so that his back was to the gunship, and the boy was where his back had been. The Jew squeezed off two more shots, dropping a man about to fire on Katzhak from his perch behind a low wall. Shots rang out from a dozen locations, sounding like fists slamming into a mattress. The chain-link fence was alive with

261

sparks and flying bits of twisted wire, and the Israeli was cut down by that withering barrage.

Sensing rescue close at hand, the boy began dragging his feet, and the exhausted Katzhak pulled him the final distance toward the helicopter. Two snipers fired almost at once, one of the bullets slamming into the fuselage and ricocheting off, painfully nicking Katzhak's ear as it whizzed past. The boy screamed and nearly fell, the second slug blowing a huge hole in his lower leg. Almost tripping himself, Katzhak caught him and pulled the wounded boy aboard from behind. He had barely hauled him in when the pilot produced a gun, as anticipated. Katzhak was ready for this move in advance, and he slumped back gratefully as the pilot tossed it out the door and lifted the awkward machine into space.

"Get this bird the hell out of here! Set it down at the airbase. There'll be a jet all fueled and ready to go. Get this thing as close to that airplane as you can. Once we're aboard, take it up and head back the way you came." Katzhak turned to the writhing, blubbering child. "You're lucky you weren't killed back there; what are you crying about? Here, for Christ's sake. Bite down on this as hard as you can. It'll help cut the pain." Katzhak shoved the boy's sleeve in his own mouth, and the youth's face turned red with the effort exerted on it.

He still had a monumental problem. How would he stay protected while he and the boy slowly lowered themselves into the small cockpit of the jet? Katzhak glanced around the helicopter for something that would help. He smiled in triumph as he saw some hand grenades. Quickly he pulled the pin of one of them and held it in his left hand with the lever depressed. If they killed him, the boy would be killed or maimed too, and this knowledge was security enough. In no time at all the copter began its hovering descent, touching down almost too close to the interceptor plane.

"Tell them I've got a live grenade."

While the nervous pilot radioed, Katzhak watched the struggling young Communist fight back the tears.

"You don't have to be brave with me. No one else will know. The pain is always worst the first time."

"My leg . . . is fine," the boy stammered.

"Who said anything about your leg? The other wound is

262

more serious. That's the one that's really hurting you, isn't it?"

The boy bit his lip, but his chin quivered anyway, and he nodded as the hot tears of outrage and resentment were wrung out of his eyes and rolled down his cheeks.

"I never thought my father would let them shoot," he sobbed, bewildered and betrayed.

"He didn't let them shoot, boy—he *made* them shoot."

"You mean," he choked bitterly, "that they weren't trying to rescue me? They were trying to kill you."

"Swallow it, now, son, and save yourself a lot of grief. It won't do anything for the pain, but it'll scar up faster that way. They wanted to save you, sure. I'm sure he didn't want to see you hurt. Your escape was just a by-product. It was secondary to what they really wanted."

"They will kill you." This sincere statement of belief was neither a threat nor a boast. It was not even an opinion. It was simple fact. Katzhak looked at the earnest face, disdainful and disapproving, and yet, somehow, suddenly concerned. A memory of Tash saying much the same thing stabbed at his heart with icy pangs of terrible loneliness.

"I know," he said softly. "You should be out of danger now. I don't think they'll try it again. Especially since they hit you the first time."

"What do you intend to do with me?"

This brought a burst of ironic laughter from Katzhak. "Do with you?" He rolled his eyes and grunted cynically. "If all goes well, I'll put you on this jet in a few hours and send you home."

"And if it does not go well?"

"I'm sorry" was all he would say.

The helicopter pilot reported that the ultrafast interceptor was manned, fueled, and ready. Katzhak gestured for him to come back and open the door. Trembling, the pilot popped the latch, pulled back the bolt, and very, very slowly rolled back the door a few inches.

The sky was darkest black, with heavy clouds that rumbled and rolled ominously. It was almost as dark as an overcast winter night, and the air was the coldest and sharpest Katzhak could remember. What light there was,

263

was muted, yellow, and diffused. With a sudden steady rush, the wind rose and buffeted every blade of grass, every barren tree that dared to challenge the drifts of smudged gray snow that smothered the ground and buried every living thing. Marching the wounded boy in front of him, Katzhak stepped down from the helicopter and onto the crunchy snow.

A square of gray-coated men, rifles poised and sights on the two figures alone in the snow in front of them, stood shoulder to shoulder, forming a perimeter that surrounded the men, the helicopter, and the jet. Like statues, they stood unflinching, unyielding, unblinking, oblivious of the savage wind. They were fierce and frightening, faces hard as stone, fur caps making them resemble some kind of animals rather than a group of unsympathetic men. The helicopter engines roared like a hungry beast, and the clumsy thing lifted off in a whirl of snow, in a flurry of murderous blades and flashing steel. Katzhak and his captive were almost blown over by the man-made hurricane, blinded by walls of icy white. No one moved, as if all were suddenly transfixed as part of a frozen tableau of potential violence and reckless carnage. No one moved.

Finally, his side aching diabolically, Katzhak nudged the boy into halting movement. Their first tentative steps did not seem to have been noticed by the grim griffins who steadfastly maintained their weird vigil. Katzhak pushed the wounded boy now, at last reaching the ladder that stood beside the nose of the airplane. His heart pounding, every step an effort, Katzhak followed the son of the Russian premier achingly up the countless rungs, innumerable, torturing, icy. It hurt like hell to breathe, and Katzhak wished for some air to thaw his lungs. With frozen fingers he dragged himself higher and higher, the rungs growing farther and farther apart with every step.

The boy was made to stand in the second seat of the cockpit, while Katzhak somehow twisted his body into place behind him. The boy was then pulled onto the edge of the contoured seat, half in Katzhak's lap and half out. It was an impossibly tight squeeze, but at length the belts were pulled around and tightened. The cockpit cover closed and locked into position and the jet-killer fired its engines and whined in deafening impatience. It was only then that the honor guard of stones began to move away from the front of the plane, defiant, unhurried, unconcerned.

The entire aircraft shuddered for a long moment, alarming Katzhak into thinking that it might break up and shake apart at any moment. Instead, it catapulted, as if fired by a slingshot or shot out of a huge cannon, and it hurtled almost straight upward into space. Katzhak blacked out briefly as he was held flat against the back of his seat by the sudden thrust of the aircraft's multi-G acceleration.

Meanwhile, far below the surface of the earth, the premier thanked the caller and hung up the red phone.

"My son is still alive. The interceptor should be appearing on our screens now."

The two men turned and looked back at the giant radar screens. The Soviet planes were not far from their unprepared destination, and the first tiny blips that meant Katzhak's pursuit craft were beginning to appear over the area near Moscow. The men watched the fast-moving object in silence.

The premier shook his head in worry and deep sadness. "How will he get out alive? How will we ever get him down, now?"

"Comrade," the first secretary prompted, "he must not come down. He is lost."

"Must not? But . . . he is my son. My only son. Don't say that. Don't say that about my boy."

"Katzhak could never stop the attack, you know that. There is a chance, though, that he might wreak havoc with our planes for a few moments, that someone, somewhere, might take warning. We must not let that happen. There is much too much at stake."

"No—"

"You know what must be done. For the people. For the cause of socialism . . ."

"For the good of the state."

"Yes. Your son is a hero in the spirit of Lenin. No one could make a greater contribution. You must see that, don't you? You must be proud."

The premier hung his head in mute assent. "Proud," he said to his feet, as a tear fell and trickled across the shine of one shoe. The first secretary had not heard him. He turned his head to the side and spoke in a low voice to a controller at his left.

"Shoot it down," he said.

Already, a thousand miles away, the advance Soviet war planes were flying into . . . rain.